Best Wishes !

D0594000

THE BLIND PIG

MURDERS

FRANK L. GERTCHER

Wind Grass Hill Books

Terre Haute, IN

Although fiction, *The Blind Pig Murders* rings true to the fascinating history and colorful characters who lived, loved and died in Chicago, the 'murder capital of the world,' during the heyday of Al Capone, speakeasies and Chicago-style jazz. Any similarity of the storyline characters in this novel to persons living or dead is purely coincidental and not intended by the author.

The Blind Pig Murders © 2020 Frank L. Gertcher
Hard cover EAN-ISBN-13: 978-0-9835754-6-7
E-book EAN-ISBN-13: 978-0-930546-32-5
Paperback EAN- ISBN-13: 978-1-930546-31-8

Cover design by Phil Velikan

Cover art: 1920 flapper silhouette ©Incomible/Shutterstock.com; backgroup image © Bildagentur Zoonar GmbH/Shutterstock.com

Packaged by Wish Publishing

Printed in the United States of America
10 9 8 7 6 5 4 3 2 1

This book is dedicated to my wife, Linda.
Her continued encouragement, research efforts and editing skills
helped turn the concepts for my books into finished products.

ALSO FROM FRANK L. GERTCHER

In 1841, the con artist Worthingtons lure wealthy and sinister Black John Murrow to the dark cabin. Murrow disappears. What happened? Years later, two of the three now wealthy Worthingtons are murdered in their mansion. Who and Why? Jeremiah and James, father and son, solve the mysteries. Should they keep the terrible secret of Thomas Worthington? The author weaves an exquisitely crafted Civil War era murder-mystery that includes good detective work, romance between key characters and insight with regard to the battle of good and evil within the human soul.

"...*An imaginative morality tale about free will, crime, punishment, and the possibility of redemption.*" — **Kirkus Reviews.**

"*Readers of murder mysteries will relish the many facets of* The Dark Cabin Murders, *which is anything but singular, involving readers in probes of inner being as well as mysteries and events that ultimately examine wider issues of the impact of life choices.*" — **Midwest Book Review.**

After the murder of her friend Alec in 1921, Caroline Case, a Wabash Valley madame, becomes an amateur but extremely resourceful detective. She meets the mysterious Hannibal Jones, and the pair work with an odd assortment of local characters to solve several murders. The group adapts the name 'River Rats.' As the Rats pursue justice, they become involved in the war between Al Capone and the North Side gang over control of the booze trade. There are shootouts, kidnappings and daring rescues. Selected as a Distinguished Favorite, Mystery Category, **Independent Press Award** 2020.

"*Surprisingly and pleasantly lighthearted for a tale involving prostitution, bootlegging and murder. The author skillfully alternates action scenes...with his focus on the gently evolving relationship between Caroline and Hannibal. Detailed descriptions of developments in forensic techniques and equipment add a historical bonus.*" — **Kirkus Reviews.**

ACKNOWLEDGEMENTS

My thanks to all who contributed historical information about the Wabash Valley and Chicago during the roaring 1920s. My father, Frank Gertcher Senior (1910-1998), was my primary source about the Wabash Valley. He made moonshine whiskey during Prohibition, and he told me many stories. There really was a madame who lived on a houseboat, and my father would hide his 'product' in her trash pile on the river bank for pick-up by the Capone people from Chicago. During my childhood, I was also a Wabash 'river rat,' and I know the river and its colorful people.

In Chicago, the Spencer Hotel (1927-1945) was my setting for a fictional murder and later, a wedding. The Spencer was purchased by Conrad Hilton in 1945. John G. Wells, the manager of the Hilton Chicago (2019), provided a personal tour, architectural drawings and many details about the Hilton when it was the Spencer. Jessica Vanpoperinghe, Hilton Chicago Sales Liaison & Media Relations Service Manager, set up meetings and tours.

My wife Linda and I also visited the Green Mill Jazz Club and The Hideout. Both were Chicago speakeasies during Prohibition, and both play important roles in my fictional story. My thanks to Patrick Romanowski for details on the Green Mill and Tim Tuten, Alice Blander, Sully Davis and Tim Samuelson for information on The Hideout and its surrounding mills and industries.

Source materials on ethnic neighborhoods, the Chicago Police Department, speakeasies and gangsters during the roaring 1920s were provided for my review by Ellen Keith and her colleagues from the Chicago History Museum.

The details provided by the above kind-hearted people were, I'm sure, factually accurate. Any errors in this book concerning the above locations, organizations and historical persons are strictly my own.

THE BLIND PIG MURDERS

PROLOGUE

I am Caroline Case, and you are reading the second volume of my diary.

If you read the first, you know that in the summer of 1928, I moved from my Wabash Valley home to a penthouse near Lakeshore Drive in Chicago.

In the beginning, I was a poor, river rat Madame. Due to hard work in my chosen 'profession,' prudent saving and roaring twenties investments, I am now quite wealthy, thank you. Recently, I moved my money into cash and conservative holdings; this crazy stock market can't last forever.

My path up, out and into a new life was difficult, but it was worth the effort, sacrifice and intrigue. I took advantage of every opportunity, legal and otherwise. Wealth has brought freedom.

I am free to be a private detective, and I love it. I specialize in blind pig murders. According to the newspapers, there are over seven thousand blind pigs in Chicago. Not the barnyard kind with dirt on their faces, but the speakeasy kind, with not-so-secret passwords, jazz musicians and lots of illegal booze.

Prohibition has unleashed a crime wave of epic proportions. Speakeasies, ranging from simple, dimly lit blind pigs to elegant, upscale salons, provide thirsty consumers, male and female, with booze, a place to meet and greet and opportunities to break the law and social mores with uninhibited abandon.

In addition to the usual crimes of passion, rival Chicago gangs fight bloody battles over control of the illegal booze trade. Murders are frequent, and I investigate.

1

MURDER ON MY MIND

Saturday evening, October 20, 1928

Playboy Sydney Albert Meltzer may have been murdered last night. His mother asked me to investigate. I said that I would. What happened?

Ruth, Sydney's widowed mother, lives two floors down in our apartment building. When my partner Hannibal Jones and I moved in a few weeks ago, Ruth introduced herself and offered friendship. We spent time together on several occasions. One day, we went for a walk in the nearby city park. On another day, we shared tea in her apartment. She has a poodle named Frenchie. Both Ruth and Frenchie are adorable.

I know from the newspaper society pages that thanks to Sydney's grandfather and father, the Meltzer family has loads of money. Both men passed away some time ago. According to Ruth, she has been a widow for over five years.

Ruth also told me that she has two sons, Charles Everett, the eldest at thirty-five, and Sydney Albert, who was twenty-eight last month. According to Ruth, Charles runs the family industrial chemical business, and Sydney manages the Meltzer family charitable trust.

I saw photos of Charles and Sydney in Ruth's apartment, but I have yet to meet them. Ruth didn't say much about Charles, except that he works all the time. According to Ruth, Sydney attended an Ivy League school for a while but dropped out to "find himself."

Just after my visit to Ruth's apartment, I saw photos of Sydney in the newspaper. He was attending a fund-raising event for a new hospital. Some of the photos showed Sydney with a beautiful young lady, who, according to the newspaper, was Sydney's socialite fiancé.

So, what happened to Sydney? Ruth called me on the phone this morning. I was still in bed when the phone rang. Ruth was nearly hysterical.

"Oh, Caroline, the police came, and they said they found Sydney!" There was a pause and then sobs. I heard Frenchie barking in the background.

Finally, Ruth continued: "Caroline, please come!"

"Ruth," I responded, "are the police with you now?"

"Yes," replied Ruth. "They are detectives, or so they said." Ruth's breathing was interspersed with sniffles and more sobs.

Ruth was fighting for control. Frenchie, on the other hand, was out of control. I could hear his incessant barks and whines. I could also hear two male voices, one was apparently talking to Ruth, and the other was trying to calm Frenchie.

"I'll be there in ten minutes, Ruth," I said. "Please try to be calm." I hung up the phone, rolled out of bed, shed my black silk designer pajamas, ran into the bathroom and then out in half a minute. I scrambled into my clothes from the previous afternoon. Fortunately, my dress was a blue Lanvin with a modest neckline, flutter sleeves, a long waist and a midi tea length hem. It was the latest in fall fashion. I had been shopping in the Loop on Friday, and I had dressed appropriately. However, my hair was a mess. "Comb, make-up, shoes," I muttered. "Where are my shoes?"

Finally, I was more or less presentable, I think. I ran to my apartment's front door, then out and down the hallway to the elevator. It was a new self-operating type, with no attendant. I pushed the button on the wall, and the elevator door soon opened. I opened the cage door, got in, closed the cage and pushed the correct floor button. A large mirror covered the back wall, and I primped my hair and smoothed my clothes as the elevator descended to Ruth's floor. "OK, Caroline," I said to myself, "be calm, cool and poised."

The elevator stopped. I took a deep breath, gave one last look to the mirror and made minor adjustments. I then opened the cage door and stepped quickly out into the hallway. I forced myself to walk slowly down the hallway toward Ruth's apartment. I could hear Frenchie, but his barks were less frequent.

I knocked on Ruth's door. A large man in a suit opened it. He had a no-nonsense, slightly exasperated look. Frenchie started barking again, slipped past the man and saw me in the hallway. He started wiggling all over. His tail had a ball of fur at the end, and it swished back and forth as fast as it could go. He stopped barking, whined and sat down in front of me. The tail stopped. Frenchie gave me an expectant, pleading look. I reached down and petted his fuzzy head and ears. He whined again, and then the noise stopped. The man in the suit gave a sigh of relief.

I straightened up, looked the man in the eyes and said: "I'm Caroline Case, Ruth's neighbor."

"Detective Sergeant Watts," replied the man. He smiled briefly. "Please come in." He stood aside and opened the door wide. Frenchie and I walked into Ruth's spacious receiving room.

The other man was standing near Ruth, who was sitting on a couch in her robe. The second man introduced himself. "Detective Mulvaney, ma'am," and he nodded in greeting.

Ruth looked at me and said: "Oh, Caroline!" She dabbed her eyes with a white silk handkerchief, stood and walked unsteadily over to me.

I hugged her tenderly, and she sobbed for a while. We both returned to the couch. I glanced at the modern-looking clock on the fireplace mantle over Ruth's shoulder. "Eight o'clock," I thought to myself. "Great way to start a morning and I haven't had my coffee yet."

Mandy, Ruth's live-in maid, entered the room from the kitchen, which is located in the back of Ruth's apartment. She had a large silver tray with a coffee pot, several cups, saucers, sugar, cream and linen napkins. "Perfect timing," I thought, and smiled.

"I'm so glad you're here," said Mandy, and she smiled at me in return. She put the tray on the coffee table and then served: first Ruth, then me and then the two detectives. Watts sat in a chair on the other side of the table, and Mulvaney stood nearby. Everyone sipped coffee in silence for a few moments. Mandy returned to the kitchen. Even Frenchie was quiet as he lay on the floor next to me.

I looked at Watts. I'm sure that the look on my face expressed the obvious questions. I waited.

After a moment, in a quiet voice, Watts said: "We found Sydney Albert Meltzer early this morning in his downtown hotel suite." He looked at me with a steady gaze. "He was deceased."

Ruth stifled a sob. I patted her hand. "How was he found?" I asked.

"A tip from an unknown caller," replied Watts. He pulled out a notepad and looked at it. "The Central District Station received a phone call about six this morning. After district officers made the initial discovery of the body, we were called." He paused and looked at me closely. "You said your name was Caroline Case?"

I nodded. Watts' eyes narrowed, and he asked: "Do you know Eddie Valenti?"

"Yes," I replied. "Eddie works for the Jones Forensic Laboratory; he is the lab's most highly trained crime scene investigator." I paused and then added: "Hannibal Jones is my business partner."

"Of course!" Watts replied. "Your reputation precedes you, Miss Case. It's an honor to meet you." He paused and then added: "We heard about your detective work in the Wabash Valley and in Key West." He smiled openly and continued: "Also, the Jones Lab has many contracts with the Chicago Police Department."

Ruth stopped sniffling and looked at me, then at Watts and then back to me. Her face had a puzzled expression. After a moment, she queried: "Caroline?"

I couldn't help but smile. "Sometimes I work with the police," I answered. "You have already met Hannibal, and he also works with the police."

Watts looked at Ruth, smiled, and said: "Miss Case and Mr. Jones are private detectives, the best in the city."

Watts turned to me, smiled wryly and said: "You know how things are in Chicago. The department needs all the help we can get."

"Tough situation," I thought to myself. "A few honest cops, low pay, political corruption, prohibition and gangsters." To Watts, I smiled and replied: "I understand."

I turned to Ruth. After a moment, she responded: "Oh." Her eyes widened a little. I could tell by her expression that she was evaluating the implications of Watts' revelation.

Watts looked back to me and said: "We found Mr. Meltzer in his Steven's Hotel suite, and the evidence surrounding his death has inconsistencies." He paused a moment and then added: "Mr. Meltzer had fallen, and he has injuries, possibly from the fall. However, we also found other evidence that suggests that the fall was not the cause of death."

"Murder or suicide?" I asked.

"Possibly," replied Watts. "We need an expert analysis of the scene."

"My Sydney wouldn't commit suicide; he just wouldn't," Ruth stated emphatically. "Not my Sydney." She looked first at Watts and then at me. She started sniffling again.

Watts and I gave Ruth time to regain her composure.

After a minute or so, Ruth looked at me and asked: "Can you help me?" She looked over at Watts and added: "Would you mind?"

"I would be happy to let Miss Case look into this situation," Watts stated with a smile. His eyes said more than his words.

I smiled at Watts and then Ruth. After a moment, I said: "Of course I will help."

"And I will pay you," Ruth replied emphatically. "I know your time is valuable."

And so, it began. I am alone, and Hannibal isn't due back from Pittsburgh for another week. I miss him.

Sunday evening, October 21, 1928

Before leaving Ruth's apartment, I arranged with Watts and Mulvaney to meet them at the opulent Stevens Hotel on Michigan Avenue between Seventh and Eighth Streets. The crime scene was a suite near the top floor. After arrangements were made, I left Ruth with Mandy, returned to my apartment and called Eddie Valenti. Fortunately, he was at home.

After I explained the situation, Eddie said: "I'll be right over."

I replied: "I'll meet you out front," and I hung up the phone. "It will take Eddie 30 minutes to get here," I thought to myself. "I have time to shower, put on fresh clothes and make-up. I also need to fix my hair, for goodness sakes!"

A quick look through my walk-in closet revealed my Hartnell-designed business outfit. "Donegal tweed dress, wine-colored with black piping: perfect!" I said to myself. I also chose dark silk hose and low-heeled black shoes. "It's cold, so my simple black Persian lamb coat, matching hat and gray cashmere scarf will do nicely," I added.

I finished in record time, left the apartment in a mess and made it to the front door downstairs just as Eddie drove around the corner.

Harris, the elderly doorman for our apartment building, opened the passenger door on Eddie's new Ford Model A Roadster as it rolled to a stop. Harris touched his cap and said: "Have a good day, Miss Case."

"He is such a nice man," I mused to myself, as Eddie and I drove away.

As we moved into traffic, Eddie glanced at me, grinned and said: "Nice to see you again, Caroline!" He paused a moment and then added: "Do we get paid this time?" His grin turned into a chuckle.

"Yes, Smarty," I replied. "Mrs. Meltzer has put us on retainer." I knew Eddie was alluding to the case with Scottie McDonald's murder the previous February. We didn't get paid then, but Hannibal and I had the opportunity to meet, work with and hire Eddie, who was a cop at the time, for his new position with our lab. "Now tell me about Sydney Albert Meltzer's suite at the Steven's Hotel."

Eddie was silent for a few moments as he navigated traffic. Finally, he shifted the Model A into third gear. Soon we were racing down Lakeshore Drive. The road became Michigan Avenue as we approached downtown.

"Well," said Eddie, "The Steven's Hotel is the fanciest hotel in Chicago, and if you believe the newspapers, the biggest and best in the world. The hotel has ninety suites and about three thousand rooms. I checked, and young Sydney has one of the nicest suites on the 27th floor. The 28th and 29th floors are reserved for the Stevens family, heads of state and so on."

"I have only seen it from a distance; it must be quite a place," I responded.

Eddie nodded and said: "It's virtually a city within itself, with shops, ballrooms, restaurants, a theatre, a bowling alley and even a mini-golf green on the roof." He double-clutched the peddle and down-shifted as we rolled to a stop at the corner of Michigan Avenue and Seventh Street. After looking both ways, he pulled up to the Steven's Michigan Avenue grand entrance. He turned to me and said: "Your boy Sydney lives in style."

"Well, he did anyway," I replied. "According to Detective Sergeant Watts, Sydney's body is still in his suite where they found it."

"I'll drop you off here, and then I'll park in the lot behind the hotel," said Eddie. "Meet you in the lobby."

Just then an attendant opened my door and said: "Good morning Madam, welcome to the Steven's Hotel." He touched his cap, stood to the side and motioned me toward a doorman who held open one of the massive, gleaming brass doors. The attendant then closed the car door.

Eddie drove off, turned right at the corner of Eighth Street and headed toward the parking lot on Wabash between Eighth and Seventh Streets.

Before heading to the open door, I looked up at the massive Steven's Hotel, which filled the entire space between Seventh and Eighth Streets and halfway from Michigan Avenue to Wabash Avenue. "Wow!" I thought to myself. "What a palace!"

I finished staring, walked forward and passed through the main door. The doorman smiled, touched his cap and said: "Welcome!"

I smiled in return and walked inside, across the East Corridor and between the two grand staircases that led to the mezzanine level.

I couldn't help it; I stopped and stared again. Stately Doric columns lined the grand staircase hallway. Gold gilding gleamed everywhere. Original renaissance style frescoes decorated the walls near the ceiling. "Beautiful," I said to myself.

I walked into Colchester Lane, the main north-south corridor. The Oak Room entrance was across the corridor to the left. I walked over and peeked in the door. The room gleamed with gold gilding and crystal chandeliers in the latest American version of the French Beaux-Arts architectural style. The room was a beehive of activity; hotel staff members were setting up tables for a 'small' banquet.

While I was gazing in amazement, Eddie walked up behind me and said: "Nice, huh?"

I jumped a little and then tried to recover. "Beautiful," I finally uttered. Eddie just grinned. I stopped gawking and concentrated on the business at hand.

Eddie carried a heavy leather case, and I followed him north along Colchester Lane. We passed the elevator lobby opening on the left.

Fourteen elevators lined three sides of the lobby, five on each side and four in back. Several were open, each with a uniformed elevator attendant. The half-moon dials above the others had moving pointers; those elevators were between or at other floors.

Past the elevator lobby, also on the left, we arrived at the cashier's lobby. We turned in, walked past the marble cashier's counter and arrived at a suite of offices.

Just outside an office labeled 'Assistant Manager,' I saw Watts and Mulvaney. They were accompanied by an impeccably dressed, nervous-looking middle-aged man. "Assistant Manager," I thought to myself. I was right.

I smiled at the trio. Watts' face brightened as Eddie and I walked up. Both Watts and Mulvaney knew Eddie from previous encounters. I glanced up at an ornate clock on the wall behind the cashier's counter. "Ten o'clock," I mused to myself, "Two hours since Ruth's phone call."

Watts introduced the assistant manager. "Miss Case, Mr. Valenti, this is Mr. Willard Smolle, the on-duty manager."

Smolle offered his hand, first to me and then to Eddie. His palm was sweaty. He looked back and forth between us several times and then said: "I'm glad you are here; Detective Sergeant Watts told me about you."

Smolle then looked at Watts and said: "I hope we can clear this up very quickly and quietly, the hotel doesn't need notoriety in the newspapers." He looked back at me and continued: "We opened last year, and business has not yet taken off." He paused and then added: "But we have high hopes for the future."

Smolle's voice had a slight accent. "English," I thought to myself. I smiled and said in a soft, soothing voice: "Yes, well, shall we go to Mr. Meltzer's suite? Quietly, of course."

I think the woman's touch helped; Smolle seemed to calm down a little.

Watts saw the effect of my voice and nodded. He then motioned for Smolle to lead the way. We all followed Smolle toward the elevators.

The polite, uniformed elevator attendant let us off on the 27th floor. After we got off, the attendant closed the door. The elevator hummed as it headed down. Then silence reigned.

Finally, Smolle said: "This way." He turned the corner and headed to the left, down the hallway.

The hallway was quiet. Sconces along the walls gave off a golden light. The décor blended from Beaux-Arts by the elevators to a subdued, tasteful Art-Deco. "Reminds me of a funeral parlor," I thought to myself.

We passed several double-door suite entrances. I saw a uniformed policeman sitting in a chair outside a suite door down the hall. He saw us and stood.

"Hello, Joe," said Watts as we approached. "Everything OK?"

"Yessir," replied Joe; "Kinda spooky up here all alone, with a dead guy inside." Joe gestured with a turn of his head toward the door. He then looked first at me and then Eddie, with uncertain glances.

"We need to check out the room," responded Watts. "Miss Case and Mr. Valenti need to see everything." He paused and looked at Mulvaney and Smolle. "Wait here," he said. Mulvaney nodded in response and looked at Smolle, who was fidgeting a little. Smolle plainly didn't want to go in the room.

Joe fished a key out of his pocket and unlocked the door to the suite. Watts, Eddie and I stepped inside and closed the door. Silence again.

I glanced around. The suite had a large, comfortable, carpeted, Art-Deco style sitting area with a couch, several easy chairs and a wall unit with a fold-out writing desk. Several coffee tables, end tables and lamps had been placed in key locations. The lamps were on.

Two large windows on adjacent walls let in the late morning light. Accent drapes hung on both sides of each window, and Venetian blinds were pulled up near the top. The windows gave sweeping views of the city in one direction and Lake Michigan in the other.

Several modern art paintings decorated the walls. "Probably originals," I thought to myself.

I looked closely at the tables. A decanter and two glasses rested on a silver tray on one of the coffee tables. The decanter was full of a golden liquid. The glasses appeared unused.

Several sheets of paper and a fountain pen lay on the floor near the desk. A spot of ink stained the carpet under the pen. A metal pocket flask lay on the carpet next to the pen. The cap, attached by a little chain, was screwed shut.

Steam radiators had been installed under each window. The room was cool; the radiators were not producing heat.

The cool air had a slightly sour smell. I sniffed. I looked closely next to the writing desk. A messy, yellowish stain with flecks of green lay on the carpet near the desk.

Watts noticed my expression. "Vomit," he stated matter-of-factly.

French doors to the left provided access to a large bedroom. The doors were open. The bed was still made up. Lamps glowed on two night tables.

I could see something to the left of the bed. Feet and legs, fully dressed in slacks and shoes, extended past the bed on the far side.

"Sydney Albert Meltzer," I surmised in a soft voice.

"Yes," responded Watts, "Dead as a doornail."

2

DEAD AS A DOORNAIL

Monday, October 22, 1928

What a weekend! On Saturday morning, I comforted a grieving mother, raced on crowded city streets to the fanciest hotel in town and examined a dead body. On Sunday, Eddie, along with Susie, my trusted administrative assistant, and I planned a possible murder investigation.

Eddie and I arrived at Sydney Albert Meltzer's apartment at ten o'clock on Saturday morning. After a cursory check of the living room, we walked carefully from the main reception area to the bedroom. Sydney lay face down on the floor by the left side of the bed. He was dressed in shoes, slacks, dress shirt and tie. The tie had been pulled loose and the collar of the shirt was unbuttoned. His sports jacket lay on a nearby easy chair.

Eddie's large leather case contained his evidence collection tools. He set the case near the body and opened it. I was fascinated. Watts looked on from the bedroom doorway.

Eddie lifted a 35 mm camera out of the case. Light streamed through the bedroom window, and the lamps were still on, so the light was sufficient for photography. Eddie took a dozen pictures. Some were from a few feet away from the body, others were close-ups. When Eddie finished, he put the camera back in the case and took out a small sack that contained surgical gloves.

"Put these on," said Eddie, and he handed me a set of the gloves. His tone was matter-of-fact, as if he had examined many dead bodies. He slipped on his own gloves in a practiced fashion.

"OK," I responded. I tried to act professional, as if I were an old hand at this. I fumbled a little, but I got the gloves on. Eddie paid no attention to me; he was peering intently at poor Sydney.

"Hummm," Eddie muttered. "Sydney has a nasty, swollen lump on his right temple and forehead." Eddie then gingerly raised Sydney's right eyelid and looked closely. "Pupil is widely dilated," he muttered. He pulled out a notebook and wrote carefully and quickly.

While Eddie was inspecting Sydney's head, face and eyes, I looked first at Sydney's head and then the rounded corner of the nightstand next to the headboard of the bed. "Probably smacked his head when he fell," I said. "Looks like an oily smudge on that rounded corner; I can see it by looking at it from the right angle in the light."

"I see it," responded Eddie. "From the looks of Sydney's slick hair, it's probably his hair oil. I'll take a sample." He peered closely at Sydney's head, the floor and the nightstand. "No blood on Sydney, or the floor or on the nightstand," he added. He paused and looked again at the lump on Sydney's forehead and temple. "The smack on his head didn't kill him, the swelling occurred while he was still alive." Eddie wrote again in his notebook.

"His lips are blue," I replied. "What does that mean?"

"Oxygen deprivation," stated Eddie. "Sydney died after he fell; he couldn't process oxygen into his bloodstream."

"I see," I said. "Notice the substance by his mouth?" I bent over and looked closely. I could smell faintly the sour stench that I detected in the living room. "It looks like the same stuff on the floor by the desk; it's yellow with flecks of green."

"Yes," replied Eddie, as he peered at Sydney's mouth. He reached in his case and took out a test tube and a small, disposable wooden spatula. He took the glass stopper out of the test tube and gingerly used the spatula to take a sample of the substance on and by Sydney's mouth. He carefully placed the sample in the open test tube and then closed it with the glass stopper. He put the stoppered test tube in a little wooden rack inside the case. I noticed that the test tubes were labeled 1, 2, 3 and so on.

Eddie placed the spatula in an empty paper sack, also inside his case. "Trash bag," he stated for my benefit. He took out a notepad and wrote: 'Test tube 1, substance by victim's mouth.' He then placed the notebook back in his case and stood up.

I continued to peer at Sydney's body. "Did Sydney choke on his vomit or did he just stop breathing?"

"The latter, I think," replied Eddie. "There are no contortions that would indicate a struggle for air."

"The body looks completely relaxed," I responded. I looked closely at Sydney's posture, clothing and the carpet around his body. "I don't think he moved much after he fell and hit his head."

"Yes," responded Eddie. He knelt down by his case and fished out a syringe. "Let's draw some blood."

After Eddie prepared the syringe, he pulled down the sock above Sydney's right shoe and exposed a vein just above his ankle. Soon Eddie had a blood sample in another stoppered, labeled test tube. He placed the syringe in a paper bag and placed the bag back in the case. "I'll clean and sterilize it later," he stated.

Eddie finished with the blood sample, and he got out a pair of scissors and another test tube. After a minute, he had a sample of Sydney's hair from his head in a new labeled test tube. Eddie looked at me, grinned and said: "You would be surprised at the tests we can do with human hair."

Eddie stood up again. "Let's take his fingerprints and scrapings from under his fingernails and then inventory his pockets," he stated. "Afterwards, I will take readings of Sydney's body temperature and the ambient room temperature."

"Temperature?" I asked.

"Helps determine time of death," replied Eddie. "Also, I will check for the level of rigor mortis."

Soon it was done. I helped with the pockets and fingerprinting. Sydney's pockets contained a wallet with identification, one hundred ten dollars in small bills, some loose change and a handkerchief. We left the body exactly like we found it, except for loosened clothing where the blood sample and temperature had been taken. The medical examiner would do the autopsy and the associated tests.

As Eddie and I backed up toward the bedroom door, we looked around. Nothing else appeared out of the ordinary, not even the bed. It had not been slept in.

Watts saw me as I looked at the bed and said: "According to Smolle, the sheets, blankets, pillows and bedspread have not been disturbed since the maid service on Friday."

We also looked in the bathroom adjacent to the bedroom. Again, nothing unusual; it was clean as a whistle. We checked the medicine cabinet. It contained a bottle of aspirin, a bottle of mouthwash, a toothbrush, a tube of toothpaste, a safety razor, a mug with shaving soap and a shaving soap brush. Fresh, unused towels and washcloths hung on convenient racks. We returned to the bedroom where Watts was waiting.

"There's a small kitchenette in back," said Watts. "According to Smolle, Meltzer had it set up special." He paused and then added: "Smolle also said that it's the only kitchenette on this floor. The others are on the 28th and in the penthouse on the 29th."

"Let's take a look," I replied.

Eddie, Watts and I walked back through the living room and into the kitchenette at the back of the suite. Eddie carried his case. We stopped just inside the doorway and looked around.

"Sink, counter, a small Frigidaire, an electric hotplate, an electric coffee pot, cabinets for dishes, a pantry in back, a small table and four chairs," mused Eddie.

Light streamed in from the window over the sink and counter, and the overhead light was still on. "Very modern and beautifully done," I responded. "Our Sydney had excellent taste."

I paused a moment and looked closely at the table. "Someone had a light meal," I stated. I pointed to the table.

"Yes," replied Watts. "Looks like a half-eaten salad, some rye bread, cheese and a tumbler of some clear liquid. We noticed it just after we discovered the body." He looked first at me and then Eddie. "I assume you want photos and samples."

"Yes," I responded. "We'll also check the contents of the Frigidaire and pantry." Eddie went right to work. I observed every detail. For me, it was a learning experience. Eddie finished in about ten minutes.

"Shall we go back to the living room?" Eddie stated as he finished packing up his kitchenette samples.

"Sounds good," I replied. We need samples of the vomit on the carpet, the contents of the flask on the floor, the liquid in the decanter and a look at the sheets of paper that are scattered around." I paused, thought, then added: "Are you going to dust for fingerprints?"

"The entire suite," replied Eddie matter-of-factly. "I'll do that last, it will take some time."

"OK," I responded. "While you are finishing up here, perhaps Sergeant Watts, Detective Mulvaney and I can follow up with Smolle and get a list of hotel employees that we should interview, like the elevator attendants, doormen, maids and so on." I thought a moment, and added: "Come on down to Smolle's office when you are done.'

"Right," replied Eddie. "I'll need a couple of hours here."

I looked at Watts. "OK with you?" I said.

"Sure," he replied with a grin. "You two are very efficient; would you like a job with the department?"

I chuckled in response, so did Eddie.

"I didn't think so," said Watts. He shook his head and smiled with a slightly resigned look.

Watts and I stepped out from the suite door. Mulvaney, Joe the uniformed policeman and Smolle were still there.

Mulvaney looked to Watts. "I have a list of names," he said.

"Good," replied Watts. "Let's go to Mr. Smolle's office, except for you, Joe. Wait here for the coroner's team; they'll pick up the body soon."

"Yessir," responded Joe. He didn't look very enthusiastic; the hallway was still spooky and quiet.

Watts, Mulvaney, Smolle and I headed down the hallway toward the elevators. A few minutes later, we were seated around a plush table in Smolle's office. I looked at the clock on the office wall. "Eleven-thirty," I thought to myself. "We spent less than an hour and a half in Sydney's suite." My tummy growled. "Hungry," my thoughts continued. I fidgeted.

Smolle noticed and smiled. "Perhaps everyone would like some lunch," he said. "I can have my secretary bring in some sandwiches, coffee and tea. We can eat while we work."

"The perfect host," I thought to myself. Perhaps a little too quickly, I replied: "That would be very nice." The others in the room all smiled.

Smolle gave orders to his secretary outside his office. Lunch arrived in about fifteen minutes. We continued our meeting and washed the food down with coffee.

Between bites of a sandwich, Mulvaney began with a quick review. "Mr. Smolle and I identified employees who may have had contact with Mr. Meltzer on Friday," he said. "The obvious people include: the doorman, elevator attendants, desk clerks, dining service staff and maids."

"Let's see your list," Watts stated, as he looked at Mulvaney.

Mulvaney placed his list on the table where we all could see.

"Hummm," mused Watts: "Names, job title and location. Good!"

I peered at the list. "Looks pretty comprehensive," I stated, and I smiled at Mulvaney. "It's a good start. Of course, as we do interviews, we'll probably come up with additional names." Everyone nodded.

"Did you identify any visitors or companions who were with Mr. Meltzer, perhaps on Friday or earlier?" I asked.

"Yes," responded Mulvaney. "Mr. Smolle remembers that Charles Everett Meltzer, Sydney's brother, visited recently; we'll probably get more names from other hotel staff members."

"Right," added Smolle. "Charles Meltzer came into my office several times over the past few months. He had questions about his brother's bills."

"How much were the bills?" I asked.

"Quite high, as a matter of fact," replied Smolle. "I remember that for last month, his incidental charges were over two thousand dollars." He paused a moment and added: "Mr. Smolle's suite cost four thousand per month."

"Wow!" Mulvaney exclaimed. "That total is almost twice as much as I make in a year, and I've been on the force over twenty years."

Watts glanced at his partner with a frown. Smolle just smiled.

"Can we get a record of Sydney's bills and payments for the past year?" I asked.

"Of course," replied Smolle. "I can give you records from the time Mr. Meltzer rented his suite to the present." He paused and then added: "We opened on May 2nd last year, and Mr. Meltzer has been our guest since the beginning. In fact, he signed a lease in late 1926, and he had modifications done to his suite during hotel construction."

"I'm particularly interested in who pays the bills," I responded.

"I understand," replied Smolle. Watts nodded approvingly.

And so, the afternoon passed. Eddie joined us at about two o'clock, and we compared notes. After the usual pleasantries, we all agreed to keep in touch by phone. Eddie planned to take his photos and samples to the lab as soon as he dropped me off at my apartment. Watts promised again to let us know when the medical examiner's report was ready. Smolle passed the list of employees developed by Mulvaney and himself to his secretary for proofing, corrections and typing. He promised to deliver copies to both Watts and me by courier on Monday. I was exhausted. It was time to go home.

I resolved to try to reach Hannibal by phone as soon as I could. In the meantime, I would also call Susie, my assistant. I needed her fine administrative touch. "We must set up one of our offices at the apartment to manage this investigation," I concluded to myself.

Eddie and I walked to the parking lot, got into his car and headed back to my apartment at about four o'clock. The traffic was heavy for a Saturday, and Eddie came up with a few new words with regard to other drivers. I tried not to laugh. Eddie saw me, grinned and shook his head. "Sorry about that," he said.

On the way, Eddie asked: "When will Hannibal be back?"

"This weekend, I hope," I replied. "He's working in Pittsburgh; he has banking business that has to be done."

"I understand," responded Eddie. He didn't pry; he was well aware that Hannibal had many responsibilities.

We arrived safely at the apartment at about a quarter until five, and Eddie drove off with a wave of his hand. Harris was gone for the day, and I let myself in the building.

I trudged to the elevator, got to my floor and into my apartment.

Fortunately, Silvia, my maid who lives in the quarters just below our penthouse, had made a nice cold plate for me and left it in the Frigidaire. I found her note on the kitchen table.

Silvia had also picked up my mess from earlier this morning and put clean sheets and pillowcases on the bed. The lamps were on, and everything looked very neat and cozy. "Very thoughtful," I said to myself.

I poured myself a glass of chardonnay from the open bottle in the Fridge and set it on the coffee table by the window that looked out over Lake Michigan. I then cleaned up in the bathroom, put on my silk pajamas and robe and returned to a soft chair next to my glass of wine. "To prohibition," I said aloud, and I raised my glass in a toast. The evening view out the window was beautiful.

Sunday was better. I got up at about eight o'clock, made some coffee and sat by the window that looked out over Lake Michigan. Silvia arrived at about eight-thirty, fixed breakfast, and cleaned up my messy bedroom and bathroom.

In the meantime, I called Ruth, made sure Mandy was present, and re-assured Ruth that I was working hard on her case.

She told me that her son Charles had arrived and had spent the night. "Charles is making arrangements," she said.

I was relieved. "I'll talk with Charles later," I told Ruth. After a few more re-assurances, I hung up the phone. "Time to have breakfast, get cleaned up and dressed," I said to myself. "I'll call Susie afterwards."

"Breakfast is ready," Silvia called out, right on cue.

I called Susie about ten o'clock. "I'll be over at about one," she said. She arrived, right on time. I was already dressed in slacks, a simple blouse and comfortable shoes. I had also finished lunch and had regained some of my composure.

Susie and I spent the rest of the afternoon setting up a workroom in my apartment office. She left about five, and again, I was exhausted.

"This private detective work isn't for sissies!" I exclaimed to Silvia. She laughed and served me a very nice supper. Silvia cleaned up, turned down the bed, and left for the night. I had a glass of chardonnay, watched the lights come on in the city to the south and went to bed about nine PM.

3

TESTING, TESTING AND MURDER

Saturday evening, October 27, 1928

Early this morning, I was warm and cozy in bed. Sunlight was just beginning to illuminate the bedroom through the window at the far end. A soft, yet insistent knock on my door impinged upon my consciousness. My mind slowly, reluctantly drifted up from deeply personal dreams.

Knock, knock! There it was again. I then heard a soft voice. "Caroline, it's time to wake up!" It was Silvia.

"Silvia," I responded in a grumpy, slightly slurred voice: "It's too early. Go away!" I burrowed down in the bed under the warm covers and pretended that the knock and the voice didn't happen.

Knock, knock: there it was again. "Oh, Caroline," I heard Silvia say, "Rise and shine!" I then heard a giggle. "I have your coffee, and your door is locked."

I opened one eye and looked at the clock on the nightstand. After a minute or so, my other eye opened and I focused. "Silvia, it's only seven-thirty!"

"Coffee will get cold, Caroline," replied Silvia.

"OK, OK, I'm coming," I replied. I flipped off my covers, rolled to a sitting position and rubbed my eyes. After a minute, I slowly got to my feet and stumbled toward the door. I didn't bother with a robe. My ivory silk lounging pajamas from Saks in Palm Beach hung loosely over my willowy frame. My hair was a mess and down in my eyes.

31

"The coffee had better be perfect," I muttered, loud enough for Silvia to hear. The only response was another giggle.

I opened the door. Hannibal stood there, smiling at me. Silvia stood back a little. She had a silver tray with coffee service for two. She burst out laughing.

"You!" I uttered. "You weren't supposed to be back until tomorrow!"

Hannibal chuckled, and in his deep resonant voice, said: "Surprise!"

"Oh, Hannibal, it's so good to see you!" I reached around his waist and up to his shoulders. I hugged him close. He was warm, and I snuggled. "You're better than the bedcovers," I said.

Silvia stopped laughing and said: "Ahem! I'll just put this on the dresser." She walked past Hannibal and me, completed her errand and left discretely.

"It's so good to see you!" I said again, and I began kissing Hannibal over and over.

Much later, Hannibal and I sat across from each other at the kitchen table. We both were fully dressed, and I had combed my hair. We had just consumed a light breakfast, and we were sipping our third cup of coffee. After preparing breakfast earlier, Silvia had disappeared. Hannibal and I were alone. I had a stack of reports, which I had placed on the kitchen table, along with a notepad and a couple of pencils.

"I have so much to tell you," I stated.

"Oh, good," replied Hannibal with a smile. "I was wondering when you would get around to it." He sipped more coffee and watched me over the rim of his cup.

"OK, Smarty," I responded. I giggled a little; I couldn't help it. I paused a moment, sipped my coffee and collected my thoughts. Hannibal waited patiently.

"I told you about Ruth, the death of her son, Sydney, and the investigation that Eddie and I have started, over the phone on Tuesday," I began.

Hannibal nodded, and I continued. "While the detectives and I were at Ruth's apartment, Sergeant Watts said that the Police Central District Station received an anonymous tip about Sydney at six in the morning on October 20th."

"On Thursday, I got the Cook County medical examiner's report and Willard Smolle's list of hotel employees that we should interview. On Friday, I got Eddie's preliminary lab report. I have read all three."

"What did the medical examiner have to say?" Hannibal asked.

"Well, to begin, the report gives a brief summary of how the body was found," I said. I paused as I looked at the first couple of paragraphs of the report. "It verifies the time of the phone call as six-ten, and it adds that the caller's voice was female. The report cites police switchboard and desk sergeant logbooks as sources."

"Hummm," responded Hannibal. "What exactly did the caller say?"

I read a little further and replied: "The caller simply said: 'The police should check on a Mr. Sydney Meltzer at the Steven's Hotel,' and the report says the caller then hung up."

Hannibal nodded and said: "Not much to go on, except that the voice was female; she knew Sydney and where he lived, and that something happened that required police attention."

I looked further down in the report summary and continued: "Death from asphyxia, oxygen deprivation due to paralysis of the respiratory system." I paused and then added: "Also, the stomach contents included substantial amounts of both ethyl and methyl alcohol, and tests of the blood, liver and kidneys showed substantial traces of formaldehyde."

"Hummm," responded Hannibal. "Methyl alcohol is highly toxic." He paused a moment and then added: "The human body metabolizes methanol, the common term for methyl alcohol, into formaldehyde over a period of several hours."

I looked at the report closely and said: "Here it is. The report says that the estimate of blood alcohol levels and the presence of formaldehyde, indicates the consumption of at least 250 milliliters of methyl alcohol over a period of several hours."

"Lethal," replied Hannibal.

"How did he get methanol, as you call it, into his system?" I asked.

"Ingestion of methanol is not unusual nowadays," Hannibal stated with a sigh. "Most folks call it 'wood alcohol.' It's highly poisonous, and it often shows up in moonshine, along with ethyl alcohol, which is the usual alcohol used for human consumption."

"Poison in the moonshine?" I asked.

Hannibal nodded and said: "It shows up in moonshine naturally in small amounts and also as an additive." He paused a moment and then added: "Methanol is readily available. I know that DuPont and Commercial Solvents Corporation manufacture it for medicinal, laboratory and industrial uses."

"So, someone spiked the moonshine with extra methanol?" I asked.

"Probably," replied Hannibal. "Also, given that some of the methanol had metabolized into formaldehyde, Sidney had begun to ingest bad booze several hours before his death." He paused a moment and then added: "The unprocessed ethyl and methyl alcohol in his stomach indicates that he continued drinking it until just before the end."

I thought a moment and then said: "I have heard the term 'formaldehyde' before, but I thought it was used by funeral homes to embalm bodies."

"Yes," replied Hannibal with a grim expression. "Embalming fluid is a mix of formaldehyde, methanol, disinfectants and solvents. With formaldehyde in his bloodstream, Sydney essentially was in the process of being embalmed while alive."

"Wow," I responded. "However, the report also shows something else."

Hannibal raised his eyebrows and said: "Oh?" He took another sip of coffee and looked at me over the rim of his cup.

I looked carefully and then read the words slowly from the report. "Blood tests and kidney analysis show the presence of piperidine alkaloids." I paused and then added: "These alkaloids are listed as conine, N-methyconine, conhydrine, and gamma-conhydrine." I stumbled over the unfamiliar words.

"Interesting," replied Hannibal. "If I remember my classwork in chemistry and biology correctly, those alkaloids are present in conium."

I looked further down in the report. "Yes," I said. "Here it says: Estimated dosage of conium was 120 milligrams." I gave Hannibal a questioning look and added: "What does that mean?"

"Conium maculatum," Hannibal replied. "It's the Latin term for hemlock." He paused and then added: "Any dosage over 100 milligrams in an adult human is fatal."

"Oh," I responded. I thought a while and recalled my readings of history. "Socrates, the Greek philosopher, was poisoned with hemlock."

"Yes," Hannibal replied. "So goes the story anyway." He paused, leaned back in his seat and added: "Hemlock is an invasive species of flowering plant, and it has become quite common in and around Chicago."

I know my face had a quizzical expression. "How do you know this?" I asked.

"Lots of reading at the lab," Hannibal replied modestly. "Our lab guys have encountered hemlock poisoning before. The Illinois State agricultural people involved the lab with an investigation that showed hemlock poisoning in livestock last year."

"Oh," I responded. I thought a moment and then added: "The report had something else." I leafed through the report and found what I had read earlier. "Stomach contents included unidentified masticated green leaves, cheese, common rye bread, vinegar, lettuce, tomato and cucumber."

"Humm," mused Hannibal. "Except for the unidentified leaves, it appears that Sydney ate a salad, bread and cheese before his death."

"I agree," I replied. "Eddie and I found a half-eaten plate of salad, cheese and bread on the table in Sydney's kitchenette."

"Interesting," said Hannibal, and he leaned back in his chair: "Anything else from the medical examiner?"

"Nothing in terms of findings," I replied. "The rest of the report provides procedures used for the autopsy and the analysis of samples, instructions for preservation of evidence and so on." I leafed through report again to be sure. "Nothing," I repeated.

"How about Eddie's lab report?" Hannibal asked.

"Eddie's report essentially corroborates the findings of the medical examiner," I replied. "It also adds information on the vomit sample." I paused as I looked to places I had marked in the report. "In addition to confirming the stomach contents, the unidentified leaves from the medical examiner's report were also in the vomit and in the salad on the table. The lab identified them as conium maculatum."

"Good," said Hannibal. "Our guys would know; they have samples taken during our livestock poisoning research."

I nodded and responded with "The other new findings were an estimate of time of death, an analysis of the contents of a hip flask that we found on the living room floor, the results of an examination of the body, an analysis of the papers lying on the living room floor and a list of fingerprints found in the apartment, including an unknown set on the flask." I paused and added: "Eddie also included lots of photos with his report."

Hannibal looked at the photos while I leafed through Eddie's report again and found the correct passage.

I read it aloud. "As of 11:00 AM, October 20, 1928, the temperature of the body was 80.4 degrees F. The ambient room temperature was 68 degrees F. The body exhibited modest rigor. Based on an average drop in body temperature of about 1.5 degrees per hour and assuming a steady state ambient room temperature, death occurred after 10:30 PM and before midnight, October 19, 1928."

"And the hip flask?" Hannibal queried.

I leafed through the report, looked up and stated: "The hip flask has an eight-ounce capacity." I looked down the page and added: "The contents of the flask included about one ounce of liquid with a mix of 50 percent ethyl and 40 percent methyl alcohol in a water solution."

I looked up at Hannibal, who nodded. I then looked back to the report and continued. "The remaining flask contents included water and small traces of particulate matter, including lead. The mixture indicates a 100-proof, homemade alcoholic beverage, with fermented corn as the source of the ethyl alcohol. The methyl alcohol was an additive."

"Did you or Eddie find any other source of bad booze in the apartment?" Hannibal asked.

"No," I replied. "There was a full decanter of what looked like an alcoholic beverage and two glasses on a coffee table in the living room, but the decanter was full and the glasses appeared unused."

I looked at Eddie's report again. "Here it is," I said. "Eddie had the contents of the decanter analyzed. It was good quality scotch whiskey."

Hannibal picked up a pencil from the table and started scribbling on the notepad. I watched in silence.

Finally, he put the pencil down and looked up. He then said: "Based on 250 milliliters of methanol consumed, the ratios of the two alcohols in the flask and the proof estimate, Sydney consumed a little over two pints of contaminated moonshine in about two hours or so."

I thought a few moments and then said: "Given that the flask capacity was eight ounces, which is about half a pint and the fact that one ounce remained in the flask, Sydney consumed most of his poison moonshine from another source."

Hannibal nodded. "Sydney came home drunk, drank more from his flask, tried to eat a salad, vomited in the living room and somehow made it to his bedroom."

I nodded and said: "As the photos show, he fell, hit his head on the nightstand and died sometime afterwards. I paused, thinking, and then added: "The bump on the head probably rendered him unconscious, and he simply stopped breathing as he lay on the floor."

Hannibal leaned forward in his chair and reached over to the nearby coffee pot on the table. He filled my cup and then his own. We both sipped and thought for a while in silence.

Hannibal finally asked: "What about the papers on the living room floor?"

I read more in Eddie's report and said: "Eddie found ink stains on the index finger of Sydney's right hand. Apparently, Sydney tried to write something on the paper while at the desk, dropped the pen and scattered the papers on the floor. The only writing was a scrawl of 'Sus' on one sheet." I paused and added: "No suicide note."

"Hummm," replied Hannibal. "Sus could be the start of a name. What about fingerprints?"

"Sydney's prints, of course," I responded, and I looked at Eddie's report. "There were five other sets, sources unknown. One set was on the hip flask, two sets were on a ceramic container in the Frigidaire, a fourth set on an unopened bottle of scotch in the pantry and a fifth set on the counter in the bathroom, the back of a chair in the kitchenette and on the doorknobs to several rooms. The container in the Frigidaire also had some residue of the same salad that we found on the table."

"The fifth set of fingerprints in several locations probably belongs to the maid," observed Hannibal. "But we will check."

After another minute or so of silence, I asked: "So what killed Sydney? Was it methanol or hemlock? He had lethal doses of both."

"Good question," replied Hannibal. "Certainly, the hemlock was an attempt at murder, and the intake of methanol could either be just bad booze inadvertently consumed or bad booze administered by someone with murder as the intent."

"We need to follow up with interviews of the people on Smolle's list," I replied.

"Yes," responded Hannibal with a smile. "You have been a busy lady during my absence."

4

ASK THE RIGHT QUESTIONS

Saturday, November 3, 1928

Burrr! People don't refer to Chicago as the 'windy city' for nothing. Yesterday morning at about eight-thirty, Hannibal drove his new burgundy and black Ford Model A two-door coupe around to the front of our apartment building. Harris, our doorman, helped me as I hurried from the building vestibule to the car. The wind blew from Lake Michigan and low gray clouds scudded across the sky from the direction of the lake. Drops of rain pattered all around.

"Early winter," I muttered as I climbed in next to Hannibal. My beige mink fur hat, fur-lined black gloves, high-top black leather boots and my second, more elaborate black Persian lamb coat with beige mink trim kept me reasonably warm, but the cold lake wind found ways to get inside and give me the shivers. In addition to my purse, I carried a nice leather notecase. Inside, I had a writing pad, pencils, Smolle's list and my notes on findings from the reports by Eddie and the medical examiner.

As Hannibal drove away from the building toward Lakeshore Drive, I fiddled with the little door in the firewall under the dash so the manifold heater could warm the passenger compartment. Finally, I got it about right, and the warm air off the engine helped a little. Hannibal drove at a moderate speed; not like the breakneck pace that Eddie accomplished during our ride less than two weeks ago. Still, we seemed to hit the new traffic lights and old-fashioned stop signs at just the right moment to keep a steady pace.

Hannibal and I headed to the Steven's Hotel. Working with us by phone after our meeting, Willard Smolle and Amy, his secretary, had set up interviews with key hotel employees beginning at ten o'clock in the morning and ending just after five in the evening. Our objective was to take statements and pare down the list to employees who merited second, more in-depth interviews.

"Twenty-two names," I said in a voice that Hannibal could hear over the sounds of the car engine and traffic noise. I took the list from my note case and looked carefully: "Two doormen, five elevator operators, two maids, three front desk clerks, two club attendants, an account manager, two waiters, a delivery boy, two bellmen and two hotel-based taxi drivers," I added.

Hannibal nodded and replied: "Smolle provided a good annotated list, with names, job titles, work hours and likely circumstances with regard to contact with Sydney."

"Yes," I responded. "Thanks to Amy, we have appointments with each, twenty minutes apart, all day long. I paused and then added: "According to Amy's last phone call, she set us up in a small conference room near Smolle's office."

Hannibal nodded and said: "Busy day ahead."

We arrived at the hotel about nine-thirty, and we made it to the plush little conference room a few minutes later. Amy had brought us a tray with a large coffee pot, a pot of tea, condiments and little sweet snacks. We also had two racks of twenty-four clean coffee cups and plates in a cabinet under the counter where Amy set the tray, coffee pot and tea pot. The slots in the two racks were numbered. The counter where we placed the tray had a nice little built-in sink and faucet. After getting settled, we were ready to start.

Our first interviewee, a thin young man in his early twenties, entered the conference room. "You are Joseph Smith, and you are a front desk clerk, evening shift," I said, as the young man stopped and stood on the other side of the table from Hannibal and me. I looked at Joseph with a steady gaze, but also with a smile.

Joseph fidgeted a little and replied: "Yes, ma'am, most folks call me Joe."

"Please have a seat, Joe," I responded in a soothing voice. "Want some coffee or tea?"

Joe nodded as he took a seat on the other side of the conference table. "Yes, ma'am, coffee please," he replied.

I took out a cup from the rack in the cabinet and poured him a cup from the nearby coffee pot. "Cream? Sugar?" I asked.

"Just a little sugar, ma'am," Joe responded. He relaxed a little.

After Joe had sipped his coffee, Hannibal and I asked questions. The interview went well, and we finished in about fifteen minutes. Joe left. I picked up his half-empty coffee cup by holding the rim and the bottom gingerly, emptied it in the sink, and replaced it in the rack spot labeled number one. Hannibal and I were ready for interview number two.

And so, the day progressed, with interview after interview. Hannibal and I both took notes, and we maintained a steady pace. Amy kept us supplied with fresh coffee, tea and snacks, and we had sandwiches at noon. We finished number twenty-two just after five in the evening.

"Whew!" I exclaimed as Mary Jane McGregor, a maid and the last interviewee, left the conference room and closed the door. "Let's compare notes and see what we have."

Hannibal smiled. "OK, but let's keep it short. I made dinner reservations in the main dining room for seven o'clock. We won't get home until nine or so."

"Long day," I agreed. "Let's finish it."

"Well," responded Hannibal, as he glanced through his notes: "We got relevant comments from Joe Smith the front desk clerk, Winston Brooks, a doorman, Antonio De Melza, an elevator operator, Mary Jane McGregor, a 27th floor maid, Anna Lombardi, a hotel telephone switchboard operator and Vincenzo Parelli, a taxi driver who is a regular at this hotel."

"Yes," I replied. "I have those names, plus Arthur Smythe, an employee of the Colchester Grill in the lobby, and Andrew Sullivan, a bellman."

"OK," said Hannibal. "Let's start with Joe Smith."

I nodded and replied: "Joe said that he received calls from Charles, Sydney's brother, on several occasions, asking the whereabouts of Sydney." I paused and then added: "This is consistent with Smolle's comments concerning Charles' questions about Sydney's bills."

Hannibal nodded, flipped through his notes and said: "The last call from Charles was on Friday, October 19th, the day Sydney was poisoned." He paused and added: "Joe said the time was mid-afternoon."

I looked through my notes and replied: "Anna, the hotel switchboard operator, logged the call at four-fifteen."

"Agreed," replied Hannibal.

I studied my notes for a few moments and then said: "Joe also recalled that over the past few weeks before Sydney's death, he got calls from three females. They all wanted to talk to Sydney. Several calls came from a lady named Jaqueline Dumas, who identified herself as Sydney's fiancé. Another call was from Mrs. Elizabeth Meltzer, and the third came from a woman who did not give her name."

Hannibal nodded and then responded: "Jaqueline Dumas is from a wealthy family. I saw her name several times in the society pages of the Tribune. Her father is a Chicago banker."

"Didn't know you read the society pages," I replied with a smile.

Hannibal blushed a little and grinned. "Yes, well, only occasionally," he responded. After a moment, he added: "Elizabeth Meltzer is Charles' wife; she also shows up in the society pages."

I couldn't help it; I continued to smile at Hannibal for a moment or so. He fidgeted.

After a moment, Hannibal recovered his composure and continued. "Both Joe and Anna said that the third female had a 'working class' accent, whatever that means."

"When did she call?" I asked. I leafed through my notes but couldn't find anything.

Hannibal was back on his game, and he scanned his notes. "Joe said all three females called the hotel on Friday," he stated in a matter-of-fact tone. "Anna logged the times as follows: Jaqueline at twelve-thirty-five, Elizabeth at three-fifteen and the 'working class' female at nine o'clock that night. According to Anna, all three asked to speak to Sydney, who didn't answer Anna's rings to his suite."

"The last phone call is especially interesting, given that Sydney died in his suite between ten-thirty and midnight," I replied.

"Anything else from Joe and Anna?" Hannibal asked.

"No," I replied. "The next person in my notes is Winston Brooks, the doorman."

"Agree," responded Hannibal. "Winston recalled quite a few nights when Sydney arrived at the hotel front entrance in a taxi, drunk and hardly able to navigate through the door."

"Yes," I replied. "The last time was about eight-thirty on Friday evening, October 19th." I paused and then added: "The Friday arrival time was confirmed by Vincenzo, the taxi driver, and Andrew, the bellman."

Hannibal studied his notes and then said: "Fortunately, Vincenzo brought his logbook to the interview. He said that he picked Sydney up at the corner of North Throop Street and West Wabansia Avenue just after eight o'clock."

"Yes," I said. "I remember. Vincenzo said that the driving distance is about four and one-half miles, and the drive from the pick-up point to the Stevens Hotel took less than 20 minutes." I thought a moment and then added: "He also said that he had taken Sidney to and picked him up at the same location several times over the past few months."

"Vincenzo also said that Sydney sang during the entire ride back to the hotel," Hannibal mused, almost to himself.

"Yes," I responded. "Oh, Susannah, don't you cry for me, or some variation." I paused and then added: "It must have been quite a show. At least Sydney was happy."

Hannibal leaned back in his chair. I could tell the wheels were turning in his mind. I waited patiently.

After a minute or so, Hannibal asked: "What did Sydney write on the paper you found on the floor in his suite?"

I thought a moment. "Sus," I responded." So?"

"Coincidence, maybe," replied Hannibal. "Sydney was singing about a female named Susannah."

"We need to find Sydney's watering hole near North Throop and West Wabansia," I stated. "In addition to poison booze, who knows what we will find?"

"OK," responded Hannibal. "Let's look up the intersection of North Throop and West Wabansia on a map."

"Good idea," I replied. I got up and stepped out of the conference room. I soon found a desk clerk who gave me a city street map. He also kindly located the intersection of North Throop and West Wabansia for me. I returned with the map to the conference room.

I spread the map on the table, pointed to the intersection and said: "After giving me this map, the clerk out front stated that this intersection is in a rather seedy, industrial part of town."

"Interesting," replied Hannibal. He looked closely at the map. "It's definitely a working-class neighborhood." He turned away from the map, leafed through his notes and added: "Andrew escorted Sydney to his apartment between eight-thirty and eight forty-five. He then reported Sydney's condition to Joe Smith, the front desk clerk."

"Hummm," I responded. "Yes, here it is in my notes: Joe was a little more succinct. To quote Joe: 'Mr. Meltzer was drunk as a skunk when he arrived Friday evening,' end of quote."

Hannibal chuckled a little and said: "I remember Joe's description."

I waited as Hannibal read. Finally, he said: "Antonio, the elevator operator, confirms Andrew Sullivan's story about escorting Sydney to the 27th floor at about eight-thirty."

"Antonio also said that he saw Andrew leave another elevator in the lobby after eight forty-five but prior to nine o'clock, when Antonio's shift ended," I replied.

I then asked: "Do you have anything from Mary Jane, the maid?"

Hannibal smiled and said: "Not much, except that she cleaned and picked up Sydney's suite on Friday from about noon until two in the afternoon." Hannibal paused and then added: "Mary Jane said the suite was a mess, as usual."

I replied: "Sydney was careless about his suite, but not so in his dress. I saw his closet, and Eddie took photos." I took out a couple of photos from my note case and handed them to Hannibal.

"Expensive tastes," Hannibal agreed. "Did Mary Jane say anything about the contents of the Frigidaire?"

"I remember your question during the interview and Mary Jane's answer," I responded. "When she wiped down the condensation inside the Fridge, she saw a salad in a ceramic container." I paused and then added: "Mary Jane also said that no one came to the suite while she was there, and she was alone the entire time."

"Hummm," responded Hannibal. "That means that the salad was placed in the Frigidaire before noon on Friday."

Hannibal and I paused in our conversation. We each made few more notes.

After a few minutes, Hannibal put his pencil down, looked up and said: "You mentioned Arthur, the Colchester Grill guy. I didn't write down anything during his interview. What did you observe?"

I thought a moment and then said: "I remember that he looked down and fidgeted when I asked him about his relationship with Sydney."

"Hummm," responded Hannibal. "I recall that he said Sydney stopped by the grill for a sandwich on occasion, but that was all. What does your intuition tell you?"

"I think that Arthur and Sydney had more than a casual relationship. It's a hunch, but I will follow up."

"We also need to find out the identity of the working-class female caller and where the salad in Sydney's Frigidaire came from," replied Hannibal.

"Yes," I responded. "In addition, we don't know exactly where Sydney got 'drunk as a skunk' on Friday before eight in the evening, and we have yet to identify the four sets of fingerprints in Sydney's suite."

Hannibal leaned back in his chair and folded his hands behind his head. He looked at me for a long moment with his characteristic, steady, blue-eyed gaze. I squirmed a little in my seat.

Finally, he said: "Looking for a source of poison booze in the neighborhood of North Throop and West Wabansia could be dangerous. It's an industrial area with tough neighborhoods." He paused and then added: "Even the police send a large force if they have to go in."

"I know," I replied. "I've been in tough neighborhoods before." I thought a moment and then added: "I expect that the source will be someone who was with Sydney, probably in a blind pig style speakeasy."

Hannibal smiled, nodded his head and said: "Yes, well, Wabash Valley establishments are tame compared to those in Chicago." His eyes seemed to be searching for some sign in my expression. He then added: "Also, this is Al Capone's backyard, and his local competitors are not all dead yet."

"It will be an adventure," I responded, as I tried to look confident. Inside, my emotions were a mix of excitement at the prospect of adventure, but there was also a tinge of fear. Hannibal was right, of course.

Hannibal smiled again, and he seemed to come to a conclusion in his mind. He then said: "OK, blind pig first, followed by fingerprints and the hemlock-laced salad. We have lots to do."

Hannibal leaned forward and pulled out his pocket watch. "Six forty-five," he said. "Eddie will stop by shortly to pick up the racks of used cups and plates under the counter and take them to the lab. Amy knows not to touch them. He paused and then added: "We are both in business attire, and you look beautiful. Are you ready for dinner?"

"Flattery will get you a date," I replied with a grin.

So, our long day drew to a pleasant close.

5

QUEST FOR BLIND PIG

Wednesday morning, November 7, 1928

On Monday, Hannibal and I started our hunt for a blind pig. We suspected that one was hiding in the jumble of junk yards, machine shops, industrial plants and run-down neighborhoods that surrounded the intersection of North Throop and West Wabansia.

Given the nature of the area, we decided to dress for the occasion.

The previous Saturday, Susie had found some dowdy clothes for me in a second-hand store on West Erie Street. My outfit included a plain black woolen coat, matching warm hat and gloves and a simple dress. I already had some old lace-up shoes with moderate heels. Everything fit reasonably well. I added a cream-colored woolen scarf for warmth and flair.

"You still look pretty good," observed Susie as I modeled my new outfit.

"Well," I replied, as I thought about my lovely, expensive designer clothes in my large walk-in closet: "Chalk it up to inner beauty showing through. My hypocrisy only goes so far."

Susie laughed.

Hannibal met Susie and me in the kitchen after he dressed in his own bedroom on the other side of our suite. I looked him over carefully and said: "You are dressed exactly like you were when we met in 1921."

"Same clothes," responded Hannibal with a smile. "These are perfectly good jeans, flannel shirt, work shoes, old leather jacket and my old slouch hat."

Hannibal raised his hands, palms toward me. "My callouses are gone, so I'll wear gloves."

"What a pair!" Susie exclaimed. "I better let Harris know to let you back in when you return."

"Thanks," replied Hannibal, and we both laughed.

"I've arranged to take a taxi about five o'clock to a spot about a block from the corner of North Throop and West Wabansia," said Hannibal. "I've also arranged with the same driver to pick us up about nine at the same location." He paused and then added: "I chose Vincenzo from the Stevens as our taxi driver. What do you think?"

"Good choice; he knows the area," I replied. "I liked Vincenzo from the start during our interview." I lifted my purse and added: "I have my Smith and Wesson in my purse: How about you?"

"I have my forty-five," Hannibal responded. "Thanks to our detective friends, we also have the appropriate city and state gun permits."

"Right," I replied. "It's nearly five, are you ready?"

Hannibal nodded and said: "Vincenzo should be out front."

Susie took a sharp breath. "Be careful," she said. There was a tinge of trepidation in her voice.

Vincenzo was waiting as Hannibal and I walked out the front door of our building. He got out of his cab and opened the door for us as we approached. "Good evening, Miss Case, Mr. Jones," he said, with a slight bow and a touch of his cap.

As we got in, Hannibal said: "Our destination at the corner of North Throop and West Wabansia is a seedy place, Vincenzo." He paused and then added: "Are you sure you want to drive us there?"

"No problem, Mr. Jones," Vincenzo replied. "I've been there before."

As we drove away, I said: "Tell us about your trips with Sydney Meltzer." I paused and then added: "Do you know what he did after you dropped him off?"

Vincenzo shifted into third gear as we drove west on North Avenue. After a moment, he replied: "Well, Mr. Meltzer always went to the same place. I watched in my rearview mirror a couple of times as I drove away, and he headed toward an old frame house on Wabansia, about half a block down."

After Vincenzo negotiated traffic for a few minutes, he continued: "The house was set back from the street on the right, and he turned toward it. I saw him go up the steps a couple of times."

"About what time did you drop him off?" Hannibal asked.

"Oh, usually about six," replied Vincenzo. "It was always getting dark, and there aren't many street lights in that neighborhood."

"Did you see anyone else?" I asked.

Vincenzo slowed the car down and turned right on North Throop. After shifting gears, he said: "Yes, I always saw several people, usually in work clothes, on the street. Some were headed toward the same house as Mr. Meltzer." He glanced back at Hannibal and me, grinned and said: "Popular place."

Vincenzo slowed down after a few more minutes of driving and turned left on West Wabansia. After about a dozen feet, he stopped the cab near the curb on the right. Hannibal gave Vincenzo a twenty-dollar bill.

"Gee, thanks Mr. Jones!" Vincenzo said with a low whistle.

"One more thing, Vincenzo," I said. "How did you know when to pick up Mr. Meltzer for the trip back to the hotel?"

Vincenzo thought a moment and then said: "Except for the night Mr. Meltzer died, I always picked him up about midnight." He paused a moment and then added: "The dispatcher would get a phone call, and I would get word through the bellman at the Spencer." He looked at Hannibal and added: "I make it a point to park at the front of the hotel until I get calls."

After a moment, I said: "That night, you said earlier that you picked Mr. Meltzer up just after eight o'clock. Why?"

Vincenzo thought a moment and then said: "Well, at about quarter 'til eight, the Spencer bellman came out to my cab and said that Mr. Meltzer wanted to be picked up right away, so I headed to the usual pick up point." He paused, thought a moment and added: "Mr. Meltzer was at the curb when I got there, and he was very drunk."

"Interesting," Hannibal replied. "Can you be here to pick us up tonight at nine o'clock? We won't be calling the dispatcher."

"No problem, Mr. Jones," Vincenzo replied. "Have a nice evening!"

We got out of the cab. Vincenzo made a U-turn at the next intersection and drove back the way he came. I could hear the cab engine as he turned at the corner, shifted gears, and headed south on North Throop. The car sounds diminished in the distance.

No other cars were moving on the street. I could see a few parked cars on Wabansia, and a few people walked here and there on the street; there was no sidewalk.

Across the street to the east, a huge industrial complex loomed. Lights scattered throughout the complex gave an eerie glow. Men moved about here and there, and a constant low roar echoed from the buildings. Smoke billowed from tall chimneys.

Hannibal saw my stare at the complex. "Steel mill," he said. "It borders the north branch of the Chicago River. It probably has open-hearth furnaces, from the sound of the place." He paused and watched for a minute or so. "From the looks of the activity, they run both day and night shifts."

"You can tell from this vantage point?" I asked.

"Yes," Hannibal responded, and his eyes squinted a little as he watched the men moving about in the complex. "My family heritage," he added.

"Of course," I replied, you are a Pittsburgh boy." I paused and then added: "It's so different than life on the Wabash." Hannibal glanced at me and smiled.

The evening light was fading, and a lone street lamp came on as we stood on the corner for a minute or so. "Spooky," I thought to myself. I gave a little involuntary shiver. Hannibal noticed and gave me a hug.

"Shall we go?" Hannibal asked.

I nodded in response and replied: "See that frame house just down the street on the right?"

"Ummm," Hannibal responded. "I think we have found Sydney's watering hole." He then offered me his right arm. I slipped my arm under his, and we headed toward the frame house.

Three people on the street were headed toward the house just ahead of us. Two were men in work clothes; the other was a young woman in a plain-looking outfit. "I am better dressed," I thought to myself. I looked up at Hannibal. He was smiling at me. "He knows what I'm thinking," my thoughts continued. I smiled sweetly.

The trio ahead reached the step of the house. One man knocked on the door.

Hannibal and I stopped and watched from a moderate distance. I could hear occasional laughter from inside the house. The spookiness of the area abated a little.

As we watched, a little hatch opened at eye level in the narrow door. I could see a face through the hatch. One of the men on the outside leaned over and said something to the person looking out from the hatch. I saw lips move, but I couldn't make out the words. The door opened and all three people went inside. The door closed.

"Let's go," said Hannibal in a soft voice, and he stepped forward.

I looked up at Hannibal as I walked by his side. His face had a confident look. "Hope you know what you're doing," I muttered.

We walked up the steps. Hannibal knocked on the door. The hatch opened. Hannibal leaned toward the hatch and said: "We're here to see Susannah." I held my breath.

After a few seconds, the door opened. A large, beefy man in an ill-fitting suit and tie stood there. He squinted his eyes as he looked first at Hannibal, then at me and then back to Hannibal.

The large man smiled. "Come in," he said. He then looked at me and added: "Beautiful ladies are always welcome." I liked him instantly.

We stepped inside. Lights gleamed. A long bar lined the left side of the room. It had an L-shape at the far end. A dozen tables were arranged from the middle of the room over to the right wall. About twenty patrons were seated, either on bar stools or at tables. Most were hardened men dressed in work clothes.

"Quiet place, working men stopping by for a drink before going home," I mused to myself as I scanned the room. "It's a neighborhood bar."

"May I take your coat?" I heard Hannibal say. He looked at me with a smile.

I nodded, unbuttoned my coat and let Hannibal slip it off. Hannibal handed the coat to our host, who in turn gave it to a young lady who had approached discretely.

As Hannibal leaned over, I whispered: "How did you know the password?"

"I read lips," Hannibal replied softly. His smile broadened a little, and he added: "Also, remember Sydney's song?"

I smiled in response. "Why didn't I think of that?" I thought to myself.

The big man was talking to Hannibal, and I caught the conversation in mid-sentence. "…the bar or a table?" He asked.

"Table," Hannibal replied.

"This way, please," replied the man. He looked at me and smiled again. "My name is Connor O'Brien, and this is my place."

I smiled in return. "Pleased to meet you Connor," I replied. "I'm Caroline."

Hannibal also smiled at Connor and said: "I'm Hannibal." He then offered his hand. The two men shook hands.

Hannibal and I were soon seated where we could listen to the conversation and see the front door, the back of the room and the bar across the room.

I glanced toward the front door. A staircase just inside led up. I could hear female voices and laughter.

Connor saw my glance to the stair. "My dice girls work upstairs," he said. "They roll dice in the twenty-six game with the customers."

"Twenty-six, game?" I asked.

Connor nodded and replied: "Ten dice in a cup, thirteen rolls, bet on a number to come up twenty-six times. The customers love it." He paused and grinned. "Usually, customers bet a quarter or a dollar. If they win enough times, they are paid in drinks of their choice." He paused again and then added: "There is another room upstairs for high rollers, who play other games." He winked at me.

I smiled in return and replied: "Sounds like fun."

"What can I get you?" Connor asked.

Hannibal looked at me and asked: "Would you like a glass of beer, or something stronger?"

"Scotch on the rocks, if you have it," I replied. I preferred a glass of chardonnay, but this place felt like a beer, scotch or moonshine establishment.

"Make that two," responded Hannibal as he looked first at me and then Connor. "Good Canadian, if you have it."

"Coming up," replied Connor, "Right off the boat." He paused and then added: "Only the best for Miss Caroline."

He then walked over to the bar and spoke to the bartender. Soon the bartender brought two generous glasses with scotch over ice to our table. Connor went on to mix with his other customers.

Hannibal and I sipped our drinks, looked around and listened to the low chatter of friendly conversations around the room. "Nice place," I said in a soft voice. "I can see why Sydney liked it."

"Yes," replied Hannibal. He paused and then added: "Perhaps he found attractions other than gambling and drinks."

I nodded and said: "I'd like to check out the upstairs rooms."

Before we could rise, voices rose at the front door. Connor was there, and he had opened the door. Three men in suits pushed their way in. One shoved Connor back to the corner of the bar nearest the door. The conversations stopped.

"Gangsters," I thought to myself. My body tensed.

"Let's have a conversation in your office," one of the newcomers snarled at Connor. He reached up and grasped Connor's jacket lapels with both hands.

The other two stepped to Connor's sides and shoved him toward the back of the room along the bar. As the three gangsters, with Connor between them, passed our table, Hannibal became a blur of motion.

After a couple of seconds, the nearest gangster sprawled on the floor next to me, face down. Blood sprayed from a smashed nose. He had knocked over the adjacent empty table in the process of going down.

A melee ensued between the remaining two gangsters, Connor and Hannibal. As this was going on, I reached for and found my purse. I scooted my chair forward.

The gangster on the floor started to rise. I could see a gun in a shoulder holster under his left arm. He reached his right hand across.

"I wouldn't do that if I were you!" I said in a clear voice above the noise. I had already pulled my revolver from my purse. I smacked the side of it across the gangster's temple and then held it against his left ear. I reached over with my left hand and grabbed a handful of greasy hair and jerked his head around so he could see both me and my revolver.

The room was suddenly silent. The other two gangsters were on the floor. I pulled the hammer back on my revolver. The click-click of the turning cylinder sounded very loud.

"One wrong move and your brains will be all over the floor," I stated matter-of-factly. I meant it; my blood was up.

The man eased back down. "Hands where I can see them," I said. "Spread-eagle, palms down." The man complied with a groan; I'm sure his nose and his head were throbbing; at least I hope so.

As this was going on, Hannibal and Connor pinned the other two gangsters to the floor. Both had guns, but not for long.

The bartender came over. He had a baseball bat. Soon he had the three guns from the gangsters. Two other hard-looking patrons also came over as back-up.

Within a few minutes, the three gangsters, minus their artillery, were escorted to the door and tossed out in the street. The bartender and the two patrons stepped outside to make sure the vanquished foe departed. Soon it was done.

Hannibal and Connor walked back to our table and sat down across from me. I put my revolver back in my purse. Other customers set up the overturned furniture. After a few minutes, the bartender and his two companions returned and closed the door. The quiet conversations started again, as if nothing had happened.

Hannibal, Connor and I looked at each other for a long minute.

Connor grinned and said: "You did well, Miss Caroline." He paused and glanced over to Hannibal. "And she didn't even get up from her chair."

Hannibal chuckled and commented: "Caroline has a way of handling emergencies."

"Thanks," I responded. I began to calm down a little.

Connor looked at Hannibal, then at me and back to Hannibal. "Who are you, really?"

I saw no reason for hiding our identities, and I replied: "I am Caroline Case, and Hannibal Jones is my friend and business partner. We are private detectives."

Connor eased back in his chair, looked at me and then Hannibal carefully and asked: "Why are you here?"

Hannibal followed my lead and answered: "We are investigating the death of Sydney Meltzer." He paused and returned Connor's steady gaze. "Sydney's mother has put us on a retainer."

"Ah, Sydney," mused Connor. "I remember." He was silent a moment and then added: "Rich playboy. He came in on a regular basis for nearly a year. I saw in the newspapers that he died."

"Yes," I replied. "Sydney died within a few hours after leaving this place."

Connor nodded, leaned forward and said in a low voice: "Sydney spread a lot of money around. He was friends with a young Irish lady from this neighborhood."

"Name?" I asked.

"Molly," is all that I heard, replied Connor. "Come to think of it, I haven't seen her since Sydney left that night."

Hannibal also leaned forward and asked: "Why did those three men try to muscle you tonight?"

"North Side Gang," Connor replied: "I buy my booze from Capone."

"Ah," responded Hannibal. "That explains a lot."

"Yes," replied Connor. "Thanks for your help; I owe you one." He paused and then continued: "My suppliers will take it from here; I don't think those three will be back." He grinned and added: "Tough neighborhood."

"Does your place have a name?" Hannibal asked.

Connor grinned again and said: "We call it The Hideout."

"What an appropriate name," I thought to myself. To Connor, I said: "I see. Hannibal and I will come back tomorrow night." I paused and then added: "We want to find Molly."

"I'll see what I can do," replied Connor. He then got up and mingled with his other customers.

Hannibal and I finished our drinks and left about nine. Vincenzo was waiting. We arrived home at about nine-thirty. Busy evening!

6

SWEET MOLLY

Wednesday evening, November 7, 1928

Hannibal and I returned to The Hideout on Tuesday, November 6. Vincenzo picked us up at our home and drove us to the corner of North Throop and West Wabansia at about five o'clock. We arranged for Vincenzo to pick us up at nine. We walked the half-block to The Hideout.

Connor was there, and he greeted us as friends. Conversations in the room stopped as we walked toward our table. Several men at the bar nodded. Soon we each had a scotch on the rocks. The conversations around us returned to normal. Still, there were occasional glances in our direction.

"I think we have become the talk of the neighborhood," I whispered to Hannibal.

Hannibal nodded as he looked around the room. He then said in a low voice: "Your performance last night was especially memorable." He grinned and raised his glass in a mock toast.

Connor joined us at our table. After the usual pleasantries, Hannibal and I waited for him to speak.

Connor looked at each of us, in turn, for several moments. Finally, he leaned toward us and said: "I've asked around about Sydney and Molly."

Hannibal and I both nodded.

"Molly is a working girl, if you know what I mean." Connor continued. "She was infatuated with Sydney; I think she had marriage in mind."

"And Sydney?" I asked.

"No," Connor responded. "He was playing her along." Connor paused and then continued: "Come to think of it, she got very angry a week or so before Sydney died. She said, rather loudly, that she saw Sydney's picture in the newspapers."

"She probably saw the society pages, with Sydney and his socialite fiancé," I replied.

"That makes sense," said Connor. "Molly made threats. Lots of customers heard."

"Can you help us find Molly?" I asked. "We have questions."

"I'll see what I can do, Connor replied. "In the meantime, do you want another scotch? It's on the house."

I smiled and responded: "Thanks, but no, one is my limit."

Hannibal also smiled and said: "Perhaps on our next visit; your scotch is very good."

Connor nodded and grinned in return. "You're on duty; I understand." He stood and added: "I'll find out more about Molly." He then turned and walked over to the bar.

Soon Connor was in a low-key conversation with a patron. The patron was a hard-looking man, probably in his early thirties. He wore a rough denim jacket, a work shirt, overalls and heavy shoes. As Connor asked questions, occasionally the other man glanced our way. Finally, he walked over to our table.

"May I join you?" he asked. "My name is Mike."

Hannibal replied: "Sure, Mike. Have a seat. I'm Hannibal, my companion is Caroline."

I nodded and smiled. Mike sat down and then looked me up and down with a steady stare. I squirmed a little.

Finally, Mike looked over at Hannibal and then back to me. After a moment, he said: "I like the way you handled yourselves last night." He grinned and added: "Those three gangsters got what they deserved."

I nodded my head, relaxed a little and continued to smile. So did Hannibal.

After another moment, Mike asked: "Why are you interested in Molly Malone?"

"Ah!" I thought to myself: "A last name!" I then spoke to Mike: "She may know something about the death of Sydney Meltzer."

Mike nodded his head and said: "Sydney was the life of the party." He paused and then added: "He was also an overdressed playboy with too much money." He glanced over to Hannibal and then back to me. "Molly was sweet on him; at least until that visit a couple of weeks ago."

"What happened?' I asked.

"I was sitting over at the bar with my usual after-work beer," responded Mike. "Molly and Sydney were sitting at this table." He paused and then added: "Molly had a copy of the Chicago Tribune, and she kept pointing to a picture on a page. Her voice got louder and louder."

"Did Molly make any threats?" Hannibal asked.

"Oh, yes," replied Mike as he turned to Hannibal. "If words could kill, Sydney would have been dead on the spot." Mike looked at me with a steady gaze. "Molly wanted a way out of this neighborhood, and I think she believed that Sydney was her ticket." Mike paused and then added: "At least until she saw that picture."

"Does Molly have a family?" I asked.

Mike continued to watch my face carefully. After another long moment, he choked a little, and then continued: "Molly does what she has to do to get by. As far as I know, she doesn't have a family."

I could tell that Mike's knowledge about Molly was based on personal experience. My heart immediately reached out, and I'm sure that Mike picked up on my sympathy. "Molly is your friend?" I asked.

Mike looked away for a moment, as if he saw another time and place, and then back to me. "She used to be, before Sydney," he said in a low, sad voice. "I didn't have much to offer, except a steel mill job and a small house in this neighborhood."

Hannibal said: "Sydney died on Friday, October 19th. Do you recall when Molly made her threats?"

Mike leaned back in his chair and thought a moment. "Let's see," he replied. "Yes, I was here on the 19th. I was also here the Friday before, and that's when Molly confronted Sydney with the Tribune." Mike looked up toward the ceiling and made some mental calculations. "So, Molly's fight with Sydney was on Friday, October 12th."

"What happened on Friday, October 19th?" I asked.

"That was a strange night," replied Mike. Sydney came in, and he had a box of candy. Molly was here, and she was sitting with another customer." Mike paused and then added: "His name was Sean, I think. He's a new neighborhood man."

Hannibal and I waited. Obviously, Mike would tell us more.

After a moment, Mike continued: "Sydney went over to the table where Molly and Sean were sitting. Sydney was his usual smooth-talking self, but at first, Molly wasn't buying it. For that matter, Sean wasn't either, I could tell by their expressions."

"Did Sydney drink anything?" Hannibal asked.

"Yes," replied Mike. "Sydney ordered a round of drinks from the bar as soon as he sat down." He paused a moment then added: "Molly and Sean both accepted the drinks, Scotch I think. Sydney quickly downed his. Molly and Sean sipped theirs."

"Did Molly make any threats?" I asked.

"No," replied Mike. He paused and then said: "Funny thing, after a few minutes of conversation, Molly and Sean seemed to get friendly with Sydney. At least Sydney thought so; he chattered on about how Molly was a wonderful, beautiful girl. Sean left for a while, and then returned."

"Did Sydney drink anything else?" I asked.

"Well," replied Mike; "I turned away for a while, minding my beer. Later, I glanced over to the table where Sydney, Molly and Sean were still sitting." Mike paused a moment and then added: "The three had an old-fashioned jar with a screw-on lid, like the jars that farm folk use for canning fruits and vegetables. Molly poured Sydney a full glass from the jar as I watched."

"Did Molly or Sean pour drinks for themselves from the jar?" I asked.

"If they did, I didn't see it," responded Mike. "In fact, the drinks in their glasses were dark, like scotch, and the stuff in the jar and in Sydney's glass was clear, like pure moonshine."

"Did Sydney get drunk?" Hannibal asked.

"Oh, yes," replied Mike with a grin. "He got drunk and very loud." Mike's grin progressed to a chuckle. "In fact, he got so loud that Connor walked over and told Sydney to tone it down, or he would be tossed out on his ear."

"Did Sydney get tossed out?" I asked.

"Don't know," Mike replied. "I finished my beer and left."

Hannibal and I asked a few more questions, but Mike didn't add anything new. After a few pleasantries, he got up from our table and left. Hannibal and I watched him go in silence. We both sipped our drinks for a while, each immersed in private thoughts.

I began to form a mental image of Molly Malone. "Molly makes a living by selling herself," I thought to myself. "She's wants to move out of her situation, but doesn't know how." I felt a kinship, given my own history, and I couldn't help but sympathize.

I could see that Hannibal was watching me carefully. After a few minutes, he said: "Molly had motive and opportunity, and we already know that Sydney had a fatal dose of methanol."

At that point in our conversation, we heard the bartender's voice above the low murmur of conversation in the room. He was standing near the front door. "Hey, Connor," he said.

Connor looked up from his seat near the L-shape in the bar. The bartender pointed to the front door. Connor got up, walked across the room and peered through the little hatch. After a brief moment, he opened the door.

Two men entered. Both were wearing expensive-looking suits and Fedora style hats. Both smiled at Connor, and one whispered in his ear. "Not local working men, but they seem friendly enough," I thought to myself. Nevertheless, I tensed a little.

Connor looked in our direction, smiled and walked over to our table. The two men followed.

"Hannibal and Caroline," said Connor, "Meet Joe, who is an attorney, and Albert. Both work for our supplier." He paused and then added: "I called Joe yesterday and told him about last night. He seemed to already know about you." He looked first at Hannibal and then me. He then stepped back.

Joe stepped forward. Hannibal rose from his seat and offered his hand. He towered above both men. "Pleased to meet you," he said in a non-committal but friendly tone.

Joe smiled and shook hands. "The pleasure is mine, I assure you," he replied.

Albert stepped forward and said: "Likewise." He and Hannibal shook hands.

Both men turned and looked at me. Both removed their hats and smiled.

"Of course, we know all about the lovely Miss Case," said Joe.

Albert said: "Your reputation as a lady to be respected is well known to us." He paused and then added: "You are lovely, like Joe said." He bowed slightly. His lips smiled but not his eyes.

I was taken aback a little, but I tried not to let it show. I took a breath and let it out slowly. The tension left my body. "Thank you, I'm sure," I responded with a slight smile.

Joe then said: "May we join you for just a few minutes?"

I glanced at Hannibal and he gave a slight nod. I could tell that he was curious. The two men obviously had sought us out for a purpose. "Of course," I responded.

Soon the four of us were seated around our small table. Connor went back to his seat at the bar. Hannibal and I waited for Joe and Albert to begin the conversation.

After a few moments of mutual assessment, Joe said: "I know from a friend that you do not get involved in kinds of activities that occupy the time of my client." He then grinned and added: "Except, at the present time, as consumers."

I caught the irony in Joe's statement. In our detective work, we wanted to stay on the right side of the law. However, we visited speakeasies and consumed illegal booze. "We're like most people," I justified the inconsistency to myself. I chose to ignore the fact that in my shady past, I owned speakeasies and houses of ill-repute. Nevertheless, I squirmed a little, glanced at Hannibal and saw his knowing smile.

Joe continued: "My client has a friend who is a prominent Chicago businessman." He paused and then continued: "This businessman needs your help." He smiled as I raised my eyebrows. "He has problems that may or may not be associated with the business of my client," he added.

"Your work would be strictly on the up and up," said Albert. "My boss will see to it." Joe gave Albert a quick glance. Albert hung his head a little, but his eyes retained a steely look.

Joe looked at Hannibal, then back to me, and said: "Anyway, my client would be pleased if you would meet with this businessman. He will be at the club at this address Friday night at about eight o'clock." Joe reached into his jacket pocket, took out a slip of paper, and handed it to me.

I looked at the paper. It gave an address: 4802 North Broadway Avenue. It also had a phone number. I handed the paper to Hannibal. After he looked at it, I could tell he knew about the place at the address. He handed the paper back to me.

Hannibal gazed at me for a long moment, as if assessing my reaction to what he already knew. He then looked at Joe and said: "I will discuss your proposition with Miss Case," he said. "We still have unresolved issues on our current assignment."

"Of course," replied Joe. "I look forward to your phone call." With that statement, he and Albert stood, smiled, and without another word, turned and walked back through the front door.

After the door closed, Hannibal looked at me and said: "The club at the address on the paper is called the Green Mill. It is a speakeasy, and it's a favorite hangout for Al Capone."

"Aha," I responded. "I suspected a Capone connection when Connor introduced Joe and Albert as men who worked for his supplier."

"Connor told us last night that he gets his booze from Capone," Hannibal agreed.

We both sat back in our chairs and thought about the implications of our conversation with Joe and Albert.

I returned to the present from my reverie. "Yes," I replied. "Let's do it."

Hannibal chuckled and said: "Sounds like fun. I will call Joe and set up a meeting for Friday night." He paused a moment and then added: "We can always back out if we don't like the details."

I then focused my mind on our current case. "However, our next step is to meet Molly." I paused and then continued: "We can work two cases at a time, provided we stay on the right side of the law."

"OK," replied Hannibal. "I bet the bartender has Molly's phone number and address, given that the Hideout was her base for contacts." He then rose from his seat and walked over to the bar.

Soon it was done. Hannibal returned to the table with a scrap of paper. He showed me a phone number and an address. "According to the bartender, Molly lives in a two-room flat over a store just down the street, he said. "He confirmed that Molly used the Hideout to make contacts."

I understood. My own beginning in the profession was similar. Molly just hadn't progressed and moved up. I asked: "Anything else?"

"Yes," responded Hannibal. "Molly hasn't been in, as far as the bartender knows, since the night Sydney died. Also, the bartender said that Sean McBride, the local man that escorted Molly that night, stays with her when she doesn't have other customers. He also said that Sean has a good job in the industrial chemical plant about a half mile from here, so he probably pays Molly's rent."

"Interesting," I replied. "Shall we call Molly's phone number?" Hannibal nodded. I paused, thinking. I then added: "You call. If Molly answers, say that a friend gave you her name and you would like to stop by. If Sean answers, say that you have business with Molly as soon as she's free."

"That could work," replied Hannibal. "Both of us could then visit her flat and take it from there." Hannibal looked around, rose, walked over to the bar and whispered in the bartender's ear. I watched as the bartender nodded and pointed to the alcove behind the bar. Hannibal walked into the alcove. After a few minutes, he returned to our table and sat down.

"A man answered," Hannibal stated. "When I asked: Are you Sean? He said yes. Anyway, after a short conversation, we can go over tonight. Molly will be free at eight. Sean confirmed the address and said he would leave before eight."

"He sounds like a real prince," I replied. I looked up at the clock on the wall behind the bar. "It's seven o'clock, and we have plenty of time." We sat and slowly sipped our drinks.

According to Hannibal's watch, we arrived at Molly's address at five minutes after eight o'clock. The street was dark on the way over from the Hideout, except for a few street lamps. The steel mill roared in the distance. We were alone.

The building at Molly's address had a second-hand clothing store that fronted on North Throop. A rickety, steep set of steps on the left side of the building led up to a landing and a door at the second-floor level. Smoke rose from a chimney on the roof. The place was heated with a coal furnace in the basement; we could see the ground level coal chute near the stairs. We could smell the smoke, and coal dust lay all around the chute entrance. The place had a seedy appearance.

The stairs creaked as we climbed up. When we reached the landing, Hannibal knocked on the door. I stood back a little, out of the line of sight from the doorway. At the second knock, the door opened a crack. A woman's face appeared. She saw Hannibal.

"Are you Molly?" Hannibal asked. "I called earlier."

"Why yes, handsome," the woman replied. "I'm Molly." The door opened wider, and an exquisitely beautiful face framed in red-gold hair moved into the pale light from the street lamp on the corner. Molly was wearing a loose robe, and obviously nothing underneath. She couldn't have been more than twenty years old.

I stepped forward so Molly could see me. Molly's face showed surprise. I then said: "Molly, I'm Caroline. My friend here is Hannibal." I then added: "Hannibal and I would like to talk with you." Before Molly could reply, I continued: "We will pay you well for your time." Hannibal took three twenty-dollar bills from his pocket and held them where Molly could see them.

Molly's eyes widened. Sixty dollars was a lot of money, three times her normal fee.

"Just questions, nothing else," Hannibal said in a soft voice.

"May we come in?" I added.

After moment's hesitation, Molly replied: "Yes, I suppose." She couldn't take her eyes off the sixty dollars in Hannibal's hand. She stepped back. Hannibal stood aside and let me go in first.

I looked around. "Bed, dresser and mirror, to the left, closet, sofa, two chairs, two lamps on end tables to the right and probably a small kitchen and bathroom through the doorway, also on the right," I thought to myself. The place was small, but it looked surprisingly clean and neat. "Reminds me of my old houseboat," I mused under my breath: "Seedy on the outside, nice on the inside."

Molly motioned to the sofa. "Please sit," she said.

Hannibal and I took off our coats and sat down. Molly sat in a soft easy chair across from us and waited. Hannibal placed the sixty dollars on the end table next to the sofa.

I began by stating: "We know you were friends with Sydney Meltzer." Molly's eyes widened and she took a sharp breath. I then added: "We are friends of Connor at the Hideout."

Molly let out her breath a little.

"Did Sydney promise to marry you?" I asked.

A look of pain and then anger passed across Molly's face. "Yes, he did, that two-timer," she replied.

"We are here on behalf of Sydney's mother," I said. "You know, of course, that Sydney died just over two weeks ago."

Molly nodded her head slowly. "I read something in the newspaper," she said in a very cautious manner.

"Did Sydney leave anything here that his mother would want as a keepsake?" I asked.

"He left some clothes, but I threw them out when he jilted me," Molly replied. Anger returned to her face. "He gave me a box of candy, but I didn't eat it." She paused, and ground her teeth. I could see the anger build.

"Did he leave anything else?" I asked softly. "We would be happy to pay for it." Hannibal took out two more twenty-dollar bills and held them so Molly could see.

Molly's eyes widened again. After a moment, she said: "I think he left a cigarette case and a lighter. I was going to sell them to the pawn shop down the street."

Hannibal took out another twenty.

"I'll see if I can find them," responded Molly. She got up, walked over to the dresser, opened a drawer and took out a silver lighter and a matching cigarette case. I looked closely. I could see 'Sydney A. Meltzer' engraved on the front of both.

Hannibal took out another twenty. Molly brought the lighter and case over and held them out. I picked up my purse and opened it. "Please just drop them in," I said softly. "I'm sure Sydney's mother will cherish them." Molly walked over and dropped the lighter and case in my purse.

Hannibal gathered up the entire one-hundred forty dollars and handed the bills to Molly. "Thank you, Molly," Hannibal said.

Molly took the money and held it tightly in her fist, as if Hannibal might try to take it back.

"Do you have any more questions, Hannibal?" I asked.

"Just one," Hannibal responded. "Do you have Sydney's phone number?"

"Yes," replied Molly. "We talked on the phone occasionally; I called him when I was available a few times." Her expression grew apprehensive and she added: "Lots of people probably have his number."

"Yes, well, thank you so much, Molly," I said. Hannibal and I both stood, put on our coats and walked to the door.

Molly followed, still clutching the money. She opened the door. Hannibal and I stepped out, and Molly closed the door behind us. We walked carefully down the creaky stairs and to the street corner. It was nearly nine o'clock, and we saw Vincenzo's taxi turn on to North Throop about half a block away. Soon we were in the taxi and on our way home.

7

THE GREEN MILL

Saturday morning November 10th, 1928

Hannibal and I arrived by taxi at 4802 North Broadway a few minutes before eight o'clock, precisely the time that he had arranged with Joe by phone. We got out of the taxi on the corner of West Lawrence and North Broadway. We could see two doors, one on the West Lawrence side and another on the North Broadway side.

We walked around to the Broadway side. The exterior of the two-story building had a plain red-brick facade, with a narrow green door on the right. The windows were darkened on the street level. A sign above and to the left of the door advertised a jewelry store and that was all.

I could hear music from within. "Jewelry store, my foot," I thought to myself.

The new Uptown Theater marque lit up the street half a block north on Broadway, and another theater gleamed in the distance to the south. Well-dressed men and women walked on wide sidewalks on both sides of the street; we were in an upscale area of town.

"Very different from the neighborhood of the Hideout," I thought.

Hannibal had described the area before we left home, so we were both appropriately dressed.

This time I wore my knee length black Chanel evening dress. It was made of silk of course, and it featured a rouched silhouette and a halter neck with self-tie detailing at the back. I had matching long black gloves, stiletto shoes, my long, triple-strand white pearl necklace and matching pearl pendant earrings.

It was cold, so I carried my black silk brocade evening shawl for inside and wore my dark mink coat with silver fox collar and trim for outdoors. I also wore my matching silver fox hat. I was very stylish, if I do say so myself.

Hannibal wore his dark, charcoal gray single-breasted suit with a matching vest, a gold silk tie and traditional black shoes. For outer wear, he wore his dark gray trench coat, matching hat, light gray cashmere scarf and matching gloves. He looked the part of a gentleman of means, out on the town.

We walked up to the door just behind another well-dressed couple. The man knocked on the door. A little hatch opened at eye-level and a face appeared. Words were exchanged. The door opened and the music got louder. The couple went inside.

Hannibal and I stepped up before the door closed. A large, beefy man held the door, and eyed us carefully.

"Joe sent us; we have an eight o'clock appointment," said Hannibal.

The man looked back into the room, said something, got a response and turned back to Hannibal. "You and Miss Case are expected," he said with a smile. "Come in." He then opened the door wide. Golden light and music streamed out and all around us.

I recognized the music. "It's Rhapsody in Blue, by Gershwin," I said to myself. The pianist was especially good; but the rhythm of the soft percussion, the sax, the trombone, the clarinet and the trumpet wove a spell in and around the tinkling of the piano.

We stepped inside, and the door closed quickly behind us. My eyes took a few moments to adjust to the golden light. As I focused, I saw a long bar on the left, a stage at the back and booths between the bar and the stage.

I could see six men of color on stage. "I've never heard such complex and multifaceted music before," my thoughts continued. "How beautiful."

The place was packed with well-dressed people. Through the crowd, I saw three men in the booth nearest the far end of the bar. Based on newspaper photos, I instantly recognized the one on the right. The man was Al Capone.

Capone saw us and raised his hand in greeting. As an automatic reaction, I waved back.

Joe and Albert appeared, seemingly out of nowhere, and walked through the crowd along the bar toward us. People shifted, and I could no longer see Capone.

"Good evening," said Joe, as he approached. "Welcome to the Green Mill." At the same time, a cute, scantily dressed young lady slipped up behind us on the right and said: "May I take your coats please?" Hannibal and I turned to comply.

After the tedious operation with the coats, hats and so on, I turned back to Joe and Albert, who waited patiently. I peered around them toward the booth nearest the end of the bar. Capone and his two companions were gone.

"We have a booth in a quiet corner," said Albert. "Our friend who needs your help is waiting for us."

The musicians finished Rhapsody in Blue and began a tune that I didn't recognize.

As we made our way slowly along the bar toward the booth, Joe saw my puzzled expression. "Rhapsody in Blue is the favorite of my client," he said with a smile. "Now that he has departed, Armstrong and his 'Hot Five' band are playing another house favorite." He paused a moment, listening. "I think it's called West End Blues."

Albert piped up and said: "Armstrong and his band play mostly at the Grand Terrace Café, but they come over to this place sometimes." He paused and then added: "The boss likes Armstrong and the boys."

"Who are the boys?" I asked.

"Well," responded Albert, "Louis Armstrong plays the trumpet, Jimmy Strong has the clarinet and tenor sax, Fred Robinson plays the trombone, Mancy Carr is on the banjo, Zutty Singleton plays drums and percussion and that great piano player is Earl Hines."

The room was crowded, and it took a while to work our way through. Albert continued to chatter. "Louis' wife Lil used to play the piano, but she and Louis are on the outs."

Joe gave Albert a quick glance that said: "Enough gossip."

As we made our way to the side of the room and headed for our booth, Joe added: "Armstrong has taken a shine to several of our regular musicians," said Joe. "He is a very talented man, and the younger set tries to learn from him."

The music wove a magic spell for me, and, I think, for everyone in the room.

As Hannibal, Joe, Albert and I approached a corner booth, a slender, older gentleman with gray hair rose to greet us. He was wearing a tasteful suit and tie, the kind a businessman would wear to work every day.

"Good evening," he said as we approached. "I'm Giuseppe Costanzo." He held out his hand to Hannibal, who took it in greeting.

"Hannibal Jones," replied Hannibal.

I approached just behind Hannibal. Giuseppe turned to me and smiled. "Ah, the lovely Miss Case, I presume." I offered my hand, expecting the usual handshake.

Instead, Giuseppe bowed formally and kissed my hand lightly. He then stood erect, and his old eyes twinkled merrily.

I instantly liked Giuseppe. "The pleasure is mine, I'm sure," I replied with a big smile.

Hannibal looked at me and grinned broadly. "That rascal, he always knows what I'm thinking," I thought. I gave him a quick dirty look.

Soon Giuseppe, Joe, Hannibal and I were seated in the booth. The bar extended a few feet past a wall that ran behind it. I could see around the L-shape at the end of the bar near Capone's booth. The bartender walked back and forth, serving customers. Dozens of bottles with many labels lined shelves behind and underneath the back of the bar.

Albert stepped away, turned right and went out the door that must have opened on West Lawrence Avenue. "Capone must have gone out that door," I concluded.

The music played beautifully in the background, above the murmur of the patrons. Hannibal and I waited for Joe and Giuseppe to speak.

Joe began by saying: "Giuseppe runs a string of bakeries all around Chicago. His business serves many restaurants and clubs as well as private consumers."

"I have three neighborhood bakeries and a central commercial operation near West Erie Street and Ashland," volunteered Giuseppe. "All are in quiet, Italian neighborhoods. Sometimes I help friends who frequent the Green Mill with money transactions."

I understood. "Giuseppe launders money for Capone," I thought to myself. "So that's the connection."

Joe saw my knowing expression and smiled. "Giuseppe had a serious incident at his bakery on Chicago Avenue in Little Sicily, just last month," he said. "Men came in, demanded weekly payments, and threatened his youngest son Michael, who manages the store."

Giuseppe nodded vigorously. "It's my smallest store, and it serves a Sicilian neighborhood," he said. He paused and then added: "I asked around, and those men are from the North Side Gang."

After a moment to let this revelation sink in, Joe said: "After consulting with Albert, Giuseppe told Michael to refuse. He also told Michael to say that his father, the store owner, has friends who frequent the Green Mill."

"However, two weeks ago, shots were fired into my son Michael's nice new apartment on Chicago Avenue just east of his bakery," said Giuseppe. "It may have been a message from the North Side Gang." Giuseppe's face had an expression of both fear and anger.

"On the other hand, Michael has other problems and enemies," responded Joe.

"Ah, yes," said Giuseppe. "My Michael had been seeing a young society lady from a prominent Italian family." He paused and added: "He is also seeing several other ladies."

"The family found out about the other ladies," Joe said. He tried his best to suppress a smile. "Brothers have sworn a vendetta as a matter of honor."

"I see," said Hannibal. "So, the question to us is: "Who is trying to kill Michael?"

"Yes," replied Joe. "If it's the North Side Gang, my client, who you saw briefly tonight, has a very serious problem. If it is one of the families of the ladies in question, the case is very different."

"If it's the latter, a diplomatic solution might be best. If it's the former, more vigorous action might be required," I responded.

Joe and Giuseppe looked at me. Joe smiled and said: "You understand perfectly." Giuseppe nodded vigorously.

The conversation ended for a few minutes. We all listened to the music. The song was low, soft, sad and somehow soothing.

"What a unique sound," I whispered to Hannibal. He nodded.

Joe overheard and said: "The boss is part owner of both the Green Mill and the Grand Terrace Café." He paused and then added: "You are always welcome at both clubs." He then leaned back in the booth and waited.

Hannibal and I looked at each other. I nodded. Hannibal then turned to Giuseppe and said: "We will take your case."

Giuseppe gave a big sigh and replied: "Thank you so much; thank you, thank you!" He turned from Hannibal and looked into my eyes. Impulsively, he reached across the table, took my hand, and kissed it.

I was startled again, but I quickly recovered. I let Giuseppe caress my hand for a very brief moment and then slowly withdrew it. As I did so, I gave him a gracious smile.

Hannibal and Joe both grinned. I gave Hannibal a snooty look.

"Joe saw my expression, suppressed a chuckle and said: "Of course, I will cover your expenses and retainer."

After a few more pleasantries, Joe and Giuseppe took their leave. Hannibal and I listened to Armstrong and the Hot Five for a while. The bartender brought us two scotch-on-the-rocks drinks. "Word gets around," I mused. Hannibal smiled.

As we finished our drinks, Albert returned and stood by our booth. "The boss sends his thanks," he said with a smile. "Whenever you are ready, I will have the bartender call a taxi for you."

"Now would be fine," said Hannibal. Albert nodded and headed around the bar toward the Broadway door. He stopped and talked to the bartender, who turned and made a phone call.

After a few minutes, Hannibal and I got up from our booth, walked around the end of the bar and headed toward the Broadway door. As we turned the corner by the bar, I saw a door in the floor behind the bar open. A man appeared from below and placed a case of full bottles of booze on the floor behind the bar. He then reached over to the door handle, and closed the door as he disappeared under the floor.

Albert saw my startled look and came over. "That door in the floor has lots of uses," he said with a grin. "It leads to tunnels." He paused and then added: "The boss likes it."

I looked at Hannibal, who nodded in recognition of the implications.

Albert nodded, smiled, turned and walked along the bar and out the Broadway door. He stepped outside. A few moments later, he came back in and raised his hand. Hannibal and I saw the gesture, walked to the door, got our coats and accessories from the coat check girl, and stepped outside. We could still hear the music as we got into our taxi.

8

FRESH FROM THE GARDEN

Sunday morning, November 18, 1928

Last Thursday after breakfast, Hannibal and I spent the morning laying out the facts of our Meltzer case in our plush workroom at the apartment. Susie and I had set up a portable blackboard next to a large mahogany table with soft chairs around it. Notepads, pencils and various reports littered the table. Sconces and lamps provided a warm, inviting ambiance. We also had a new-fangled electric coffee pot on a nearby counter, along with healthy snacks of fruit, mixed nuts and veggies. After all, we had to keep slim and trim.

After a few sips of coffee, I began the conversation. "We have an eyewitness account that Molly, probably with Sean as an accomplice, gave Sydney a clear beverage from a fruit jar while they were together at the Hideout the evening of October 19th. Sydney received a fatal dose of methanol that evening. The source was almost certainly the liquid in the fruit jar. We also know that Molly had Sydney's phone number."

"Agreed," replied Hannibal. "Molly was, by her own account, a jilted lover, and eyewitnesses say she threatened Sydney the week before his death." Hannibal paused and then added: "motive, method and opportunity."

"We also have Molly's fingerprints on the lighter and the cigarette case," I added.

"Eddie will check it out; I'll deliver the lighter and case to him at the lab," replied Hannibal.

"By the way, did Eddie finish lifting fingerprints from the racks of cups and plates we gave him after our interviews at the Steven's Hotel?" I asked.

"Yes," replied Hannibal. "I have his supplemental report here somewhere." He looked through the stack of reports on the table. "Ah! Here it is." He read through it quickly. "The prints on Mary Jane McGregor's cup matched the fourth set of prints we found at several locations in Sydney's apartment. The prints on Arthur Smythe's cup matched the set found on the bottle of scotch in' Sydney's pantry. There were no other matches from the cup and plate prints."

"The maid's prints in the apartment make sense, no problem," I replied. I paused, thought a moment and added: "Arthur's prints on the bottle of scotch probably means that he was Sydney's supplier of the good stuff at his apartment."

"Yes," responded Hannibal. "That's why he was nervous during the interview."

I laughed a little and said: "Interesting, but not related to Sydney's murder."

"I agree," replied Hannibal, also with a chuckle. "Smolle will be glad to know that his staff didn't have anything to do with Sydney's death."

Hannibal then leaned back in his chair and stared up at the ceiling. I waited for the expected comment. After a moment, he said: "We have two unmatched sets of prints from the ceramic container in Sydney's Frigidaire and one unmatched set on Sydney's flask found on the floor in his living room."

"Yes," I replied. "I would be willing to bet that the set on the flask will match Molly's prints on the lighter and cigarette case, but we shall see." I paused for a moment and then said: "Who made the salad and gave it to Sydney?"

"Brother Charles had motive," responded Hannibal. "But did he have opportunity?"

"Time to visit Charles," I replied. "I'll get his address and phone number from Ruth." I paused a moment, thinking. "I'll tell Ruth that we are making progress, and we need to talk to Charles to better understand Sydney's habits and whereabouts before he died."

"Sounds good," responded Hannibal. "If Ruth asks questions, tell her that we know that Sydney was murdered, and we have a very strong case with regard to a suspect." Hannibal paused and then continued: "I'll visit and brief Watts and Mulvaney on our findings to date after I visit Eddie at the lab."

"Please ask them to wait with regard to inquiries at the Hideout," I said. "We don't want to spoil our relationships with Connor and Mike." I grinned and added: "Speakeasies are illegal, don't you know?"

Hannibal chuckled and said: "I'm sure Watts and Mulvaney will understand. They are investigating a murder, not vice." He then added: "There are thousands of speakeasies in this town, and for the most part, the cops don't care if folks consume illegal booze, unless there is a violent crime at a given speakeasy."

"Or some speakeasy owner misses a payoff," I responded.

Hannibal laughed. "Yes, that's an issue."

"OK, let's each do our tasks," I said. "Through Ruth, I'll see if we can visit Charles, perhaps at his home; he probably would feel more comfortable there."

I met with Ruth Thursday afternoon at her apartment. She was alone except for Frenchie. Ruth met me at the door. Frenchie was glad to see me; his tail wagged and he wiggled all over until I held up my right hand and looked him in the eyes. He sat down in front of me, looked up and waited. I reached down and rubbed behind his ears, softly, gently. If a dog could purr, he would have.

Ruth, on the other hand, looked worn. Three weeks had passed since Sydney's funeral. A cane leaned against the end of the coffee table near the sofa. I walked over, and we sat together on the sofa. Frenchie joined us and lay at my feet. Mandy silently and efficiently brought us tea and condiments on a silver tray, and then returned to the kitchen.

After we each fixed our tea, I asked: "How are you doing, Ruth?" I reached over and caressed her ancient, folded hands.

"Oh, Caroline," Ruth replied. "I'm trying to be strong for Charles, but it's hard." Tears welled in her eyes.

"I know, Ruth, I know," I replied.

After a moment, Ruth took a deep breath and let it out slowly. Her eyes changed to a steady gaze. Her chin stopped trembling and her face acquired a hard look. "Was Sydney murdered?" She asked in a soft voice.

I was taken aback a little. "There's more to Ruth than a doting old lady," I thought to myself. To Ruth I said: "Yes, he was, Ruth. We have a strong suspect, and we are gathering evidence."

"I know that Sydney had his faults," Ruth stated matter-of-factly. "He probably got involved in something that he shouldn't have." She paused and then added: "I want to know, Caroline." She continued to look at me with a steady gaze. The tears were gone.

"Hannibal and I will get to the bottom of it," I replied. "We need to see Charles and Elizabeth; perhaps they can shed light on Sydney's habits and whereabouts before the day of his death."

Ruth got up, walked slowly over to a small secretary's roll-top desk on the other side of the room, found a pen and paper and wrote a note. She returned to the sofa, sat down and handed me the note. "Charles' home phone and address," she stated. "They live in the old Meltzer mansion just north of the city along the lake." She paused a moment and then added: "I will call Charles, give him your name and tell him that you are working for me. He will expect your call."

"I will call Charles this evening, if it's alright with you," I replied.

"Yes," replied Ruth. She then stood up. The conversation was over. I rose from my seat, smiled, turned and walked toward the door. Mandy appeared from somewhere and opened the door for me. I glanced back, and Ruth was still standing by the sofa. "Goodbye, Ruth," I said softly with a smile. I then turned and stepped out into the hallway.

Mandy smiled and said: "Good hunting, Caroline." She then closed the door.

"Humm," I thought to myself. "Ruth has steel underneath that sweet old lady exterior."

Hannibal returned to the apartment later Thursday afternoon. Silvia had replenished the coffee pot in the workroom, so Hannibal and I sat at the table and compared notes. I told Hannibal about my visit with Ruth and the impending phone call to Charles later in the evening.

Hannibal described his visit to Eddie at the lab. "Eddie got Molly's prints off the cigarette case while I waited. They were a match to a set taken from Sydney's flask."

"That's strong evidence," I exclaimed.

Hannibal nodded. "That was a nice touch, having Molly drop the lighter and cigarette case directly in your purse. Eddie got very clear prints, no smudges."

Hannibal then described his visit with Watts and Mulvaney. "Both were pleased with our progress," said Hannibal. "They would like a full report when we are ready." He paused a moment and then added: "They understand about the Hideout, but we need to emphasize that we want to protect our sources." Hannibal chuckled and continued: "Mulvaney did mention that he had his own favorite off-duty watering hole. The three of us laughed."

"I'll call the Meltzer mansion after five o'clock," I said. "Ruth will have contacted Charles by then."

"Good," replied Hannibal. "Today is Thursday; see if we can visit them at home, perhaps on Saturday or Sunday." He paused, looked at the address on Ruth's note and added: "I'll look at a map to be sure, but I think the Meltzer estate is about an hour's drive north of the city."

Later Thursday evening, I called the phone number that Ruth gave me. Hannibal sat nearby and watched my performance.

A man with an English accent answered the phone. "Meltzer residence, Higgins speaking," said the voice. I introduced myself.

Higgins, it turned out, was the Meltzer butler. He had already been given instructions. "Mr. and Mrs. Meltzer would be very pleased if you would join them at the estate on Saturday for lunch," he said formally.

"Perfect!" I answered Higgins in a formal tone. "Please inform Mr. and Mrs. Meltzer that we would be pleased to attend. Would twelve noon be appropriate?"

"Yes, madam," responded Higgins. "How should I announce you when you arrive?"

"Major Hannibal Jones and Miss Caroline Case would be fine," I replied in my best hoity-toity voice.

"Of course, madam," responded Higgins.

"Good evening," I replied, and hung up the phone.

Hannibal burst out laughing. I joined him. We took a couple of minutes to recover. Finally, Hannibal said: "Our visit to the Meltzer mansion should be interesting!"

"We should visit Eddie at the lab before we go," I said. "We need a few things, and we should give him a heads up on our plans."

"Good idea," Hannibal replied.

On Saturday, November 17th, Hannibal and I planned our trip on the highway to the Meltzer estate north of Chicago. The weather was clear and very cold. The manifold heater in the Model A would provide some warmth, but not much.

At first, I couldn't decide whether I should wear my British-style light tan Donegal tweed dress with dark brown trim or my Chanel black crepe satin dress. I finally decided on the Chanel; it was dressier and less businesslike.

The black crepe dress was classic winter season Chanel, with simple lines, long, billowing sleeves and high, squared neckline. The trim was made with the same satin material, with the reverse crepe side out. A narrow scarf draped my right shoulder. A small cluster of embroidered red, blue and yellow flowers decorated the left shoulder. Three vertically arranged silver buttons gave the front of the bodice a minimalist, yet elegant look. I wore a double strand choker of white pearls tightly about my neck.

For outdoors and the car ride, I chose my medium-length black Persian lamb coat with light beige mink trim. I also wore matching black gloves, dark silk hose, medium-heeled black shoes with small silver buckles and a black Persian lamb hat with a small Ostrich feather. I wanted to be fashionable as well as warm.

Hannibal wore a charcoal-gray, worsted-wool single-breasted suit with a matching vest. A gold watch rested in a vest pocket and a gold chain draped from the watch across the front of the vest. The trousers had a pleated front, and the legs had medium-widths and cuffs at the bottom. Hannibal also wore simple black shoes and a dark-red silk tie with a gold clip for accent.

For outerwear, he had a slightly darker cashmere single breasted overcoat and a matching charcoal-colored hat with the front brim turned down. His hands were protected with black, fur-lined gloves. He had a light gray cashmere scarf around his neck, and it was tucked inside the neckline of the overcoat.

We were prepared for the weather, a long drive, a formal luncheon and of course, Higgins, the stuffy-sounding butler.

After an hour or so in the car, we drove up the long gravel lane to the palatial Meltzer mansion. Hannibal reached through his unbuttoned overcoat and checked his watch.

"Five minutes until twelve," said Hannibal with a tone of satisfaction, as he replaced his watch.

"Only one chance at a good first impression," I replied.

Our car rolled to a stop at the front entrance. A formally attired attendant waited at the base of the steps to the main front door. He opened the car door for me a moment after the car stopped.

I stepped out and waited for Hannibal as he walked around to my side and handed the attendant the car keys. I took Hannibal's arm, and we walked with a confident air up the lightly colored sandstone steps to the mansion door. The door opened precisely at the moment we cleared the top step.

A tall, thin, silver-haired man, dressed in formal black and white, stood in the doorway. "Major Jones and Miss Case, I presume," said the man in a deep voice and grave, formal tone.

Hannibal nodded and smiled. I could see his eyes; they indicated much inner amusement at the pretense of the moment.

"I am Higgins," said the tall thin man, with a slight, formal smile. "Welcome. Please come in." He opened the door wider and stepped to the side.

"It's like being welcomed to a funeral parlor," I thought to myself. I looked directly into Higgins' eyes and smiled sweetly as I stepped inside.

A footman stood just inside the vestibule with a silver tray held out in a formal fashion. Hannibal was ready, and he placed his beautifully designed calling card on the tray. The footman bowed and without a word, scurried off. A uniformed maid stepped up to take his place.

The maid gave a brief curtesy and said: "May I take your coats and hats please?" Hannibal assisted me with my coat and then shed his own. After this tedious operation, the maid, piled up to her nose with our garments, gave another curtesy and departed. I kept my purse. We were left with Higgins.

"The Meltzer's are in the library," said Higgins. "Please follow me."

Higgins then proceeded slowly, almost ceremoniously, through the cavernous receiving area into a long, dark oak-paneled hallway.

After about thirty feet, he stopped at set of double doors. "The library," Higgins announced. He opened the doors.

Inside, I immediately saw Ruth and a middle-aged couple. All three rose from their seats. They were appropriately dressed for a formal luncheon. I recognized Charles from his picture in Ruth's apartment. The other lady had to be Elizabeth, Charles' wife. Ruth's presence was a surprise, but I was happy to see her.

"Miss Case and Major Jones," Higgins formally announced. He stood aside, bowed slightly and motioned us in. Hannibal and I stepped into the library. Higgins quietly closed the doors behind us.

"Oh, Caroline, I'm so glad you could come," said Ruth. "Please meet my son Charles and his wife, Elizabeth. Charles and Elizabeth, this is Hannibal and Caroline, my very good friends."

"Hello," I replied. I smiled. "Thank you so much for inviting us."

Hannibal said: "Hello, I'm pleased to meet you." He nodded politely to Elizabeth, and stepped forward. He offered his hand to Charles.

Charles met Hannibal halfway, smiled and shook hands. His face had a strained look, and he appeared older than his thirty-five years. He then turned to me and said: "Caroline, my mother told me so much about you." He smiled again, and his eyes had a steady gaze.

I returned Charles gaze and smiled. "Not sure about him," I thought to myself. "First impression: Charles has many responsibilities, and he works hard. The dark circles under his eyes show lack of sleep."

I then turned to Elizabeth, who nodded her head formally, first to me and then to Hannibal. "Enchanted, I'm sure," she responded in an icy, high-pitched voice. Her look appeared cold and calculating.

I instantly disliked Elizabeth. "Careful, Caroline, you must reserve judgement," my private thoughts continued. To Elizabeth, I smiled sweetly and said: "You have a beautiful home."

"Thank you," replied Elizabeth.

Hannibal said: "We are so sorry about your loss." He paused a moment and then continued: "Caroline and I are making progress on resolving the manner of Sydney's death." Ruth and Charles both nodded. Elizabeth maintained her icy demeanor.

I glanced at Charles and then returned Elizabeth's stare. After a moment, I said: "I have two items that we found during our investigations. Perhaps you could identify whether or not they belonged to Sydney." I opened my purse and took out a silver cigarette case. I was careful to hold it so that my fingers touched only the thin edges. I handed it to Elizabeth, who took it in both hands, turned it over and looked at both sides. She then handed it back to me.

"No," Elizabeth replied: "Sydney's cigarette case had his name engraved on it. This is not Sydney's."

I took the case from Elizabeth. Again, I was careful to touch only the edges. I returned the case to my purse. "Thank you, Elizabeth. You have helped greatly in our investigation."

I then took a silver cigarette lighter from my purse. I held it by the edges, turned to Charles and said: "We also found this lighter. Did it belong to Sydney?"

Charles took the lighter, turned it over and looked carefully at both sides. "No," he said. "Sydney's lighter also had his name engraved on it. It matched his cigarette case. I don't think he had one like this." Charles handed it back to me. His face had a puzzled look.

I took it, again holding it only by its edges. "Thank you," I replied, and returned the lighter to my purse.

Hannibal looked at me. His eyes said all that needed to be said.

Ruth looked first at Hannibal and then me. She gave a slight smile and said: "Shall we adjourn to the garden room for lunch?" She then stepped to a nearby table, picked up a little hand bell and gave it a shake.

The bell tinkled loud enough to be heard outside the library. Instantly, Higgins opened the door and said in his grave, formal voice: "Lunch is ready, ladies and gentlemen. Please, this way." He stepped to the side and motioned with his hand down the hallway. Elizabeth led the way, followed by Hannibal, Ruth and me. Charles, the gracious host, brought up the rear.

The spacious garden room was beautiful. Three of the four walls and the high ceiling were made of glass. The air was moist and warm. Flowers of every color filled built-up stone-lined beds. Short palm trees, tropical ferns and several other plants reached high above us. Orchids in purple, white, yellow and mauve graced the trunks of the palms and laced themselves through bamboo frames.

A glass-topped wrought-iron table with six chairs rested in the middle of the garden on a stone floor. A side table had a variety of meats, vegetables, lettuce, fruits, breads and wonderful desserts. Plates, white linen napkins and silverware rested on one end of the table. A maid stood at another table with tea, coffee and condiments.

Higgins turned and said: "Please serve yourselves from the side table; Maria will bring drinks of your choice to your table after you are seated."

"What a novel way to have lunch," I thought to myself. I'll follow Hannibal's lead to see how it's done."

Soon the Meltzers, Hannibal and I were seated and enjoying a sumptuous lunch. Higgins and Maria stood by, attentive to our needs.

Between mouthfuls of exquisite flavors, I said: "What a wonderful setting and lunch; thank you again for inviting us." I paid particular attention to the desserts; the date candy was delicious.

Maria was very attentive; yet Elizabeth made several haughty comments to her when she did not respond immediately or whenever Elizabeth's glass of iced tea was half-empty. It was rude; but I couldn't interfere. My initial dislike strengthened.

When Maria poured tea in my glass, I made it a point to complement her. "Thank you, Maria," I said. "You and your colleagues have done a marvelous job with lunch." I paused, smiled and asked: "Do you work in the kitchen?"

"Yes ma'am," replied Maria, and she gave me a grateful smile. "We all worked together this morning; I'm glad you like it." She glanced up at Elizabeth and moved quickly on.

I looked over at Elizabeth and saw her frown. I smiled sweetly in return.

I could tell Ruth saw the exchange. She smiled and said: "Elizabeth has a greenhouse out back. She grows flowers, tropical fruits and vegetables of every kind." She paused and then added: "She supplies many of the vegetables and flowers for the household."

At her mention of her garden, Elizabeth produced her first genuine smile. "It's my hobby," she responded. "Charles is always working at the office, and he stays in our town apartment during the week. I prefer my garden and my garden club here at the estate. The city is so far to drive."

"Perhaps after lunch, we could visit your greenhouse," said Hannibal. "I'm sure it's fascinating."

"Of course," replied Elizabeth. She smiled again and opened up a little more. "My garden is such fun."

After lunch, Elizabeth and Charles gave us a tour of the greenhouse. It was located just behind the main mansion; we didn't need our coats. As we walked to the greenhouse, Hannibal and I asked several questions about Sydney's social life, but neither Charles nor Elizabeth said much.

Charles did say that Jacqueline, Sydney's fiancée, was devastated. "Sydney was a free spirit," added Charles. "Still, he managed our family trust and funded several worthwhile charities." He choked a little as he ended his comment.

Charles cared about his brother," I concluded to myself. I then looked intently at Charles and asked: "Did Sydney visit this estate often?"

"Occasionally," replied Charles. "We spent our childhood here, with Father and Mother." He looked at Ruth with a wistful smile. "Those were good times."

Ruth smiled at Charles in return and said: "Yes, they were." She then looked at me and said: "Too many memories for me to stay here, although I visit often." She sighed deeply and then added: "Sydney and I were both here the weekend before the police came to my apartment." Tears formed in her eyes. I could tell she saw another time and place.

Charles hung his head but didn't say anything.

In response to my question about Sydney's social activities, Elizabeth said: "Sydney moved in different social circles compared to ours." She paused and then added: "Sometimes he associated with an unsavory element."

Elizabeth gave Charles and Ruth a cold stare. Her demeanor clearly showed that she didn't approve of Sydney.

I glanced at Hannibal. His look indicated that he had similar thoughts about Elizabeth's attitude. Sydney's visit the weekend before his death was also a revelation.

The afternoon in the greenhouse was filled with small talk, descriptions of flowers, varieties of lettuce, tomatoes and so on. I noticed that several of the beds in the greenhouse were vacant.

Hannibal also noticed the empty beds, and asked: "Are you planning new plantings?"

"Oh, yes," replied Elizabeth. "We had a local variety of flowers in the now empty beds, but I decided to re-plant with tulips and daffodils for spring." She turned and walked quickly toward the other side of the greenhouse.

"Hummm," I muttered to myself. "I wonder what grew there."

As we followed Elizabeth, I noticed that Hannibal lingered behind, stooped over and picked up something from the stone floor. No one else noticed, and Hannibal quickly caught up.

After the tour, we returned to the library and sat in comfortable chairs. Charles asked a few more questions about our investigation; he seemed genuinely concerned.

Hannibal provided straightforward answers, but no details. "The evidence indicates that Sydney consumed a fatal dose of methanol," he said. "The source was probably contaminated liquor." He paused and then added: "We are working closely with the police to be sure that we can identify whether or not the methanol poisoning was intentional, and who might have been responsible."

"We want to build a case for prosecutors," I said. "We will keep you informed."

Charles seemed satisfied. "If you need anything from me, please call," he said.

I looked at Elizabeth and Ruth, in turn, as Hannibal explained about the methanol. Elizabeth had a puzzled look at first, and then she gave a slight sigh and a furtive smile. She quickly recovered and resumed her icy reserve. Ruth listened carefully, but gave no sign of emotion. "Interesting," I thought to myself. "Elizabeth seems pleased about the methanol."

Ruth eyed Elizabeth closely and then looked at me. I returned her gaze. She nodded and said nothing.

A large grandfather clock in the hallway chimed four o'clock. "My goodness," I said. "Hannibal and I better return to the city; it gets dark early now."

Hannibal responded to my hint and stood. "Yes," he said. "Thank you so much for a wonderful lunch and conversation."

After the usual pleasantries, we gathered our coats, said our goodbyes and prepared to depart. The Meltzers remained in the library; Higgins escorted us to the front door.

As we entered the vestibule by the front door, Maria stepped quietly out of the shadowy hallway. She curtsied quickly and handed me a small box and said: "It's the date candy, ma'am, I noticed you liked it at lunch."

"How very kind," I responded. "Thank you so much." I took the box, and Maria stepped back. I felt a little guilty, knowing that I would give the box to Eddie to obtain fingerprints.

Higgins frowned and harrumphed, but his eyes twinkled. Maria quickly scurried back into the shadows.

"Higgins is an old softie behind that perfect butler exterior," I thought to myself. I couldn't help it; I grinned a little.

The outside attendant brought our car around. As we stepped out the door, Higgins leaned over to me and said: "Good luck with your investigation, madam. Call me if you need anything." He gave me a long, steady look. "I have been with the Meltzer family for many years."

"Thank you, Higgins," I replied. "I will."

Soon Hannibal and I were on the road. After Hannibal turned on to the main highway, he said. "We can compare facts and impressions when we get home." He paused and then added: "By the way, nice touch with the cigarette case and lighter." He looked at me and smiled.

"Thanks," I replied. "I borrowed them from Eddie. He should be able to get fingerprints from both, plus this little box." I held up the box of date candy. I thought a moment and then asked: "What did you find on the greenhouse floor?"

"Seeds," replied Hannibal. "I think I know what they are, but the lab will tell me more."

9

REASONABLE DOUBT

Wednesday evening, November 21, 1928

Hannibal was quiet during dinner on Tuesday. I could tell that he was thinking. After dessert, he got up from the table and walked over to his briefcase that was sitting by the front door. He fished out a couple of thin newspapers. He then returned to his chair at the table.

After taking his seat, Hannibal held up the newspapers so I could see. "Local Italian," he said. Hannibal smiled as he observed my expression. "I spotted these on the newsstand downtown today," he added.

"You read Italian?" I asked. I'm sure surprise was written all over my face.

"Learned in France during the war," Hannibal replied modestly. "We had Italians on our staff." He paused a moment and then added: "My Italian is a bit rusty, but I think I can still read these newspapers well enough."

I smiled and sipped my coffee. So many surprises, even after all this time together! "A man of many hidden talents," I replied quietly.

My language skills included the ability to understand spoken Italian and to speak a few phrases slowly and carefully. After all, my old home town of Clinton on the Wabash was also the home of many immigrant Italian coal miners. Of course, we were also friends with Mom and Pop Valenti in Clinton, and with Eddie, our crime scene guy, who knew many Italian swear words. However, I had never tried to read Italian newspapers.

"A photo on the front page of this one caught my eye," said Hannibal. He held up one of the newspapers so I could see.

I squinted and peered at the photo. It was Giuseppe Costanzo. He was smiling and apparently presiding at some social occasion.

"I have already looked at the headline captions of several articles. They may provide information on our friend Giuseppe and his son, Michael," Hannibal said. "If it's OK with you, I'll find a comfortable chair and read." He smiled and added: "I'll give you a synopsis if I find anything of interest."

"Good idea," I replied. I searched my mind for a way to contribute. After a moment, I continued. "I'll call Detective Sergeant Watts in the morning and see if I can get the police reports on the shooting at Michaels's house." I then added: "I'll study the lab reports on the seeds tonight before I go to sleep."

"Sounds like a plan," responded Hannibal. After a third cup of coffee, I retired to my bedroom, and Hannibal went down the hall to our workroom. Silvia cleaned up the dishes in her usual quiet, efficient way.

"Don't know what we would do without her," I thought to myself as I headed to my bedroom. I undressed and took a warm bath in my adjoining bathroom. Afterwards, I put on my new Jeanne Lanvin cream-colored silk negligée and matching robe that I ordered from the Saks Fifth Avenue store in New York.

I felt warm and cozy as I slipped into bed about nine o'clock. My nightstand had a stack of lab reports, and I read for a while. I turned out the light about eleven. Moonlight through the window provided a silver glow. I left my door open; I could see the golden light in the hallway.

Hannibal worked far into the night. Much later, I woke and saw Hannibal's silhouette in the hallway light. I raised up slightly and smiled. The golden light went out; only the moonlight through the window remained. The night passed softly, gently. Morning would bring new challenges.

Saturday evening, November 24, 1928

On Thursday, I called Detective Sergeant Watts, explained our interest in the Costanzo shooting, and asked if I could read the police reports. I also told him that we were ready to sit down with him and present our findings on the Sidney Meltzer murder.

"Your place or downtown?" said Watts. He seemed very glad to hear from me.

"Downtown might be best," I replied. "We'll bring our Meltzer files."

"I'll see what I can find on the Costanzo shooting," responded Watts. "Can you be here at noon?"

"Yes, of course," I responded.

Hannibal and I discussed our planned presentation to Watts and Mulvaney during breakfast. At about ten-thirty, we drove to the new downtown police station at 1111 South State Street. We arrived just before noon. Typically for Chicago, the November weather was cold and windy. I fiddled with the manifold heater vent during the entire drive downtown.

We both wore business attire under our winter coats and hats. Hannibal wore a plain charcoal-colored suit and conservative blue striped tie, and I wore a classic navy knit dress made in Paris by the new designer Elsa Schiaparelli.

My dress had a conservative midi length, long plain sleeves, a high neckline and a smooth, form-fitting waist. A silver silk scarf knotted at the neck provided accent. The back of the dress had one of those new-fangled zippers instead of loops and hooks. Of course, I had matching navy low heeled shoes and a gold-trimmed navy-blue purse, but no jewelry. Since I was going to a police station, I also left my revolver at home.

We parked in the small lot at the back of the building just off 11th Street. Several of the Detective Bureau's new, specially designed, high-powered Cadillac touring cars were parked nearby.

As we pulled into a parking space, I looked at the Cadillacs closely. Hannibal noticed my curiosity. "The Detective Bureau got new cars a couple of years ago," he said. "I think each detective squad has one, and they are equipped with shotguns, tommy guns and tear gas bombs."

"Do the cops need both the cars and all that extra firepower?" I responded.

Hannibal nodded and replied: "The detectives are now a better match for the booze gangs that fight in the city streets. I heard they have over 600 detectives now, assigned to 30 zones in the city. There's even talk of putting two-way radios in the cars." He paused a moment and then added: "The increases in manpower, cars and equipment were all the result of reforms made during Mayor Dever's administration."

I reflected on the changes and said: "Dever lost to Thompson in the 1927 election. I wonder how Watts and Mulvaney are doing, now that the fox is back in charge of the chicken coop."

Hannibal laughed, but his expression was grim. "Not well, I expect. Both are honest cops." He paused and then added: "As everyone knows, including the cops, Big Bill Thompson has re-set his old tone of tolerance for the booze trade."

"Plenty of corruption to go around, even in a spiffy new police headquarters," I agreed.

We got out of our car and walked west on 11th Street around to the State Street entrance of the headquarters building. A dozen or so cops passed us, and several nodded to Hannibal in recognition. The wind found ways to get inside my black Persian lamb coat. I shivered as we walked.

We passed a couple of cops who gave me the once-over, with typical male expressions of appreciation. Somehow their looks gave me a smug feeling, and I smiled coyly. "After all, I am a good-looking female, if I do say so myself," I thought. Hannibal saw my expression and grinned. I gave him a snooty look.

As we turned left at the corner on State Street, I glanced up to the towering new building. The bottom four stories were limestone, and the remaining nine were red brick. The place had a no-nonsense, fortress-like look. I shivered again, but not from the cold.

We checked in with the desk sergeant just inside the gleaming main entrance. The sergeant recognized Hannibal. "Watts and Mulvaney are waiting for you; they reserved a conference room away from the top brass, the main squad rooms and the noise."

I looked around; the lobby was a beehive of activity. I smiled at the sergeant.

He smiled in return; I'm sure he read the expression on my face. He then said: "You'll have peace and quiet." He motioned to the bank of six elevators behind him. "Just take an elevator up; they are all the new, self-operating type. The conference room is on the 6th floor, down the hall to the left as you leave the elevator lobby."

Hannibal and I rode the elevator to the 6th floor. As we got off the elevator, we saw Mulvaney talking to a uniformed officer. Mulvaney's saw us, smiled and motioned us over.

"Good to see you," said Mulvaney as we approached. "How do you like our new headquarters?"

"Very nice," replied Hannibal, "It's much better than your old place on South Clark Street. When did you move?"

"Mid-September," responded Mulvaney. With a grin, he added: "We left the old place to the rats and roaches."

Hannibal and I both laughed. "The precinct guys remain in the old place. I'm sure they envy you," I said. "Are you ready for us?"

"You bet," replied Mulvaney. "Watts is already in the conference room over there." He pointed, and we could see an open door just down the hall on the right. "Go on down; I'll be there in a minute."

Hannibal and I walked into the conference room. Watts was seated in a straight-backed wooden chair next to a long, plain-looking wooden table. Five additional wooden chairs were arranged around the table. The walls of the room were painted a pale green, and a few pictures, mostly of police dignitaries, adorned the walls. Everything looked new and pristine, but the atmosphere was definitely institutional.

Watts had several reports open on the table. He glanced up as we entered and smiled.

"Welcome to our new building," said Watts. "It's not as plush as your usual haunts, but it's a big step up for us." His look was a mixture of pride tempered by a knowledge of how the décor of his place of business compared to private sector establishments.

"The place looks great, Sergeant Watts," I stated. My sincerity was genuine; I remembered my own very humble beginnings. "If you have coffee, I think we are all set to go."

Watts' expression showed appreciation for my kind words. "Coffee is the one thing we have in plentiful supply," he responded. "Cops can't function without it." He paused and looked over at Mulvaney as he walked in the doorway. "Can you get Miss Case and Major Jones their coffee?"

"Sure," replied Mulvaney. He looked first to me and then to Hannibal and said: "How would you like it?"

"Black, please," Hannibal and I said, almost in unison. "And hot," I added. I was still cold.

Mulvaney departed. He soon returned with a beat-up tin tray that held mugs, one teaspoon, a crusty bowl of sugar and a steaming pot of very black coffee.

We each fixed our own coffee. Watts, Hannibal and I took ours straight. Mulvaney added three heaping teaspoons of sugar. I smiled; I couldn't help it. The four of us got as comfortable as we could in the hard, wooden chairs, with our coffee cups and files scattered on the table. All eyes turned to Hannibal.

In practiced military fashion, Hannibal leaned forward, placed a large leather-bound briefing easel on the table where everyone could see and began flipping pages. I marveled at his summary charts and smooth, informative delivery.

"Sydney Albert Meltzer was murdered," Hannibal began. "Our report identifies two possible causes of death by respiratory system failure. He ingested two poisons. We collected forensic evidence and obtained several eyewitness accounts. We identified four suspects who could have administered the poisons."

Watts and Mulvaney both leaned back in their chairs and focused their attention on Hannibal and his flip charts. I watched their faces for reactions to Hannibal's presentation.

Hannibal continued. "Sydney died after 10:30 PM and before midnight on Friday, October 19, 1928. He was poisoned by methanol, commonly called wood alcohol, and conium maculatum, which is the scientific term for hemlock."

"Methanol poisoning is pretty common these days," said Watts. "Was the source contaminated booze?"

"Yes," replied Hannibal. Sydney ingested 250 milliliters of methanol over two to four hours. Any dose over 150 milliliters over that time period is lethal." He paused a moment and then added: "Our evidence shows that Sydney got his fatal dose from spiked moonshine."

"You mentioned hemlock," said Mulvaney. "I haven't heard of any cases of hemlock poisoning, except in history books. How did Sydney get it?"

Hemlock is a flowering plant native to Europe and western Asia," Hannibal replied. "Somehow it got to the United States during the last century. It is now quite common in the countryside around Chicago." He paused for effect and then added: "All parts of the plant are poisonous. Sydney ingested 120 milligrams of hemlock leaves that were placed in a salad intended for his consumption."

"Lethal dose, I suppose?" Responded Mulvaney.

"Quite lethal," answered Hannibal.

"So which poison got him first?" asked Watts.

"Don't know," responded Hannibal. From Sydney's point of view, it doesn't matter." He smiled grimly and looked directly at Watts and then to Mulvaney and then back to Watts. "However, attorneys will have a field day with the question."

Both Watts and Mulvaney nodded. Watts then grinned. "That question is beyond my pay grade to answer; let the lawyers have it."

Hannibal then turned to me and said: "Caroline has insight into the human element associated with Sydney's murder."

I leaned forward in my chair and folded my hands comfortably on the table. I then said: "We have two suspects for the methanol poisoning and two for the hemlock poisoning." I looked at Watts and then Mulvaney directly in the eyes for effect. Both were paying rapt attention.

After a moment, I continued: "Forensic evidence and eyewitness accounts show that Molly Malone and possibly Sean McBride had motive, method and opportunity to poison Sydney with contaminated moonshine on the evening of October 19th."

I then briefly explained about Molly's relationship with Sydney, the events at the Hideout on October 19th and the results of our fingerprint analysis. "The details are all in our report," I summarized, and I pointed to the file Hannibal had just laid on the table.

"What about the hemlock?" asked Watts.

"In addition to Sydney's fingerprints, Elizabeth Meltzer, the wife of Charles Everett, Sydney's brother, left fingerprints on the dish that contained the salad with hemlock leaves," I replied. "Another set of fingerprints on the dish belonged to Maria, a kitchen maid in the Meltzer home."

Watts and Mulvaney both nodded. "Two suspects," Watts mused.

"At the request of our client, Ruth Meltzer, Hannibal and I attended a lunch at the Meltzer mansion." I paused for effect and then added: "Ruth, Charles Everett, Elizabeth and their household staff were present. We had a very interesting luncheon in the greenhouse."

Both Watts and Mulvaney leaned forward and watched me intently. I continued: "Hannibal found hemlock seeds on the floor in Elizabeth's greenhouse at the Meltzer mansion, but no hemlock plants." Watts and Mulvaney both raised their eyebrows. I then added: "Sydney also visited the Meltzer mansion a few days before he consumed the salad."

"I can see method and possibly opportunity, but what about motive?" Mulvaney asked.

I nodded and replied. "Elizabeth was the only one present who clearly disliked Sydney and showed no sorrow with regard to his death."

"Not much to go on," stated Watts. "Do you have witnesses that would testify that Elizabeth prepared the salad?"

"No," I replied. "We just have Elizabeth's and Maria's fingerprints on the salad container. Anyone in the Meltzer household could have laced the salad with hemlock. I thought a moment and then added: "But I think I know how we might obtain a witness or two."

The four of us spent the next two hours devising a plan. "Watts and Mulvaney seemed very pleased with our ideas, the detailed report and our summary presentation. As we were about to finish, Watts smiled and surreptitiously slipped me a thick file folder.

I opened the folder and quickly glanced at the first page. It was a carbon copy of the Costanzo report. I smiled at Watts and slipped the folder into my leather-bound notebook. No words were needed.

After a moment, I looked first at Watts and then Mulvaney. "There is one other topic," I said quietly. Both men returned my look and waited.

"Our witnesses saw Molly Malone and Sean McBride slip Sydney his spiked booze at a place called The Hideout," I continued. "We don't want to cause problems for the owner and the patrons; yet we would like to see them cooperate with regard your police murder case."

"Watts caught on instantly. He looked over at Mulvaney, smiled and said: "Isn't that area of town Clancy's beat?"

"Why yes, I believe so," Mulvaney replied. He then looked at me with a twinkle in his eyes and said: "I think Clancy can take written statements from your witnesses without prying into their drinking habits or the nature of The Hideout."

I breathed a sigh of relief. "Thank you," I replied.

"We are homicide detectives, not the vice squad," stated Watts. "We have no desire to even open that can of worms."

Mulvaney grinned and then said: "I understand that The Hideout serves a pretty good, perfectly legal near beer. Just let your friends know that when Clancy shows up, near beer is all that's available."

"Done," I replied, and gave both men a grateful smile.

Watts stood and said: "Thank you for your help, both of you." I could see that he really meant it. "I will keep you informed, but I think we can take it from here with regard to Malone and McBride." He paused a moment and then added: "Good luck on your plans for the Meltzer part of the investigation."

Hannibal and I both stood, and we all shook hands. Mission accomplished! Hannibal and I put on our coats, hats and gloves and found our own way down to the lobby. The friendly desk sergeant was still there, presiding over the buzzing of activity that filled the area around him. He looked in our direction and waved goodbye.

We walked outside into the windy winter evening. It was bitter cold. Hannibal spotted a nice-looking, Italian restaurant on the other side of State Street, so we popped in for an early dinner or late lunch, whatever you might call it.

After an excellent meal, we walked back to our car in the dark, got it going in the cold and drove home. Harris, still on duty, let us in and we took the elevator up.

We entered our suite, and the lamps were on. They gave out a warm glow. Silvia had set up everything for a pleasant evening, and she had retired to her apartment on the floor below for the night. Hannibal and I had the place to ourselves.

Hannibal went to his rooms and I entered mine. I was very happy to have a nice warm bath, and Hannibal did the same. Afterwards, we had a glass of chardonnay together and watched the city lights through the window. The wind howled outside.

Our discussion centered on plans for briefing Ruth and another visit to the Meltzer mansion. We retired for the night at about 10 o'clock and slept soundly. It was a good day.

10

LOOSE ENDS

Sunday evening, November 25, 1928

At about noon today, I phoned Ruth's apartment. Mandy answered.

"Hello Mandy, it's Caroline," I began. "Is Ruth available?"

"Hello, Miss Case," Mandy replied. "Mrs. Meltzer will be home from church shortly. Can I take a message?"

"Please ask Ruth to give me a call; Hannibal and I would like to meet with her at her convenience," I responded. "We have new information concerning Sydney."

"Certainly," replied Mandy. We ended our brief conversation, and I hung up the phone.

Ruth called within the hour. She invited us for tea at three o'clock.

Hannibal and I arrived at precisely three. Mandy met us at the door, invited us in and escorted us to the parlor. The apartment was warm enough, but the pale afternoon light through the big windows gave the place a wintery ambiance. Ruth, hot tea and scones were waiting for us.

I noticed that Ruth used a cane when she stood to greet us.

Ruth saw my glance, and said: "Last week, the doctor said I should use a cane for balance." She smiled and added: "I can still walk just fine."

I smiled in return; Ruth is such a nice lady.

After the usual pleasantries, the three of us sat in comfortable chairs by the window. Mandy efficiently served tea.

Our conversation lasted over an hour. Hannibal and I brought Ruth up to date on our investigation. Ruth was warm, friendly and grateful for the information. She asked many insightful questions. Hannibal and I answered them all.

Ruth nodded occasionally and seemed very thoughtful. I could tell the wheels of her mind were turning.

We then made plans. As we talked, I noticed that Ruth's eyes had acquired a hard gleam. I could tell she had fully absorbed the implications of our findings, and she had plans of her own. The afternoon passed.

"I will set up a visit for the three of us at the mansion," said Ruth. "Charles will certainly accommodate us." She paused a moment, thinking. "Would next Sunday work for you?"

"Sunday would be fine," I replied. Hannibal nodded. Ruth rose from her seat, using her cane. The tea was over.

Hannibal and I took our leave. Mandy escorted us to the door. "Ruth is quite a formidable lady," I thought to myself, as the door closed behind us. "Wonder what she'll do?"

Tuesday evening, November 27, 1928

At breakfast this morning, Silvia handed Hannibal a copy of the Tribune. "Go to the second page," said Silvia. "I think you both will find the picture and story of interest."

Hannibal took the newspaper and replied: "Thank you, Silvia." He then moved his chair around so we both could read, and he opened the newspaper to page two.

A photo of Molly Malone stared back at us with big sad eyes. In spite of a slightly disheveled appearance, she was beautiful. A no-nonsense police matron stood next to her.

The bold caption and story below the photo read:

ARREST MADE IN THE
SYDNEY MELTZER MURDER

'Miss Molly Malone from the near north side was arrested at her home on North Throop Street on Monday, November 26. A police spokesman confirmed that their investigation was on-going. Quoting the spokesman: "We have evidence that on the evening of October 19, Miss Malone poisoned Mr. Meltzer with illegal whiskey spiked with methanol. Mr. Meltzer, a scion of a prominent Chicago family, was found dead in his apartment the following morning." The spokesman also said: "We are searching for an accomplice." However, the spokesman would not give out a name.

This reporter obtained an exclusive interview with Miss Malone in her cell at Cook County Jail shortly after her arrest. "I didn't know the booze was bad," she said. "I'm innocent of murder." Miss Malone joins a series of females implicated in murder who have graced the cells of the rat-infested Cook County lock-up over the past few years. Just four years ago, in April 1924, Beulah Annan was arrested for the murder of her lover, Harry Kalstedt. She was acquitted in May. Other females who were arrested for murder and later acquitted include Belva Gaertner, who was arrested for killing her married lover Walter Law in March 1924. She was acquitted by an all-male jury in June, three months later. Will the beautiful Molly Malone have the same fate? This reporter will keep the public informed on this sensational case!'

We both finished the article and looked at each other.

"Trial by newspaper," Hannibal mused. "I'm sure the defense attorneys will use the reasonable doubt approach. The police have McBride as a plausible suspect and evidence on the hemlock, which could have been the poison that killed Sydney."

"If recent history provides precedent, Molly could very well beat the rap," I agreed. I thought a moment, and then added: "However, this newspaper story could work to our advantage next Sunday."

Hannibal looked at me a long moment. "Yes, I see," he said, and nodded.

"Exactly," I responded. "Our visit at the Meltzer mansion should be most interesting."

Thursday evening, Thanksgiving Day, November 29, 1928

Thanksgiving was a welcome and very pleasant interlude. It also gave Hannibal and me an opportunity to evaluate our close friends for possible sleuthing assignments.

We had already invited Silvia, Susie, Harris and Eddie over a few days earlier. Why not? All four were single and had no local family. I had learned long ago that friendship and work relationships need not be mutually exclusive. The disparity in our wealth had no relevance at all; I was very familiar with humble beginnings and circumstances.

Early in the morning, Hannibal and I prepared Thanksgiving turkey and all of the trimmings ourselves. As usual, Hannibal displayed hidden talents; he is a master chef. Not to be outdone, I prepared cinnamon-flavored hot apple cider and laid out a lovely dining table with fine china, crystal glassware, gleaming silverware and white linen napkins.

Hannibal and I finished our preparations at about eleven. We just had time enough to dress properly before our guests arrived.

We decided on casual. Hannibal wore light grey slacks, black shoes, a light blue shirt, gold tie and a light grey, white and blue Norwegian holiday sweater with silver buttons. I wore lovely flowing black slacks, simple low-heeled black shoes, a white blouse and a black and white trimmed Norwegian sweater, also with silver buttons. For accent, I also had a white silk kerchief knotted tightly around my neck. We were stylish, but not overdressed. We adjusted the room temperature so everyone would be comfortable in their holiday clothes.

By noon, our guests had all arrived. After a period of pleasant conversation, jokes, laughter and hot apple cider, everyone helped set the food on the table. We all gathered in comfortable seats around our dining room table. Eddie surprised us all by leading us in a thankful prayer. Hannibal carved the turkey, amid many hilarious suggestions. We polished off the feast with Hannibal's homemade pumpkin pies, ice cream and coffee.

Late in the afternoon, we girls cleaned up the dishes. Hannibal, Harris and Eddie divided up the leftovers; there was plenty for everyone.

By six o'clock, our guests had departed. Hannibal and I settled in by the parlor window with glasses of chardonnay, and we watched the lights of the city wink on in the cold, clear evening. What a beautiful day!

Saturday evening, December 1, 1928

Back to work! Ruth called on Friday; she had spent the holiday at the Meltzer mansion. She was still there.

"A recent family member death, Elizabeth's suspicious behavior and a frightened servant," I thought to myself. "I can imagine how that holiday passed."

However, Ruth's voice was clear and precise, and she asked if we could join the Meltzer family at the mansion at noon on Sunday. We expected the invitation, and we said yes.

Monday morning, December 3, 1928

Hannibal and I had to dress for our visit to the Meltzer mansion. I chose another Chanel dress, this time in knit burgundy trimmed with black satin. It had simple lines, long sleeves and a high buttoned collar. A narrow black scarf draped my right shoulder.

For outdoors and the car ride, I had my second medium-length black Persian lamb coat, the one without the mink trim. I wore matching black gloves, dark silk hose and medium-heeled black shoes with small gold buckles. I also put on my old black Persian lamb hat with a small Ostrich feather; which reminds me, I need a new winter hat.

Hannibal wore his charcoal-gray, worsted-wool single-breasted suit again, this time without a vest. He had a new-fangled gold Rolex wrist watch instead of his pocket watch. He also had on simple black shoes and his old dark-red silk tie with a gold clip for accent. For outside, he had his cashmere overcoat, matching hat and fur-lined black gloves. "Men have no sense of clothing variety," I thought to myself. Oh, well.

An attendant came out the front door when Hannibal and I drove up to the Meltzer mansion just before noon.

The attendant opened the car door for me the moment after the car stopped. Soon he had the keys and Hannibal and I walked up the steps to the mansion front door.

Higgins opened the door. "Welcome," he said. He smiled and his eyes had a knowing look.

"Ruth has done her job," I thought to myself. "Nice to see you again, Higgins," I replied.

"Are we ready?" Hannibal asked.

"Yes sir," responded Higgins. "Everyone, including key staff members, are in the library." He paused and then added: "No lunch today, I'm afraid." He smiled grimly.

"Thank you, Higgins," replied Hannibal.

A maid appeared and took our coats. Hannibal kept his leather notebook. After the maid departed, Higgins said: "Follow me, please."

Higgins then proceeded slowly down the hall toward the library. He stopped at the library double doors. "The library," Higgins announced formally. He opened the doors.

Inside, I saw Ruth, Charles, Elizabeth, several maids, a chef and two young ladies who appeared to be dressed for work in the kitchen. One was Maria, who Hannibal and I met during our previous visit. Maria had an apprehensive expression.

The Meltzers were seated, and the staff stood nearby. "After all, class distinctions must be maintained," I thought to myself. I'm sure my face had a wry smile. Higgins discretely joined the staff. I watched him for a moment; but he gave no expression of emotion.

Ruth used her cane and rose from her seat. She smiled and said: "I have asked everyone to be here." She paused, glanced around the room and then returned her steady gaze to Hannibal and then me. She added: "We all saw the newspapers with regard to the arrest of Molly Malone and the on-going police investigation. I have told everyone that you have more information concerning Sydney's death."

Charles also rose from his seat as his mother finished and sat down. His eyes had a moist, pleading look. "Yes," he said. "We are all most anxious to learn what happened to Sydney." He paused and then added: "The Tribune article said that Sydney had consumed methanol."

Elizabeth remained seated. Her face had a confident, haughty expression. In an icy, formal tone, she said: "Ruth asked staff members to be present today, although I can't imagine why." She gave the staff members a sweeping, imperious look.

"Everyone here knew Sydney," responded Ruth. She gave Elizabeth a brief, sweet smile. "I'm sure they want to know what happened." Her voice quavered a little at the end of her statement.

I could tell that Ruth, in spite of her cool demeanor, had churning emotions inside. "What a brave lady," I thought to myself.

I looked at Charles and then Elizabeth and said: "Thank you for inviting us." I paused and then added: "Indeed, we have much information to share, and we have a few questions."

"Please, have a seat," said Charles. He motioned to two comfortable-looking chairs that faced the others in the room. A coffee table rested between the chairs.

Hannibal and I walked across the room to the two chairs. Charles, being the considerate host, waited until we were seated before taking his own seat. "Nice arrangement," I thought to myself. I glanced at Higgins, and he nodded.

Hannibal opened his notebook and laid it on the coffee table. He looked at his notes for a moment. I knew he was just pretending to read; he wanted to give me a chance to assess the reactions of the others in the room. His actions had the desired effect; several people in the room squirmed a little.

Finally, Hannibal rose from his chair and began to speak. "Sydney was murdered," Hannibal began. "We identified two possible causes of death by respiratory system failure. There were two ingested poisons."

I watched the expressions on the faces in our audience.

At first, Charles looked totally devastated. He gave out a low moan and put his hands over his eyes. After a moment, he put his hands down, looked intently at Hannibal and said: "Two poisons? The newspaper only mentioned methanol." His face expressed surprise and puzzlement.

Ruth maintained her stoic expression; she knew the story from our earlier discussion.

Higgins remained impassive, the perfect butler.

At first, the other members of the staff, including Maria, expressed shock, just like Charles. I watched Maria's expression intently, but it did not change, except that she put her hands up to her face and whispered, almost to herself: "Oh, no," she uttered.

Elizabeth's expression was most interesting. She took a deep breath, and released it slowly. Her face acquired a puzzled and then an apprehensive look. I could tell she was reacting to the mention of two poisons.

Hannibal continued. "Sydney died after 10:30 PM and before midnight on Friday, October 19th. He was poisoned by methanol, commonly called wood alcohol, and conium maculatum, which is the scientific term for hemlock."

"Good heavens," said Charles. "I understand how he got the methanol from the newspaper report." He looked at Hannibal intently. "How on earth did he consume hemlock?"

"Hemlock leaves were in a partially eaten salad that we found in Sydney's apartment," replied Hannibal. "He consumed most of the salad during the evening of October 19th." Sydney died a few hours later." Hannibal's gaze touched everyone in the room, in turn. He then continued: "The autopsy showed that he had consumed lethal doses of both methanol and hemlock."

"The newspaper said that Molly Malone gave Sydney the methanol," responded Charles. "Who gave him the hemlock?"

"I had hoped the people in this room could shed some light on that," replied Hannibal in a low, steady voice. "I found hemlock seeds in your greenhouse."

I glanced at each person in the room, in turn, noting each expression. Except for Charles, Elizabeth and Maria, nothing changed. Charles' mouth opened as if he was about to speak, but nothing came out. He looked over at Elizabeth with a shocked expression, which changed to bewilderment. Elizabeth's expression turned apprehensive. Maria looked extremely scared. "Oh, oh," she uttered.

Elizabeth's expression changed from apprehension to fear and then to anger. "You didn't find any hemlock plants or leaves in my greenhouse," she said fiercely. "I have no idea how the seeds got there." She paused a moment, gathering her thoughts. "Maybe some animal or bird brought them in; the door is open at night on occasion."

"Perhaps," replied Hannibal. He then looked over at Higgins.

Higgins took a deep breath, looked at Elizabeth with a steady gaze and said: "I remember the plants in the now empty spaces in the greenhouse." He paused and then continued: "I also remember they produced seeds like these." He opened his hand. It held seeds. He turned to Hannibal and asked: "Are these hemlock seeds?"

Hannibal walked over to Higgins. Higgins handed over the seeds. Hannibal looked closely and then swept the room with his gaze. "These are the same kind of seeds that I found during our previous visit," he stated in a matter-of-fact tone. "They are indeed hemlock."

Elizabeth took a sharp breath and sniffed: "Well!" she finally uttered.

"I think we can conclude that the greenhouse contained hemlock plants," said Hannibal. "The remaining question is: How did hemlock leaves get into Sydney's salad?"

Elizabeth's expression became cautious and cagey. "Maria made the salad in the kitchen," she blurted out. "I saw her."

Maria sobbed a little, looked at me and then responded in a shaky, scared voice: "Yes, but Mrs. Meltzer gave me greens from her garden." She paused, collected her thoughts, looked at Elizabeth and added: "You told me it was lettuce!"

Not to be outdone, Elizabeth retorted: "I gave you lettuce, tomatoes and cucumbers, nothing else. Besides, you flirted with Sydney on many occasions, I saw you!" Elizabeth's face contorted into a sly expression, and she added: "Of course, Sydney spurned your advances!"

"Ah, motive," I said in a clear but soft voice. "Possibly a spurned and disappointed maid." I glanced at Maria and then stared directly at Elizabeth. "However, I have the impression that you didn't approve of Sydney."

Hannibal turned to me, smiled and sat down in his chair. It was my turn to press home with the human element. I took a deep breath, relaxed back in my chair and waited.

In the meantime, Charles looked intently at his wife. His expression changed from bewilderment to a hard look. "You never approved of Sydney," he said quietly.

"Sydney was a rake and a spendthrift, and he associated with undesirable society," Elizabeth responded angrily. "My friends laughed and made sly comments, and you constantly complained about his spending!"

Silence reigned for a few moments. I then said in a soft voice: "What we need is a witness." I looked directly at Higgins.

Higgins stepped forward, took a deep breath, harrumphed a little and faced the Meltzers. "I have served in this household for over forty years," he began with quiet dignity. "I remember happier times, when Master Charles and Master Sydney were little boys."

Higgins then looked over to Charles and then to Ruth. Both had tears forming in their eyes. Ruth sobbed a little.

Higgins continued: "I have observed many things in this house. For example, I saw Mrs. Elizabeth Meltzer gather lettuce, tomatoes, cucumber and yes, hemlock leaves in the greenhouse on the afternoon of Monday, October 15th." He paused, sighed and added: "Mrs. Meltzer delivered them to the kitchen. Maria then prepared the salad."

Stunned silence permeated the library. After a moment, I asked: "Who gave the salad to Sydney?"

Higgins turned to me and replied: "On October 16, Elizabeth Meltzer gave Master Sydney a ceramic dish containing salad in the hallway near the front door. He took the dish and then left through the door. He talked briefly with our driver, and the pair drove off down the lane."

Stunned silence again, but only for a few seconds. Elizabeth erupted in a loud voice: "You! You spied on me!" She then jumped up from her seat and started toward Higgins. However, she only made two steps before she sprawled face down on the floor.

Everyone in the room was aghast for a few seconds. Ruth shifted in her chair slightly and withdrew her cane from an extended position. She looked directly at me and smiled sweetly.

"I love that old lady," I thought to myself.

Elizabeth rose to a sitting position on the floor. No one moved to help her. She sobbed softly.

Higgins broke the silence. "I will phone the sheriff," he said in a dignified voice. He turned to leave the room.

"No, Higgins, I will do it." Everyone turned to the sound of the voice. It was Charles.

11

METHODS OF JUSTICE

Friday Evening, December 7, 1928

On Sunday, Charles took over after the revelations about the murder of Sydney. The Lake County sheriff soon arrived. After a brief explanation of our presence, all the sheriff needed from us was our names and how to contact us. Discretion on our part seemed appropriate, and we prepared to leave.

Higgins escorted us to the door and the outside attendant brought our car around. As we put on our coats, Higgins said: "Thank you both." He smiled in a genuine way.

As we drove back to Chicago and home, we speculated on Elizabeth's future. After some discussion, Hannibal mused, almost to himself: "Families at the Meltzer level in society handle such affairs differently."

I wasn't sure how to respond, since my background was certainly not high society. After a moment, I responded: "We will have to wait and see." I paused and then concluded: "In any case, our role, I think, is finished."

"Yes," responded Hannibal. He looked at me and smiled. "Ruth will keep us informed."

I saw Ruth briefly when I left our building on Wednesday, December 5th. She smiled and waved as we met in the lobby. I was on my way to the Loop; I needed a new winter hat. My taxi was waiting.

"I just got back from the mansion," said Ruth. "Frenchie needs a walk." She seemed surprisingly light-hearted, given her ordeal at the mansion over the weekend.

I noticed that she didn't have her cane. "Her balance problem must be cured," I thought to myself. I know Ruth saw my look, and she just smiled. Frenchie was bouncing around, and the pair left after we exchanged pleasantries.

"I will wait," I thought to myself. "Ruth will bring me up to date when she's ready."

Sure enough, Ruth called on Thursday. "Can you and Hannibal come to my apartment on Friday for tea at three o'clock?" she asked. "I want to bring you both up to date on the situation with Elizabeth."

Of course, we accepted. Neither of us had seen anything in the newspapers since we left the Meltzer mansion on Sunday afternoon, just after the Lake County sheriff arrived.

I fidgeted and speculated to myself all day Thursday. Hannibal watched me, smiled in his knowing way, and on Thursday evening after wine time, said: "Patience, my dear." I gave him a dirty look.

Finally, Friday arrived. I was antsy all morning. However, I forced myself to wait until two forty-five before badgering Hannibal to head toward the elevator. Hannibal was good natured about it, which, of course, is infuriating. We arrived at Ruth's apartment right on time.

Mandy opened the door. "Welcome," she said in her usual gracious manner. "Mrs. Meltzer is in the parlor." She closed the door behind us and then led the way to the parlor.

Ruth rose to greet us. Tea, scones and other sweets rested on a side table. Soon we were all seated. Mandy served everyone and discretely left.

After a few moments of small talk, Ruth leaned back in her chair, looked intently at Hannibal and then me. "First," she said, "I have a check for your services." She picked up an envelope from an end table next to her chair. "Please look at it; I had to guess about your expenses." She leaned forward and handed the check to me.

I have never been shy about counting up money for services rendered. Old habits, I suppose. I opened the envelope. The check was for twenty-five thousand dollars. My mouth dropped open.

"Oh Ruth," I exclaimed. "This is too much!" I expected less than half that amount. Hannibal looked at me and smiled.

"No, it isn't," replied Ruth. "You two are worth every penny." She leaned back in her chair, smiled warmly and continued: "Now that we have settled that, I have an update on Elizabeth."

Hannibal set his teacup down, looked at Ruth intently and said: "I'm sure Charles handled the situation appropriately." There seemed to be an unspoken understanding between Ruth and Hannibal.

I looked back and forth between the two. I remembered Hannibal's remark about how families at higher levels in society handled such things. Hannibal and Ruth both came from wealthy backgrounds. "Patience, Caroline," I thought to myself. "Listen and learn."

Ruth also set her teacup down. "Yes," she replied to Hannibal, with a glance at me. Her eyes twinkled a little. "Of course, the sheriff took Elizabeth away, and she spent the night in jail."

"Sounds good so far," I thought to myself. I smiled. Both Hannibal and Ruth noticed and smiled in return. I could tell both knew what I was thinking.

"The next day, about noon, Charles posted bail," Ruth continued. "The Lake County authorities cooperated nicely." Ruth paused, Mandy refreshed her tea, and Ruth picked up her cup and took another sip.

I fidgeted. Ruth, of course, noticed and her eyes twinkled again. My thoughts raced. "How frustrating! Elizabeth the witch should have stayed in jail!" I smiled sweetly, but I fidgeted again.

"Elizabeth was brought home by the sheriff mid-afternoon on Monday," said Ruth. "She was quite broken and disheveled." A look of satisfaction crossed her face. "The attorneys were waiting at the mansion, along with Charles, Higgins, Maria and me."

Now I was really puzzled. Ruth set her tea down again, and continued: "After some discussion, Elizabeth was given a choice."

I leaned forward in anticipation; I couldn't help it.

Ruth continued: "Based on the advice of our attorneys, Elizabeth could not be convicted of murder unless Higgins and Maria testified. The seeds, fingerprints and Elizabeth's reactions would not be enough."

Ruth paused while Hannibal and I digested this information. Ruth was right, of course. I nodded in response, so did Hannibal.

"Also, we have the problem of methanol poisoning," added Ruth. "A good defense attorney would certainly point out that methanol, not hemlock, could have been the poison that killed Sydney." Ruth's voice had a catch in it when she mentioned Sydney's name. "Even with the testimony of Higgins and Maria, conviction would still be uncertain."

"What remarkable control," I thought to myself. I'm sure Ruth's emotions were still raw underneath.

Ruth saw my look and smiled. "I have come to terms with Sydney's death," she said. "The pain will never fully go away, but neither will anything bring my son back." She had a brief moment when tears formed. She removed a silk handkerchief from her sleeve and dabbed her eyes. She quickly recovered her poise and added: "We must move on."

"So much was said in those few words," I thought to myself. I looked directly into Ruth's eyes and tried to smile in sympathy. I think Ruth understood my emotion and smiled in return.

"Anyway," she continued, "Elizabeth could either face a very public trial with Higgins' and Maria's testimonies, or she could accept a speedy divorce from Charles." Ruth paused and a look of satisfaction passed briefly across her face. "Of course, the divorce would stipulate that Elizabeth would get no money, property or compensation of any kind." Ruth paused again, and then added: "Elizabeth, upon the advice of the attorneys, accepted the divorce."

"Sounds good," I thought to myself. However, another thought crossed my mind, and I asked: "Does Elizabeth have a wealthy family she could turn to?"

"No," responded Ruth. "Elizabeth's family had name, titles and prestige, but unfortunately, earlier generations had squandered the money." Ruth's look of satisfaction returned, and she added: "Elizabeth will be quite penniless."

I leaned back in my chair and pondered for quite a while. Ruth and Hannibal waited patiently. Finally, I said: "Justice is different for Molly Malone."

It was Ruth's turn to be taken aback a little. After a few moments, she responded: "Yes, I see." She looked at Hannibal, who had a slight smile. I think he expected my reaction, and he probably already saw the path forward.

"Well," replied Ruth. "Would it be possible for me to meet Miss Malone?"

I thought a moment, and then replied: "Yes, I suppose, but she's still in the Cook County jail."

"Oh, I think we can take care of that," responded Ruth. Her old eyes twinkled again, and she continued: "Perhaps after she's out, we could meet in a place where she would feel more comfortable."

"The Hideout," I blurted out without thinking. "Molly worked out of a place called The Hideout." I'm sure my face had a slight apprehensive look; I didn't know how Ruth would react.

Hannibal laughed. "The Hideout is a working-class speakeasy," he said. "Molly was a working girl."

Ruth looked at him with a puzzled expression, but only for a moment. "I see," she finally responded with a mischievous look. "Sounds like fun!"

Saturday, December 15, 1928

Well! Friday evening was an eye opener. Hannibal had made many phone calls during the week. Vincenzo drove Ruth, Hannibal and me to The Hideout about six o'clock. We all dressed in plain-looking clothes for the occasion, even Ruth. I wore the same clothes that I had on during my first visit to The Hideout.

"You have dressed for the occasion," I said to Ruth as we entered Vincenzo's taxi.

Ruth smiled and replied: "I'm full of surprises, aren't I?" Her old eyes twinkled.

Hannibal, dressed in his old jeans and leather jacket, said: "Fascinating." He grinned broadly. "You and Caroline make a fine pair."

"Yes, we do," I replied with a little giggle.

The key players in our unfolding drama were all waiting as Ruth, Hannibal and I passed through the front door. Connor was his usual hearty, straightforward self, and he pointed to a table near the back corner away from the bar. Molly, fresh out of jail on bail, was already seated at the table, along with a man dressed in a business suit. Mike, Molly's former boyfriend, sat on a barstool nearby. Sean was not there.

The man in a suit rose from his seat as we approached. "I'm James Simpson Brandt," he said. He looked totally out of place in The Hideout. "Mrs. Meltzer, I presume," he continued, and he looked at Ruth.

"Yes," responded Ruth. "Our attorneys said you would be here." She extended her hand.

Brandt took Ruth's hand gently in a formal manner, released it, and said: "Please, have a seat." He motioned to a chair across from Molly, looked at Hannibal and then me.

"Thank you," replied Ruth, but she made introductions before taking her seat. "Please meet my good friends Caroline and Hannibal."

Brandt, who had remained standing, responded with courteous greetings and handshakes. "Please have a seat," he said, and he motioned to two chairs next to the chair for Ruth.

Before we took our seats, Hannibal and I looked to Ruth.

Ruth looked for a long minute at Molly, who squirmed a little. Finally, Ruth said: "You must be Molly Malone."

Molly replied: "Yes ma'am." Her eyes were wide in the presence of the aristocratic Ruth.

I confess, I was also a bit in awe of Ruth. She had, by her presence and quiet, yet forceful personality, taken charge of the meeting.

Ruth then took her seat. I took the seat next to Ruth. Hannibal and Brandt, being perfect gentlemen, waited until Ruth and I were seated and then took their seats, in turn. Connor joined Mike on a nearby bar stool. The stage was set.

Ruth continued to stare at Molly. After another long pause, she said: "Caroline and Hannibal told me about the poisoned moonshine." Everyone in the group looked at Molly.

"I didn't know it was poison," she blurted out. She looked around the group wildly, with a scared expression. "I told the police."

"Yet you and Sean McBride were there the night Sydney consumed the poisoned moonshine," I said. It was my turn to look Molly in the eyes.

Ruth glanced at me, gave a nod of approval and returned her gaze to Molly.

"Witnesses saw you give the moonshine to Sydney, who drank it," I continued; "Yet you and Sean didn't drink it."

Tears formed in Molly's eyes and she sniffled a little. "It was supposed to make Sydney sick, not kill him." She looked wildly around again. "Sydney jilted me, the two-timer." She took a deep breath and added: "Sean said Sydney needed a lesson, and he got the moonshine."

Molly gained a little control after the last statement. I could tell she was thinking and planning her defense.

"Beautiful girl, reasonable doubt and a good defense attorney," I thought to myself. "She won't be convicted of murder, and she might not even be convicted of being an accomplice."

I looked over at Ruth. Her face had a hard look for a long time. Finally, her look softened a little. "Hannibal and Caroline told me about your background," she said in a soft voice. Her expression softened a little more. After a long pause, she asked: "What would you do if you were given a way out of your current circumstances?"

Molly's face had a puzzled look. After a long moment, she asked: "You mean out of jail?"

"No," replied Ruth, "I mean a way out of your current job and lifestyle."

"Oh!" responded Molly. She paused, and then added: "But Sean is gone, and I don't know anyone." She looked around at our faces and said: "I don't know any other way." Her expression changed to one of genuine sorrow.

Instantly, I felt a sense of pity. Based on my own background, I knew exactly how Molly felt. In my early days, I had many such moments of feeling trapped with no way out.

Connor and Mike had been listening intently. Connor spoke first. "Sean won't be back," he said. We all looked at Connor as he got up from his bar stool. Connor looked first at Hannibal, who nodded. There seemed to be an understanding between them.

Connor folded his brawny arms. He gazed around our little group. His eyes twinkled as his stare touched me. He then said: "Industrial accidents are common over at the mill next to the Chicago River." He then looked over at Mike.

"That's right," responded Mike. "Rumor has it that Sean sleeps with the fishes." He then looked over at Molly, whose mouth dropped open. I could tell by her expression that, slowly, the meaning of Mike's words crystalized in her mind.

My mind raced as I added up the nuances of the conversation. I then looked over at Ruth.

Ruth took a deep breath and then looked intently at Molly. I could tell that she understood. "Well," she finally stated. "I think, Molly, that you have a way out." Ruth looked from Molly to Mike and then back to Molly. "Hannibal told me that Mike has feelings for you."

I looked over at Hannibal. "You old softy," I whispered. Hannibal just smiled.

There was a long pause. Finally, Brandt harrumphed. "Well!" he stated. "I will work out the legal details." He then turned to Molly. "I think you can be confident that the case will never go to trial, and the charges will be dropped due to insufficient evidence."

Ruth stood up from her seat. She looked at Molly. "The rest is up to you, Molly." Take advantage of your opportunity." Ruth then looked around the little group and asked: "Is there anything else?"

Her question was greeted with silence.

"Very well, then," she added. She then sat back down, looked at Connor, and asked: "May I have a scotch on the rocks, please?"

12

WINTER INTERLUDE

Sunday, December 16, 1928

Hannibal, Harris, Silvia, Ruth and I set up and decorated a Christmas tree in our parlor on Friday morning. We invited Eddie and Susie, but Eddie had to work overtime at the lab, and Susie had a date with her current boyfriend. Harris was still on duty; he was only able to help Hannibal carry the tree up the stairs to the apartment. Silvia and I cleaned up the pine needle mess.

After we got the tree inside the apartment, Harris said his goodbyes and returned to work. It was a cold, blustery, winter day, and he waited just inside the building front door, next to his little office. The opening and closing of the door created a cold draft, and I'm sure he was miserable.

For the tree, we used new-fangled strings of Noma colored electric lights, intricate glass ornaments from Marshall Fields and lots of tinsel. When he bought the tree, Hannibal also bought a stand that allowed the base of the tree to sit in a little tub of water. What a novel idea!

Ruth, Silvia, Hannibal and I dressed in festive winter fashions. Like Thanksgiving, it was the right time to be dressy-casual and to forget social distinctions.

Ruth wore a long-waisted, long-sleeved burgundy dress with simple lines. It had a low waist, a black belt with a small silver buckle in front and a hem just below the knee. Her accessories included short, double strands of white pearls, dark silk hose and low-heeled black shoes. The colors of her outfit contrasted beautifully with her silvery hair, which was coiffed in the latest fashion for mature ladies. Her cane stayed at home, and she was as spry as a person half her age.

Silvia left her maid's uniform in her apartment. She wore a holiday-green, all-wool low-waisted velour dress. The collar, flowing tie, cuffs and sash were white with holiday green dots. Pin tucks and pearl buttons trimmed the front of the bodice. The skirt sides were pleated, and the front and back were plain. She wore simple, low-heeled black shoes and no jewelry. Her dark hair was bobbed in the latest fashion. She was a lovely young lady.

Hannibal wore grey pleated slacks, a simple white shirt with an open collar, black shoes and a grey and white Norwegian holiday sweater with silver buttons. His short dark hair was parted on the side, and the grey at his temples accented his clothes and framed his handsome, chiseled face. What a guy!

Of course, I had to keep up with my companions. My outfit was straight from Jane Régny, 11 Rue La Boétie, Paris. It embodied the latest in ladies' holiday sportswear. My high-waisted, worsted wool tan slacks accented my trim figure at the top and blended into wide, flowing legs. A loose, narrow, black belt with a small gold buckle defined my waist. I also wore an ivory-colored, silk, V-necked blouse. In tune with the season, I topped my outfit with an open, powder blue cashmere sweater. It had patterned holiday decoration and trim. The tan color of the trim matched my tan slacks. Finally, I wore low heeled, medium-topped brown leather boots. My dark hair was short and turned under at the ends. I was a fashion model, or so I felt. How delightfully daring!

Ruth brought a tree skirt made of deep red velvet with embroidered sprigs of evergreen and white snowflakes. I could tell she had made it herself, perhaps long ago. She had a wistful look when Hannibal arranged it around the base of the tree. We topped the tree with a silvery, lighted star. It was beautiful, and the smell of spruce filled the room.

Afterwards, we sat around and sipped hot apple cider, flavored with a touch of cinnamon. We talked about Christmas seasons past. Each of us had private memories, but our conversations dwelt on the good times. It was a pleasant, nostalgic morning.

We finished with a light lunch. I took a Christmas box with sandwiches, cookies, hot cider in a thermos and other goodies down to Harris. He set it in his little office next to the front door, with many thanks. I made a mental note to send a similar box to Eddie on Saturday.

After lunch, Ruth returned to her apartment, and Silvia busied herself in the kitchen. Hannibal and I kicked off our footwear and lounged on the sofa. We then discussed Giuseppe Costanzo.

"Our client is Sicilian," said Hannibal. "He arrived through Ellis Island in 1890, and he traveled west to Chicago almost immediately." He paused, flipped through his notes that were stacked on the coffee table next to our two cups of hot apple cider and then continued: "He lives with his wife of 38 years just off West Taylor Street near Sheridan Park." He flipped through the notes again. "As he told us, he owns three retail bakeries and a commercial operation." Hannibal smiled wryly. "Old Giuseppe has done well in the new world."

"And you've done your homework," I replied and returned the smile. "Where did you get your information?"

Hannibal responded: "Giuseppe is a charter member of Italian-American Chamber of Commerce and several social clubs." He leafed through more notes and then continued: "He is also well-known to Italian language newspapers published in Little Italy, and his family and business backgrounds are generally available from several public sources." He smiled and added: "Also, Watts and Mulvaney were very helpful."

I gave Hannibal a quizzical look. "Little Italy?" I asked.

Hannibal nodded and replied. "There are several Italian neighborhoods in Chicago. The largest is in Chicago's near west side, centered on West Taylor Street between South Ashland on the west and South Morgan on the east." He paused, opened another folder, took out a detailed Chicago map, pointed and continued: "There are several other smaller Italian neighborhoods, here, here and here."

I leaned over and looked closely at the map. Hannibal pointed to Grand Avenue between Aberdeen Street and Washtenaw Avenue, then to 24th Street and South Oakley on the lower west side and finally to the area between Division Street and Chicago Avenue and between LaSalle Boulevard and the Chicago River.

"This last area on the near north side is known as Little Sicily," Hannibal explained. "Sometimes the newspapers call it Little Hell." He paused and then added: "Lots of gangster activity."

"Bootlegging?" I queried.

Hannibal nodded. "Everything," he replied. "Bootlegging, gambling, lower-end speakeasies and so on."

Hannibal didn't need to add brothels; I understood the unspoken connotation. I squirmed a little as I recalled my earlier days.

Hannibal looked at me closely; he seemed to read my thoughts. He then eased my discomfort by shifting the conversation. "Giuseppe has a small bakery there, on Chicago Avenue near Orleans Street," he said. "Michael, Giuseppe's youngest son, manages that store."

I smiled; Hannibal was such a thoughtful man. I then asked: "Is that the bakery where Capone sends his money?"

Hannibal grinned and replied: "Very perceptive. Yes, I think so."

"On the other hand, Little Italy and the area around Grand Avenue are generally upscale, with nice homes for more affluent families," Hannibal continued. "There are several large Catholic Churches." He pointed to a couple of hand drawn circles on the map. "For example, Our Lady of Pompeii is on West Lexington and the Holy Guardian Angel is on Arthington Street."

"Does Giuseppe have bakeries in those neighborhoods?" I asked.

Hannibal nodded. "He has one on West Taylor Street near the corner with South Morgan and another on Grand Avenue near the corner with Aberdeen." He paused and then added: "Giuseppe's second son Antonio manages the store on West Taylor and his third son, Alberto, manages the one on Grand Avenue."

I did a quick analysis and smiled. "You imply that Giuseppe has another son besides Antonio, Alberto and Michael," I said. "What does the eldest son do?"

"Right again," replied Hannibal. "Santino is the eldest, and he manages the commercial bakery on Erie Street near Ashland Avenue."

"Competitors?" I asked.

"Three major competitors and several minor Mom and Pop establishments," replied Hannibal. "The big three are Scafuri Bakery at 1337 West Taylor, Ferrara Bakery at 2210 West Taylor and Giordano Bakery on Chicago Avenue near Hudson Street, just two blocks from the establishment managed by Michael."

I thought a moment, then stated: "In addition to gangland ties, old Giuseppe has serious legitimate competition." I thought a moment and then added: "Perhaps one or more of the competitors has a violent tendency."

Hannibal nodded, looked at his notes and added: "All three main competitors have retail and commercial operations. The competition to serve individuals, restaurants, social clubs, church functions, weddings and so on is, by all accounts, fierce."

"I wonder if competition includes gangland activities," I mused.

"Could be," replied Hannibal. "We need to find out."

"Agreed," I replied. "What have you found out about the Costanzo family social connections?"

"The Costanzos hold memberships in several church and social clubs," responded Hannibal. "The entire family participates as active parishioners at Our Lady of Pompeii. Also, Giuseppe and his sons are members of the Italian-American Chamber of Commerce and the Unione Siciliana, which has well-documented gangster connections." He flipped through his notes and added: "The three older sons are married with children. Michael remains an eligible bachelor."

He grinned a little and added: "From what I've been told, old Giuseppe sometimes thinks he's still a bachelor."

I giggled a little. "The old goat; that explains his attention to me," I replied. "Did you find out anything about Capone's involvement with our client?" I asked.

Hannibal leaned forward, picked up another file from the coffee table, opened it and read a few moments.

Finally, he answered. "As far as the police are concerned, there is no known direct connection between gangsters, Capone or otherwise, and the Costanzo family." Hannibal paused, read a moment and then continued: "However, the Unione Siciliana does have known criminals among its members."

"And our boy Giuseppe and his sons are members," I replied. "Interesting." I thought a moment, and then asked: "Who are the bad guys among the members?"

"Well, currently, Giuseppe "Joe" Aiello and his brothers Salvatore and Pietro are trying to run the Unione Siciliana," responded Hannibal. "Past leaders have been murdered or run out of town."

Hannibal paused and then added: "The six Genna brothers, Angelo, Antonio Mike, Peter, Sam and Vincenzo, used to dominate the organization, but Angelo, Antonio and Mike were murdered in 1925, probably by the North Side Gang."

"Really?" I exclaimed. "Any proof? Was anyone convicted?"

"No and no," replied Hannibal. "Our friend Sergeant Watts seemed frustrated when I asked about the murders. No doubt honest cops have a hard time getting things done in the department."

"What about the other three Genna brothers?" I asked.

"They disappeared," replied Hannibal. "Watts thinks they are hiding, and for good reason. It has been all out war between the North Side Gang and the Gennas, who are allied with Capone."

"Ah," I said. "I see why Capone has an interest in the problems of Giuseppe and son Michael. North Siders may be trying to muscle in on Giuseppe's money laundering operation for Capone."

"Yes," responded Hannibal. "Also, Watts thinks that the Aiello brothers now run the Genna organization. In 1921, the Gennas obtained a federal license to legally manufacture industrial alcohol at a plant at 1022 West Taylor Street in the heart of Little Italy, and Watts thinks the Aiellos run the plant now."

"Let me guess," I responded. "This industrial alcohol gets converted into a drinkable version and it is sold through speakeasies in Little Italy."

"That's the rumor," agreed Hannibal. "Lots of money involved, and our boy Giuseppe funnels cash through his bakery business accounts. The money comes out clean on the other side, probably in accounts that are accessible to Capone and his allies at some major bank."

I smiled, and said: "We should follow the money." I thought a moment and then added: "We need to know if some of the money goes elsewhere, either as payoffs or into accounts accessible to Michael or the other members of the family."

"Agreed," replied Hannibal. "I have friends in banking that might be able to help us."

"Do you have more on the Unione Siciliana?" I asked.

Hannibal leafed through his notes. "The police have quite a file. Originally, the Unione Siciliana was a social organization for males of Sicilian birth or descent. In 1925, the name was changed to the Italian-American National Union, although most folks refer to it by the old name. After the name change, it was opened to all Italian males." He paused a moment, then added: "The organization sponsors social and sporting events, delivers Italian votes in elections and provides 'insurance' to individuals and businesses against extortion by outsiders."

I thought a moment. "The insurance sounds like a protection racket to me."

"Yes," replied Hannibal. "Although the police have no proof, Watts thinks the whole organization is controlled by Capone."

"What's the evidence?" I asked.

"Lots of changes at the top, among other things," replied Hannibal. "Presidents of the Unione have been murdered. The police have no proof, but Watts thinks the murders were either casualties of the war between Capone and the North Side Gang or ordered by Capone himself."

"Names?" I replied.

Hannibal read from his notes. "Being president of the Unione is hazardous duty. President Angelo Genna was murdered on May 27, 1925, President Samuel Amatuna was murdered on November 13, 1925 and President Antonio Lombardo was murdered on September 7, this year."

"Let me guess," I said. "No one has been arrested or charged with the murders, right?"

Hannibal nodded, flipped a couple of pages and continued: "The first two were probably killed by the North Side Gang and the Lombardo murder may have been ordered by Capone over disagreements about peacemaking efforts. Pasqualino Lolordo is the current president, but the police think that Joe Aiello is angling for Lolordo's job."

"I can see why Capone is interested in the source of Costanzo family problems," I replied. "Possibilities include bakery competitors, North Side gangsters, internal fighting within the Unione Siciliana, or something personal unrelated to the Capone-Costanzo relationship."

"Agreed," said Hannibal. "Giuseppe Costanzo is scared, and both Capone and old Giuseppe want to know who is behind it."

"OK," I responded. "Now to the personal part. What do you have on Michael's romantic entanglements?"

Hannibal laughed. "Nothing, other than what Giuseppe told us." He leaned back on the sofa, put his hands behind his head, and watched me for a moment. His face had a knowing grin. "Snooping for information on Michael's love life is your department."

"OK, Smarty," I replied. "I think Ruth and I can do the necessaries."

Hannibal raised his eyebrows. "Ruth?" he queried. "Have you been a nefarious influence on that sweet old lady?" His eyes twinkled.

"I'm not sure what 'nefarious' means, but Ruth has her mischievous side," I responded. "I expect to learn a few things from that old gal."

Hannibal laughed again. "You're probably right," he responded. "Just stay out of jail."

"Will do," I replied with a grin. "You know me."

"Precisely," Hannibal responded with a chuckle. "I know you very well." He moved over on the sofa and gave me an affectionate hug. He then added: "I'll give Watts and Mulvaney a heads up."

I giggled, snuggled a little and replied: "OK, let's lay out a plan."

"Good idea," replied Hannibal. He grinned broadly. I suppose we should take care of business first."

I gave out a mock sigh and said: "OK, if we must."

"Ahem," replied Hannibal. "Well, to begin, I think we have to be discrete. Family honor is a major feature of Sicilian culture."

"How so?" I asked.

Hannibal leaned back and was silent for a long moment. "Whether the attempt on Michael's life was related to bakery competition, the gang wars or something personal, family honor may play a role as an excuse for past or for future violence." He looked at me intently. "Again, please be careful as you probe into Michael's personal relationships."

The implications of Hannibal's concern slowly crystalized in my consciousness. He was right of course. "I will have a long talk with Ruth, and we will be careful," I replied.

"I'll see what I can do to get you and Ruth into a social situation with the Costanzos," said Hannibal.

We sat silent for quite a while. Dusk arrived, and the light outside the window slowly dimmed. Inside, the lights of our Christmas tree glowed brightly. Silvia came in from the kitchen, said her goodbyes and discretely left for her apartment downstairs.

Finally, Hannibal said: "We need a team for our investigation."

"I agree," I replied. "We can't operate in Little Italy alone." I paused and then added: "I speak enough colloquial Italian to get by." I thought a moment and continued: "I suppose you are fluent?"

"Yes, well, I do have a bit of an accent compared to Sicilians; my Italian companions during the war came from northern Italy," responded Hannibal.

"I think that if we are careful, we can get by in Little Italy," I replied.

"Agree," said Hannibal. "We can also use Eddie; his Italian has a Napoli accent; his parents came from Naples."

"What about Ruth?" I asked.

"She hasn't told you?" responded Hannibal. "Her maiden name is Canossa, and she is descended from one of the oldest aristocratic families in Italy."

"That old gal is full of surprises!" I exclaimed. I paused a moment and then asked: "Fluent Italian?"

"Oh yes, replied Hannibal with a grin. "Her family still owns villas and vineyards in Tuscany." He grinned and added: "Of course, her accent is northern Italian."

"OK, what other surprises do you have for me?" I asked.

"Well, Harris Brown's father and mother are Italian, in spite of his Americanized name. His father's name was Bruni, but it got changed when he came through Ellis Island."

"That happened a lot," I agreed. "Many of the folks of Italian descent in Clinton, my home town, have Americanized names."

"What about Susie?" Hannibal asked.

"No," I replied. "She's Scots-Irish, I think." I paused, then added. "Still, she might play a role in our little schemes; she's very resourceful and good observer."

Hannibal and I were silent for a while, thinking. As we watched through the window, the streetlights came on.

I looked closely. "Oh, look!" I said. "Snowflakes!" Indeed, snow was gently falling outside; the parlor was warm, and Hannibal and I were together.

Hannibal turned to me, and we kissed. "Enough work for today," he whispered.

"Are you sure?" I said with a mocking smile.

Hannibal smiled in return and kissed me again.

13

HOLIDAYS WITH SWITCHBLADES

Christmas Evening, Tuesday, December 25, 1928

Hannibal and I celebrated Christmas at home today. We started early; I was so excited! I wore my warm, ivory-colored lounging robe with a silver fox collar over my matching silk pajamas. My feet were toasty in velvet slippers. Ever the early bird, Hannibal was already dressed in gray slacks, light blue flannel shirt and a navy-blue cashmere sweater. His concession to the early hour was a pair of soft leather slippers over his thick, navy-blue cotton socks.

We fixed coffee in the kitchen; Silvia would join us later. With cups in hand, we adjourned to the parlor with our lighted Christmas tree. The sky outside the window was just getting light; the street lamps were still on. New snow had fallen overnight; the sky was now clear, and the scene was perfect for Christmas morning.

We each found our gifts under the tree. Mine was in gold wrapping paper with a red ribbon. Hannibal's gift was in green paper with a white ribbon. I wrapped it myself, and I did a great job, thank you. We sat on the sofa with gifts in hand.

I opened mine first. I tried to take the paper off without tearing it, with moderate success. Hannibal laughed. Finally, I got the paper off and found a lovely rosewood box. I opened the box, and on a red satin liner, I found the most beautiful necklace I had ever seen.

Hannibal gave me a triple-strand pearl necklace with an enormous solitaire ruby, which was set in a platinum frame. The frame that held the ruby fastened in the middle of the pearl strands in front. "It was my mother's," he said with a wistful smile. "I would be pleased if you would wear it."

"Oh, Hannibal, it's beautiful," I responded. Tears misted in my eyes for a moment. Finally, I wiped away a tear, smiled and simply said: "Thank you." I fumbled with the fox collar of my robe and the necklace as I tried to put it on.

"Here, let me help," said Hannibal.

Between the two of us, we finally got the clasp fastened. I walked over to our full-length hallway mirror and opened my robe and pajama top so the necklace would show. I saw a slim young woman, with tousled dark hair, in lounging clothes, wearing an elegant, gorgeous necklace. What a picture! I turned and giggled.

Hannibal joined in with a chuckle. "You are beautiful," he said.

"Now it's your turn," I said. I returned to the sofa, necklace and all.

Hannibal's gift was in a small box, very carefully wrapped. He deftly slipped off the ribbon, then produced a small pocket knife, and cut the cellophane tape that held the wrapping paper at the package ends. The paper came off without a tear.

"OK, Smarty," I said, and I gave him a dig in the ribs. Hannibal just smiled, with his usual twinkly-eyed look of inner amusement.

Hannibal opened the box. Inside, he found a gold, double strand watch chain with a dime-sized, solid gold pendant in the middle. The pendant was engraved with his initials.

"It's both elegant and very useful," Hannibal said. He held it up to the light, and it sparkled. "A new family heirloom." He put the chain back in its box and set it on the coffee table. He then turned to me, put his arms around me and kissed me, long and warmly. I tingled all over.

After a long moment, Hannibal leaned back on the sofa, smiled and said: "Merry Christmas."

After about an hour, Hannibal and I dressed appropriately and prepared for guests. Silvia, Ruth, Susie, Eddie and Harris arrived about ten o'clock. We exchanged small gifts, and everyone laughed and said thank you over and over.

Silvia, Susie and Ruth had made side dishes. Silvia had prepared cranberry-maple carrots and candied sweet potatoes; Susie brought slow-cooked green beans and mashed potatoes with a touch of butter, and Ruth brought a tossed salad with lettuce, sliced tomatoes, cucumbers and radishes. I supplied traditional stuffing made with turkey giblets, celery, onion, turkey broth, bread, sage and parsley.

The men also contributed. Eddie brought newly baked Italian cannoli. He also brought almond biscotti, just right for dipping in hot coffee. Harris and Eddie also brought six bottles of wine, carefully selected, and "straight off the boat," as Harris said. Two were hearty 1922 Bordeaux Château Lafite premier crus, which was a red blend, two were Olivier Leflaive Meursault-Charmes first cru chardonnays, and two were full-bodied Lambrusco di Sorbara, from the village just north of Modena, Italy.

Roasting the 20-pound turkey was Hannibal's purview, along with his usual pumpkin pies. He got lots of supervision from Eddie and Harris. Eddie, the consummate forensic scientist, provided hilarious guidance on the proper temperature inside and out, the proper mixture for the gravy and so on. Harris calmly suggested basting the turkey with a special mixture of butter and herbs. Hannibal remained calm in spite of all the 'help.' Fortunately, he had made the pies the day before.

We had everything ready by two o'clock. I had set the dining room table on Christmas eve, and we used side tables for the food, except for the turkey. After we were all seated, Eddie gave thanks in a dignified way. All of us remained silent with private thoughts. I had much to be thankful for, and I gave a silent, personal prayer. I think others did the same.

After the prayer, Hannibal carved the turkey. Again, he got guidance from Eddie and Harris. We all laughed, and it was finally done. We ate, talked and had a wonderful afternoon together.

Evening arrived. Like Thanksgiving, we girls cleaned up the mess and the dishes, and the guys divided up the leftovers. Everyone had enough for several days of snacking.

Afterwards, we all sat in the parlor, enjoyed final glasses of Lambrusco and planned our invasion of Little Italy. Eddie, Susie and Harris got detailed street assignments. Silvia would stay at home and coordinate any emergencies by phone. Ruth would work with Hannibal and me to meet the Costanzos. Soon all was settled, except for details on the Costanzo meeting.

Our guests all said their goodbyes by six o'clock. Laden with gifts and leftovers, everyone left for their respective homes.

It had been a wonderful day. Hannibal and I poured ourselves final cups of coffee and returned to the parlor. The light outside faded; only our Christmas tree glowed with its lovely lights. We curled up on the sofa together and began our discussion of the Costanzo case.

"In addition to our plans with Eddie, Susie and Harris, we need to think through our plans with Ruth," I began. I paused a moment and then added: "We all agreed at the meeting that we should meet the Costanzos in a social setting," I began. "Old Giuseppe and his family might feel more at ease, and we might gain insight into their activities associated with the shooting at Michael's home." I paused again, then said: "The question is: How?"

"I agree," replied Hannibal. "Would you and Ruth like to attend a ball sponsored by the Unione Siciliana the evening of January 6th?"

I was taken aback a little, and I'm sure my face had a blank look. What else had Hannibal been up to? I quickly regained my composure and replied: "Oh? Sounds like fun." My mind raced. "How do we get invited?"

Hannibal smiled and said: "I talked with Joe and Albert at the Green Mill a few days ago, and they were able to get three tickets for us." He leaned back on the sofa and added: "The ball will be in the evening, after the Feast of the Epiphany parade down West Taylor Street."

Again, I'm sure I had a blank look, but for just a second. "Parade?" I finally said.

"Part of the traditional Italian Christmas season," replied Hannibal. The Feast of the Epiphany commemorates when the Magi, or three Wise Men, visited Jesus in Bethlehem." He then added: "January 6th falls 12 days after Christmas. Little Italy celebrates with a parade and evening parties, including the one sponsored by the Unione Siciliana."

I must admit; I have little knowledge of church holidays, except for Christmas and Easter. Other than my mother's brief attempts when I was very young, I hadn't attended church for ages. "What should I wear?" I blurted out.

Hannibal laughed. "Well, the witch's role is already taken by La Befana, the Italian Christmas witch, who will fly in on her broom and give candy to all of the kids."

I gave Hannibal a dig in the ribs. "OK, Smarty, answer the question."

"Conservative clothing, with your usual flair, will be fine," Hannibal replied with a chuckle. "Be prepared to dance with Giuseppe, I'm sure he will ask."

"I will brief Ruth, maybe the old boy will dance with Ruth instead," I replied.

Hannibal laughed. "You distract Giuseppe. Ruth, I think, can talk with his wife, Margherita."

Hannibal was right, of course. Ruth should play the elderly confidant.

Monday, January 7, 1929

I didn't know the Feast of the Epiphany parade could be so exciting! About three o'clock yesterday, Ruth, Hannibal and I took a taxi from our apartment building to the corner of West Taylor and South Carpenter Streets. Harris, Eddie and Susie were already there somewhere, according to plan.

We three were dressed in overcoats, hats and gloves over our party clothes. I noticed that Ruth had her cane. "That's good," I thought to myself. "Hannibal and I are also prepared."

Vincenzo drove his taxi; he was very familiar with Little Italy. It was good that we had him; the streets were crowded with people, all bundled in winter dress, waiting for the parade.

Vincenzo had to make several detours to get around the throngs of people. Taylor Street was closed for the parade for a dozen blocks. We came south on Michigan, turned right on Harrison, left on Racine, left on Polk and right on Carpenter. We drove south on Carpenter to Taylor; nothing else was open; the other north-south side streets were crowded with pedestrians. Ruth and I got out of the car, and Hannibal made arrangements with Vincenzo for a pick up at midnight.

Vincenzo made a beautiful, illegal U-turn and headed north on Carpenter. It was the only way. The parade on Taylor was a few blocks away, and it was headed in our direction. We could hear the music.

We walked around the corner toward Miller, and we saw floats, with a marching band in front. The band was led by a smiling, overweight grand marshal, probably some local politician.

The first float had a setting of a stable with Joseph, Mary and the Christ child. These three were flanked by adoring Maji in rich costumes. White lights were strung above the scene and along the edge of the float. I could hear an engine underneath; the whole float apparatus was set on a small truck made from a modified Ford Model T. I could see several floats behind, all with religious themes. The band blared a slow march, but I had no idea of its name. The whole scene was colorful and rich with religious overtones.

I began to observe the crowd. Most folks were families with children, all in simple winter dress. "Working families," I thought to myself. Many of the mothers crossed themselves in Catholic tradition as the first float passed.

I also saw men and women who were better-dressed. Some had children, but most were middle-aged or older. I saw gold earrings and a few fur coats among the women. The men were invariably dressed in suits, most with bowler or homburg hats, plain overcoats and gloves. "Shopkeepers, with shops closed for the holiday," I thought.

Here and there in the crowd I saw other men in well-made suits, rich-looking overcoats and fedora hats. Most had hard-looking expressions on their faces. Some smiled condescendingly at working men and especially shopkeepers, who invariably greeted them with deference. After the greetings, the working men and shopkeepers quickly walked away.

"Not working-class folks or shopkeepers," I concluded to myself. I nudged Ruth, who stood in front of me, and nodded toward the nearest of the well-dressed men. "Gangster," I whispered in her ear. Ruth nodded.

I then looked up at Hannibal. He was watching carefully. I could tell he was well-aware of our surroundings, especially the sinister men in expensive suits, hats and overcoats.

Hannibal gave me a nudge. I looked at his face, and he said softly: "Eddie and Susie are just down the block to your right."

I glanced right and saw them just as they walked down the street and around the corner. "OK, today is Sunday, and the stores are closed," I thought to myself. "Ah," I muttered. "They are following someone." I looked back to Hannibal and nodded.

Hannibal leaned down and said softly: "According to plan, Harris probably visited the Giordano Bakery on Chicago Avenue yesterday."

I nodded and replied: "I'm sure Eddie and Susie made it to the Ferrara and Scafuri bakeries yesterday as well."

The parade reached our vantage point on the street. The band and the first float were greeted with cheers from the crowd, and the noise was deafening.

I looked directly in front, near the curb. The crowd parted a little, and I saw a slender, elderly, expensively dressed man in an overcoat, a homburg hat and fur-lined leather gloves. He stood next to a dignified, silver-haired woman, and they were talking volubly and smiling.

The woman was late-middle-aged, and she was dressed in an ensemble of mink, gold earrings and a dark hat with a veil. She had high-topped black shoes and dark hose. She was fashionable, in a conservative way.

The couple clearly received deference from the crowd around them. Three younger couples stood next to them. I could see several children.

The old man turned, and I could see his face. It was Giuseppe. "This is lucky; how can we use this chance meeting?" I thought to myself.

I leaned down and whispered in Ruth's ear. "That's Giuseppe Costanzo directly in front."

Ruth looked back at me, then forward. She nodded. "Is that his wife next to him?" She asked.

"I think so," I replied. "His wife's name is Margherita."

Suddenly, I felt a close presence on my right. Since Hannibal was on my left and Ruth was just in front, the hair on the back of my neck prickled, and my body tensed. I took in a sharp breath and looked over. It was Albert from the Green Mill. Joe stood next to Albert. Both had hard, stern looks on their faces.

"Hannibal!" I uttered.

Hannibal looked over and moved swiftly to my right side, just behind Albert and Joe. He towered over both men.

It was Albert's and Joe's turn to look startled. Both looked back at Hannibal.

"Can I help you gentlemen?" said Hannibal in soft but clear voice, just audible over the noise of the crowd.

Joe recovered first. "North Side Gang members, on the sidewalk, behind, to your left and right!" He stated. He looked around, searching the crowd. "We may have trouble today," he added. He slipped his right hand in his coat pocket, slowly. "Be careful! They are after Giuseppe."

I looked left. I saw three well-dressed men, about twenty feet away, in the crowd. Both were staring at Giuseppe, with steely looks in their eyes. I swiftly noted their features, dress, approximate height and weight, and so on.

I had seen them before, at the Hideout. They were the ones who tried to muscle Connor O'Brian. However, the trio didn't seem to notice Hannibal and me.

I then looked right and then directly behind. Two other well-dressed men lounged against the wall of the nearest storefront, about ten feet away. They were also watching Giuseppe. I repeated my memorization exercise. I would forever remember all five men.

"What is going on?' I thought to myself.

From first glance to last, my whole recognition process took less than ten seconds. I took a deep breath and relaxed my body. My purse hung under my left arm. I unfastened the top, slipped my right hand inside and found my revolver. I kept it hidden in my purse, but I was ready for instant action.

I leaned over and whispered in Ruth's ear. "Ruth, we have unwanted company behind us on both sides. They are watching Giuseppe." Ruth turned slightly and looked up at me. Her eyes squinted a little, but she showed no fear. I then added: "The two men next to me are friends." I nodded in the direction of Albert and Joe.

"I see," said Ruth in a calm, soft voice as she looked both left and right and behind us. She moved her cane from her left hand to her right, lifted it up a little and turned back toward the marching band in the parade.

"Five men at least," I thought to myself. "They won't be afraid of Giuseppe, and there may be more."

I was right about their boldness. The five moved forward through the crowd, directly toward us, but with their attention on Giuseppe in front. Hannibal saw them coming and moved over behind Ruth and me and turned slightly. Albert slipped left and Joe remained on the right. I turned to face the on-coming assailants.

Hannibal leaned first to Joe, whispered something, and then repeated the process with Albert. Both men nodded. I saw a switchblade flick out in Joe's right hand as he moved forward and to the right. I couldn't see Albert's hands, but he moved forward toward the opponent on the left. Hannibal stayed in the middle. I slipped my right hand, with revolver, out of my purse.

Scuffles occurred on my left and right. Knives flashed, low and swiftly. Joe's opponent groaned and dropped to his knees. Joe held a knife to his throat. Albert bent over slightly as his opponent hit him hard in the abdomen. I glimpsed brass knuckles. Albert returned the blow, but his hand had a long thin knife. Albert held his opponent close. The man's mouth opened in a silent scream, and he broke free. He then staggered back, holding his abdomen with both hands. He bumped into unsuspecting bystanders. Three men remained, and they shifted their attention from Giuseppe to Hannibal. Two had knives in their right hands, held low and ready.

"They should know better," I thought to myself, as I steeled for action.

Hannibal grabbed the right wrist of the man on his left and twisted him around to the right toward the man in the middle. He then raised and slammed his left foot behind his opponent's right knee. The man dropped his knife, collided with his partner in the middle, and both men went down.

The third man on the right remained standing. His attention was on Hannibal. He also had a knife. I moved forward, raised my right hand high and hit him hard on the side of the face with my revolver. The man staggered back and to my right. However, he quickly recovered. Eyes blazing, he headed straight for me, knife ready. I raised my revolver.

A shot wasn't necessary. With my peripheral vision, I saw a swift blur at my left side. It was Ruth. With a two-handed stroke, she swung her cane down hard on my opponent's knife hand. Crack! The knife dropped to the sidewalk. She then moved forward slightly and swung the cane up between the man's legs.

"Oh!" The man screamed, and his face contorted with pain. I could barely hear his scream above the noise of the band and the crowd. I finished him off with another thump of my revolver right between the eyes. He went down for the count.

As my opponent landed on his back, I looked up. Hannibal had finished his opponents; both were on the sidewalk out cold. Joe was whispering something in the ear of his opponent, as he scraped his knife along the man's neck, just behind his ear. He nodded in agreement to whatever Joe said, and got up slowly. Joe backed off slowly and carefully, and he put his knife away.

I looked back toward the curb and Giuseppe. His mouth was open in surprise and dawning fear. He clearly recognized the three men lying on the sidewalk. He looked up at me, then over at Hannibal, then again down to the men on the sidewalk. I could tell from his changing expression that he had figured out what had just happened.

His wife also looked first at the men on the sidewalk and then up at her husband. "Giuseppe?" She uttered.

I glanced around at bystanders. Several stared, mouths wide open in surprise. Most moved away slightly and pretended not to notice. After all, they were there for the parade. None interfered. Two other well-dressed men to my left, about thirty feet away, turned and walked down the street. I discretely put my gun away.

My mind raced. "They will report this fight to their superiors," I thought to myself. "Why Giuseppe, in public, with hundreds of witnesses?" I pondered. "A message to the community?" I thought a moment. "How did Joe and Albert know to be here?" So many questions!"

My attention shifted back to the street. Joe and Albert moved over toward Hannibal, Ruth and me. Albert was breathing heavily, but he was OK. "Nicely done," said Joe, and he grinned. "Shall we move on down the street? The parade is almost over."

He then looked over at Giuseppe. No words were exchanged, but Giuseppe clearly recognized Joe.

Giuseppe whispered to his wife, who now had a frightened look. He then looked at the three young men who were standing nearby. "Partire!" He said clearly, and he pointed down the street. The entire Costanzo group moved quickly away and faded into the crowd. As he passed, Giuseppe looked at Hannibal and me and said: "Grazie, grazie!"

Hannibal looked closely at Ruth and me. "Are you ladies OK and ready to go to a party?"

"Of course," replied Ruth. "I think those ruffians have had enough." She pointed with her cane to the three men still lying on the sidewalk.

I laughed; I couldn't help it. Hannibal, Joe and Albert joined in. The five of us moved on down West Taylor Street, the parade passed, and the band played on.

14

A MATTER OF HONOR

Monday, January 7, 1929 (Continued)

It's getting late, but I want to write this down while it's still fresh in my memory.

The street fight had provided an impromptu encounter with the Costanzo family, and I intended to make the most of it. We still had to go to the Unione Siciliana party.

Joe and Albert escorted Hannibal, Ruth and me to building where the party had already started; it was only half a block away. Joe and Albert said their goodbyes as we reached the doorway.

The door was open, and we could see stairs leading up to the second floor. The sound of violins and a mandolin drifted down. I recognized the music; it was a Vivaldi concerto, with violins and mandolins dominating the melody. A well-dressed young man stood by the entrance to the ground floor of the building; he was collecting tickets from guests just ahead of us.

Hannibal presented our tickets. The young man smiled and said: "Buona sera, signore." He then turned to Ruth and me, bowed slightly and added: "Ah, buona sera, signore!" He smiled and motioned with his hand toward the open door and stairway.

"Buona sera," Hannibal replied graciously, and he motioned for Ruth and me to precede him.

Both Ruth and I nodded, gave condescending smiles to the young man and swept by him toward the stairs. We both pretended as if going to a Sicilian ball was 'old hat' to us.

"Qualcuno prenderà i vostri cappotti e cappelli in cima alle scale, signori," added the young man as we passed.

"Grazie," answered Hannibal over his shoulder, as he followed Ruth and me as we headed up the stairs.

Sure enough, a coat check station was set up at the top of the stairs to the left. Hannibal assisted Ruth and me with our coats, took off his own outer wear and completed the coat check process.

I looked around. The ballroom was huge; it encompassed almost the entire second floor. I could see waiters coming and going through swinging doors at the back, and a little hallway to the left. "Kitchen, powder rooms," I concluded.

The main room was ringed with circular tables with white cloths and chairs, six to eight per table. Several groups of guests had pushed tables together to form larger seated groups. At least a hundred people filled the room, most engaged in animated conversation. The center of the room had an open dance floor. Strings of white lights hung from the ceiling in rows from the front to the back of the room.

Several young couples were dancing to the music. I watched for a quick moment; the dancers were doing an Italian version of a waltz, with slight variations to the box step. "I can do that," I thought to myself.

Many of the tables had glasses and bottles of wine. "All red," I thought to myself. "I wonder if they serve a pinot grigio?"

I looked right, and spotted a small orchestra. With a quick glance, I recognized two mandolins, an accordion, a violin, a viola, a cello, a double bass, a clarinet, an oboe, a flute and two muted French horns. The music was soft, slow and soothing.

I also noticed that the musicians were dressed in tuxedos. The maestro was a large man with huge mustachios, and he dominated his small kingdom with imperious grace and style.

"What a wonderful setting!" I whispered to Ruth.

"Yes," replied Ruth. "And I think we are about to be welcomed to the party." She nodded in the direction of a man who was walking across the dance floor toward us. It was Giuseppe.

Giuseppe's face was pale, and his eyes showed residual fear from the encounter on the street. However, he made an effort to smile as he approached.

"Ah, good evening, my friends," said Giuseppe.

He shook hands with Hannibal, who nodded and replied: "Good evening, Signor Costanzo."

Giuseppe then turned to me, smiled broadly, bowed and then formally kissed my extended hand. "Ah, L'adorabile Signorina Case," he said. He then gave a curious look at the aristocratic Ruth.

I returned Giuseppe's greeting with: "Buona sera, Signor Costanzo," and smiled in return. "Per favore, incontri la Signora Ruth Meltzer, la nostra cara amica."

Giuseppe turned to Ruth, bowed and said: "Ah, Signora Meltzer, mi fa molto piacere conoscere una signora così simpatica."

"The old boy is back on his game," I thought to myself. Indeed, the fear had faded from Giuseppe's eyes, and the old twinkle was back.

Ruth smiled, extended her hand and replied: "Buona sera, Signor Costanzo." She raised her eyebrows just enough to let Giuseppe know that there were formal boundaries to the pending relationship.

Giuseppe got the hint. He reached out, took Ruth's hand, bowed again and did not quite touch Ruth's hand with his lips. "Incantata, Signora Meltzer," he responded.

"Well done, Ruth, I must learn your technique," I thought to myself.

I glanced over at the distant table from which Giuseppe had come. I could see the lady who I assumed was Margherita Costanzo. She was watching Giuseppe's performance. She smiled wryly, shook her head from side to side a couple of times and then turned back to the others at the table.

"Resigned to her husband's flirtations," I mused silently. I glanced at Ruth, who just smiled. I could tell she had also noticed Margherita's reaction.

Giuseppe had returned his attention to Hannibal. "Please," he said. "Would you and the ladies join my family and me at our table? I will get extra seats."

Hannibal smiled, looked to me and then Ruth and said: "Ladies? Shall we join the Costanzo family?" Of course, Ruth and I both nodded yes. And so, our evening at the party began.

As we approached the table, Giuseppe motioned to a waiter for extra seats. The waiter scurried about, and three young men got up from the table. The older lady, who I assumed was Margherita, and three young ladies remained seated.

Giuseppe made introductions. "Major Hannibal Jones, Miss Caroline Case and Mrs. Ruth Meltzer, please meet my wife Margherita and my sons Santino, Antonio and Alberto," Giuseppe announced. "Next to each are their wives Maria, Angelica and Sofia." Giuseppe paused a moment, smiled broadly and said: "Ah, figlie così adorabili!

I smiled in return, nodded and said: "È un piacere incontrari." Hannibal and Ruth also responded appropriately. I noticed that two of the daughters-in-law rolled their eyes a little as Giuseppe made his grand introduction, but they recovered nicely and smiled as we responded to the introduction.

We all took our seats, and I looked around the family group. "Is Michael with you this evening?" I asked.

"Alas, no," responded Giuseppe. The twinkle in his eyes faded for a moment. "He had business to attend."

I glanced at Margherita, and I noticed she hung her head a little. I glanced at Ruth, and she nodded. Margherita would be a source of more information on Michael.

I responded to Giuseppe with a smile and said: "Perhaps we can meet him some other time."

"Of course, of course," replied Giuseppe. The twinkle returned to his eyes. "But the evening is young, and we are safe here."

Margherita gave Giuseppe a frown, turned to me and said: "Thank you for your actions on the street earlier." Her voice was low and soft, with a moderate Italian accent.

"Her English is quite good," I thought to myself. I looked into her eyes, and saw sincerity. "Glad we could help," I replied.

Ruth turned to Margherita and asked: "Did you know those men?"

I turned back to Giuseppe to distract him. "You are right about the evening; the setting is lovely, and I so enjoy the music."

Ruth got my cue, and continued her conversation with Margherita.

I smiled sweetly to Giuseppe, and he responded as expected. His attention was now fully on me. I gave a quick glance to Hannibal.

Hannibal also got the hint, and he turned to Santino. "We saw many shops, including bakeries, from the street," he said. "From the holiday crowd, I expect that this is a busy season for you."

Santino smiled and replied: "Ah, yes, we have many customers. In addition to Christmas celebrations, many weddings occur this time of year." He paused, and gave Hannibal an appraising look. "You know about bakeries?"

Hannibal had done his homework. Soon he, Santino, Antonio and Alberto were engaged in an animated discussion about the bakery business.

I could also hear Ruth, who was speaking in Italian to Margherita about families in the 'old country.' Soon the daughters-in-law joined in. After the initial shyness, they seemed quite taken with the aristocratic Ruth.

"Perfect!" I thought to myself. I returned my attention to Giuseppe, who had been blathering on about something. I concentrated and finally caught the drift.

Years of experience with men during my former endeavors on the Wabash had prepared me for the moment; I knew just how to handle the old boy. "I smiled sweetly and pretended that Giuseppe was the most important person in the room.

Finally, after coyly deflecting Giuseppe's compliments, I said: "I noticed how your sons and others in the room treat you with great respect." I paused as Giuseppe's mind shifted gears. "You must be a very important man in the community."

Giuseppe puffed up a little and responded: "Well, my family and I have many social duties in our church, in this Unione Siciliana and in the business community." He leaned back in his chair, put his thumbs behind the lapels on his coat and added: "I am also a past president of our local chamber of commerce."

"Oh, my," I replied. "I'm sure that the respect you receive is well-earned."

"Yes, well, family honor and social obligations are very important in Sicilian society." He paused a moment, as if reflecting on his exalted position in the community. "So it was in the old country, and it is the same in our community in America."

"Tell me about Sicilian honor and your family," I responded.

That did it. Old Giuseppe talked about his family, his position in the community, where he came from in Sicily, the nature of family honor and so on for an hour. The dialogue continued through three glasses of wine, dinner and continuous music.

I listened carefully for clues to explain the attempts on Giuseppe and his family on the street and the shootings at Michael's home. I was not disappointed.

Finally, Giuseppe ran out of self-important things to say. I could tell his mind was returning to flirtation.

The background music changed from slow and soothing to a faster pace. I remembered the music of the Italian community in the Wabash Valley and recognized a Lazio saltarello tarantella. A dozen couples moved to the dance floor. "Oh, good heavens, I hope Giuseppe doesn't ask me to dance," I thought to myself.

He did. It was an offer I couldn't refuse. I glanced over at Hannibal, who was grinning from ear to ear. I gave him a dirty look. Fortunately, I had half-a minute to refresh my memory of the saltarello tarantella.

I watched the couples assemble on the dance floor as Giuseppe explained to Margherita that he had a duty to dance with his guest.

At first, Margherita had a resigned look, but then her expression changed to one of appraising curiosity. She gradually smiled and watched.

"OK, Caroline, you can do this," I told myself firmly. The accordion in the orchestra took center stage as Giuseppe led me to the dance floor. Fortunately, my skirt was not too tight and it had a flair from the hips down.

The music started slow, and Giuseppe was an excellent dancer. I quickly picked up his footwork and followed his repetitive high steps and spins.

After a few spins and postures, I picked up the rhythm and loosened up. I alternated having my hands on my hips and lifting my skirts as I swayed, high-stepped and spun around in time with the gradually increasing tempo of the music. Giuseppe, spun, high-stepped and waived his arms about in an evocative manner as I whirled in front and all around him. A female voice sang to accompany the accordion and mandolin. I began to enjoy the dance.

After a couple of minutes, I noticed that Giuseppe and I were the only two dancers in the center of the floor. All of the others stood in a semi-circle about us and were clapping their hands in time with the music and laughing. A tambourine joined in with the accordion and mandolin. We whirled, high-stepped, spun and gestured with our hands. It was fun!

We danced for perhaps five minutes. Finally, the music faded, slowed and drew to a close. Giuseppe stopped, stood erect with a broad smile on his face and bowed to me in a formal manner. I extended my hand. Giuseppe bowed again and kissed my hand. The entire audience in the room stood and gave us a standing ovation. I was breathless!

Hannibal, Ruth and the entire Costanzo family stood, laughed and clapped their hands while Giuseppe led me back to the table. My lungs gasped for air for a full three or four minutes. Even Hannibal had an expression of surprise and amusement on his face as I gradually caught my breath.

I looked over at Giuseppe. He too was out of breath. Gradually he recovered. He laughed and said: "Signorina Case, sei lei é fantastica! Che danza meravigliosa!"

I looked at Margherita. She was smiling; and her smile was genuine. What a nice lady!

The dance with Giuseppe was the social highlight of the evening. I also obtained facts and insights from Giuseppe with regard to our investigation. I will find out what Ruth and Hannibal and the others from our team learned at our next meeting tomorrow.

Ruth, Hannibal and I left on excellent terms with the entire Costanzo family. After our dance and four more glasses of wine, even my attitude toward old Giuseppe softened.

15

MORNING AFTER

Tuesday, evening, January 8, 1929

I finally got to bed on Sunday night at about two in the morning, which made it Monday, I think.

Silvia was cruel and unsympathetic at an unbelievably early hour on Monday. Her cruelty began with a persistent knock on my bedroom door.

"Caroline, oh Caroline," I heard Silvia's voice along with another knock. "It's time to get up; you have a meeting at one o'clock this afternoon!"

I rolled over in bed, snuggled, covered my head with my pillow, and pretended I didn't hear. It didn't work.

"Caroline, I have coffee ready," Silvia continued.

"Go away!" I muttered. My voice came out slurred.

I heard Silvia giggle, she knocked on the door again and said, in her sweet voice: "The coffee smells good, Caroline. I also have some warm cinnamon rolls with butter."

That sounded better. "OK, OK," I muttered. I removed the pillow, rolled over and tried to sit up. Oh! My head, lower back, butt and the calves of both legs hurt. I'm in good physical condition, but dancing the saltarello tarantella exercised a totally different set of muscles. The wine, lots of it, contributed to the misery.

I opened one eye. The light from the window was blinding. I opened the other eye and slowly focused. I then looked at the clock on the nightstand. Ten o'clock! There was nothing I could do except get up. I made a mental note to speak sharply to Silvia about her unrelenting cruelty.

I finally sat up on the edge of the bed, rubbed the sleep from my eyes and then stood up. The room moved around for half a minute, but finally stopped. I slowly shuffled into the bathroom.

"I'm up, I'm up," I said, this time in a non-slurred voice.

Silvia heard. "The coffee and cinnamon rolls are in the kitchen, Caroline!" I heard another giggle.

I stood in the warm shower for a long time. Finally, I turned the cool water up and stood a while longer.

My mind began to work again. "OK," I thought to myself. "The wine last night explains the headache." I paused, thinking: "Oh yes, the dance with old Giuseppe explains the sore muscles." I paused again and muttered aloud: "I hope that old goat is sore, too."

I finally completed my toilet, combed my hair, made up my face, walked to my closet and selected my clothes for the day. "Dressy casual," I thought to myself.

I dressed in a silk, long sleeved blouse, grey, worsted wool slacks and a warm, burgundy-colored pullover cashmere sweater with a new style turtle neck. Everything came from Mandell Brothers, who get the latest fashions from Paris. I added diamond stud earrings and a necklace with a platinum chain and a single diamond in front. A few final touches made my hairdo presentable.

I walked out of my closet area, sat on the edge of my bed and put on comfortable, satin-lined black shoes with low heels. The headache faded, and my muscles felt better with use.

I was ready to face the day. "I will not let Silvia see me looking like I have a hangover," I muttered, as I stood up, left my bedroom and headed for the kitchen. Ah, coffee!

The meeting began promptly at one o'clock. Everyone was there, including Hannibal, Ruth, Eddie, Susie, Harris and of course, Silvia, who had been forgiven. We met in our workroom. Silvia provided coffee and refreshments.

Hannibal presided as we sat around our large table. "Let's begin with you, Harris. What did you find out about the Giordano Bakery on Chicago Avenue?"

Harris flipped through some notes for a moment and replied: "Well, Giordano's is just two blocks from the Costanzo Bakery run by Michael. I strolled the street, listening to customers as they entered and exited both bakeries. It's amazing what can be learned by just listening."

"In front of the Giordano store, I heard comments like: 'They have much better cannoli at Costanzo's,' and 'Did you know about the wedding cake for the Olmi family? Costanzo made it, and old Leonardo Giordano was furious.' I also heard comments like: 'Yes, Costanzo's cakes are better, but the prices! Oh, good heavens!' There were others, but you get the idea."

Harris paused a moment, smiled and added: "I heard similar comments, praising Giordano's, from customers leaving the Costanzo store."

"After comparing prices at both stores, I bought some bombolone at Giordano's. When I mentioned that the price at Costanzo's was less, the clerk, a young man named Francesco, immediately lowered his price to match, and I could hear him muttering curse words in Italian as he wrapped my bombolone in a page from a stack of newspapers." Harris grinned and added: "There's no doubt that the two stores are fiercely competitive."

Harris paused, looked at his notes and continued. "Inside Giordano's, I saw a framed page from an Italian language newspaper. The story on the page praised Giordano's Bakery and told the story of the Giordano family."

Harris paused and then said: "I copied key phrases, the gist of which is: the store is owned by Leonardo and Nina Giordano; they have two sons named Francesco and Josef, and they have two daughters, one named Maria and the youngest named Constanza. The store was opened in 1908, and the date on the newspaper article was Sunday, May 21, 1922." The article had a photo of the entire family standing in front of the store."

Harris paused again, smiled broadly and said: "Now for the big news. While I was reading the framed newspaper article, two elderly women sitting at a table nearby noticed my concentration.

One whispered to her companion: 'That man is reading old Leonardo's article.' She paused and then added: It's a beautiful picture; the family was so happy then. See them smiling?' Her companion shook her head sadly and replied: 'Such a shame that beautiful Maria married that Costanzo boy.' Both women noticed that I was listening, and they continued their conversation in whispers."

Harris grinned broadly and announced: "I took the hint, and I did some checking of church records at the Lady of Pompeii Church. Maria married Santino Costanzo on Sunday, May 30, 1926." He smiled triumphantly. "Baptism records show that they have two children: Salvatore, born November 21, 1926 and Anna, born September 10, 1928."

I did some quick calculations and exclaimed: "Maria was pregnant before she married Santino!"

"Yes," replied Harris. "The animosity between the two families is more than just business."

Silence reigned for a few moments. Hannibal then said: "Anything else, Harris?"

"Just two more items," responded Harris. "I asked around the neighborhood, and Michael's apartment address is on Chicago Avenue." He leafed through his notes and added: "It's 444 West Chicago Avenue, Apartment 206, just a block from his bakery."

He paused a moment, and said: "I walked to the apartment building. It's the nicest building in the block. I went in; the front door to the building became unlocked." He grinned a little. "Anyway, the apartment doors have names on them. Michael's apartment is on the second level, and it has windows that face the street. From the street, I saw that one window has two bullet holes."

"Apparently, repairs take a while," Hannibal responded. "I wonder if Michael is staying there since the shooting."

Ruth spoke up. "No, I don't think so," she said. "During our gossip session at the party, Maria mentioned that Michael was their house guest." Ruth smiled: "Apparently, the brothers are close, and Michael is afraid to spend the night at his apartment." She then added: "Maria doesn't like Michael very much."

"Well, no one was home last Saturday," said Harris. "The door to Apartment 206 became unlocked, and I went in." He grinned again, fished in his pocket and held up a lock pick.

"Very resourceful," I said. I made a mental note to remember Harris' special skills for possible future adventures. I then asked: "What did you find while you were inside?"

Harris fished in his pocket again. "Just these," he replied. He held out his hand. He had two slightly deformed bullets. "They were in the crown molding around the ceiling across from the window with the bullet holes."

Eddie then piped up. "Harris called me at home on Saturday, and I drove over to West Chicago Avenue."

"I went along for the ride," added Susie with a big grin. "I became a lookout."

Eddie then said: "Harris had described the situation over the phone. I took some string with me, and we stretched a string from each hole in the window to the bullet holes in the crown molding. After checking each possibility for matching the holes in the window to holes in the molding, we were able to sight along the strings to a single location. The bullets were fired by a person hiding in a narrow alleyway just across the street. We went to the alley and found two nine-millimeter bullet casings. One had a clear fingerprint."

"It doesn't appear to be a gangster style hit," mused Hannibal. "Based on patterns of previous shootings during the current gang war, I think gangsters would shoot to kill, most likely at close range."

"I agree," said Eddie. "I also checked the bullets at the lab. They came from a nine-millimeter cartridge that made European style grooves in the bullets, which is not a common weapon among gang members."

"A German Luger handgun?" Hannibal asked.

"Probably," agreed Eddie. "I won't know for sure until I have the actual weapon."

The room was silent for a moment, everyone was thinking. Finally, I said: "Can we check war service records?" Perhaps one of the Giordano sons served in Europe during the war."

Hannibal immediately caught the implications. "Good," he responded. "Many Lugers were brought back by servicemen at the end of the war." He thought a moment and added: "I know some people, and I will check."

"Of course, you do," I responded with a smile. Our guests all chuckled. Hannibal blushed a little and just grinned.

"Eddie, did you and Susie find out anything at the Ferrara, Scafuri or Costanzo bakeries on West Taylor Street?" I asked.

"Well," replied Susie: "All three bakeries make excellent torcetti and sprinkle butter cookies." She gave a big sigh, and we all chuckled. Susie then continued: "We sat in the three bakeries on Saturday, had cookies and coffee and listened to conversations among the customers. We made it a point to identify members of the three families while we were in their stores."

Everyone nodded, and Susie continued: "From what we could tell, the Ferraro, Scafuri and Costanzo families all attend the Lady of Pompeii Church. The three bakeries on West Taylor Street are over half a mile apart and serve different small neighborhoods. There may be some competition, but we didn't detect any animosity."

"Susie and I went back to West Taylor Street on Sunday, the day of the parade," said Eddie. "We recognized Salvatore and Serafina Ferraro on the street. They were greeted by many as they passed by. Obviously, they are well-known in Little Italy and well-liked by everyone they encountered."

Eddie added: "While we were at Ferraro's on Saturday, I heard a customer refer to Serafina as the 'Angel of Halsted Street.' Apparently, she works with many charitable organizations in the Italian-American community."

Susie then said: "The Scafuris have a similar reputation. Luigi Scafuri, his wife Carmella, their first child Frances and Luigi's father Giovanni immigrated from Calabria, Italy to Chicago in 1901. Since then, they had six more children. They are very active in the community, and their bakery seems to do a substantial business."

"We couldn't detect any friction between the Scafuri, Ferrara and Costanzo families," Eddie confirmed.

Susie then said: "I also think the Capone people have good relations with all three businesses."

"How do you know this?" I asked.

Susie replied: "While we were visiting all three bakeries on Saturday, well-dressed men came in that were obviously not working class or local business people. I'm pretty sure those patrons were gangsters."

Eddie nodded in agreement and added: "They chatted with members of the Ferrara, Scafuri and Costanzo families, bought and paid for breads, cookies and other pastries and then left. I could detect no fear or apprehension on the part of any of the three families."

"How do you know they were Capone people?" Hannibal asked.

Eddie replied: "I recognized Pasquale Lolordo while we were at the Costanzo Bakery. He was jovial and obviously on friendly terms with everyone in the bakery."

"Interesting," I responded. "Pasquale Lolordo is an important person in the Unione Siciliane. Are you sure he's associated with Capone?"

"Yes," responded Eddie. "Lolordo is well-known to the police as an associate of Al Capone. His photos have appeared in several newspapers." He paused and then added: "I also recognized the gangsters who visited the other two bakeries. They were associates of the Genna brothers, who are known associates of Capone."

"The surviving Genna brothers were on the run," Hannibal responded. I wonder if they are back in town."

"Possibly," replied Eddie. "The war between Capone and the North Side Gang has been quiet for a while. A new confrontation, I think, may be brewing."

"Everyone please be careful," Hannibal said. "We don't want a high profile in our investigations."

Everyone nodded in agreement.

I then asked: "Ruth, you spent time with the Costanzo ladies at the party. Any news?"

"Well," Ruth began, "In our discussion about families, I could tell that Margherita is very concerned about Michael. She let slip a few comments about his fast and loose social life. Apparently, he takes after his father with regard to flirtation, and he is still a bachelor."

"Oh, boy," I replied. "Giuseppe must have really been something when he was younger, and perhaps the apple doesn't fall far from the tree."

"Yes," responded Ruth. "Also, something is going on between Maria, Santino's wife, and Michael. I observed her gritting her teeth every time Michael's name was mentioned." She paused a moment and then added: "Maria is, after all, a Giordano."

"Interesting," I mused. "Santino and Maria married after she became pregnant." I paused and thought a moment. "And Maria doesn't like Michael for a reason."

Ruth picked up on my train of thought instantly. "Giordano resentment of the Costanzos may have a current personal basis, not just family history or business. We need to find out."

Everyone was silent for a while. Finally, Eddie said: "Hannibal, you said that you had banking friends that could follow the Costanzo money."

"Yes," responded Hannibal. "My friends checked the Costanzo accounts. The deposits from Michael's bakery far exceed the receipts that could normally be expected from a relatively small business." Hannibal paused, looked at his notes and added: "For example, deposits of over two and a half million dollars, all in cash, went into the bakery account in the past six months."

"Impressive," said Harris. "Baking must be a lucrative enterprise. What about money leaving the account?"

"Good question," replied Hannibal. "Every month for the past six months, two other banks, both outside of Chicago, draw on the account for a total of over three hundred thousand per month."

I did a quick calculation and said: "Based on the remainder, Michael's bakery makes about sixteen or seventeen thousand per month, and the remainder is just passed through the account."

"Yes," responded Hannibal. "Perhaps less than half of the sixteen thousand is legitimate, the remainder is a fee for services rendered."

"Clearly, Giuseppe knows about the money laundering," I stated. "We picked up on that during our meeting at the Green Mill."

"And the North Side Gang wants a piece of the action," said Ruth. "They may also have friends in the banking business."

Everyone in the room looked at Ruth in surprise. I was the first to respond: "Ruth, you continue to amaze me!"

Ruth smiled in her aristocratic way and replied modestly: "Yes, well, my family has over a thousand years of history in banking." She paused, and her eyes twinkled as she looked at me and then at

Hannibal. "You already know my maiden name is Canossa, one of the oldest names in Italy."

Susie openly gasped. Harris and Eddie sat with their mouths open. I couldn't help but laugh at their expressions. Ruth just smiled demurely. After a few more minor details, our meeting ended.

After our guests left, Hannibal and I settled in for a quiet evening. After a light supper, Silvia left for her apartment. I decided to forego wine, the morning episode was still fresh in my memory.

Hannibal smiled in a knowing way, but he didn't say a word. It was a good thing for him, I was ready with a cutting response. How does he always know what I'm thinking?

We decided to follow up on the nine-millimeter pistol and Maria's unexplained dislike for Michael the next day. We finished our evening by sitting on the comfy sofa in our parlor, and we watched the city lights come on through our big windows.

16

CLOSING THE RING

Wednesday evening, January 9, 1929

I was already at our dining room table sipping coffee this morning when Hannibal came in with the morning's newspaper. I was still dressed in my silk lounging pajamas and robe with a silver fox collar. Hannibal walked in, fully dressed of course. I poured him a cup of coffee from the pot on the table.

"I think the article on the front page will be of interest to you," Hannibal said, as he handed me the newspaper.

I took it and looked at the front page. After a moment, I exclaimed: "Eddie was right!" The article read as follows:

PASQUALE "PATSY" LOLORDO MURDERED

Pasquale Lolordo, a well-known businessman in Chicago's "Little Sicily," was shot to death in his home yesterday on Chicago's near west side. A police spokesman confirmed the murder, but offered few details, except to say that "the investigation into the crime is on-going."

Lolordo was the current president of the Unione Siciliana, an Italian-American social organization. He was also widely rumored to have connections with gangsters who engage in the illegal alcohol trade. For example, Lolordo was a known associate of Al Capone, the rumored kingpin of organized crime on the southside of Chicago.

This reporter was able to get a brief interview with Mr. Capone on the street as he exited the Four Deuces Club on South Wabash. When asked about Lolordo's murder, Capone said: "It's a shame that prominent businessmen ain't safe in their homes."

When pressed on if he knew who might have killed Lolordo, Capone muttered: "Criminal elements from the north side." One of Mr. Capone's associates then whispered something in Mr. Capone's ear, and the interview abruptly ended.

This reporter watched as Capone got into his limousine with several associates and drove down Wabash Avenue. This newspaper will continue to keep readers posted on this sensational case.

I put the newspaper down, sipped my coffee and leaned back in my chair. After a moment, I said: "I think Capone and his people have their answer about the North Side Gang's efforts to muscle in on their territory in Little Sicily." I paused and took another sip. "I wonder how this will affect Capone's money laundering operation with our boy Giuseppe?"

"Well," responded Hannibal, "We know about the attempt on the Costanzo family during the parade the other day, and no doubt Giuseppe is scared."

I thought a moment and then said: "Yes, but who shot into Michael's apartment?" That's the question we were asked."

"Agree," replied Hannibal. "Our investigation should include finding out who may have a nine-millimeter handgun."

"Should we gather fingerprints to build a file?" I asked.

"Good idea," replied Hannibal. "Who knows what might turn up."

We were both silent for a few minutes, thinking. I poured us each another cup of coffee. Silvia arrived from her apartment downstairs and started fixing breakfast in the kitchen.

"Maria intrigues me," I finally said. "I think I know how to get fingerprints of all of the Costanzo women."

"How so?" Asked Hannibal.

"Ruth can host a tea party," I replied. The Costanzo women were obviously fascinated with Ruth, our Italian aristocrat, during the ball the other night." I paused and then added: "I'm sure they would be flattered if Ruth invited them to her home."

Hannibal laughed and replied: "I bet Ruth would love it."

I thought a few moments and said: "Mandy and Silvia could set up the tea party, do the formal invitations, and prepare tea and refreshments." I grinned back at Hannibal. "Ruth could play the society lady hostess."

"Teacups with fingerprints?" asked Hannibal.

"Of course," I replied. We'll make a labeled collection and Eddie can do the analysis."

Hannibal leaned back in his chair, thought a moment and said: "Eddie and Susie can gather fingerprints from the Costanzo and Giordano men at their respective bakeries." He sipped his coffee and then grinned. "I'll set it up; watching the men and surreptitiously lifting prints from counters and tables shouldn't be a problem."

"And you will also follow up on the handgun?" I asked.

"Will do," replied Hannibal.

I got up from my chair, walked into the kitchen and retrieved a calendar. I then returned to the dining table, pulled my chair around where both Hannibal and I could view the calendar and sat down.

"Let's do the tea a week from next Saturday, on January 19th." I looked over at Hannibal. "Do you think that you, Eddie and Susie can do your tasks by that date?"

Hannibal studied the calendar for a moment. "No problem," he replied. "Let's give Eddie a few days after the tea to do his fingerprint analysis. I think we will be ready to present our case by Saturday, January 26th."

"Great!" I replied. Let's have breakfast." Silvia arrived with a tray, right on cue. She had eggs Benedict, Canadian bacon, orange juice and sweet rolls. Hannibal and I shoved aside our papers and began our meal. Planning our investigations is such hard work!

Sunday, January 27, 1929

Two days ago, our little investigative group finished up on schedule, and we had our big get-together Saturday afternoon, January 26.

We held the meeting at the same building where the Unione Siciliana held their ball on January 6th. The building had a large, comfortable, wood-paneled conference room on the third floor above the ballroom.

Giuseppe made the reservation for the room. He was very interested in discovering the nature of the threats to his family. Hannibal gave him some information on the scope of the meeting, but not all. Giuseppe was not informed about the meeting 'guest list,' except for members of his family. The meeting was scheduled to begin at ten o'clock in the morning.

Hannibal and I arrived at about nine-thirty. We thought about having other members of our team attend, but decided not to reveal their identities. Ruth wanted to come; she was known to the Costanzo family and to Joe and Albert. However, there was no point in exposing her role to some of the other attendees.

Hannibal and I set the stage for our little drama. We both stood at the far end of the long conference table, awaiting our guests. We had a waiter, who had set up a side table with coffee, tea and light snacks, including cannoli, chocolate covered almond biscotti and sprinkle butter cookies. All of these goodies came from the Costanzo bakery, of course.

Our guests began to arrive just before ten. The Costanzos arrived first: Giuseppe and Margherita, sons Santino, Antonio and Alberto, and their respective wives all filed into the room. They took off their outerwear and seated themselves. The waiter served them refreshments, and the group relaxed a little, which was our intent.

Michael followed. Giuseppe made the introduction. As far as the Costanzos knew, we had never seen Michael before. Michael was a bit of a dandy, dressed in an expensive suit. He laid his fedora hat, gloves and fashionable overcoat on a chair just inside the door. He had a hard look, very different than his three older brothers.

Joe and Albert arrived next, and quietly sat at the opposite end of the table from Hannibal and me. Both men had looks of expectation; they wanted answers.

A few minutes after ten, the Giordano family arrived. Gasps came from many of the Costanzos. They had not expected this, and looks of astonishment, animosity and bewilderment appeared on many Costanzo faces. Joe and Albert both nodded toward Hannibal, who had briefed them ahead of the meeting concerning the guest list.

Old Leonardo Giordano was accompanied by his wife Nina, sons Francesco and Josef, and daughter Constanza, the youngest. Constanza looked to be about 17 or 18, and she was beautiful.

I observed the interplay of glances and expressions. Constanza looked over at her sister Maria, who sat on the opposite side of the table. Both appeared surprised to see the other.

Constanza then looked at Michael, who returned her demure glance with a surprised and slightly apprehensive look.

The Costanzo and Giordano men glowered at each other. If looks could kill, none of the men would have survived. Joe and Albert just smiled; they thought they knew what was about to happen.

Hannibal stood next to me at the head of the long table as the Giordanos filed in. When the newcomers were seated, he said: "Ladies and gentlemen, please remember that I intend to keep the peace while you are all in this room."

His voice was commanding; his look was stern, and he towered above everyone else. Even Joe and Albert had looks of respect on their faces.

Hannibal continued: "On Friday, November 9th, Miss Case and I accepted an assignment to answer the question: 'Who is trying to kill Michael Costanzo?' Our purpose today is to present our findings on this question as well as other facts that we discovered during our investigation."

Hannibal then looked over to me. I stepped forward and said: "To facilitate our work, we obtained fingerprints from everyone in this room."

There were several gasps and comments that expressed: "How? When? Where?"

I let the murmurs subside and then said: "Those questions are irrelevant; the point is this: We have everyone's fingerprints." I paused, and then said: "We have two nine-millimeter Parabellum shell casings from the gun that fired the bullets that we dug out of the crown moldings across the room from the window in Michael's apartment." We found fingerprints on one of the shell casings."

I stepped back and Hannibal stepped forward. "We also discovered the gun that fired the bullets." Most of the glances around the room indicated astonishment. However, Maria's expression had a tinge of fear. Both Hannibal and I stared at Maria for a long moment, and she squirmed in her seat.

Hannibal then continued: "Santino Costanzo, public records show that you served in France during the war. Did you bring back a German Luger pistol?"

"Yes," replied Santino. His face showed utter bewilderment. "I keep it in my office at our commercial bakery for protection; the neighborhood is known for crime."

"We thought that might be the case, and one of our operatives was able to retrieve the gun," responded Hannibal. "For the future, I suggest you install a better security system for your place of business." Hannibal looked directly into Santino's eyes. It was Santino's turn to squirm in his seat.

I smiled a little, I couldn't help it. "Good old Harris with his lock pick," I thought to myself.

"We dusted the gun for fingerprints, matched the bullets retrieved from Michael's apartment and returned the gun to its place in your office desk." Hannibal paused while this news was digested by the audience. I am nearly certain that you never knew it was missing for over 24 hours."

Santino's expression turned angry, and he retorted: "Are you saying that I shot at my own brother?"

Hannibal smiled and replied: "No, not at all." He looked over at Maria, and said: "Our taking of Santino's Luger for tests was not the first time it had been taken. Isn't that correct, Maria?" Hannibal paused a moment and then said: "We found your fingerprints on the gun."

Santino looked at Maria in utter astonishment. Finally, he said: "Maria, what did you do?"

Maria's eyes flashed; she stood up, and she pointed an accusing finger at Michael. "You terrible man! You are toying with my little sister! She's only seventeen!"

Everyone in the room turned to Michael, who now looked very scared.

After noting Michael's expression, I glanced around the room. Old Giuseppe and Margherita had tears streaming down their faces. "How very sad," I thought to myself. A lump formed in my throat. I swallowed convulsively and tried to concentrate on our task.

I glanced at Hannibal. He nodded. I stepped forward and said, in a low voice: "As I said earlier, we found a fingerprint on one of the shell casings." I looked over at Francesco and stared into his eyes for a long moment. His expression had changed from anger to consternation.

"The fingerprint was yours, Francesco," I stated quietly. "You fired Santino's Luger through Michael's window from the alley across the street from his apartment." I paused a moment, and then added: "Maria supplied you with her husband's gun and ammunition."

The room became so quiet we could hear the low sound of traffic on the street outside. Finally, Hannibal said: "Maria, you returned the gun to Santino's office, probably the day after the shooting. Santino never knew it was missing."

After a long moment, I looked first at Giuseppe and then at old Leonardo. "Family honor is a strange thing," I began. "People have died as a result of perceived insults." I paused while my words sunk in. "Giuseppe, Leonardo, for the sake of your families, don't you think it's time to make the peace?" I paused again and then added: "You both could lose sons over this."

I watched both old men carefully. Tears were streaming down Giuseppe's face. Leonardo was taking deep breaths, trying to control his emotions.

Finally, Giuseppe slowly rose from his chair. He looked over at Michael and said: "Michael, you will leave that young girl alone!" His eyes flashed, and there was steel in his voice.

"If I were Michael, I wouldn't cross that old man again," I thought to myself. I then looked at Santino, Antonio and Alberto. They were staring at Michael with single-minded intensity. I looked over at Michael. His face was pale and he was clearly scared. "I think Michael got the message," my thoughts continued.

I then returned my attention to Giuseppe, who had turned to Leonardo. Giuseppe drew himself up, stood very erect and said: "Signor Giordano, per favore accetti le mie scuse per le azioni di mio figlio Michael e anche per quelle di mio figlio Santino molto tempo fa!"

Leonardo slowly rose from his chair, stared at Giuseppe and said in a choking voice. "Signor Costanzo, per favore accetti le mie scuse per le azioni di mio figlio Francesco e di mia figlia Maria. Molto tempo fa, la colpa non era interamente quella di Santino."

"Very good," I thought to myself as I followed the two apologies in Italian. "I think we have a basis for peace between the families."

Leonardo looked at Francesco and then Maria. There was fire in his eyes. Both son and daughter squirmed and hung their heads.

The room was silent for a long time. Finally, Hannibal said: "May no one break the agreement made here today." His gaze swept the room.

He then looked first at Giuseppe and then Leonardo. "I think, gentlemen, you should continue your discussions in private." He paused and then added: "Your business interests can be worked out so both can share equitably in the bakery market and in other markets."

I looked up at Hannibal, smiled and whispered: "Are you thinking of both the bakery and the laundry business?" He returned my look with a twinkle in his eyes.

I looked over at Joe and Albert. I could see that both men caught the drift. Both smiled.

Hannibal then turned to Joe and Albert and said: "Miss Case and I answered the question in our assignment. However, your boss has other problems." He paused for effect and then added: "I know you are well aware of the other danger facing the Italian-American community and especially the Costanzo family."

Joe and Albert both nodded. "We understand," said Joe. "The boss has plans."

Joe glanced at Albert, who said: "Thank you for all you have done, Major Jones, Miss Case." He paused, grinned and added: "Mr. Costanzo will send you a most generous check."

Giuseppe heard, looked at me, and said: "Of course I will send a check." He paused and added: "I will add a bonus for the wonderful dance we had at the ball, Miss Case. I shall never forget." The old twinkle had returned to Giuseppe's eyes.

Everyone in the room chuckled, even Margherita. It was a good ending to a very emotional meeting.

Tuesday, January 29th, 1929

On Monday, Hannibal and I had two meetings. The first was with Giuseppe and Leonardo. The second was with our little team.

To Giuseppe and Leonardo, we explained what we knew about the threats of the North Side Gang and the dangers of the money laundering business. We mentioned the recent murder of Lolordo, and the North Side Gang's continuing attempts to take over the Unione Siciliana. Both men understood.

Giuseppe spoke of plans for retirement and signing over his business interests to his sons. Leonardo was especially attentive to Giuseppe's retirement ideas; he revealed that he had similar thoughts. I hope both men follow through. We presented the facts as we understood them. Whether or not the pair make wise choices is up to them.

We also shared the details of our meeting with the Costanzo and Giordano families with our little team. All were pleased with the results, and we thanked everyone for their hard work. Of course, we would compensate everyone when we got Giuseppe's check.

On Monday evening, Hannibal and I relaxed on the sofa in our parlor with glasses of chardonnay. I had a couple of questions.

After we were cozy, I said: "I understand how you discovered that Santino had been in the Army in France during the war; it's a matter of public record. It's also obvious that you discovered that neither Francesco nor Josef had been in the Army."

I paused and then asked: "How did you know to send Harris to Santino's place of business to find his gun?

Hannibal grinned and replied: "I didn't know. Harris burglarized both Santino's home and then his place of business. When he didn't find anything at Santino's home, he went to the next most likely place."

"How resourceful," I responded. I thought a moment, then asked: "Did Harris have help?"

Hannibal laughed and said: "You don't have a need to know!" He then looked at me with warmth and said softly: "It's for your own protection."

"I understand," I replied. "I have one other question. Do you think that we are in any danger from the North Side Gang?"

Hannibal was silent for a long time. Finally, he said: "Yes, I do. We encountered them at The Hideout and on the street in Little Italy. We are known to them."

I thought a moment and then asked: "What do you think Capone will do?"

"I'm not sure, but I expect it will be very violent," replied Hannibal. "He may reduce the potential threat to us, but I don't think he can eliminate it." He gave a sigh and added: "Please be careful, and don't go out alone."

I snuggled closely for warmth. I was quiet for a long time.

17

JAZZ CLUB MURDER

Saturday Morning, February 2, 1929

Friday evening after dinner, I was in the kitchen, rummaging through our Frigidaire. I had already changed into my cream-colored silk lounging pajamas and matching robe with a white fox collar.

I was also barefoot; I couldn't find my matching slippers. The Frigidaire door was open. I was bent over, and I was peering inside. I couldn't find the chardonnay.

"I know we have half a bottle left," I muttered. I moved a bottle of ketchup and a jar of mayonnaise.

"Ah ha!" I exclaimed. "There you are!" I was about to extract the chardonnay when the phone rang.

The ring startled me. I rose up, banged my head on a shelf, and the ketchup bottle fell out. It landed on my right big toe. "Oh!"

The phone rang again. With remarkable presence of mind considering my excruciatingly painful toe, I extracted the chardonnay, picked up and replaced the ketchup bottle and slammed the Frigidaire door. The whole unit wobbled for a moment.

I then hobbled over to the phone on the counter across the room, set the chardonnay next to the phone and picked up the receiver. "Hello!" I said, a little too loudly.

There was a long pause. "Miss Case?" An uncertain voice asked.

"Yes!" I replied, again, too loudly.

Another pause, and then: "This is Mel Johnson. I'm a jazz musician at the Green Mill. I called Joe, and he said I should call you."

"Yes?" I responded.

"My friend Sammy Washburn was murdered after our performance last night."

I put the thought of my throbbing toe in the back of my mind and tried to focus on the phone call. "Are the police involved?" I asked.

"Yes," Mel responded. "I found Sammy backstage in the dressing room this afternoon about three o'clock when I returned to the club. The bartender called the police."

Mel was quiet a moment and then added: "The detectives are here now."

My mind was now focused; the pain in my toe was under moderate control. "When did you see Sammy last?" I asked.

"About ten thirty last night," responded Mel. "He was in the dressing room when I left the Green Mill." Mel quickly added: "The bartender and I left at the same time, and I caught the trolley toward home."

I noted the reference to an alibi and asked: "How do you know Sammy was murdered?"

I heard a muffled, choking sound. Finally, Mel replied: "He was stabbed." There was another choking sound, and then: "There was lots of blood."

I thought a moment and then said: "Tell the detectives everything you know." I thought a moment and then continued: "Did the detectives give their names?"

I heard a brief side conversation that included a familiar voice. Mel then answered my question.

"The Sergeant said his name was Watts." Mel paused a moment and then added: "He said that you and Hannibal Jones are most welcome to visit the club."

"I will speak to Hannibal and call you back within five minutes," I responded. "What is your phone number?"

Mel gave me the number. I then hobbled to the workroom, smoothed my robe and hair, regained my poise and opened the door.

Hannibal was sitting at our work table and writing on a scratch pad. He had a stack of reports in front of him. He looked up as I opened the door.

"I think we could have another case." My explanation was brief, and Hannibal agreed that we should investigate.

"I will call Eddie on our second phone," he said. He thought a moment and added: "When you call this 'Mel Johnson' back, see if you can speak to Watts and get more details." He then looked at his pocket watch. "I think we can be at the Green Mill within an hour, provided you get dressed." He smiled and his eyes twinkled.

"Humph," I responded. I gave him a snooty look. I then returned to the kitchen, made my phone call and headed to my bedroom and closet. My toe still hurt.

Eddie was already at the Green Mill when Hannibal and I arrived. We parked right behind Eddie's Ford on North Broadway between the Uptown Theater and the disguised Green Mill entrance.

An unmarked Cadillac police car was parked right in front of Eddie's Ford. "Watts and probably Mulvaney arrived in the Caddy," I said to myself as Hannibal shut down the car engine.

Hannibal opened the car door for me, and we walked up to the doorway marked only with a jewelry store sign. Hannibal knocked. Mulvaney opened the door.

"Welcome," said Mulvaney with a strained smile. "Eddie is already inside."

Hannibal and I shed our outer winter coats, hats and gloves and stacked them on a stool at the near end of the long bar. I recognized Eddie's coat, hat and gloves on the next stool over. As I took off my coat, I saw a handsome man, with dark hair, age mid-thirties. He stood at the end of the bar. He wore dark trousers, a white shirt and a bow tie. "Bartender," I surmised to myself.

The man looked at Hannibal and me with steady eyes. He had a white apron in his hand, and he was folding it as we took off our coats. A uniformed policeman stood nearby. As I walked along the bar, I looked over to the shelves. All of the illegal booze was gone. Only 'near beer' and soft drinks lined the shelves. "Interesting," I thought to myself. "Bet the good stuff was gone before the cops got here."

Mulvaney introduced us to the bartender. "Major Jones, Miss Case, this is Bruno Gatti. He's the person who called the police."

Both Hannibal and I said our hellos. Gatti nodded and said: "Pleased to meet you. Detective Mulvaney told me about you." His gaze remained steady.

"Continue past the bar," said Mulvaney. "The dressing room for the performers is the door to the left just beyond the stage."

As the three of us walked past Gatti toward the stage area, Mulvaney added: "The dressing room is small, only about six by fifteen feet. It's pretty cramped in there. Be careful when you open the door; the room has stuff on the floor and of course, a dead body."

Hannibal knocked on the dressing room door. A familiar voice said: "Open the door slowly." It was Eddie. Hannibal opened the door. It swung in and to the right.

We both peered in. Eddie and Watts stood to the right just inside the door. Both wore surgical gloves. Eddie's open case sat on the floor by his feet.

Both Eddie and Watts had grim expressions on their faces. "First impressions?" Eddie asked. Both he and Watts were looking at me.

My eyes were immediately drawn to the body. It was on the floor, about a dozen feet away. "A black male, dressed in dark suit pants and white shirt, face down, in a pool of blood," I mused aloud. "Blood on the shirt in back, low, man's right side. Probable wound site."

I peered intently. "The blood pool is too large for the single wound in the back," I continued. "Probably more in front."

"Yes," responded Eddie. "We checked, and there are two wounds in front, centered, just under the victim's diaphragm. Afterward, we returned the body to the way we found it."

I looked at the victim's hands. Both had cuts on front and back. Blood seeped from the wounds. "Defensive wounds," I mused aloud.

"Yes," responded Eddie. He paused, and his voice remained calm and professional. "What do you see in the room?" He asked.

I glanced around for a quick visual survey. The far end of the dressing room was a mess.

"Four chairs, one at each dressing table," I responded. "The chair at the far end is overturned."

I looked at the floor and said: "Containers of make-up and talcum powder and a trumpet on the floor. I also see white talcum powder on the floor."

"Probable struggle between the victim and one or more assailants," said Hannibal softly.

"Yes," replied Watts. "The victim put up a fight."

I scanned the row of four dressing tables, each with a mirror, along the left wall. I looked at the body again. It lay face down, diagonally across the floor from the last table, facing the wall to my right.

"Two lights above each mirror. One broken light bulb on the left above the mirror at the far end. The bulb base and glass remnants remain in the socket," I spoke softly, but loud enough for Hannibal, Eddie and Watts to hear. "Bulb glass fragments on the dressing table and floor."

All three of my companions looked and nodded in agreement.

I then said: "Smears of red on the corner of the mirror, just below the broken light, probably blood."

"Up high," added Hannibal. "Probably made when someone banged into the lightbulb."

"Yes," said Eddie. "I'll get a sample."

I looked at the victim and the wound in his back. "Knife as a murder weapon?" I asked.

"Probably," replied Eddie. "I will have to take measurements, but the width of the puncture cut in his back and the two in his abdomen are about three quarters of an inch wide, which is consistent with a knife."

"Any slash wounds other than the victim's hands?" I asked.

"No," replied Eddie. "The knife-wielder knew what he or she was doing." He paused a moment added: "The wounds in back and in the abdomen are all placed to kill."

"Could the killer be a woman?" I asked.

"Possibly," replied Eddie. "However, the victim is a large, relatively young man, and he clearly put up a struggle."

"More than one assailant?" Hannibal asked.

"I think so," responded Eddie. "Two of the victim's shirt buttons are ripped off on the front and the blood on the back of the shirt is smeared."

"Hummm," I mused aloud. "The victim was stabbed from behind as he rose and knocked over the chair. He turned and tried to block the assailant's knife. Someone grabbed him from behind, smearing the blood coming from the wound in his back."

I paused and then added: "The buttons on front popped as the victim's arms were pulled back."

I looked closely at the broken light above the mirror. "The light is about head high," I continued. "There is no wound on the victim's head."

"Agree," responded Eddie. "The victim shoved backward, slamming the person holding him from behind against the dressing table and light."

"Interesting," said Hannibal. "The knife-wielder stabbed the victim twice in front, probably up through the diaphragm and into his heart. The struggle then ceased, and the victim was released by the person behind. The victim then dropped to the floor, face down."

"The person who held the victim from behind probably has a wound on the back of his head from the broken light," I said.

"He?" Watts asked.

"I think so," I replied. The broken light is over six feet above the floor, and most females are not that tall." I was quiet for a moment and then added. "However, the knife-wielder could have been male or female."

"Good theory," responded Eddie, "And probably correct. However, I will conduct tests."

"Yes," I responded. "I am especially interested in the type of the blood below the light compared to the blood on and under the victim."

I then looked at the powder on the floor. "Two faint footprints," I said, and I pointed to the near end of the dressing table. "Left and right shoes, same person, toes pointed toward the victim."

Eddie and Hannibal looked to the side of the dressing table where I was pointing.

"Good eye," replied Eddie. He then looked at the victim's shoes. "The footprints are not those of the victim; the shoe size isn't the same."

I looked closely. "Agree," I responded. "Also, look in the corner across from the dressing table. We have two different sets of prints. The footprint size by the side of the dressing table is larger than the single footprint in the corner." I peered at the print. "The toe is pointed toward the victim."

"I see it, responded Hannibal. "Much smaller shoe, and it's the left shoe only."

I peered again. "The single print in the corner could have been made by a female shoe; it has a small heel and a narrow-pointed toe."

"Or a small man," replied Eddie as he looked at the single print. "I will take measurements and photos of both sets."

Hannibal then asked: "Witnesses?"

"None that we know about," replied Watts. "Mel Johnson said he found the body at about three o'clock this afternoon, and he immediately reported his findings to Bruno Gatti, the bartender. Gatti then called the police."

Watts opened his notebook and flipped a page. "The call was received at the station at three-ten."

He paused and smiled. "I suppose you would like to speak with both Gatti and Johnson."

"Yes, please," I replied. "Are they available?"

"In the club manager's office," replied Watts. "A uniformed cop is with them."

"Who is the club manager?" asked Hannibal.

"Danny Cohen, but he's on 'vacation,'" replied Watts with a grin; "In Florida, according to Gatti." He paused a moment, thinking. "Gatti runs the place in Cohen's absence."

"I'll finish up here," said Eddie. "I need to collect samples, dust for fingerprints, take photos and make measurements."

"How long?" asked Watts.

Eddie looked at his wristwatch. "Three hours at least," replied Eddie. "It's nearly seven-thirty now; I should be finished by ten or ten-thirty."

Watts looked out the door and said: "Mulvaney, tell Gatti that this place is closed indefinitely. No one gets in without my permission."

"Right," replied Mulvaney.

Watts then said: "Major Jones and Miss Case are coming up to talk to Gatti and Johnson."

"Got it," responded Mulvaney.

Hannibal and I stepped out of the dressing room and moved away from the door. Watts and Eddie remained inside.

"Let's talk to Gatti and Johnson separately," said Hannibal. "Perhaps their stories will match, perhaps not."

"Agree," I replied. "Let's also have a plan for our questions."

Hannibal nodded. "We will have follow-up interviews, but we need to establish a preliminary timeline and get names of potential witnesses and possible assailants while memories are fresh."

"Yes," I replied. "Eddie will provide an estimate of time of death later, but we need to confirm when both Gatti and Johnson left last night, when they arrived today, and what they did before and after Johnson said he found the body."

"Agree," said Hannibal. "Why did Sammy Washburn stay after Gatti and Johnson left?"

"Good question," I responded. "Also, we should ask whether or not Gatti or Johnson saw anyone besides Washburn in the club when they left last night."

"In addition, let's find out if Gatti and Johnson can produce proof of when they left the club last night and arrived today," replied Hannibal.

"Yes," I replied. "Later, we can check destinations and arrival times after they left the club, and so on."

After our brief conference, Hannibal and I walked toward Mulvaney, who was waiting for us by the bar.

"Gatti and Johnson are in the office," said Mulvaney. "I guess you want to talk to each separately, correct?"

"You read our thoughts," replied Hannibal with a smile. "We'll have a go at Gatti first, Johnson can wait in the bar area."

"Sounds good," responded Mulvaney. "Our uniformed cop will sit with him. In the meantime, I'll nose around the place." He grinned and added: "Who knows what might turn up?"

18

UP FROM THE SOUTHSIDE

Saturday evening, February 2nd, 1929

Most of today was spent organizing my notes from the interviews on Friday night. I was sitting at our table in the work room at home when the phone rang. I answered, and it was Eddie.

Eddie had news. Without preliminaries, he said: "Based on temperature measurements of the body, the ambient room temperature and a normal rate of body cooling, Sammy Washburn died early on Friday, February 1, between midnight and one o'clock in the morning."

"Thanks, Eddie," I replied. "I'm working on a timeline, and this helps." I paused, thinking. I then asked: "Any luck with fingerprints, shoe prints and blood?"

"I need a couple more days," responded Eddie. I'll have prints and blood types, but we need a data base of names, fingerprints, shoes and blood samples to compare to my findings."

"Working on it," I said. "I'll get back to you." Our conversation ended, and I returned to my notes.

Our interviews lasted from about seven-thirty until after ten on Friday night. We talked with Gatti from about seven-thirty until nine. He gave us lots of information. We talked with Johnson from about nine until just after ten. His responses were more complex; we will need follow up interviews.

Just after we were introduced to Gatti on Friday, I made a mental note that he walked with a limp. I also saw that his left shoe was built up, and it had an unusual shape. When I asked, he said the special shoe compensated for a war wound, but he didn't give any details.

On Friday night, we conducted our interviews in the club manager's office. The office was small and very utilitarian. We sat in hard oak chairs around a small oak desk. The chairs were very uncomfortable. We began with Gatti while Johnson waited in the bar area.

Hannibal and I took out notepads. Gatti leaned back in his chair and watched us carefully. He eased his left leg out straight, wincing a little as he did so. We could see the details of his built-up left shoe.

I turned to Hannibal, and he nodded. Both of us had seen the foot prints in the dressing room. Gatti's shoe didn't match any of them.

When I asked Gatti about his whereabouts on Thursday evening and Friday, he said that he took a taxi when he left the club on Thursday night at about ten forty-five. He also said he arrived in a taxi on Friday afternoon about three o'clock.

Gatti then got up and took us to the front door of the club. He pointed to a taxi parked on Broadway, near the Uptown Theater, about twenty feet from the Green Mill entrance.

While Gatti and I watched from the doorway, Hannibal walked over to the taxi and introduced himself to the driver.

I heard Hannibal say that he was a criminal investigator. He briefly explained that an incident in the club earlier involved police action. He then asked questions.

The driver seemed somewhat awed by Hannibal, and he answered questions freely. Hannibal took out a writing pad and made some notes.

After a few minutes, Hannibal returned toward the Green Mill door. He smiled as he approached.

As we stepped back inside the club, Hannibal said: "The driver's name is Tony Olmi. He said that he was outside the club and theater Thursday night as well as this afternoon, waiting for customers."

"Does he know Mr. Gatti?" I asked. I gave Gatti a quick glance.

"Yes," replied Hannibal. He then looked at Gatti and said: "Tony said that you are a regular customer." Hannibal paused a moment, smiled and then added: "Tony also wrote your name and pickup times in his logbook. The times match your statements."

Gatti nodded. He didn't seem surprised.

I thought to myself for a moment. "So, Gatti's times are confirmed by one witness, at least for now." I also smiled at Gatti, and asked: "Did you see others leave the club?"

"Mel Johnson," replied Gatti. "He left just before me." He thought a moment and then added: "Before that, I didn't see anyone else leave after the performance ended at ten. However, I was in the storeroom behind the bar, counting inventory. I didn't check the back rooms. Sometimes band members stay overnight, sometimes they don't."

Hannibal, Gatti and I then turned to go back to the club manager's office to continue our discussion.

However, just as we turned, Mulvaney walked up past the bar. "You need to see this," he said. He motioned for us to follow him.

The three of us followed Mulvaney past the dressing room. We heard Watts and Eddie talking; they were still in the dressing room.

Mulvaney led us to another door near the back of the club. He opened the door. Hannibal and I stepped inside. Gatti waited in the hallway.

I looked around the room. It was about fifteen feet wide and twenty feet long. It was drab, but neat and clean. There were no windows. Two standing lamps provided dim light at both ends on the right side of the room.

The room contained four sleeping cots against the long wall on the right. All had been made up with sheets, pillows and blankets. Clothes, all male, hung on a central rack across from the beds.

A door stood open at the far end of the room, directly across from the entry door. I walked over and looked through the doorway.

I could see a light hanging from the ceiling with a string switch. I stepped forward and pulled the string. The light turned on.

I looked around. The little room was a water closet. It had a washstand with a small sink, a mirror above the sink, a rack for towels and a toilet.

I observed every detail. No towels were on the rack. However, I spotted a used washcloth beside the doorway, and the sink had S-shaped drain trap.

I also sniffed the air. "Chorine," I muttered. The water closet had been scrubbed, and it smelled of bleach.

"Mulvaney, could you please call Eddie?" I asked.

"Will do," replied Mulvaney.

A couple of minutes passed. Eddie arrived with his bag, followed by Watts. After a short discussion, Eddie put the washcloth in an evidence bag. "I'll also check the room and the water closet for fingerprints after I finish the dressing room," he said.

"I think we should also check the contents of the drain trap," I replied, and I turned to Mulvaney.

"Good idea," responded Mulvaney. "I'll call for a plumber."

"There's a phone behind the bar," said Hannibal.

"Right," replied Mulvaney, and he headed for the bar.

As Eddie and Mulvaney continued their tasks, Hannibal, Watts and I turned to Gatti, who was still waiting in the hallway. The four of us walked back to the club manager's office.

As we took our seats, I asked: "Who uses the sleeping room?"

"The room is for our black entertainers," said Gatti. "They all live on the south side of town."

I thought a moment. "Black entertainers, no nearby housing and a long commute from south side homes to work," I replied. "I understand."

"Yes," responded Gatti. "With transfers, it takes over an hour by trolley for them to come to work. After a long evening on the stage, several of them often sleep over rather than catch a trolley home."

"Does anyone besides your black entertainers use the sleeping room?" Hannibal asked.

Gatti thought a moment. "Not as far as I know," replied Gatti. "When we have white entertainers, they find local housing without a problem."

"Seems unfair," I responded.

"Yes," said Gatti. "Many white folks in this town love jazz music, but they don't want black people living in their neighborhoods."

He paused, looked away a moment, gave a sigh and then added: "That's the way it is."

"Can you give us a list of all of your employees?" Hannibal asked.

"Of course," replied Gatti. "I'll include names, addresses and positions."

"Who owns the club?" I asked.

Gatti smiled and said: "That's a complicated issue. The paperwork shows that the owner is Vincenzo Antonio Gibaldi." He paused a moment and then added: "The police can check."

"I'm sure they will," I replied. I looked over at Watts, who made a few notes.

A smile crossed Hannibal's face, and he said: "Gibaldi goes by the name Jack McGurn. The newspapers have had many stories over the past couple of years."

"Ah ha!" I uttered spontaneously. "I remember reading a newspaper story that said McGurn is the guy who cut Joe E. Lewis's throat about two years ago and left him for dead."

Hannibal, Watts and I looked at Gatti, who squirmed a little. "I read that story," he responded. His voice had a cautious tone. "Lewis used to work here, but he left."

Hannibal nodded, turned to me and said: "McGurn works for Capone."

Gatti squirmed again, but said nothing. Watts made a few more notes.

I could see that Gatti was nervous and might clam up. "Time to change the subject," I thought to myself. I then asked: "Tell me about your current entertainers."

Gatti gave a little sigh and relaxed a little. "Well," he said. "Melvin Johnson leads a jazz band that plays every night except Sunday and Monday."

"Names?" I asked.

Gatti paused a moment and then said: "Mel plays the clarinet and serves as leader. Sammy Washburn played a trumpet, Jimmy Brown plays trombone, Willie Bender is the piano player, and Bo Carol plays the banjo and sometimes the bass."

He paused again and then added: "Until a few weeks ago, Bel Washburn, Sammy's wife, was the band's composer, arranger and singer."

"Is Bel still with the band?" I asked.

"I'm not sure," replied Gatti. "She hasn't performed for a couple of weeks." He was silent a moment and then added: "Something is going on between Mel and Bel, but you will have to ask Mel about it."

"We will," said Hannibal. "Do you have any other employees?

"Just old Billy McBride and his wife Maude, they help me with washing glassware and they clean the place," replied Gatti. He paused and then added: "Both Billie and Maude are in their sixties, and they need the income. They have a small apartment just down the street on Lawrence, and they walk to work."

"Do they clean restrooms, the sleeping room and dressing room as well as the common areas?" I asked.

"Yes," replied Gatti. "They do a pretty good job."

"What are the work hours for Billy and Maude?" Hannibal asked.

"They normally come in about four o'clock in the afternoon and leave about ten-thirty or so, just before me," replied Gatti. "After I called the police, I called Billy and told them not to report to work today. I also told them that the police were coming, and we would be closed tonight."

Hannibal then asked: "Who has a key to open a door into the club?"

Gatti thought a moment and then answered: "Quite a few people have keys. I have keys to both doors, and I lock up when I leave. We keep a key for the Broadway door in the sleeping room for the entertainers. Old Billie has keys to both doors. Mr. Cohen, the regular manager, has keys, and so do the owners."

"Lots of access," I thought to myself. "Keys are not controlled." I then changed the subject. "Do you employ any other entertainers?" I asked.

"Not currently," responded Gatti. "Louis Armstrong used to stop by and play with Mel's band; he even brought in his 'Hot Five' band a few times."

I nodded and replied: "Yes. Major Jones and I watched Armstrong and his Hot Five perform at this club a few months ago." I paused and then added: "They are very good. Will they be back?"

Gatti gave a sigh and added: "I heard that Louis broke up with his wife Lil. I was told that he left for New York about a month ago." He paused and then added: "I don't know if Lil is in town or not."

Silence reigned for about a minute. I looked at Hannibal and then Watts. "I don't have any more questions," I said. "We can follow up later if necessary."

"Agree," replied Hannibal.

Watts looked at his watch. "Nine o'clock," he said. "We need to talk to Mel Johnson." He looked over at Gatti. "You can go on about your business, but don't leave town." He gave Gatti a steely-eyed look.

"Yes, sir," replied Gatti in a quiet voice. He then got up and walked slowly, with a limp, out of the room.

I watched with sympathy. "Not our murderer," I said to myself.

Johnson was sitting with the uniformed cop in the bar area.

As Hannibal, Watts and I approached, I said: "We'd appreciate it if you would come with us to the club manager's office." I gave him a long, steady look. "We have questions."

"Sure," replied Johnson. His voice had a nervous edge, and his eyes cast about, as if he were looking for a way out of his situation. He got up from his seat by the bar, looked to the uniformed cop who nodded. He then followed Hannibal, Watts and me to the office.

We all took seats. I looked at Johnson and said: "I'm sure you are very upset about Sammy's death." I paused and watched Johnson's face for reactions. "We want to find out what happened, and we need your help."

Johnson relaxed a little. "I'll tell you all I know," he replied. I smiled, and Johnson took a deep breath and let it out slowly. He stretched out his legs a little, and I looked closely at his shoes. They were far too large compared to the footprints in the dressing room.

"What time did you leave the club on Thursday evening?" Hannibal asked softly. I noted that Hannibal was following my lead about getting Johnson to relax.

"I left between ten-thirty and ten forty-five," replied Johnson. "Our performance ended at ten, and I had to catch a trolley home."

He then added: "Bruno saw me leave. So did Billie and Maude, the cleaning crew. They followed me out the door."

He paused a moment and then added: "I always catch the trolley as it turns right from Lawrence Street onto Broadway, just outside." He paused again and then said: "The last trolley heads toward Halsted Street between ten-thirty and ten forty-five."

"How long does it take you to get home?" I asked.

Johnson leaned back in his chair. "Let's see," he said. "I catch the trolley outside the club, do a transfer at Broadway and Halsted, another transfer at Halsted and Division and another at Division and State. I arrive at State Street South and 24th Street about an hour and a half later."

"A long ride," I said with another smile. "Do you live near the last stop?"

"Yes," replied Johnson. "My apartment is in a nice building near the corner of Indiana Avenue and 24th, just three blocks east of State."

"Do the other members of your band live in the same area?" Hannibal asked.

"Except for Bo, we all live in the same apartment building," responded Johnson. "I live in the first-floor apartment, Willie and Jimmy live on the second floor, and Sammy lived on the third." He paused and then added: "Bo lives down the street a couple of buildings away."

"After your performance on Thursday night, did the other members of your band leave?" I asked.

Johnson nodded. "Everyone except Sammy." He paused and then added: "Willie and Jimmy left before me; they said they were going to catch the ten-fifteen trolley." He paused, smiled and then added: "They ran out the Lawrence side door; I think they made it."

"How about Bo?" Hannibal asked.

"He also left about ten-fifteen, but a car was waiting outside," replied Johnson. "I saw him go out the door on the Broadway side. Before the door closed, I saw him get into a car."

"What kind of car, and did you see the driver or other passengers?" Hannibal asked.

Johnson thought a moment and then said: "The car was a Model T. I couldn't see the driver; he was on the other side." He paused again and then said: "There may have been a passenger, but I'm not sure."

I wrote names, times and modes of transportation in my notebook. Hannibal also made notes. I then looked at Johnson and asked: "Are you all bachelors?"

"Well, no, not exactly," responded Johnson, and he squirmed a little. "Sammy was married to Bel Lee, but they split up. Sammy lived with Essie Harlan before his death." Johnson gave a big sigh and then continued: "Bel now lives with Bo."

"Interesting," I mused softly. "Did Sammy and Bel divorce?"

"Not yet," replied Johnson. "They fought over money and rights to music." He paused a moment then continued: "Bel was a successful song writer. She knew Sammy in New Orleans before she moved to Chicago in 1923. She brought Sammy to Chicago from New Orleans in '25, and they married."

"Who is Essie Harlan?" Hannibal asked.

Johnson's expression changed to one of distaste, and he replied: "Sammy's girlfriend."

"Tell me about Essie," I said. "Is she an entertainer too?"

"A singer," responded Johnson. "She has a wonderful voice. Mostly, she performed over at the Gardens before it closed."

"Did she perform with your band?" Hannibal asked.

"No!" Johnson responded emphatically. "I didn't want to get involved in the goings-on between Sammy, Bel and Essie."

"Did Bo and Sammy get along?" I asked.

"They were friends before the female problems," responded Johnson with a sad look on his face. "Professionally, they still worked together. However, I could tell the relationship was strained."

I thought a moment and then asked: "Other than personal relationships, did Sammy have enemies?"

"Sammy played the horses at Washington Park and Arlington Park on Sundays and Mondays," replied Johnson. "He sometimes missed our rehearsals. I think he owed lots of money; he constantly complained about bookies and asked for advances on his salary."

"We can follow up on his wife, girlfriend and horse betting later," I thought to myself. I then asked: "Why did Sammy stay at the club on Thursday night?"

"Well, he often stayed instead of going home," replied Johnson. "So did Jimmy and Willie." He thought a moment, then continued: "It's a long ride home, late at night. With Sammy, I also think he wanted to get away from his female problems."

We were all silent for a long moment. I looked at Hannibal.

Hannibal then said: "I have no more questions at the moment." He looked at Watts.

"Right," responded Watts. "You can go now, Johnson. Don't leave town; we will have more questions later." Watts then got up, walked out and conferred with the uniformed cop waiting by the bar.

"Yes," replied Johnson. He got up and hurriedly left the room. I heard the main door out to Broadway open and close.

I looked at Hannibal. "Long day," I said.

Hannibal pulled out his pocket watch and looked at it. "After ten," he said. "We have lots of work to do, but it can wait until morning. I'll check on Eddie. If he's finished, let's go home."

As Hannibal finished his sentence, Eddie's face appeared in the office doorway. "All done," he said. "Shall we call it a day?"

19

TANGLED WEBS

Sunday evening, February 3, 1929

Sunday morning began in the kitchen over coffee. Silvia had the day off, and Hannibal and I started at seven-thirty. Neither of us could sleep; our heads were full of observations and possibilities concerning Sammy Washburn's murder.

I was dressed in my cream-colored silk lounging pajamas and robe with a white fox collar. I also wore my matching velvet-lined slippers; they had been hiding under my bed. Hannibal was fully dressed, as always.

My right big toe had a blackened nail, and it was still sore. However, I had no intention of letting Hannibal know how the damage occurred. Still, I think he knew; I saw him smile when I hobbled about. I gave him a dirty look whenever I observed his half-hidden grin; he knew better than to say anything.

Hannibal began by reading from his notes out loud, between sips of coffee. "Johnson said that Willie Bender, Jimmy Brown and Bo Carol left the club at about ten-fifteen. Willie and Jimmy caught the ten-fifteen trolley. Bo got into a Model T Ford just outside the Broadway exit door at about the same time. Again, according to Johnson, he left at the same time as Billie and Maude McBride. He caught the ten-thirty trolley and headed for home."

"Yes," I replied. "Gatti confirmed that Johnson left at the time that Johnson gave us. According to Gatti, Billie and Maude also left at about ten-thirty. He said they always walk toward their home on Lawrence Street."

Hannibal turned a page of his notes. "Gatti said he left at about ten forty-five to catch a taxi home. Tony Olmi, a taxi driver, confirmed that Gatti got in his taxi at ten forty-five."

"Agreed," I replied. "Gatti said that he locked the doors before he left. Apparently, Sammy Washburn was alone in the club. He planned to stay the night, as he often did."

"Yet at least two assailants murdered Washburn in the club dressing room between midnight and one o'clock," responded Hannibal. "The assailants were either hidden in the club or gained access between ten forty-five Thursday night and one o'clock Friday morning."

"Lots of keys to the doors, so someone could have gotten a key and gained entry," I added. "I doubt that identifying a specific key, if one was used, is even possible."

"Agree," said Hannibal. At this point, we don't know if anyone observed the two club doors from ten-thirty until one o'clock, although we can do more research." Hannibal thought a moment and added: "Perhaps Watts and Mulvaney can help. I'm sure the police are aware that the club is a hangout for gangsters, and they may keep an eye on it."

"Good," I replied. "Also, I think we can rule out Mel Johnson and Bruno Gatti as likely suspects," I said. "They each have witnesses for the time that they left. I looked closely at their shoes, and neither has shoes that match the footprints in the dressing room."

"Agree," said Hannibal. "We know that Washburn had relationship problems with Bel Lee Washburn, his estranged wife, and possibly Essie Harlan, his current girlfriend. Bo Carol is Bel's current boyfriend. Washburn also had gambling debts from playing the horses."

"Eddie will have fingerprints, blood types and exact footprint measurements. He may also find something on the washcloth and in the sink drain trap in the water closet," I said.

"We need a data base of fingerprints, footprints and blood to compare to Eddie's findings," responded Hannibal. "Who are our suspects?"

"Bo Carol, Bel Washburn and Essie Harlan may have motive. Jimmy Brown and Willie Bender are possibilities, but as far as we know, they have no motive," I said.

"Yes," replied Hannibal. "Let's work with Watts to set up interviews."

I thought a moment and then said: "How about a conspiracy with Watts to collect fingerprints and footprints during the interviews?"

"Devious, as usual," replied Hannibal with a grin. "I'll set it up." He paused a moment and then added: "During the interviews, we might find out more about Sammy's debt problems."

Silence reigned for a few minutes, and we sipped our coffee. Finally, I said: "Our evidence, interviews and data base will help us with motive and opportunity, but what about a murder weapon?"

Hannibal nodded and said: "Well, the wounds tell us that the murder weapon was most likely a knife. Eddie's measurements and the autopsy will give us the size and information on the type of blade."

"Yes," I agreed. "Let's work with Gatti to do a thorough search in and near the club." I smiled and added: "I have some ideas."

Hannibal raised his eyebrows and said: "Oh? Do you think that you might find the weapon?"

"It's worth a try," I replied. "I doubt that the killer would keep it as a souvenir. He or she may have ditched it shortly after the murder."

"True," said Hannibal. "I'll talk to Eddie; he can help."

"Good idea," I replied. "I'll call Susie, she and Eddie make a good team. I also think Joe and Albert at the club will get directions to help. Their boss will want the police to go away from the club as soon as possible." I smiled and added: "A closed club brings in no money."

"Anything else?" I asked.

"Not at the moment," replied Hannibal. He smiled and his eyes twinkled. "I hope your toe gets better soon."

"Humph," I said, and I gave Hannibal the snootiest look I could muster.

Tuesday evening, February 5th, 1929

Monday was a busy day. After making an appointment by phone on Monday morning, Hannibal met with Watts and Mulvaney at the new Police Headquarters. I followed up with Eddie, Susie and then Joe, our main contact with the 'owner' of the Green Mill.

Eddie gave me the preliminary findings from the autopsy over the phone. Indeed, Washburn had been killed with a knife. Based on measurements of the three stab wounds, the blade was about four to five inches long, tapered, and sharp on both sides. He said the knife probably had a stiletto blade.

Eddie added that such knives were common weapons in Chicago murders, and the stab wounds showed that the user twisted the knife around inside the victim. "Whoever stabbed Washburn was an expert," said Eddie.

I shuddered when Eddie described the wounds; Washburn died a painful death.

I called Susie and briefed her on the case. She was excited, and I could tell she was looking forward to working with Eddie again. "Romance in the future?" I thought to myself. "Get back on track Caroline," I muttered after I hung up the phone. "Cupid doesn't need my help."

Next, I called Joe. I briefed him on our findings concerning the Washburn murder. As I thought, his boss wanted to clear up the murder as soon as possible and re-open the club. He promised full cooperation in searching the Green Mill and other key locations for a murder weapon.

Hannibal arrived home about five o 'clock. Silvia had a nice dinner waiting. After dinner, Silvia cleaned up and then left for the day.

Hannibal and I showered and I dressed in my customary lounging clothes. We then retired to our workroom and made ourselves comfortable. Of course, we each had a glass of chilled chardonnay, and we sipped slowly as we compared notes.

"Watts and Mulvaney were most helpful," Hannibal began. "The new police headquarters on South State Street is only a dozen or so blocks from the homes of our current suspects." He smiled and added: "They will bring in Willie Bender, Jimmy Brown, Bo Carol, Bel Washburn and Essie Harlan tomorrow afternoon for questioning."

"Good," I responded. "Let's develop a list of questions. In addition to personal relationships, I want for find out more about Washburn's gambling debts." I thought a moment and then added: "Do we have time to prepare the conference room?"

"Yes," replied Hannibal, and his smile broadened. "We can set up in the morning. I'll have Eddie bring in a rack of very clean coffee cups. Can Susie find some decent coffee and a large coffee maker?"

"Oh, yes," I responded with a grimace. "That stuff Watts and Mulvaney call coffee would kill a horse." I then added: "I'll have Susie set up coffee, donuts, hot tea, ice water, condiments and so on." Our objective will be to make the interviewees comfortable and talkative, not poison them."

Hannibal laughed and said: "Let's bring extra; Watts and Mulvaney will appreciate the change."

"What about footprints?" I asked.

"Eddie and a janitor will be in room next to the conference room," replied Hannibal. "The floor will be newly damp with a light sprinkle of talcum powder before each suspect walks down the short section of hallway between the holding room and the conference room. After the suspect enters the conference room, Eddie will come out of his room, take photos and lift the footprints with an adhesive paper. After the interview is over and the suspect goes back to the holding room, the janitor will prepare the floor for the next suspect."

"Great!" I responded. "The suspects will be unaware that their footprints have been taken."

Hannibal then smiled and said: "Watts had another very useful item of information." He handed me a folder.

I opened it and read. The folder contained a hand-written police surveillance log. "The club has been under surveillance by the cops for over a year!" I exclaimed. 'Why?"

"Jack McGurn," replied Hannibal. "According to Watts, McGurn is well-known to the police, and they suspect that he may have been involved in over twenty murders, including three of the Genna brothers. He also is suspected in the attack on Joe E. Lewis in November 1927."

"Ah, yes," I replied. "Lewis the singer and comedian."

"He was," answered Hannibal. "According to Watts, Lewis was a star at the Green Mill. Apparently, he had a contract dispute with McGurn, who, as you know, is a club owner. Lewis was attacked in his hotel room by three men, probably including or sent by McGurn. His throat was cut and his tongue nearly severed." He paused and then added: "No one was prosecuted; Lewis wouldn't testify."

"Good heavens!" I exclaimed. "Did Capone order the attack?"

"I doubt it," replied Hannibal. "I asked both Gatti and Joe about it on the phone after I talked to Watts, and they both said Capone liked Lewis. Also, Watts said the notoriety of the attack on Lewis is what caused the police to begin surveillance of the Green Mill." He paused and then added: "Capone may eventually turn on McGurn, who appears to be a loose cannon."

"How interesting," I replied. "All is not well within Capone's organization."

"Apparently," agreed Hannibal. "Anyway, the cops have a second-floor room diagonally across the street from the club. The observers can see both the Lawrence and Broadway doors."

He paused while I looked at the report. He then added: "Look at the entries for Thursday, January 31st and Friday February 1st."

I read the entries and then mused: "According to the cops, Gatti was the last to leave the club on Thursday night, at ten forty-five, like he said." I was silent for a moment as I read further. "No one entered or left the club through the Lawrence or Broadway doors until Gatti arrived at three in the afternoon."

"Yes," replied Hannibal. "Washburn's assailants were either hidden in the club from Thursday night until after three in the afternoon on Friday, or they found another entrance and exit, unknown to the cops."

"The trap door behind the bar," I replied. "We saw it when we met with Giuseppe in the club in November."

"The passage underneath is worth a tour, don't you think?" Hannibal said with a smile.

"Already arranged," I replied with a smug look. "I thought about it even before this surveillance report."

An expression of surprise crossed Hannibal's face. However, he recovered after a second or so. I was so pleased with myself!

Our discussion continued for a while as we ironed out the details of our planned interviews at the police station the next day. In addition to untangling the web of personal relationships within Mel Johnson's jazz band, we needed to find out who might have held Washburn's gambling debts. Also, we didn't have a murder weapon, and we were still waiting on Eddie's complete lab report and the final autopsy report.

Hannibal and I finished our discussion and wine at about ten o'clock. After we were silent for a while, I yawned. "Time for bed," I said. "Tomorrow will be a busy day."

"Agreed," replied Hannibal. He smiled, leaned over and kissed me. I returned the favor.

20

HUNTING A SPIDER

Thursday evening, February 7, 1929

Today, we conducted interviews and identified leads for the next round. We also obtained fingerprints, footprints, lab reports and autopsy reports. In addition, Watts and Mulvaney consumed most of the good quality coffee and a significant share of the donuts.

I also think they both fell in love with Susie as she set up the conference room. Watts offered her a job and Mulvaney flirted at every opportunity. Susie smiled coyly. Eddie frowned as he observed Mulvaney with Susie.

Both Hannibal and I wore conservative winter attire for the occasion; impressions are important.

Hannibal dressed in a charcoal colored, worsted wool, single-breasted suit with a vest. His deep red tie with a thin navy diagonal stripe contrasted nicely with his light blue shirt.

I wore a simple Jeanne Lanvin navy-blue skirt with a long length, matching jacket. My blouse was white silk and had thin vertical navy stripes. I wore a red silk scarf knotted at my neck for flair and mid-heel black shoes with T-straps and small gold buckles. Everything came from Mandell's, of course. I styled my hair in the latest bobbed fashion.

Back to business. Watts and Mulvaney had all five suspects at the station just before noon.

"No need to keep the suspects separated," I thought to myself. "If they wanted to discuss their stories before their individual interviews, they would have done so by now." One of the uniformed cops stayed in the holding room with them, and he conspicuously had a pencil and notepad.

Hannibal and I watched as the suspects were escorted to the holding room by a couple of no-nonsense, uniformed cops. We then entered our conference room, which had been prepared by Susie earlier that morning.

Watts introduced Hannibal and me to a police stenographer named Irene, who was waiting for us in our conference room. After introductions, Irene took a seat on a chair in a corner. She had her notepad. She was an older woman, and she was dressed in a dark, plain but tasteful dress. She was so quiet that after a while, we were hardly aware that she was in the room.

"Good," I thought to myself. "Our interviewees will not pay much attention to Irene either, and the cops will have a verbatim record."

After a short discussion with Watts, Mulvaney, Eddie and the janitor on final details, we began our interviews at twelve-thirty with the least likely suspects: Willie Bender first, followed by Jimmy Brown.

Hannibal, Watts and I had seats on one side of the large conference table. An empty chair rested on the other side. Both Hannibal and Watts had notes, files and cups of coffee on the table. The table in front of the empty chair held a blank notepad and a couple of pencils.

The room was ready. Susie had set up the counter. It held the coffee urn, teapot, a pitcher of iced water and donuts. Susie had even supplied some cannoli. A few cups, water glasses and plates rested near the urn and pitcher, along with cream, sugar and napkins. Racks with more cups, glasses and plates were hidden in cabinets under the counter.

Watts leaned out the conference room door and gave a signal. He and Hannibal took their seats. I chose to stand by the counter. After a minute or so, a uniformed cop opened the door and escorted an apprehensive Willie Bender into the room. Willie stood just inside, next to the empty chair. He looked first at Watts, then Hannibal and finally, at me.

I smiled and said: "These interviews take time and effort. Would you like some coffee, tea or water? We also have some donuts and cannoli." I motioned to the counter.

Willie didn't know quite how to respond. He was clearly scared. "I guess so," he stuttered.

"Help yourself," said Hannibal. He smiled cordially and motioned with his hand toward the counter.

Willie stepped over to the counter and fixed a cup of coffee. With uncertain glances at me, he also put a donut on a plate. I smiled sweetly. Encouraged, he added a cannoli.

"Please have a seat," I said, and motioned toward the empty chair.

Willie picked up his coffee cup, plate and a napkin, set them on the table, and took his seat. He then sipped his coffee and eyed his three interrogators, in turn. I poured myself some coffee and sat down.

"We are investigating the murder of Sammy Washburn, who, I understand, worked with you in a jazz band headed by Mel Johnson," said Hannibal in a soft but firm voice. "We know that you are very upset about Sammy's death." He paused a moment and then added: "We hope you can help us bring the killer or killers to justice."

"I'll try," responded Willie. "Sammy was my friend." He took a bite of the cannoli. He visibly relaxed a little. Even Watts smiled as Willie took another bite of the cannoli.

Watts, Hannibal and I then asked questions. We began with verifying the time that Willie left the club on Thursday night and continued with easy questions about where he lived, how long it took him to get from the club to home and so on.

Willie answered politely and continued with his snacks. I heard Eddie moving about outside the conference room, but Willie didn't seem to notice.

After about five minutes of simple questions, I asked the first leading question: "How long did you know Sammy?" I smiled, leaned forward a little and sipped my coffee.

Willie ate the final piece of cannoli, discretely licked a little powdered sugar from his fingers and then politely used his napkin.

"Oh, Sammy, Jimmy, Bo and I knew each other in New Orleans," he replied. "We played together in clubs on Bourbon Street." Willie then gave a long-winded narrative on how they met, their travels to Chicago in 1925 and on and on. Hannibal, Watts and I listened politely.

After a couple of minutes, Willie ran out of steam. I then asked: "Do you get better pay in Chicago?"

"Oh, yes," responded Willie. "We can afford nice apartments, and we visit all the places allowed for colored folks."

"I heard that Sammy liked to bet on the horses at Washington Park and Arlington Park," I stated. "Did you go with him?"

"Several times," answered Willie. "We rode the special train from Dearborn Station to Washington Park. When we got to the track, Sammy bet a lot, but I didn't." He paused and then added: "Sammy used to meet Big Watson at the track and hand over his markers and bet sheets." He eyed the remaining donut on his plate.

I looked over at Watts. He nodded. "Big Watson is known to the police," I thought to myself. "Good!"

"Did Sammy win at the track?" Hannibal asked.

"Not very often," replied Willie, as he picked up the remaining donut. "Sammy asked me for loans several times. I think he owed Big Watson a lot of money."

Hannibal, Watts and I exchanged glances. We had a lead, and we would follow up. Willie finished off his donut.

I then changed my line of questioning. "I understand that Sammy and Bel are married. Do they have a good relationship?"

Willie immediately looked up at me, then Hannibal and finally Watts. "Well, no, but you'll have to ask Bel about that."

I asked a couple of additional questions about Bel and Sammy, but Willie was evasive. He kept saying that we would have to ask Bel. Willie had clammed up.

The interview ended at about one-o'clock, with no additional information. Watts finally got up and opened the door. The coast was clear; Eddie had finished his work outside in the hallway.

"You can go now," said Watts. "We'll contact you if we have more questions." He paused, smiled slightly and then said: "We will also type up what you told us and contact you for a signature." His eyes gleamed and he added: "Don't leave town."

"Yessir," responded Willie. He got up from his seat, took a last sip of coffee, put the cup down, and walked out the door.

Watts watched while Willie was escorted to the elevator. After a few moments, he said: "The coast is clear." He stepped out into the hallway. I could hear him open the door to the adjacent room. There was a brief conversation as the janitor prepared the hallway for the next interviewee.

In the meantime, I gingerly put Willie's coffee cup and plate in the rack in the cabinet under the counter, along with a label with Willie's name. Hannibal cleared the remains of Willie's snack from the table. At one-fifteen, we were ready for our next interview.

The interview with Jimmy Brown went much the same. We confirmed Sammy's gambling habits. According to Jimmy, Sammy asked everyone he knew for loans. Jimmy said he gave Sammy some money a few times, but Sammy was slow to pay it back, even to a friend. Jimmy said that he had stopped loaning Sammy money months ago.

Jimmy did provide a little more information on Bel and Sammy. "Bel loved Sammy," said Jimmy. "At least she used to."

"How long had Sammy and Bel been married?" I asked.

"They married in '25, just after Bel convinced Sammy, Willie and me to come to Chicago." He paused and then added: "Bel is a singer and composer, and she had worked with us in New Orleans before she moved to Chicago in '23."

"Did Bel have a successful career in Chicago before you arrived?" Hannibal asked.

"Oh yes," responded Jimmy. "She's big time. She knows all the club owners, and she worked with Louis and Lil Armstrong." He paused and then added: "Bel has recording contracts and owns lots of music that she composed herself."

"Was she a good business person?" Hannibal asked.

"Smart as they come," replied Jimmy. "She had a lawyer write contracts."

"Do you know the lawyer's name?" Watts asked.

Jimmy thought a moment and then said: "Brian Connolly, I think. He knows Louis and Lil, and he helps lots of colored musicians set up contracts with club owners and folks who publish and record our music."

"Another contact for questions," I thought to myself. To Jimmy, I asked: "Does Bel own the rights to her music?" I glanced at Hannibal, and he nodded.

"Yes," replied Jimmy. "She owns most of it, but she and Sammy owned some together. That happened after they married in '25." He paused and then added: "Our band made several recordings that featured Bel as singer and Sammy on the clarinet." He paused again and then said: "Beautiful songs, and they were big hits."

"I understand that Bel and Sammy were separated," Hannibal said. "Did they have problems over ownership rights to music?"

"Yes, I think so," responded Jimmy. "But you'll have to asked Bel about that."

Just like Willie, Jimmy clammed up when I asked too many questions about the relationship between Sammy and Bel. I got the impression that he was too scared to say much. "We'll have to follow up on that as well," I thought to myself, as I made notes.

The interview ended at about one forty-five. Watts told Jimmy to stay in town and be prepared to sign his statement after it had been typed. Jimmy answered: "Yessir," and then left. We put away his coffee cup and plate, cleaned up the mess on the table and verified that Eddie had completed his work in the hallway. We prepared for our next interview.

Bo Carol, the trombone player, was next. He was a big man. His face had a sullen scowl when he entered the room. Hannibal and Watts were in their seats, and I stood near the counter. Carol looked first at Hannibal, then Watts and finally, me. His eyes were steady, and he showed no fear. He walked over to the chair on his side of the table, stood, and waited. I shuddered a little as I watched him.

After a moment, I said: "Would you like some coffee? We also have tea, water and donuts." I smiled and watched Bo's face intently.

Bo turned, looked at Watts and Hannibal, and then returned his gaze to me. "Just water," he replied.

I wasn't about to get it for him, so I responded: "Help yourself, and then take your seat." My voice had a slight commanding tone, and my smile was gone. My eyes held steady.

Bo looked at me for a moment, then stepped over to the counter. He surveyed the offerings, and then poured himself a glass of water. He took a sip as he turned and walked over to his seat.

After Bo had taken his seat, Hannibal asked: "Was Sammy Washburn your friend?"

Bo looked at Hannibal for a moment before replying. "He used to be," he finally said. "We still worked together." He paused, and his eyes misted a little. "I'm sorry he's dead."

I watched Bo's face intently. In spite of my initial impression, his reply seemed genuine. "Surprise!" I thought to myself.

"I understand that you and Bel, Sammy's wife, are friends as well," I stated. "Do you live together?"

Bo looked at me, and the mist in his eyes departed. He moved uneasily in his seat. "Bel and Sammy broke up last year," he finally said. "Bel wanted a divorce. Sammy wouldn't cooperate." Bo's eyes flashed a little. "Yes," he finally said. "We lived together."

I noted the past tense in Bo's reply. Have Bo and Bel changed their relationship?

"Why wouldn't Sammy consent to a divorce?" Hannibal asked in a soft voice.

Bo turned to Hannibal and replied: "Money: Bel and Sammy jointly owned the rights to songs they composed together. They also jointly received royalties from recording contracts."

"Do you know how much money was involved?"

Bo was quiet for a while. Finally, he said. "You will have to ask Bel."

"We will," Hannibal replied. "Was the amount substantial?"

"Yes," responded Bo.

"Clearly, motive for murder," I thought to myself. I looked at Hannibal and then Watts. Both nodded.

"Do you intend to marry Bel, now that Sammy is gone?" I asked.

Bo was quiet for a long moment. "Perhaps," he finally said. He paused and then said: "I'm not sure." He paused again and then added: "Bel moved out yesterday."

"Careful with stereotypes, Caroline," I mused. "Bo Carol is a complicated man."

"We have been told that you left the Green Mill Club last Thursday evening about ten-fifteen," I stated. "You were seen getting into a Model T Ford just outside the Broadway exit door. Who picked you up, and where did you go?"

Bo was silent for a long time. Finally, he said: "Brian Connolly picked me up. We drove to the corner, turned left on Lawrence, followed Lawrence to Lakeshore Drive, turned right, took Lakeshore to Roosevelt, turned right, and then we drove to State Street and turned left. We drove to 24th Street and turned left. Connolly dropped me at home near Indiana Avenue and 24th Street at about eleven-fifteen."

"This is getting complicated," I thought to myself. I then said: "I'm impressed with your recall of the drive. Why did Connolly pick you up and take you home? Don't you normally take a trolley?"

Bo was quiet for a full minute. Finally, he said: "Bel arranged it. Connolly wanted to talk to me about a contract to compose and sell music." He paused and then added: "We talked in the car." He paused a moment and then added: "I watched the streets as we drove; I wanted to be sure that we were headed to my home."

I made a note about the evident distrust that Bo had about Connolly. I then asked: "Did you come to an agreement about a contract?"

"No," replied Bo, in a terse statement. I waited, but he didn't say anything else.

Finally, Hannibal asked: "Was Bel at your home when you arrived?"

"No," responded Bo. He looked at Hannibal with steady eyes. "She didn't come home until late Friday morning, about ten o'clock."

"Do you know where Bel spent the night?" I asked.

"No," replied Bo as he turned and looked at me. "She didn't say."

"Other than Brian Connolly, can anyone verify that you arrived at home at eleven-fifteen that Thursday night?" Watts asked.

"Yes," replied Bo. His face had a slight smile. "One of your police officers stopped Mr. Connolly at the corner of Roosevelt and State. Mr. Connolly ran a stop sign." His smile broadened a little. "The cop gave Mr. Connolly a citation."

I couldn't help it; I gave a stifled chuckle. I looked at Hannibal, who also had a grin on his face. Watts harrumphed a little and made a note. "I'll check," was all that he said.

"Still, I thought to myself, Bo Carol could have made it back from home to the Green Mill before one o'clock Friday morning in time to kill Sammy Washburn." I made a few notes. "However," my thoughts continued, "trolley service had ended before eleven, so Carol would have had to use a private car or a taxi. Both are highly unlikely," I concluded.

I looked to Hannibal and raised my eyebrows. My silent thought was: "Do you have any more questions?" Hannibal read my thought, smiled, and shook his head to indicate "No." We both then looked at Watts.

Watts evidently thought the same thing. He looked up from his notetaking and saw our expressions. He then turned to Bo and stared at him for a long moment. Finally, he said: "We are finished for now. We've made a stenographic record of this conversation. After we get it typed up, someone will call you for a signature." He gave Bo a steely-eyed look. "Don't leave town."

Bo finished his glass of water, stood up, and without a word, turned and left the room.

Hannibal, Watts and I were silent for a moment. "Finally, I said: "Bo Carol doesn't have a pleasing personality, but I don't think he's our killer."

Both Hannibal and Watts nodded in agreement. Watts then said: "I agree, but I will check out his story about Connolly and his citation with our traffic division." Watts harrumphed again.

"Good idea," I said with a smile, and we placed Bo's water glass in the hidden rack and prepared for the next interview.

Essie Harlan entered the room at three o'clock. Her facial expression reminded me of a scared rabbit; I half-expected to see her nose twitch. She was dressed in a fashionable black drop-waisted dress and matching low heeled shoes with T-straps. However, she should have left the red feathered boa at home.

From my usual position near the counter, I addressed Essie in the kindest voice I could muster. "I can only imagine how upset you are about Sammy," I said in a soft and sympathetic voice. "However, we would greatly appreciate your help in identifying Sammy's murderer."

Essie turned to me, and her eyes were as big as saucers. "Yes," was all she said.

"Would you like some coffee or tea?" I asked. "We also have some sweets."

Essie repeated herself with another "Yes."

"This is going nowhere," I thought to myself. To Essie, I said: "Come over here to the counter, and let's fix some tea."

Essie joined me at the counter. I helped her fix a cup of hot tea and put cannoli on a plate for her. Together, we walked over to her chair by the table. I made sure Essie carried her own cup. I helped with her cannoli plate and a napkin. After she took her seat and sipped her tea, she seemed to calm down a little. I walked around the table to my usual seat. After this tedious episode, we were ready to for the interview.

Hannibal started. "Sammy remained at the Green Mill on Thursday night," he stated. "Do you know why?"

"He stayed at the club sometimes," Essie replied as she looked at Hannibal. "Before he left on Thursday afternoon, he said he didn't want to be at home that night because people were looking for him." Essie paused and looked at Watts, then me and then back to Hannibal. "He was scared."

"Do you know who might have been looking for Sammy?" I asked.

"Debt collectors," responded Essie. "Once, about two weeks ago, a man came to the apartment in the morning while we were sleeping. He banged on the door and woke us up. When Sammy opened the door a crack, the man pushed his way in and threatened Sammy."

"Do you know the man?" I asked.

"Sammy called him Mr. Big," Essie replied. "I heard him say that Sammy had to pay up. After shoving Sammy around for a while, Mr. Big finally left."

"Was Mr. Big white or colored?" Watts asked.

"Colored," Essie replied. "I was really scared."

"Could Mr. Big have gone by another name?" I asked.

Essie nodded. "Later, Sammy said his name was Big Watson."

"Did Sammy say how much he owed Big Watson?" Hannibal asked.

"Twenty-five thousand dollars," replied Essie. "Sammy lost lots of money betting on the horses."

"What a motive for a beating," I thought to myself. "But a motive for murder? Dead men can't pay debts." My mind raced. "What am I missing?"

I decided to change the subject. "Are you acquainted with Bel, Sammy's estranged wife?"

Essie spilled some of her tea on the table. "Oh, I'm sorry," she exclaimed in an almost pitiful voice. She dabbed up the spill with her napkin. I waited patiently.

After a few moments of clean-up, Essie replied: "Yes, I know Bel." Her eyes gleamed for a moment. Her hands trembled a little as she took another sip of tea from her nearly empty cup.

"Interesting reaction," I thought. "Clearly, Essie doesn't like Bel."

"Did you know that Bel wanted a divorce?" Hannibal asked.

"Yes," responded Essie. "I wanted Sammy to divorce Bel, too." She paused a moment and then added: "But Bel wanted to cheat Sammy out of the money coming in from their music record sales."

"How would she accomplish that?" I asked.

Essie's eyes gleamed again. "She threatened to accuse Sammy of adultery in divorce court if he didn't sign over the music rights. Either way, Bel said, she would get the music money."

"Did Sammy give in?" Watts asked.

"No," replied Essie. "He was too scared of Mr. Big. Sammy needed the money."

Hannibal, Watts and I asked a few more questions, but Essie didn't add anything new. Essie left after Watts told her not to leave town and to be prepared to sign her statement after it had been typed. I put Essie's cup away and Eddie did his thing in the hallway.

"Five o'clock and one more to go," said Watts, as we waited for Bel to enter the room.

Bel entered through the doorway. She was well-dressed and quite attractive. I estimated her age to be mid-thirties. Like Essie, she wore a black, drop-waisted dress. She also had a double strand pearl necklace in the latest fashion. She wore a matching black Cloche hat. Her black, low heeled shoes were narrow in the toe. "I'll be very interested in Bel's footprints," I thought to myself.

All in all, Bel's fashion sense was similar to mine. I was, of course, impressed. However, her facial expression combined belligerence, half-concealed slyness and a tinge of fear. "A formidable woman," my thoughts continued. "Reminds me of a black widow spider."

Bel walked over to her designated chair, stood behind it, put her hands on its back and stared at Watts. "I want my attorney present before I answer questions," she stated fiercely.

"That's certainly your right," replied Watts in a firm voice. "However, you are not yet under arrest, but I can certainly get a warrant." He paused to let his words sink in. "This is a murder investigation, and I suggest that you cooperate."

"You should also know that your animosity toward your estranged husband Sammy is well-known and documented," stated Hannibal. "In other words, the police can establish that you have a motive for the murder of your husband."

That did it. Bel's belligerence faded and her expression changed to apprehension. She still stood behind her chair, but she shifted her weight from side to side.

I then spoke up. "This is a very upsetting time for everyone," I said in a soft, smooth voice. "Some hot tea and cannoli would be nice. May I help you fix a cup of tea and a plate of sweets?" Bel turned toward me. Her face now expressed uncertainty. I smiled and motioned toward the counter.

Soon Bel was seated with her tea and cannoli. Still, she sipped her tea carefully and eyed Hannibal, Watts and me across the table.

"I understand that your maiden name is Bel Lee, and that you came to Chicago from New Orleans in 1923, is that correct?" I asked.

"Yes," Bel replied. "I used to live in New Orleans."

"I understand that you have had a very successful career as a singer, song writer and recording artist," I stated. "You must be very proud of your accomplishments."

"Yes, thank you," replied Bel in a softer tone. She smiled a little. "I have contracts with Paramount and Brunswick Records. I also write music for several singers in town."

"I understand that you wrote music and made recordings with Sammy, your husband," I stated.

"Yes," Bel answered. Her expression became guarded.

"Your attorney is Brian Connolly?" I asked.

"Yes," replied Bel. Her attitude became even more cautious. "Mr. Connolly helps me on all of my contracts. He is also my personal attorney."

Bel rose from her seat. "If you have more questions, please call Mr. Connolly," she stated. She looked directly at Watts and added: "Unless I am under arrest, I would like to leave now."

Watts returned Bel's stare. "You are not under arrest, and you may go," he responded. "And we will certainly contact Mr. Connolly. After your statement has been typed, you'll need to return to sign it." He paused and then added in a steely voice: "Stay in town, or I will get a warrant."

Bel then turned, and without another world, walked out of the conference room.

After Bel left, Hannibal, Watts and I remained silent for a couple of minutes. Finally, I looked at Watts and asked: "Do you have contacts with the New Orleans police?"

"Yes," replied Watts. He caught my drift. "I will check with them on Bel Lee Washburn."

The three of us then finished up our notes. Hannibal and I put ours in Hannibal's briefcase, which rested in a corner. Watts conferred with Irene, who had a very full notepad. Irene left the room quickly; she had a full day's work of typing, starting the next morning. Watts turned to Hannibal and me and said: "Let's talk tomorrow. I'll give you a phone call."

Hannibal nodded and looked at his watch. "Almost six o'clock," he stated.

Just then, Eddie appeared in the doorway. "All done with the footprints," he said with a grin. "I'll also take care of the cups, plates and glasses." He paused and looked at me. "Did you label everything?"

"All done," I replied. "You have a lot of work ahead of you."

Eddie grinned again and said: "Yes. However, I just got a call from the lab. The lab and autopsy reports on Sammy Washburn are ready. I will deliver them to you at your home tomorrow."

"Thanks, Eddie," I replied. "See you tomorrow." Eddie nodded, turned and walked over to the counter. Soon he was busy with the rack of cups, plates and glasses.

And so, our day ended. I looked at Hannibal. He smiled and said: "Are you ready to go home?"

"Oh yes," I responded with a tired smile. I could hardly wait for a glass of chardonnay in our cozy parlor.

21

A KNIFE, A LAWYER AND A GAMBLER

Saturday morning, February 9ᵗʰ, 1929

Friday morning, Susie and I looked for a knife. Hannibal and Watts visited Brian Connolly. Mulvaney took a team of uniformed cops and headed for the Washington Park Racetrack; they had an arrest warrant for Big Watson. The warrant was for illegal gambling.

Susie arrived at the penthouse at nine in the morning. I called Gatti and made arrangements at the Green Mill. Harris called a taxi for us at nine-thirty. Susie and I were dressed for the event; we wore simple slacks, cardigan sweaters, warm socks and walking shoes. Our outerwear included hats, gloves and wool coats. The weather was cold; the wind was blowing off Lake Michigan again. I brought along a black canvas bag with gear inside.

Susie and I arrived at the Green Mill at ten o'clock. Gatti met us at the Broadway door, along with Joe, our contact with the Capone organization.

The club was still closed. On Thursday evening, Watts told us that the vice cops continued to watch the club from the apartment across the street. We asked Watts if we might search the club for a murder weapon. "I'll arrange it," he had said. "You'll have the place to yourselves."

Gatti had a key, and we all went inside. No one was in the club, not even the cops. The place was cold, dark and gloomy, even spooky. I shivered a little and glanced at Susie. She had a similar reaction.

Gatti walked behind the bar and flipped a light switch. The lights came on, and Susie and I both felt better.

I glanced behind the bar. As on the day of the murder, no illegal booze lined the shelves, just near beer and soft drinks. Gatti saw my glance and smiled. "We are still playing it safe," he said.

"Yes," I replied: "Good idea."

"Where do you want to start?" Joe asked.

"The cops searched this floor and the upstairs thoroughly right after the murder," I stated matter-of-factly. "No booze and no murder weapon." I paused and then added: "I want to go into your secret passage."

Gatti raised his eyebrows. "You know about that, do you?"

Joe grinned, looked at Gatti and said: "Miss Case saw the trap door behind the bar open on November 9th, during a meeting in the club with another client." He paused a moment and then added: "Open it up."

Without another word, Gatti bent over, rolled back a heavy rubber mat and exposed the trap door. Susie and I followed Joe around the bar and looked down.

I could see steep stairs leading down into the shadows. A draft of cold air wafted up through the trap door. Joe led the way down, and Susie and I gingerly followed him. Gatti remained upstairs.

At the bottom, I opened my bag and took out an Eveready flashlight. As I turned it on, Joe had already found a light switch. A row of evenly spaced overhead lights came on. The lights disappeared into the distance down a long passage way. I switched off my flashlight.

The passage way was well-made. It was about six feet wide and well over six feet high. Frames made from heavy timbers held the tunnel up, very much like mine tunnels that I had seen in the Wabash Valley long ago. However, instead of coal between the timber frames, horizontal boards lined the tunnel on both sides and above. The floor was hard-packed dirt. The overhead lights were fastened in the center of every other overhead timber, and they connected to insulated wires that ran from arch to arch.

Joe gave a brief explanation. "The lights are connected in parallel along the wires, so if one light goes out, the others will remain on." He paused a moment as Susie and I looked closely at the lights. "The tunnels are a maze down here, and they lead to a number of buildings up and down Broadway." He looked closely at me and grinned. "There are side tunnels everywhere."

"It would take forever to explore in detail," I replied. "Let's observe the floor closely as we go down the main tunnel." I gave my Eveready to Susie and took another out of my bag. "Susie, you walk down the left side, I'll take the right."

So, our search began: slowly, carefully, thoroughly. Susie and I led the way; Joe followed. Our flashlight beams illuminated the hard dirt floor, and we walked down the tunnel.

We had walked only about twenty feet before Susie exclaimed: "Look!"

I looked closely at the area illuminated by her flashlight. It was a dried blood spot, and it was still dark red. I moved my light beam around the blood spot. There were several others. "Someone was bleeding down here," I said. "Let's follow the trail."

We found blood spots about every dozen feet or so. We came to a side tunnel on the left. I turned into the side tunnel; Susie and Joe continued down the main tunnel.

After a minute or so, Susie and Joe returned. "Nothing," said Susie.

Not so in my side tunnel; I found more blood spots. "Over here," I called out.

Susie and Joe joined me. "Where does this tunnel lead?" I asked.

"Let's see," replied Joe. "We are about half a block south under Broadway on the west side of the street. This side tunnel leads to a warehouse on the east side. The warehouse is next to a new theater. Several businesses use it for storage."

"Booze?" I asked.

Joe grinned in the dim light. "Oh, yes," he replied. "Upstairs, businesses store furniture, fixtures and so on. But underneath, well, you'll see." He pointed down the side tunnel.

The blood spots continued. I remembered the broken light in the dressing room. "Consistent with a deep scalp wound," I thought to myself. I had seen many such wounds during my rowdy days on the river. "Such wounds bleed profusely," I concluded.

After about a hundred feet, the tunnel ended in a large open space. The floor changed from dirt to concrete. Boxes and barrels were stacked everywhere. Stacks had signs with labels. "All well organized," I muttered.

"Yes, it is," responded Joe, with obvious pride. "We are in the basement of the warehouse. This space stores the booze for clubs all along Broadway and Lawrence."

"Do the cops know about it?" Susie asked.

Joe laughed. "Some do, but they are well-paid." He paused a moment and then added: "We know about the vice squad operation across the street from the Green Mill." He chuckled again. "They are watching the wrong place; the Green Mill is just a retail outlet. This place is the hub of a wholesale operation."

"We are investigating a murder, not vice squads and pay-offs," I replied. "Is there an exit to the building above?" I asked. My expression was strictly business.

Joe looked a little crestfallen; he was proud of his booze operation. However, he took a deep breath and said: "Yes; we have a freight elevator over here." He pointed off to an aisle between stacks of boxes and barrels.

As we walked along the aisle, I scanned the floor for blood and found several drops. The trail ended at a table and a couple of chairs near a steel-cage freight elevator. Several wadded, bloody, torn rags lay on the floor by the table. I looked closely. "Someone made a bandage and dressed a wound here," I stated matter-of-factly. "See the torn rags?"

"Yes," replied Susie. With obvious distaste, she held her flashlight in her right hand, bent over and picked up one of the wadded rags with her left thumb and index finger. Something fell out. The three of us looked. An open switchblade knife lay on the concrete floor.

I thought carefully for a long moment about the forensic techniques that I had learned by watching Eddie. Finally, I said: "We need to take photos with my low light camera, collect blood samples from the trail on the floor, lift fingerprints and put the knife and bloody rags in evidence sacks that are in my black bag. We then should go up the elevator to the building exit."

My train of thought continued for a few moments. Finally, I said: "This is a crime scene for a murder investigation. The police will come." I looked at Joe with a steady gaze.

"Understood," replied Joe.

Joe, Susie and I started to work. We took photos with the camera I had in my bag and collected the evidence with care, including several sets of fingerprints on the table and the back of one of the chairs. When we went up the elevator, we didn't find blood, but we did find a well-used double exit door to an alley behind the warehouse.

The door opened on a loading dock. The alley led away from Broadway toward a residential neighborhood in the distance. "How convenient," I said, and looked at Joe.

"Trucks will come," Joe responded softly.

After about two hour's work, we returned the way we came, through the tunnel. Gatti was waiting for us at the trap door in the Green Mill. Susie and I took my bag full of gear and evidence and flagged down a taxi. Joe and Bruno Gatti were deep in conversation when we left.

We arrived at the penthouse mid-afternoon, and I immediately called Eddie's office to arrange for a pick-up of my bag of goodies.

Silvia had a late lunch waiting for us. After a quick bite, Susie went downstairs to catch a taxi home. We had a successful day; I could hardly wait to tell Hannibal all about it.

Sunday morning, February 10th, 1929.

Hannibal arrived home about five o'clock yesterday. Susie had already left. Sam, one of Eddie's assistants at the lab, had just stopped by for my bag of equipment and evidence. Hannibal looked inside the bag and saw the knife, camera, carefully labeled sheets with cellophane tape fingerprints and labeled glass test tubes with blood samples.

"Very thorough," Hannibal said with a smile. "Eddie will be pleased."

"Thanks," I replied. I admit I felt rather smug. Sam closed up the bag. Silvia escorted him to the front door, and he left. In the meantime, Hannibal and I retired to our respective bedroom suites and dressed in comfortable clothes for the evening. With perfect timing, Silvia called out: "Dinner is on the table!"

After a pleasant dinner, Silvia cleaned up the dining room, finished the dishes and left for the evening. Hannibal and I made ourselves comfortable in our workroom, reviewed our notes, and discussed our findings. Of course, we each had a glass of wine, this time a mellow Italian pinot grigio.

I explained the findings at the Green Mill secret passage and warehouse. Hannibal nodded when I finished and said: "I will call Watts first thing in the morning. I'm sure he will check out the warehouse."

"Yes," I replied. "He won't find much except a table, a couple of chairs and a large empty basement." I returned Hannibal's smile. "My photos will just show the table, chairs, blood spots and freight elevator."

"Good," Hannibal responded. He paused, leafed through his notes for a moment and said: "Watts and I met Attorney Brian Connolly at his office on North State Street. He was very cooperative after Watts threatened him with arrest for being a possible accomplice to the murder of Sammy Washburn."

"I suppose he had an alibi for the night of the murder," I replied.

"Yes," said Hannibal with a grin. "Connolly said he was home in bed. He said over and over that his wife would vouch for his whereabouts." Hannibal paused and chuckled. "Watts played his cards perfectly by expressions of disbelief."

"So, what did you find out?" I asked.

"Well, replied Hannibal, "The music owned jointly by Sammy and Bel produces a substantial revenue stream." He leafed through his notes. "Connolly supplied the details, but the bottom line is that their jointly owned contracts produced fifty thousand dollars this year."

"With Sammy dead, who gets the money?" I asked.

"Bel," replied Hannibal. "Strong motive for murder."

"Anything else?" I asked.

"No, except that according to Connolly, Bel was a tough lady, in addition to being a very talented songwriter and singer."

"Hummm," I mused. "Did Watts find out anything about Bel from the New Orleans Police?"

"Oh, yes," responded Hannibal. "Our Bel has a rap sheet a mile long. Among other things, she was arrested for theft, assault with a deadly weapon and threatening a Bourbon Street club owner." He paused, then added: "However, the charges were dropped because no one would testify."

"So, our gal left New Orleans under a cloud," I said. "She wanted a fresh start in Chicago."

"Evidently," responded Hannibal. "It's a shame that such a talented lady has a mean side."

I thought a moment about my own way up from 'mean streets.' "I could have turned out like Bel," I said to myself. "Was it luck or do I have an angel watching over me?" I fidgeted a little and then put that line of thought firmly in the back of my mind. To Hannibal, I said: "Anything else?"

Hannibal smiled in his knowing way and then said: "Just that Mulvaney and his crew arrested Big Watson. He's cooling his heels in Cook County Jail." He paused and then added: "According to Mulvaney, Watson has a very nasty gash on the back of his head and neck."

I thought a moment and then asked: "Did Mulvaney get a blood sample?"

Hannibal smiled and replied: "Of course. Following standard procedure, Watson's wound was treated and dressed by the medical staff at the jail. They also got his fingerprints and footprints from his shoes."

"I suppose that the blood sample, fingerprints and footprints are now with Eddie at the lab," I responded. I'm sure my face expressed a look of satisfaction.

"Yes," replied Hannibal. He smiled in return.

I thought a few moments and then said: "Then we are waiting on the analysis of all fingerprints, footprints and blood types from Eddie."

"Yes," replied Hannibal. "Eddie will also give us details on the knife that you found in the warehouse." He thought a moment and then added: "We both see where this is going, and we may get proof in Eddie's analysis."

"When will Eddie be finished?" I asked.

"I called him this evening while you were changing clothes. Even with the knife and evidence that you sent earlier today, he said he would be done by Monday afternoon," Hannibal replied.

"Shall we set up a meeting with Watts and Mulvaney on Wednesday the 13th?" I asked. "We will have all day on Tuesday to prepare." I thought a moment and then added: "Let's take Eddie and Susie with us. They should get credit for the work they have done."

"Agreed," Hannibal replied. "I'll call Watts first thing Monday morning." He then looked at his watch and smiled. "It's almost ten o'clock," he said. "Do you want another glass of wine, or shall we call it a day?"

I scooted close to Hannibal and kissed him on the cheek. "Let's call it a day," I replied with a warm smile.

Hannibal kissed me back, smiled and said: "Good idea."

22

THE ART OF CONFESSIONS

Wednesday evening, February 13th, 1929

Hannibal, Eddie, Susie and I had an appointment to brief Watts and Mulvaney at Police Headquarters at ten o 'clock this morning. I brought a tin of good quality coffee, and Susie promised to stop by a bakery for donuts and cannoli. "I think Mulvaney will gain a couple of pounds," I said to Hannibal as we left the apartment. Hannibal laughed.

Both Hannibal and I dressed in classic business attire. My new outfit came from Mandell's. They had just received their latest shipment from Paris.

We arrived in the parking lot behind the police headquarters building at about nine-thirty. Eddie drove up and parked next to us, just as we were getting out of the car. Susie was with him, and they were both well-dressed, smiling and laughing. I looked at Susie, and she gave me a mischievous grin. Where is this new relationship going?

The four of us gathered our gear and walked around the corner to the main entrance. As we entered the building, the desk sergeant saw us. He waived us over and phoned Watts. Within a few minutes, we were as comfortable as possible in the austere but new conference room upstairs. The coffee brewed and gurgled, and Mulvaney had already started on the cannoli.

Hannibal opened his briefcase and got out his set of table top flip charts. He set them up on a little stand at the end of the conference table where everyone could see. Watts, Mulvaney, Eddie, Susie and I took our seats.

In practiced military fashion, Hannibal started his briefing. His flip charts had an outline and key points in large print, and he turned pages as he talked.

"Our objective was to identify the killers of Sammy Washburn," he stated. "Based on findings at the crime scenes and from the autopsy, Sammy was murdered in the dressing room of the Green Mill Club at 4802 West Broadway on February 1st, between midnight and one o 'clock in the morning."

Hannibal looked at Watts and then Mulvaney, and he then added: "The four of us will outline our findings in this briefing. The details are in these reports." He then reached into his briefcase next to his chair, extracted a stack of reports, and placed them on the table in front of Watts.

Both Watts and Mulvaney nodded, leaned back in their chairs and waited. Watts sipped his coffee, and Mulvaney picked up the remaining piece of cannoli from a small plate on the table. I glanced at Susie, and we both smiled.

Hannibal continued: "Although the police vice squad had the club under surveillance for other reasons, our efforts were limited to the murder only." He looked directly at Watts and then Mulvaney.

Watts said: "Understood." Mulvaney nodded, between bites of cannoli. Neither wanted to open the 'can of worms' concerning the other activities associated with the Club.

Hannibal then looked at me and said: "Based on previous visits, Caroline was aware of a trap door behind the bar of the Club."

I smiled, nodded, stood and said: "We know from police surveillance reports that no one entered or left the Club through the Broadway or Lawrence doors between eleven o 'clock on Thursday night and three in the afternoon on Friday." I paused and then added: "Since the murder occurred between midnight and one o'clock on

Friday morning, the killers had to have entered and left the Club another way."

Watts mused for a few moments, then asked: "After you located the trap door, what did you find?"

I looked over at Susie and sat down. Susie nodded, stood and said: "We found stairs leading down to the basement level of the Club. A well-made, lighted tunnel led underneath along Broadway. We found blood spatters on the floor of the tunnel. We followed the trail of blood along the tunnel to the basement of a warehouse about half a block down Broadway."

Susie paused a moment and then added: "We found a knife, bloody rags, fingerprints and glass fragments on and around the table and chairs in the basement of the warehouse, next to a freight elevator. The elevator led us up to an alley exit on the first floor of the warehouse."

"So, the killers had a way in and out of the Club without being seen by the vice squad people in the apartment across the street from the Club," stated Watts. "How convenient." He smiled wryly.

"And your trap door was the only other way in or out?" Mulvaney asked.

"Yes," Susie stated. She smiled and took her seat.

"Good," replied Watts. He thought a moment and then asked: "Who would have known about the trap door and tunnel?"

"Anyone who worked at or who frequented the Club could have known," I replied. "This includes Bel Lee Watson."

Hannibal continued: "Our lab, under the direction of Eddie Valenti, analyzed the evidence from the Club dressing room, the tunnel and the basement of the warehouse. The evidence was compared to our data base of samples taken during interviews." Hannibal paused a moment and then added: "We also have Big Watson's blood, fingerprints and footprints taken when he was booked in Cook County Jail."

Hannibal then looked at Eddie, who stood and continued the briefing.

"We compared the fingerprints, footprints and glass fragments obtained in the dressing room, the blood from the tunnel and the blood, fingerprints and glass fragments from the warehouse to a data base of prints obtained during interviews of potential suspects here at this police station," Eddie stated. "Our data base includes the fingerprints and footprints of Willie Bender, Jimmy Brown, Bo Carol, Essie Harlan and Bel Lee Washburn. We also have the blood of and autopsy report for the victim and the blood, fingerprints and footprints taken from Big Watson at the Cook County Jail, and the glass fragments found in the dressing room and the warehouse."

Eddie paused and then said: "The fingerprints of all six suspects matched fingerprints taken in the dressing room. However, only Bel Washburn and Big Watson left footprints in the talcum powder on the floor of the dressing room."

"Did you find anything in the water closet sink trap or on the washcloth that we found on the water closet floor?" Mulvaney asked.

Just hair and normal refuse in the sink trap and moisture and skin flakes on the wash cloth," replied Eddie. "No incriminating evidence."

"You mentioned blood in the dressing room, tunnel and warehouse," stated Watts. "Did you find matches of blood type from your data base?"

"Yes," replied Eddie. "In addition to the A blood of the victim, we had the blood taken from a wound bandage on the back of Big Watson's head. We obtained the bandage when the Cook County Jail staff cleaned and dressed his wound. His blood type was a match to the blood found on glass fragments and a broken light fixture in the dressing room. We also matched his blood to blood found on the floor of the tunnel leading from the Club to the warehouse basement and on rags and on the table found in the basement of the warehouse. Watson's blood and all evidence samples tested O, or as originally designated in old research, type C."

"Any other evidence that ties the dressing room crime scene to the warehouse?" Watts asked.

"Yes," replied Eddie. "We found fragments of glass from the broken dressing room light fixture in one of the bloody rags on the floor next to the table in the warehouse."

"I see," responded Watts. "Glass fragments remained in the wound until it was dressed at the table in the warehouse."

"Yes," replied Eddie.

"What about the victim's blood?" Mulvaney asked.

"In addition to the type A blood from the victim in the dressing room, we found type A blood on a switchblade knife found wrapped in a rag next to the table in the warehouse basement," replied Eddie. "The stiletto blade of the knife also matched the wounds on the victim's body."

"We have proof of a murder weapon," stated Watts.

"Yes," replied Eddie.

"Any fingerprints on the knife?" Mulvaney asked.

"Only the fingerprints of Bel Lee Watson," responded Eddie. "Bel handled the knife, either during the murder, or in the warehouse or both."

"Did you find any evidence that anyone besides Bell Washburn and Big Watson were present at the table in warehouse basement during the night of the murder?" Watts asked.

"No," replied Eddie. "No fingerprints of any other person were found at the table in the warehouse, not even unknowns."

Silence reigned for a few moments while Watts and Mulvaney digested the information presented by Eddie, who took his seat.

Finally, Watts said: "OK, we have method and opportunity, what about motive?"

"Bel Washburn had motive," Hannibal stated. "We know from the statements of Brian Connolly, her attorney, and others, that Bel wanted a divorce from Sammy. She also wanted, as part of the settlement, exclusive rights to a stream of income from music contracts."

Hannibal paused and then added: "The income stream from the music contracts amounted to over fifty thousand dollars last year alone."

"I see," responded Watts. "With Sammy dead, Bel would have sole rights to the contract revenues." He thought a moment and then asked: "How does Big Watson fit in?"

I remained in my seat, there was no point in standing. I responded by saying: "From the statement of Essie Harlan, we know that Sammy owed Big Watson at least twenty-five thousand dollars in gambling debts. Based on repeated requests for loans from his colleagues, Sammy couldn't pay."

I paused and then added: "It is likely that Bel knew this, and promised Watson that she would pay the debt if he would help shake down Sammy with regard to the divorce."

"Do you have proof that Bel knew Watson and they planned the murder of Sammy Washburn?" Watts asked.

"No," I responded. "But I think I know how to get it."

"How so?" Mulvaney asked, as he eyed the donuts that remained on the table. He had finished the cannoli.

"Bel Washburn and Big Watson have not communicated since Watson was arrested," I began. "We have enough evidence to plausibly place both of them at the crime scene during the murder and at the warehouse table afterwards."

"Agreed," responded Watts. "At a minimum, we can try to get both of them as being accessories to murder." He thought a moment and then asked: "Can we go for first degree murder?"

"Yes," I replied. "Let's interview them again, separately, without allowing them to communicate beforehand." I paused and then added: "We can give each the opportunity to either betray the other by testifying that the other committed the murder, or to cooperate with the other by remaining silent."

Watts nodded slowly, as he thought about my suggestion. Mulvaney had a blank look.

Hannibal saw the expressions of Watts and Mulvaney, and said: "Let's look at the possible outcomes." Both Watts and Mulvaney leaned forward. Mulvaney even forgot to eat his latest donut.

Hannibal continued: "Suppose that both Bel Washburn and Big Watson each say that the other committed the murder. The worst case for the one that said the other committed the murder would be that they would be convicted of being an accessory and the other would be convicted of murder."

I then said: "If Bel betrays Big Watson but Watson remains silent, Bel could still hope that she may not be convicted of anything and Watson will be convicted of murder." I paused and then added: "Our evidence is circumstantial; we do not have independent witnesses. However unlikely, a good defense attorney could argue that the knife was stolen from Bel and the footprints in the dressing room were made before the murder when she was in the Club."

"I understand," responded Watts. "Reasonable doubt."

Hannibal then said: "The reverse is also true. If Big Watson betrays Bel, but Bel remains silent, Big Watson could still hope that he would not be convicted of anything and Bel will be convicted of murder." Hannibal then added: "A defense attorney could argue that the knife had Bel's fingerprints, the footprints in the dressing room belonged to someone else with the same sized shoes and he had injured his head elsewhere. Also, his blood type is O, which is quite common."

Watts thought a moment and then said: "I see. However, if both Bel Washburn and Big Watson remain silent, the best that we could hope for is that both will be convicted of being an accessory."

"Yes," Hannibal replied. "However, from Bel's and Watson's points of view, it is in their best interest to betray the other, since by betrayal, each could hope to get off Scott-free."

Susie then said: "Once Bel Washburn and Big Watson betray the other, I suggest that you ask questions that gets details on their arrangement with regard to the money."

I looked at Susie, smiled and nodded in approval. "Smart girl, Susie," I thought to myself. Susie just beamed.

The six of us spent the next hour planning our next interviews. We agreed to bring Bel Lee Washburn and Big Watson separately to the police station conference room on Thursday morning, February 14th. Watts said he had enough evidence to get an arrest warrant for Bel. Big Watson, of course, was already in jail.

Thursday evening, February 14th, 1929

Our day began with our planned interviews and ended with the worst murder in Chicago history.

On Thursday morning, Hannibal and I arrived at Police Headquarters a few minutes before nine. The desk sergeant made a call, and we were escorted to the conference room by Mulvaney. Soon Watts arrived, and the four of us took seats on one side of the table. Two empty chairs waited for occupants on the other side of the table.

By nine on the dot, Big Watson arrived in the conference room. He was a little disheveled; his jail cell was not designed for comfort. Watson didn't know enough to ask for a public defender attorney, but Watts, to his credit, provided one. Watson and the attorney sat down in the chairs waiting for them. Watts and Mulvaney did the interview; Hannibal and I listened.

The result was as predicted. Watson snitched on Bel; saying that she wielded the knife and killed Sammy Washburn. In doing so, he revealed enough about his involvement to convict him as an accessory. All the attorney could do was advise his client to be silent, but Watts skillfully outmaneuvered the attorney's advice. Good job!

Following Susie's suggestion, Watts and Mulvaney got Watson to reveal the financial arrangement between himself and Bel. As expected,

Bel told him that she would pay off Sammy's gambling debt, with interest, from the proceeds of next year's music royalties.

Watts had Irene take notes, and she had a typed statement ready within fifteen minutes. In the meantime, Watson cooled his heels in a solitary cell. Less than twenty minutes later, back in the conference room, in the presence of his public defender attorney, he signed his statement.

By nine forty-five, we were ready for Bel in the conference room. Watts and Mulvaney were armed with Watson's signed statement plus all of the evidence. Bel came in the room, along with Brian Connolly. Both took their seats.

Initially, Bel was full of bluster, but her attitude quickly changed to outright fear. Of course, Connolly realized what was going on during the interview. However, in light of Watson's statement, the evidence and his own peripheral involvement, there was little he could do, except plan a plea bargain.

In less than thirty minutes, Bel folded and tried to put the blame for the murder on Watson. Irene took notes. Shortly after ten-thirty, Watts had a signed statement from Bel that blamed Watson for the murder. Like Watson, her statement revealed much about her own actions and fit nicely with the evidence.

Combined with the evidence and the two statements, Watts had enough to arrest Bel Washburn for first degree murder and Big Watson as an accessory. Both were hauled off to Cook County Jail to await trial, without the likelihood of bail. Good day's work!

As Hannibal and I prepared to leave at about ten forty-five, we heard a commotion in the hallway. A uniformed cop came in the conference room and addressed Watts. "We have another murder," he said. "This one is big time. Our guys found six dead men and one severely wounded man at a garage at 2122 North Clark Street near Lincoln Park. According to the cops at the scene, the garage is a bloody mess." The cop paused and then added: "The Chief wants you on the investigation team."

Without another word, Watts rushed out the conference room door. Mulvaney was left to escort Hannibal and me to the elevator. "Great job," Mulvaney said as we three walked down the hall to the elevator. "We'll be in contact."

Mulvaney smiled as we reached the elevator. "In addition to your lab's usual contract fee with the department, I'm sure you will be well-paid through Mel Johnson."

I noted Mulvaney's knowing smile. "Mulvaney knows perfectly well who will actually pay our fee," I thought to myself. I smiled in return. Nothing further would be said. Hannibal and I rode the elevator down and left the building.

23

GHOSTS FROM THE PAST

Friday Evening, February 15, 1929

Busy day yesterday, so I slept late. I got out of bed about nine o 'clock, cleaned up in the bathroom and combed my hair. I then put my new, warm, cream-colored satin robe with a soft, white mink trim over my lounging pajamas, added my matching mink-lined slippers and toddled into the dining room. Breakfast, including a pot of coffee, was already on the table. I could hear Silvia in the kitchen.

Hannibal was seated at the table. He looked up, smiled and sipped his coffee as I entered the room. A folded newspaper rested on the table in front of my chair. "I think you should read the headline and the article on the front page," said Hannibal. His smile changed to a thoughtful expression. He then poured me a cup of coffee.

"Thanks," I replied as I sat down. I sipped my coffee first, then unfolded the newspaper. The headline jumped out at me with startling clarity.

SEVEN KILLED IN GANGLAND MASSACRE

Yesterday, Saint Valentine's Day, Chicago gangsters graduated from murder to massacre. Remnants of the O'Banion North Side Gang were assassinated by volleys of machine gun and shotgun fire at a garage on Clark Street at about 10:30 yesterday morning. After a few seconds of gunfire, six men were dead and a seventh lay dying. The reputed main target of the shooting was George "Bugs"

Moran, who for some unknown reason, was not present at the garage. According to neighborhood witnesses, some of the slayers wore police uniforms, and sirens cleared the path for their escape after the shooting. The victims were: Albert Kachellek alias James Clark, Frank Gusenberg, Peter "Greasy" Gusenberg, Adam Heyer alias Frank Schneider, Alfred Weinshank, Reinhardt Schwimmer and John May. Except for May, an unfortunate mechanic, all were members or associates of the North Side Gang. According to police reports, Frank Gusenberg was still alive when the real Chicago police arrived at the scene. When the police asked who did it, he replied: "No one shot me." He died three hours later in the hospital. This reporter has information that places the blame for the "Saint Valentine's Day Massacre" on associates of Al Capone, including the sinister Jack McGurn, a suspected killer in a number of gangland murders. Interviewed later by this reporter, a shaken Moran said: "Only Capone kills like that." However, Capone himself has a perfect alibi; he was at his vacation home in Florida.

After reading the article twice, I put the newspaper down. I looked long at Hannibal. Finally, I said: "I think public opinion will demand action." I paused and then added: "The police will crack down."

"Agreed," replied Hannibal. "I also think we need to be careful. Moran and the North Side Gang will go after Capone and his people with all they have left."

"Yes," I mused. We should keep our distance for a while." I thought a moment and then added: "What if Watts and Mulvaney ask for our help?"

Hannibal was quiet for several minutes. Finally, he said: "If they ask, we should give it." He paused a moment and then added: "I also think it's time that our lab and expertise transitioned to the police department."

"You mean get out of the private detective business?" I asked.

"Not necessarily," replied Hannibal. "However, it's time for the police to have their own forensic capabilities on a scale that we, as a private enterprise, cannot match."

"I see," I responded. "We take on only a few cases for which we are well-paid. There are many murders and other major crimes that we do not address."

Hannibal nodded, and said: "For the good of the city." He then smiled and added: "Also, we are in a dangerous business, and we have been extremely lucky so far."

Hannibal was right, of course. I nodded, sat back in my chair and sipped my coffee.

"I'll talk with our staff at the lab, and see what we might do," Hannibal continued. "In the meantime, please be careful, and do not go out alone."

"OK," I responded. "I'll also tell Susie." I then finished my coffee. Breakfast was a quiet affair; Hannibal and I had a lot to think about.

Friday evening, March 1, 1929

Nearly two weeks have passed since the Saint Valentine's Day massacre, and I'm lucky to be alive. On Saturday, February 16, I was kidnapped. My subsequent adventures, as I choose to call them, were the worst of my life. Writing the following narrative will take some time, but the effort may help assuage my troubled mind.

Saturday, February 16th, began on a pleasant note. The night before, I had called Susie, and we planned a shopping expedition in the Loop. We decided to visit all the big stores, including Marshall Fields, Mandell's and Carson Pirie Scott. Both Susie and I had a list of designer clothes that we wanted to add to our wardrobes. Since we would be together in a high-end area of town with lots of other shoppers, we would be safe enough. It would be fun!

Susie arrived at the penthouse at about nine o 'clock in the morning. Hannibal had already left for the lab; he planned to discuss the future with his department heads. Before he left, he again told me to be careful. "I will," I promised.

After a cup of coffee and the finalization of our respective shopping lists, I called Marshall Fields and talked to the head of ladies' fashions. The young lady was very nice, I had shopped with her many times. She said she would pick out several items that she was sure Susie and I would just love.

I then called Harris downstairs to get a taxi. By ten o' clock, we were ready to go. Silvia saw us off, and Harris opened the building and taxi doors as Susie and I exited the building. We were warmly and fashionably dressed in fur coats, hats, gloves and high-topped boots. "To Marshall Fields, my friend!" I said to the driver. He laughed and replied: "Of course!"

As the taxi drove away, Susie said: "Oh! Someone is getting flowers." She pointed to a paneled delivery truck parked not far from the entrance to my building.

I glanced as we passed; the sign on the side of the truck read 'Schofields Flowers, 738 North State Street, Chicago.' "I've heard that name before," I thought to myself. To Susie, I replied in an offhand manner: "Yes, nice." My thoughts immediately returned to our shopping trip.

We arrived at 111 North State Street and the main entrance to the Marshall Fields' South building at about eleven, as shown on the wrought iron clock on the corner of State and Washington. I looked forward to seeing the Tiffany glass in the central court inside; the place was so beautiful. Susie and I entered the building, and we laughed for the pure joy of shopping.

We found the ladies' lounge and my favorite sales lady. She was bubbly and full of charm. She had tea and scones on a tray for us. After about thirty minutes, we adjourned to the top-floor dressing rooms. Sales assistants were ready, and Susie and I prepared to try on the latest fashions.

Susie wanted new shoes, boots, gloves, scarves and other accessories. "I will go look at shoes and boots first, then you can help me pick out some cashmere scarves to go with my coat," said Susie. I'll meet you at the dressing rooms in thirty minutes."

"Sounds like a plan," I replied. After dresses, I need new scarves too." I laughed and added: "This is so much fun!"

Susie swept off toward the shoes and boots, followed by an enthusiastic sales assistant.

My interest was focused on the beautiful outfits being carried by another overburdened sales assistant. As I followed her toward a dressing room, I noticed a nicely-attired woman standing near the exit door to the hallway stairwell a short distance away. "Nice dress," I thought to myself. The woman turned away. I didn't pay much attention, and I didn't see her face. My sales assistant opened my dressing room door and left. I was alone.

All was quiet, except for the click-click of a door opening down the hallway. I didn't think any more about it; I had wonderful clothes to try on. Soon I had stripped to my slip, undergarments and stockings. I was totally vulnerable.

Suddenly, the dressing room door flew open, and I was shoved face down to the floor. As I went down, I recognized the dress of the woman who stood near the exit door earlier, but again, I didn't see her face. Muffled voices indicated at least two men. I tried to scream, but I was pinned to the floor. A rough hand with a cloth quickly covered my face. I smelled a pungent, strong odor. I struggled for a moment, but the odor was stifling. I passed out.

Gradually, I regained consciousness. My head was pounding. I was nauseous and totally in the dark. I tried to struggle, but my hands and feet were tied. My legs were bent sharply back at the knees; I was trussed up and lying on my side. I tried to scream, but a gag covered my nose and filled my mouth.

I took several deep breaths through the gag, and my head cleared a little. I felt around with my hands and body; I was in some sort of sack. "Burlap," I thought to myself. I heard a truck engine and felt the hum of wheels over pavement. "I'm in a sack in the back of a truck," I concluded.

I became conscious of pain. My wrists and ankles hurt from the bindings. My knees and elbows burned; they were raw. "OK, Caroline," I thought to myself. "You have been kidnapped." My train of thought continued; my mind was working again. "Wait, try to regain strength, and do not vomit."

I heard muffled voices and snippets of conversation. "A driver and at least two passengers up front," I concluded. "One is a woman, two are men." The voices continued. The woman's voice sounded strangely familiar: "We need to change to the big truck" and "Highway 41 south," and then "At least five hours."

"The woman is giving driving directions," I concluded: "What is five hours south on Highway 41?" My thoughts raced. "Oh, good heavens; unless we turn, we are headed south to the Wabash Valley."

I thought about Susie. As far as I could tell, I was alone in the back of the truck. "Susie was not taken; she either remained safe in the store, or, and my mind refused to follow the thought to a conclusion. "I believe Susie is OK, and she would have sounded the alarm."

Just when I thought I couldn't stand the pain in my wrists and ankles any longer, the truck turned off the pavement and onto gravel. After about a minute, the truck stopped. I heard the woman's voice say: "Untie her feet and get her out."

The back doors of the truck opened. Rough hands pulled the burlap bag off. I saw blinding lights from a vehicle; it was nighttime. A man untied my ankles. The pain was excruciating, as my legs unbent and straightened. I clenched my teeth and forced myself not to moan. The gag was removed and I took in deep breaths. The air was cold, and I shivered uncontrollably. I looked down. I was still in my slip, stockings and undergarments.

I rolled to a sitting position and squinted my eyes in the blinding light. Several men moved about. I couldn't see the woman, but I heard her voice again. "Untie her hands and feet and give her these." A man untied my hands. I gently massaged my raw wrists and looked up. A wad of clothing struck me in the face.

I looked down at my lap. I saw men's jeans, a flannel shirt, a coat and heavy cotton socks. "Put them on, a man's voice growled." I did, and I was grateful for the warmth. Gradually, with my movements and the clothes, my body warmed. The shivering stopped. My clothes were a little big, but they were functional. "No shoes," I muttered. Still, the socks warmed my feet.

"Get her in the big truck," said the woman's voice. Two men pulled me from the panel truck and half-carried me around the blinding lights to the back of a large truck. I saw duel rear wheels. Over my shoulder, I saw the side of the small panel truck that I had just left. The sign on the side read: 'Schofields Flowers, 738 North State Street, Chicago.'

I climbed and was half-lifted into the back of the big truck. I fell onto a pile of cloth that looked like the padding used by furniture movers. Cases of bottles were stacked all around. I squinted and recognized the bottles. "This truck carries Canadian whiskey," I concluded.

I remembered the flower truck and searched my memory. "Of course!" I muttered. "Schofield's Flower Shop was the headquarters of the North Side Gang!"

One of the men got up in the truck, leaned over me and said: "Stay put and don't cause trouble, or we'll tie you up again." His breath smelled of whiskey, but I couldn't see his face. I crouched down and tried to make myself small. The man stepped out of the truck and shut the door. I heard the lock click. My prison was totally black inside.

The ride seemed endless. We stopped a couple of times for short breaks at gas stations. I heard station attendants and smelled gasoline. No one responded to my calls for help.

The ride continued. My hands and feet grew numb from the cold, in spite of the clothing. The glass bottles in the cases made a tinkling sound, and the hum of the wheels droned. The truck engine chattered, sometimes loud as gears were shifted but mostly low as the truck sped down the paved road. "Highway 41," I thought to myself. I wrapped myself in one of the pads and tried to get warm.

After my body warmed sufficiently, I decided to explore my prison. On my hands and knees, I moved around. My space was roughly ten feet by three feet, and it was surrounded by cases of tinkling bottles. I felt around through the pads on the floor.

I found some cord, about four feet long. I used it to make a belt to hold up my too-large jeans; it worked tolerably well. I rolled up my pant legs and shirtsleeves. My clothing was now functional, and I felt better. I decided to explore again.

I found something made of leather and some rags under one of the pads. I felt around on the leather. It was a workman's apron, like carpenters use to hold tools. "How can I use this?"

After a moment, I decided to strip off my coat, shirt and jeans and put the apron on underneath. Soon I had my shirt, jeans and coat back on. "For now, the leather will provide extra warmth," I thought. "Later, I might be able to use it for something else." I folded the rags and put them in the pockets of my jeans.

Suddenly the truck hit a pothole in the road. I bounced up and crashed down. I heard the sound of breaking glass toward the front of the truck. Cases of whiskey bottles shifted all around me. I curled in a ball for a moment, expecting a case of booze to fall on me. Fortunately, none did. The truck slowed for a while, and my prison stabilized. "Whew, that was close," I muttered.

I felt a liquid on the floor as it trickled to the pad underneath me. I put my hand down, next to the pad, and touched the liquid. I put my wet finger to my mouth. "Whiskey," I realized. "One or more bottles have broken."

Very slowly, I felt the floor and followed the trickle of whiskey with my hand. I crawled on my hands and knees slowly toward the front of the truck. Just at the edge of the row of cases that formed one of the boundaries of my little prison, I touched the broken neck of a whiskey bottle.

I picked it up carefully. "Don't cut yourself, Caroline," I muttered. I thought a moment. "This might come in handy." I crawled back to my pads with the neck of the whiskey bottle in my hand.

"Let's see," my thoughts continued. "If they tie me up again, my hands will be behind me." I reached in my pocket, pulled out one of the rags and wrapped the glass in the rag. I then took off my coat and shirt and shifted the leather apron around so that one of its tool pockets rested against my waist in back. I then carefully stuffed the rag with the glass inside the tool pocket.

Finally, I tested my reach as if my hands were tied behind me to make sure I could get to the rag with its piece of broken glass. After a few adjustments, I muttered: "Good." I then put my shirt and coat back on.

I crawled around and continued to explore but didn't find anything else. "Get some rest, Caroline," I admonished myself. "You'll need your strength later."

I arranged a couple of the pads underneath for a mattress and covered myself with the remaining two. Soon I was relatively warm again. My mouth was dry, my throat was raw and I was extremely thirsty. I also had to urinate. I forced myself not to think about it. I dozed and had fitful dreams. The truck droned on and on.

I woke with a start; the truck had turned off the paved road and onto gravel. Hours seemed to have passed. "Right turn," I decided.

The truck bumped, bounced and swayed. The cases around me shifted, but did not fall. The driver shifted to a lower gear. Soon we were creeping along. I tried counting to estimate the time but lost my train of thought after about two thousand. "About twenty-five or thirty minutes," I estimated.

I did a quick mental calculation. "At ten miles per hour, we are about four or five miles off the pavement," I concluded. In less than a minute, the truck made another turn, this time to the left.

The truck slowed and then stopped. We had arrived, but where?

The back door to the truck opened. Dim light illuminated the scene. I looked out and around. The light came from an open door and two windows set in a small, rough-built building. "This place looks familiar," I thought to myself. A car was parked next to the building.

The woman's voice came from the side of the truck. I couldn't see her. "Take her inside and tie her to a chair," her voice said. "No mistakes. I'll interrogate her about Capone later. We need to know."

Two men climbed into the truck, grabbed my arms and roughly escorted me off the truck. "Water," I said hoarsely. "I also need to urinate." I looked over at the man on my right.

His face had a hard look, but it softened a little. "OK," the man replied. "Max, take her to the outhouse over there. I'll get her some water."

Soon I finished, and Max escorted me back to the doorway of the small building. The man who spoke earlier handed me a tin cup with cold well water. It tasted wonderful. I gulped eagerly, then sipped for a few moments. My raw throat felt much better. "Thank you," I said. The man grunted, took my empty cup and said: "Inside."

Max came up behind me and gave me a shove toward the door. I spun around and hit him with my right fist full in the face.

Max staggered back. He put his hand up to a bloody nose. He then came toward me with fists clenched and fire in his eyes. I leaned forward, hands up. I balanced on the balls of my feet, ready to strike again.

Strong arms grabbed me from behind and pinned my arms back. "Max, that's enough!" It was the woman's voice, and it came from behind me. "Sam, get her inside."

The man who held my arms laughed. "Still full of fight," he said. "OK, young lady, inside." He pushed me forward, arms still pinned. I struggled, but to no avail.

"So, his name is Sam," I thought to myself. "Max, Sam and an unknown woman." I continued to think about the woman as I was forced down into a hard, wooden chair. "I know that voice," I thought to myself.

Soon I was tied to the chair with what looked like quarter-inch hemp cord. I still had on my coat, shirt, jeans and socks. My leather apron was still on underneath. I wiggled my hands a little. The cord was not too tight, and my hands were not numb like in the flower truck. "OK, Caroline, bide your time and wait for an opportunity."

I looked around. The place was lighted by two kerosene lamps, one on a table at the front of the room and another on a stand at the back. Suddenly, it dawned on me that this was the same ramshackle old building where Hannibal, Frank Gardner and I rescued my girls Kitty and Kathy in July 1927. Max had been one of the men that Hannibal and Frank had taken down during the rescue. I was tied to a chair just like Kitty and Kathy! Why?

I heard the woman's voice again, outside. I caught bits of conversation. "Moran wants to know," she said. "This Case woman can tell us."

A third, unknown male voice replied: "OK, Chicago's too hot. We're moving our base of operations south." There was a pause, and then: "You take charge. Find out what you can, and report to me."

The voices faded, the man and woman moved away. I heard a car engine start, and the car drove off. I heard two male voices. "Sam and Max," I concluded. "The third man left in the car." I thought a moment. "Did the woman leave in the car?" I listened carefully and heard her voice in the distance. "She's still here," I concluded. "And I know that voice." But the desired memory eluded me.

Max and Sam came in the front door, sat at the table, ate sandwiches and drank coffee from a thermos. The two men kept watch, and I could do nothing. They did build a fire in a pot-bellied stove in the corner of the room, and the warmth helped. "Bide your time, Caroline." I took several deep breaths and waited.

24

MEET THE BLACK WIDOW

After an hour or so of being tied to the chair, I watched through the windows as the sun came up. Gray light illuminated the room, and I stirred a little to relieve my aching arms and legs. My mind was alert, and I did a quick summary of the passage of time.

"Susie and I were in Marshall Fields on Saturday morning, February 16," I thought. My next memory was in the flower truck. When they put me in the big truck, night had fallen. The truck drove for hours in the dark, and it was still dark when we arrived at this spot. I counted forward and summarized: "Today must be Sunday morning, the 17th."

I looked over at the table. Max was asleep in his chair, but Sam was awake. He glanced at me and smiled a little. "Sam has a soft spot," I concluded. "That could be useful."

Sam got up, stoked the fire in the stove and added some coal from a bucket. Max stirred and woke up. "What time is it?" he asked.

Sam pulled out a pocket watch. "About eight," he replied. "The boss will be here soon." He looked at me closely and said: "Do you need to go to the privy?"

"Yes," I replied. I watched Sam's face carefully.

"Max, untie her feet, get her out of the chair, but keep her hands tied," Sam said. "Then take her to the outhouse." He chuckled a little and added: "If you give her a chance, she's liable to punch you in the nose again." Max mumbled something inaudible.

250

Max complied, and we went outside. The dawn breeze was chilling, but the sky was clear. I looked around. My feet grew cold on the frozen ground; I still only had socks, no shoes. I walked slowly toward the outhouse, with Max right behind me.

I glanced around. Several other buildings surrounded the building where I was being held. Smoke came from chimneys on two of the other buildings. Another building looked like a garage. The doors were open, and I could see workbenches and tools. A car was parked nearby. "New buildings; they were not here two years ago," I thought to myself. "There are stoves inside two of them and probably more people."

I gave a sweeping glance beyond the buildings. A nearby lot contained a couple of tractors, an old truck and other farm equipment. The lot had an overgrown fencerow and trees along the far side.

In the near distance, I saw a familiar barn. Further out, the land sloped down to water-covered fields. "Winter flood water," I thought to myself. "Farm country, probably near a river."

While in the outhouse, I searched my memory. Images crystalized. "We are in the Wabash Valley, east of Clinton across the river, and just northwest of Lyford. I know this place."

When I left the outhouse, I glanced up to the sun to get my bearings and then down to the surrounding landscape.

"The road to the highway goes east, and it is above water along a ridge," I thought to myself. "These buildings are on a connecting ridge that runs north and south, parallel to the Wabash." My glance around confirmed my memories. "It's February, and the bottom land will be flooded on either side of the north-south ridge."

"Move," said Max, "Back to our building." Max was watchful, and I had no chance to escape. We soon entered the building. I was glad for the warmth of the stove; my feet were numb.

"Want some food?" Sam asked as we entered the building.

"Yes, please," I responded. Sam untied my hands gently and gave me half a fried egg sandwich. Between bites, he let me take sips of coffee. I wolfed everything down; I was ravenous.

After a few minutes of relative freedom, Sam tied me to the chair again. The bindings weren't tight, and I could wiggle my hands. "Good," I thought.

A short time passed, and I heard noises outside. Sam got up and opened the door. A woman stepped inside and looked at me.

My mouth dropped open. The woman was Anna Nuardi, the snooty wife of Fat Benny, the mayor of Clinton. "A ghost from my days in the Valley," I thought to myself. "This can't be good." I had finally put the voice of the woman I heard in the background over the past night and previous day to a face and person.

"I see that you recognize me," said Anna. Her lips smiled, but not her eyes. "You were a real pain to our operations while you lived in Clinton." She paused, chuckled a little and added: "My colleagues in Chicago told me that you have continued your habits."

My mind raced. The last time I saw Anna Nuardi was at Scottie's speakeasy in Clinton when Hannibal, Eddie, Blind Johnny and I solved Scottie's murder. She had reacted coolly when Carlo, the murderer, was killed on the spot and Louie, his accomplice, was taken into custody by the police.

"That was just over a year ago, but it seems like another world," I thought to myself. Hannibal, Eddie, Susie and I moved to Chicago shortly afterwards.

"We have a number of items to discuss," said Anna in a sinister voice. "Capone hit us hard on Valentine's Day, and Mr. Moran needs answers."

She paused and looked at me with steely eyes. "We know you worked with both the Chicago police and with Capone's people. I want to know everything about Capone's operation: names of people and speakeasies, locations of storage warehouses and of course, the money flow."

I remained silent. However, I returned Anna's look with a steady gaze.

Anna smiled again and said: "You will change your attitude when I show you what I have in mind." She turned to Max and said: "Go get my trunk, it's in my quarters in the other building."

Without a word, Max got up and went out the door. I glanced at Sam, who took a deep breath and exhaled slowly.

Max soon returned with a large black, old fashioned steamer trunk; the kind travelers used. "Set it by the table," said Anna. "Then go get three spare car batteries from the garage." Max left again, but soon returned. He had a wooden crate. I recognized three six-volt car batteries and some cables. Max had a scared look, so did Sam.

"Let me show you my equipment," said Anna. "I'm quite proud of it, actually." She paused a moment and then added: "Also, I want you to see what's coming."

She turned to Sam and said: "Drag that bench over near Miss Case's chair, where she can see it," she ordered curtly. Sam complied; the bench was about six feet long and perhaps eighteen inches wide. "Now set the batteries on the bench." Soon it was done.

Anna began to lay out items from her trunk onto the bench next to the batteries. First, she laid out a two-foot length of rubber hose, then a long thin knife, a pack of Camel cigarettes and a Ronson cigarette lighter. "These are crude instruments," Anna said, as if she were giving a lecture. "I only use them as a last resort."

She then took a set of electrical cables out of the crate. She connected the three batteries together with the cables. "Negative to positive, negative to positive," she continued to lecture. "We now have three six-volt batteries in series."

Anna took a small black box out of her case. The box had a knob on top. "This box has a rheostat and other devices," she continued in a measured, professorial manner. "It allows me to vary voltage and current from the batteries."

She turned and faced me with a twinkle in her eyes. "I generally begin with very low current, about half a milliamp," She pointed to the knob. "And I can vary the voltage from about ten thousand to nearly eighteen thousand volts."

I began to see where this was going. "Not good," I thought to myself. Toward Anna, I did my best to keep my composure. I could tell my steady gaze had an effect; Anna paused a moment and her eyes lost their twinkle. However, she quickly recovered and continued her lecture.

"Now I will connect the input side of the rheostat to the negative side of the last battery and the output side to this electrode," she continued. She held up a device with a short wooden handle and what looked like a brass piece at the end. A small metal tab connected to the brass near the wooden handle. The other end of the brass was smooth, round and about half an inch in diameter. Anna connected a cable leading from the output side of the rheostat to the metal tab.

She took out another identical electrode from her case. "This electrode connects to the positive side of the first battery," she continued. Soon the cables were connected.

Anna held an electrode in each hand and turned to face me. "You can guess where I will place these to complete the circuit, she said with a sinister, mocking smile. "Trust me, the process will be very painful."

I gulped a little, I couldn't help it. Anna continued her smile and her eyes twinkled again.

She looked at me intently.

Like in the earlier case with Bel, I was reminded of a black widow spider. However, in this case, the spider was extremely dangerous, and I was her prey.

Anna then said: "You see, I am a specialist. I'm called in for tough people just like you." Her voice had a mocking tone.

"Think overnight what you might want to tell me, and I promise that I will be relatively gentle." She paused and then added: "Of course, if I don't believe you, I may get angry." She reached over and turned the knob on the rheostat back and forth. "You wouldn't want that to happen."

Anna then turned to Sam and Max, who were standing nearby with their mouths open. "Please give Miss Case food and water," she ordered. "I want her to be fully alert when we begin first thing in the morning."

Both Sam and Max nodded. Anna placed the electrodes on the bench, turned, and without another word, walked to the door and then exited the building. The door closed behind her. The room was quiet as a tomb.

Finally, Sam said: "Max, go to the kitchen in the next building over and get some food." He paused, looked around and added: "It's cold in here; I will build up the fire."

Max left and Sam built up the fire in the stove. Max soon returned with a tin plate filled with sandwiches and a new thermos.

Sam looked at me with a steady gaze and then said: "If I untie you so you can eat, will you promise not to cause trouble?"

I thought to myself for a moment. "I can't get away, not with two of them here." To Sam, I replied: "I promise."

Sam untied me. As he finished untying my hands, he said quietly: "If I were you, I would tell Widow Nuardi everything."

I thought a moment, and then asked: "What happened to Fat Benny?"

"He died under mysterious circumstances last fall," replied Sam. "Again, tell the Widow everything she wants to hear." He shuddered a little and added: "Don't mess with her."

I got up slowly from my chair as the last cords were removed from my wrists. I then walked unsteadily over to the table. Sam and Max let me sit down. I then proceeded to eat and drink. When I finally finished eating, I asked: "May I go to the privy again?"

"Yes," replied Sam. He looked at Max, who was standing by the stove. "Take her," he said.

Max complied. While I was outside, I took another look around to verify my bearings obtained during my previous trip to the outhouse.

After we returned, Sam tied me to the chair again. Hours passed. Sam and Max talked quietly and made occasional trips outside, one at a time. I was never left alone.

As evening came, Sam broke a long silence, looked at Max and said: "Do you want to play cards? It's still early."

I looked out the window. Light was waning in the sky; it was getting dark.

"Sure," replied Max. I will go get a deck, and I'll see if I can find a bottle." He got up, walked to the door and exited the building. He soon returned.

As he entered and closed the door, he held up both hands. He had a deck of cards in one hand and a bottle in the other. "Look what I found," he said with a big grin.

"Good deal," replied Sam. "Let's play."

The game and drinking began. I dozed in my chair for a while, I hadn't slept since I was in the truck. Hours must have passed.

I woke up with a start. The sky outside the window was black. One kerosene lamp gleamed on the table between Sam and Max. Cards lay scattered on the table. An empty bottle lay on the floor, and it rolled slowly. I realized that the bottle had fallen from the table. "The thump must have awakened me," I thought to myself.

I looked closely at Sam and Max. Both were in their chairs. Sam had leaned back and stretched out his legs. He snored softly. Max lay forward with his head on the table, also sound asleep.

"OK, Caroline, I thought to myself. "It's now or never."

25

ESCAPE AND EVASION

"Think this through," I thought to myself. Cut the cords, gather supplies and slip out the back door." My train of thought continued: "It's probably after midnight, and I will have about six hours before dawn on Monday morning."

Images of the surrounding area flashed through my mind. "The highway is too far, and these gangsters would expect me to go that way. If they awake soon, they would likely catch me before I got there." My thoughts continued: "It's winter, and this ridge is surrounded by flood water, except for the road to the highway."

I searched memories of my youth in Clinton. "This narrow ridge has an inverted L-shape. It runs about eight miles north to south and then east for about five miles to the highway. This place is at the northern end, at the angle in the L. The dirt road follows the base of the L east to the highway."

My mind raced. "I know this ridge. My parents, sister and I picnicked near the south end when I was a little girl." More images flashed in my mind. "Happier days," I reflected. I put the happy memories at the back of my consciousness. "No time for nostalgia," I told myself firmly.

I then remembered the old barn along the dirt road back to the highway. "Hannibal, Frank Gardner and I used it as a base of operations during our rescue of Kitty and Kathy in July 1927. I can make a false trail along the dirt road toward the highway, double back and hide in the hayloft of the barn."

My thoughts continued: "I'll stay in the barn until tomorrow night, then backtrack to this place and head south." I continued with a risk assessment. "Hopefully, these gangsters will not search the barn thoroughly, but they will undoubtedly post someone on the dirt road near the highway. My plan is risky, but I don't have many options."

"OK, Caroline, you have a plan. Time to get out of this place." I wiggled my hands and maneuvered until I found the neck of the broken bottle in the leather apron at my back. Sam stirred in his sleep and snored loudly for a moment. I froze for a full minute. "Quietly, Caroline, don't drop the bottle neck!"

It took a full ten minutes to cut the hemp cords that bound my wrists. I then slipped the bottle neck back in the apron pocket, bent over and untied my ankles. "Might be able to use the cord later," I thought to myself, as I wadded it up and shoved it in a pocket of my jeans.

The kerosene lamp on the table provided a dim light, so I scanned the bench in front of my chair. Black Widow Anna's toys were still there. "Knife, lighter and cigarettes," I observed. "I'll take them, including the cigarettes; they can be used for tinder." I couldn't think of any use for the piece of rubber hose. "Leave it," I concluded.

I got up from my chair slowly, carefully and without a sound. My legs hurt, and my head spun around. "Don't fall, Caroline," I told myself. After a full minute, my head stopped spinning.

I then picked up the knife, lighter and cigarettes from the bench, slipped the knife through my makeshift belt and stuffed the cigarettes and lighter in my coat pockets. After one last look at Sam and Max, I turned, padded soundlessly to the back door, opened it slowly and stepped out into the cold night air. I closed the door carefully. Freedom!

The ground was damp but lightly frozen on top. "I will leave tracks in the loose dirt, I concluded. My feet, still only in socks, instantly felt the cold. "Ignore it, Caroline, you can improvise footwear later."

I padded around the side of the building toward the dirt road, making sure I left tracks. Once on the road, I walked in one of the pair of vehicle tracks at a fast pace. A pale half-moon peeked through the clouds. I could see the barn about a quarter of a mile away, on the right side of the road.

About ten minutes passed until I reached the barn. I kept going along the road, leaving a trail. I walked another quarter mile, and my feet were numb. I stopped, took some rags out of my pocket, took my socks off, and wrapped each foot in a rag. I then put my socks back on. Feeling returned to my feet. "Better," I muttered. "Now it's time to double back."

I walked a few more paces, leaving a distinct trail in the dirt along the vehicle track. I then angled my steps to the center of the road and stepped off the track onto the weeds between the two tracks. "The gangsters will think that I continued walking on the weeds in the middle of the road, in spite of no footprints," I surmised. "At least I hope so."

I stopped, turned and jumped across the vehicle track on the right into tall weeds. I then started walking back toward the barn, taking care to avoid leaving a trail. Finally, I made it back to the barn and peered in the open door. "No change since my last visit," I muttered. "Hay in the loft, scattered equipment below and a ladder up."

I pulled up an old horseweed just outside the door, back-tracked to the side of the road, and wiped out my tracks as I returned to the barn. "Good," I concluded.

I looked around the area near the barn door. A pothole next to the doorway held water. It was ice-covered. I went inside the barn and rummaged around in the dim light. I found a rusty old bucket and a tin cup. "Not the time to be picky, Caroline," I thought.

I returned to the pothole with the bucket, broke the ice with my fist and put both ice and liquid water in the bucket. "The water in the pothole will freeze again, and it will look the same as before," I concluded.

Before going back into the barn, I stepped off in the weeds for a few yards and relieved myself.

I used my horseweed to wipe out tracks and returned inside the barn. "Time to make a hidden nest, Caroline," I muttered. I climbed the ladder to the loft, carrying my bucket with the ice and the tin cup.

The loft was dark. However, enough light from the moon filtered through the cracks in the vertical boards of the barn walls for me to make out the general dimensions of the stacked hay. "The hay slopes up to the west wall, "I thought. "I'll climb to the top and tunnel down next to the wall. I can push the loose hay around and hollow out a space."

The job took a while, but I finally finished. I had my bucket with ice, the tin cup and Black Widow Anna's toys.

My nest was only about six feet square at the bottom and much narrower at the top. In addition to the opening above, I had about four feet of head room across all of my nest. I thought carefully about my tunneling activity in the hay, and decided that I hadn't left tell-tale signs of my work. "Unless someone climbs to the top of the hay pile, no one will know that I am here."

My space was small, the hay provided good insulation, and my body heat gradually warmed the space. I decided to drink water, clean up and get some much-needed rest. I felt in my bucket, and some of the ice had melted. I had enough water for a long drink and for a light sponge bath.

I used my tin cup and took a long, much needed drink. I then I stripped down to my bare skin, taking care to lay out all of my belongings where I could find them. I then dipped one of my rags in the bucket and washed myself. My skin tingled all over with the cold water, but then my body heated up.

I felt so much better. I used my clothes to make a bed, with my coat and shirt as blankets. I stretched out, took several deep breaths and fell into a dreamless sleep. My final thought before falling to sleep was: "I'm so tired."

Sounds outside awakened me. I looked through a crack in the barn wall. It was broad daylight. Several men were walking the road ahead of the car that I saw next to the garage earlier. One man was bent over as he walked slowly. "Following my tracks," I surmised.

Curses rang out. It was Anna. I saw her lean out the window on the passenger side of the car. After the curses, she shouted: "She's headed toward the highway, you idiot!" The entire entourage passed by my barn completely. "Stroke of good luck, thank heaven," I muttered. "Keep going, Anna."

I was still exhausted, and I fell back asleep. "So nice to be warm," I thought, just before drifting off.

I woke up with strong light shining through the cracks in the barn wall. I looked through one crack and located the sun. "High in the sky, southwest," I observed. "Probably just after noon."

Suddenly I heard voices. "Men are approaching the barn," I concluded. "Hope I covered my trail well enough."

Two men entered the barn below. "Check in the loft," one voice said. It was Sam. "I'll look around below." The search began. My body tensed. I heard the creak of someone coming up the ladder.

It seemed forever, but the search probably lasted about ten minutes. I heard footsteps around in the loft, the floorboards creaked. I heard poking in the hay. I held my breath. Finally, silence. After a minute or so, a voice called out. "Nothing up here." The voice belonged to Max. I heard him go down the ladder.

Sam's voice said: "She must be hiding along the road; I don't think she had time to get to the highway."

Max replied: "She was barefoot, except for socks."

"Let's check the ditches along the road," said Sam. "She can't get off the ridge to the south; the fields are flooded."

The voices faded as Sam and Max headed back to the road. I listened for sounds. "Nothing," I decided. "A good time to prepare for tonight's journey." I put on my underclothes, jeans and shirt. I then washed my face from the water in the bucket.

Refreshed, I looked at my belongings for a long time. "I need shoes," I decided. "I have leather, strands of hemp fiber from the cord that tied me up, rags, a sharp piece of glass and a knife." I thought a few more minutes. "I can make insulated moccasins."

I thought about a pattern. "Let's see," I mused. "I need three pieces of leather for each moccasin."

I cleaned the hay off the floor in a corner of my nest next to a relatively large crack in the wall. Light illuminated the floor boards. I used a sharp corner of my bottle neck and scratched a pattern of the pieces on a floor board.

I estimated measurements of my feet and did some calculations. "I'll need about three and a half square feet of leather," I decided. "The apron should be large enough, provided I don't make mistakes."

I looked through the crack in the wall to the sun. "I have about five hours of daylight." I thought a moment and concluded: "I can do this." I took another drink of water and got to work.

My stomach growled as I laid out the apron and began cutting with the Black Widow's knife. "Later, stomach," I admonished my gut. "First things first."

The light was dim through the crack in the wall as I finished my work. My moccasins were made of supple leather, had rag and hay for a liner and strands of hemp from the rope for stitching. "Not bad, if I do say so myself. Not exactly ready for sale at Saks, but very functional." I even had a little leather left over.

I looked through the crack in the wall toward the buildings in the distance. A few lights were on. "They will post a guard on the road next to the highway," I thought to myself. "I can't go that way." I continued thinking. "Sooner or later, they will come back and re-check this barn."

After another moment, I decided: "I can go along the north-south fence line, past the buildings and head south. I need food and a bag to carry stuff. I can find plenty of water along the way."

I thought a long time about food; I was ravenously hungry. "Wait until midnight and raid the kitchen. Risky, but again, not many options." I continued my train of thought. "Then head south." I took a deep breath. "In the meantime, prepare, then get some sleep."

I took another drink of water. "Time to relieve myself, and I can't do it in here, it might be noticed if they search the barn again." I crept up my tunnel to the top of the hay, using the wall as firm support. At the top, I slid down the hay to the loft floor, climbed down the ladder and exited the barn. Soon it was done. I returned to the barn and my nest.

I packed all my belongings in pockets, except for the knife, which I tucked through my makeshift belt. I was ready to go. "Busy day, Caroline, now get some rest," I muttered. I stretched out and covered my upper body with my coat. My feet were nice and toasty in my new moccasins. I faded to sleep.

As planned, I woke up after dark, probably after midnight. "Time to get supplies," I thought to myself. The idea of raiding my kidnapper's kitchen was somehow exhilarating. "Careful, Caroline," I cautioned myself: "Don't get over confident."

I put on my coat, climbed out of my nest, then filled my tunnel with hay. "Don't leave signs," I thought. "The less they know about my hiding places, the better."

Outside the barn, the weather was clear and cold. I shivered a little, and my body adjusted. A half-moon illuminated the landscape and the stars filled the sky. I looked to the buildings. "One light," I observed. "Everyone's probably asleep, except a guard."

I made my way through the weeds to the fence-line and across the lot with farm equipment, stopped by one of the tractors and observed the buildings. The single light came from the windows of the building where I was held captive. I recalled the layout of the buildings. "The kitchen is in the next building over," I remembered. "It's now or never."

The ground was frozen solid; the weather had gotten colder. "I'll leave no tracks," I thought with satisfaction. "Let's see what's for dinner." I crept through the equipment lot to the building with the kitchen.

The building had a door and a couple of windows at each end. I moved silently to the door at the back and listened for several minutes. "No sounds," I concluded. I tested the doorknob. The door unlatched, no lock. I opened the door without a sound. It was pitch black inside. I entered and closed the door.

"Time to risk a little light," I thought to myself. I took out my Ronson lighter and flicked on the little flame. I was in a walk-in pantry. Shelves lined the walls on each side. I went shopping.

After about five minutes, I left the building with a flour sack filled with canned goods, a loaf of very dry bread, a can opener and a spoon. "Not bad for a country store," I said to myself with a slight chuckle. My sack was heavy, maybe twenty-five or thirty pounds. Of course, I had taken my supplies from back rows and out of the way shelves. "No one will know I was here; at least I hope so."

I shouldered my sack, moved off into the moonlit, starry night and crossed the equipment lot. My path forward involved walking in the weeds along the fencerow to avoid leaving a trail. "South, Caroline," I thought to myself.

26

BASE OF OPERATIONS

As I walked along the fencerow with my sack of supplies, I thought about date and time. "Let's see, I escaped from the gangsters on Sunday night, February 17th and spent the remainder of the night and all day on Monday, the 18th, in the barn. This must be Tuesday morning, before daylight, on the 19th."

My train of thought continued: "By mid-day, I will have been away from Marshall Fields in Chicago for three days. Susie would have contacted Hannibal on the 16th, and he would have started a search. What would he do?"

I put myself in Hannibal's place. "In response to Hannibal's detailed questions, Susie would have told Hannibal about the flower truck. He already had concerns about North Side Gang retaliation for our detective work. Since I was kidnapped and not immediately killed, he would certainly deduce that I was taken by the remnants of the North Side Gang, and they planned to extract information from me." I developed a wry smile. "Unfortunately, I know a lot."

My logic continued. Hannibal would have contacted Watts and Mulvaney and probably Joe with the Capone organization." I paused, then continued. "Come on, Caroline, how does Hannibal think?"

I reached the end of the fencerow and stopped. The moonlight allowed me to see some distance ahead. I could see a fringe of trees leading south. Just east of the tree line on my left, flood water covered open fields as far east and south as I could see. "Follow the tree line straight south," I muttered to myself. I shouldered my flour sack and trudged off into the night.

My thoughts returned to Hannibal. "In military fashion, he would cast a wide net, gather intelligence, and act according to incoming reports. In addition to Watts, Mulvaney and Joe, he would contact every source he knew that might have information on North Side Gang operations."

Suddenly it dawned on me: "Hannibal would also contact our people in the Wabash Valley!" I enumerated on my fingers: "Blind Johnny, Jim Hansen the bookkeeper, and Frank Gardner," I summarized. "Others, including Mom and Pop Valenti and Tony and Louisa might also be contacted." I smiled as old memories came to mind. "Trusted people in the Valley would be asking questions, listening for rumors and perhaps even searching." I reviewed my logic as I walked. I could find no flaws.

My train of thought continued. "OK, Caroline, what's the plan?" The conclusion was obvious: "Evade the enemy, find a relatively safe place to hole up and prepare to fight if found. Hopefully, Hannibal will find me before Black Widow Anna." I felt comforted on the first prospect and scared about the other.

A pale light began on the eastern horizon. "Dawn soon," I muttered. "Move at night, hide by day. Better find a spot to hide and rest."

I stopped and looked back in the direction of the buildings where I started. I couldn't see them. "I've walked about two miles," I estimated. I looked into the trees and brush and glimpsed a downed tree with a big log about a hundred feet into the woods.

I walked closer and saw a clump of roots and dirt at one end of the log. "The roots form a head-high shield against a view from a distance," I observed. I looked all around. "Best spot in sight; make camp," I concluded.

I checked my back trail. "No trace," I thought with satisfaction. "This spot should be OK, unless someone comes really close."

I found a nice drift of dry leaves on the east side of the log near the clump of roots. I set down my sack. My shoulder ached. Out of sight from the western edge of the tree line, I made a thick bed of the leaves, took off my coat, lay down on my bed and covered myself with the coat. I promptly fell asleep.

When I awoke, the sun was high in the clear southeastern sky. The light was blinding, but the warmth felt good. I shielded my eyes and continued to rest for another few minutes. "OK, Caroline, time to attend to bodily functions and then breakfast."

I stood up and peered around the tree roots. "Nothing in sight," I concluded. I walked off east for a dozen yards and relieved myself. I then returned to my spot behind the log and rummaged through my sack. I found a can of peaches. Using the can opener, I soon had both sweet liquid and fruit, ready for breakfast. Using my spoon, I savored every bite and drop of moisture.

Satisfied, I took inventory. I had fifteen cans: two more peaches, two green beans, six chicken noodle soup, two beef stew and three corn. I also had a loaf of bread. "Not bad for shopping in the dark," I thought with a wry smile. "With two cans per day, this should be enough food for a week."

Having satisfied my hunger, I thought about my method of carrying my nearly twenty-five pounds of stuff. "A backpack would be nice," I decided.

I looked at my fallen tree. A number of the limbs at the far end were small, about an inch in diameter. They looked dry and strong. I looked off in the woods beyond the fallen tree and spotted honeysuckle vines in an area of low bushes. I pulled out my remaining cords, leather and my flour sack and laid them out in front of me. "I have a knife and plenty of materials," I thought. "I can make a frame for a backpack."

With knife in hand, I gathered pieces of tree branches and a small pile of stripped honeysuckle vine. The vines had a thickness of about an eighth of an inch. I added these materials to my stash of supplies, cleaned off a patch of ground and drew out a design with a stick. "OK, Caroline, get to work," I muttered.

I worked behind my log from about ten o'clock sun time until near dusk. Before dark, I had a serviceable backpack made from a cross-braced wood frame, sturdy weavings of honeysuckle, leather shoulder straps, and a neat covering made from my flour sack. My straps even had pads near the top, made of rags. "Not bad," I thought with a sense of satisfaction. Celebration included a can of green beans and all of the liquid in the can.

I lay back against my log and thought about my next move. "The farther away from those buildings, the better," I surmised. "But where should I go?"

I reviewed my memories of picnics with my parents. "Father used to drive a horse and wagon with my mother, sister and me across the wagon bridge at Clinton along the road toward Lyford," I recalled. "After a couple of miles, we turned off the main road north toward Sand Ridge in these very bottomlands."

I closed my eyes and developed a mental map. "The Sand Ridge road led onto this ridge at the south end. The southern stretch of that road was always under the flood water in winter, so I can't leave this L-shaped peninsula to the south."

I thought deeply. "We used to picnic near an old abandoned cabin near the south end of this ridge. A big shagbark hickory tree and several walnut trees grew near the cabin."

Fond memories came to the surface of my consciousness. "It was a pretty place, nice for picnics." I choked a little. "No time for sentiment," I reminded myself. "However, the old cabin, if it's still there, would be a good hiding place. It's off the road, hidden in the trees, and difficult to see."

Light in the sky was fading. I put all of my stuff in my backpack and looked around. "Make this spot look like it did when I arrived," I concluded. Soon it was done. Stars began to appear in the sky, and the moon, now three quarters full, rose slowly in the east.

I put on my coat, shouldered my pack, took one last look around and headed south. My destination was about three or four miles away.

I followed the tree line. The walk was pleasant enough. The terrain was uneven, but not bad. The ground cover was a mixture of poverty grasses, sand burrs, thistle and short grasses of some sort. Occasional fallen tree limbs required minor detours, but nothing serious.

Once I crossed a farmer's drainage ditch with a tiny stream of water. It wasn't the most desirable water for drinking, but I didn't have a choice. I drank my fill. "A glass of chardonnay would be nice," I thought to myself with a chuckle. I almost forgot that I was being hunted.

The moon was high in the sky when I topped a low ridge. The tree line ended in a short curve to the right across my path, which had been due south. I could see water to the east, south and west. I was near the end of my peninsula. On a little knoll just ahead, I could make out several taller trees. "The cabin spot, I hope." I continued forward.

My next familiar landmark was an ancient shagbark hickory tree. "I know this tree," I muttered. I looked around and saw several walnut trees and low bushes, but no cabin.

I took off my backpack and set it at the base of the hickory tree. I began a search pattern by walking in an ever-widening spiral around the tree. After gaining about a hundred-foot radius, I stumbled and nearly fell.

Looking down and around, I saw rubble, including old bricks, pieces of hewed logs, and old stones. The logs had charred, black edges. "The cabin burned," I concluded with a disappointed sigh.

I found a convenient section of log and sat down. "OK, Caroline, what's next?" I peered intently into the shadows all around, and something gleamed in the dark about a dozen feet away. I walked over to the gleam.

There, nearly covered in overgrown weeds, was a grey-white door of weathered wood. It sat at an angle in the ground. The door was secured with a simple latch. I lifted the latch, opened the door on creaky hinges and peered inside. I could see stone steps leading down into the ground. "A root cellar!" I exclaimed out loud. I walked carefully back to the hickory tree, retrieved my backpack, returned to the cellar, took out my Ronson lighter and set the backpack aside.

With the lighter flicked on, I gingerly walked down the steps. Cobwebs hung everywhere, and wooden shelves lined the sides of a space that was over six feet high, ten feet wide and fifteen feet deep.

I looked up and around. The walls and ceiling were made of mortared brick, and the floor and steps were made of flagstone. "What an excellent hiding place," I said, in complete surprise.

I explored in detail. I found old mason jars, an empty lantern, a couple of buckets, a couple of rusty metal pie-plates, some old jar lids, half an old door hinge and lo and behold, a box of long candles. I picked up a jar lid, took out a candle and lit it with my lighter.

It worked! The candle had a nice, steady flame. I quickly flicked off the lighter, picked up a jar lid, dripped wax from the candle on the inside of the lid and set the base of the candle in the melted wax. I now had a steady, portable light that didn't use up precious lighter fluid.

I set the jar lid with its candle on a nearby shelf and looked around. "I can clean this place up and make a livable hideout," I decided. "It's hidden from view, out of the weather and probably unknown to just about everyone, especially town-folk and gangsters."

I went back outside. The sky was getting light in the east. "Work quickly, Caroline," I admonished myself.

I looked around. Dead branches from a walnut tree lay nearby. I also saw horseweeds, bricks, stones and large pieces of partially burned timbers. "Clean the place first, collect bricks and stones for a fireplace, gather wood for a fire and leaves for a bed, find water and restore the outside area."

I set to work at a feverish pace. I finished just as the sun peeked above the southeast horizon. I walked off a dozen yards and completed my bodily functions before returning to my cellar door. I even had time to break and cut a foot square hole in the cellar door with my knife. I then camouflaged the entire door with leaves before I stepped inside and closed it.

In the light of my still burning candle, I took inventory. I had enough bricks and stones for a rudimentary fireplace, a stack of dry firewood and a big pile of dry leaves for a bed. I also had two buckets of fresh water from a cold-water spring that the original inhabitants of the cabin had once used. The outside area looked as natural as I could make it. "Whew!" I could now work inside at a slower pace.

"Time for breakfast, Caroline," I said to myself. I treated myself to a can of green beans and a long, cold drink of water taken from my bucket with a cleaned Mason jar. Such luxury!

I spent the next few hours building a fireplace from bricks and stones just under the hole in the cellar door. I left space to one side of the fireplace so I could step around, lift the door and exit the cellar. Fortunately, a vent pipe had been built into the ceiling at the far end of the cellar, so there was a nice draw of air through my space and out the hole in the door.

I built a small fire, using the lighter, a couple of cigarettes, dried grass and small sticks for tinder. As the flame grew, I added walnut limbs and a piece of old timber. Soon the fire burned and crackled merrily. The fire produced both heat and light. I snuffed out my candle. The sky darkened outside, so the smoke would not be seen by prying eyes.

Next, I laid a series of shelf boards over some spare bricks to make a bed above the cold flagstone floor. It was a bit rickety, but it worked. I piled the leaves on top.

Finally, I laid out my belongings and supplies on a couple of remaining shelves. I reviewed my earlier mental calculations, and yes, with rationing, my supply was sufficient for about seven days.

My little home was warm, so I stripped down and took sponge bath with my favorite rag. I even washed out my hair with a little extra water from a Mason jar. I had to use my fingers for a comb, but it worked.

As before, my skin tingled all over from the cold water. I shook out my clothes and put them back on, except for my coat. I also put my socks and moccasins back on, so my feet remained warm. I built up my fire, snuggled down in my dry leaves, covered my upper body with my coat and almost instantly fell asleep. What a day, I was exhausted.

My next moment of awareness was caused by light shining through the hole in the cellar door. I rubbed sleep from my eyes and sat up. My fire had died to embers, but it had lasted through the night. My little home was cool, but not cold.

I got up and splashed cold water from a bucket on my face. I did not build up my fire, the smoke might be seen in the daylight. However, enough embers remained to heat an open can of beef stew. Breakfast was soon served. After I finished, I lay back on my pile of leaves with my coat for a pillow.

"OK, Caroline," I thought to myself. "You are safe for now, but it's time to assess the situation and develop some contingency plans."

I began with a mental map of my peninsula. It was about eight miles long and two miles wide. Since I didn't show up along the dirt road to the highway, Black Widow Anna would leave a guard at the junction with the highway and deploy search parties south, there was no other place I could go.

That meant a thorough search of sixteen square miles. Even with a force of a dozen men, such a search could take days. I probably had time, but sooner or later, the bad guys would find me, unless Hannibal got here first.

What should I do? I thought long and intently. "False leads," I finally decided. "I could go out at night, create places that looked like camp sites away from my current location and give the searchers a reason to search elsewhere. I could also make some rudimentary weapons for a last-ditch fight," I thought grimly. "I have lots to do."

I rested all day Wednesday, February 20th. My cellar was cozy enough. Late in the afternoon, I slipped outside. No wind, but the sky was overcast. "The temperature feels above freezing, so I might get rain tonight," I thought to myself. "Better not go out."

I looked intently all around. Nothing stirred, except a flock of starlings in the distance and a couple of squirrels in the nearby walnut trees. I walked away into the bushes for a few moments to relieve myself. I then gathered more wood for my fireplace. After stashing my wood inside, I went to the spring and refilled my two buckets. I then brought in a fresh supply of dry leaves for my bed.

Afterwards, I took my knife, found a couple of hickory saplings growing near the big tree and cut them off near the ground. Both were about six feet long and one and a half inches in diameter at the base. I trimmed them of small limbs and took them inside. Last, I used a horseweed to brush the area around my outside activities. Everything was restored to its natural, undisturbed condition.

Before closing my cellar door, I looked all around. Nothing stirred. Even the two squirrels had retired for the night. Clouds covered the sky, and raindrops began to patter the ground. Daylight faded.

Back inside, I built up my fire and tidied up the place. I made a sturdy bench from a couple of shelf boards and some leftover flat stones that I had brought in when I built my fireplace. Finally, I lighted my candle and placed it on one of my remaining shelves along the wall.

Finished, I looked around. "Not bad Caroline," I said out loud. The fire crackled merrily. My little home was warm and dry.

"Time for dinner," I added, with some satisfaction. I treated myself to a can of corn, a piece of bread and a long drink of cold water from a Mason jar.

After dinner, I made a quick trip outside to the bushes and then returned to my cellar. I buttoned up the door, took off my clothes and took another sponge bath. I left my clothes off, except for my flannel shirt and my socks.

"Not my usual style," I thought, as I remembered my closet full of beautiful clothes back in Chicago. I then laughed, and it felt good. Outside, the rain changed to a steady downpour.

27

CONFUSE AND SURPRISE THE ENEMY

Thursday morning, February 21ˢᵗ, dawned. The rain had passed, but everything outside was dripping wet. I put on my clothes and went outside in the gray light. I looked all around. Nothing stirred, not even my neighborhood squirrels. After a few minutes in the nearby bushes, I returned to my cellar.

Breakfast consisted of two pieces of bread and cold water. As I sat on my bench and chewed the dry bread, I thought about my tasks for the day and for later, after dark.

"Make weapons during daylight, make false trails tonight," I concluded.

My two hickory saplings stood in the corner where I had left them the day before. I got up from my bench and retrieved one of the saplings. "I can make a spear," I mused. I picked up my knife from a shelf and began to whittle.

After about an hour, I had a clean, shaved six-foot stick with a sharp point at the small end. Embers still glowed in the fire, so I held the point of my stick in the embers and turned it slowly. "Harden the point in the fire, sharpen it again, then harden it for a final time," I said to myself. Soon it was done.

I looked back in the corner at my other hickory stick. "Make a club and a short stabbing pike," I thought.

After about four hours, I had finished. My pike was about eighteen inches long with a sharp, fire-hardened point. My club was a masterpiece. I had used my remaining strands of unraveled hemp cord, the half door hinge and three eighteen-inch sticks of hickory to make a club with a metal edge bound into the business end. "Ready for battle," I said out loud, with a sense of satisfaction.

I lay my weapons on the floor next to my bed and then slowly opened my cellar door. The sun was low in the southwestern sky, and the temperature was dropping. "The ground will freeze tonight," I concluded. "Good. Time to plan my expedition."

I put on my coat, went outside and looked all around. A few birds flitted by, that was all. I then walked down into the tree line and found a few dry limbs on a dead tree. After several trips, I had replenished my firewood.

Back inside, I used one of my metal pie-plates to scoop out some ashes from my fireplace. I filled four Mason jars with ashes and placed these in my backpack. I also packed my three empty cans left over from my meals and two Mason jars with water. I then peered through the hole in my door. The sky was clear, and the light was fading.

I took off my coat, re-built my fire and heated up an opened can of chicken noodle soup. My evening meal consisted of the soup, a piece of bread and water. It actually tasted pretty good. "Your standards are dropping fast, Caroline," I said out loud. I laughed. I finished and added my empty soup can to my backpack.

"Rest for a few hours and then leave after dark," I decided. "The moon should be nearly full, and the sky will be clear."

I dozed on my bed next to my cozy fire. After a couple of hours, the fire died down. "Time to go, Caroline," I told myself. "My destination will be the far west side of the peninsula, then about a mile or so north."

I put on my coat, hefted my backpack and exited my cellar. The three-quarter moon was just above the eastern horizon. I closed up the door, made sure that my camouflage was in order, put on my backpack and verified my bearings. My first destination was straight west to the water's edge.

The walk took about half an hour to the top of the ridge. I could see the flood water on the western side of the peninsula; it gleamed in the moonlight. I stopped, turned around slowly and scanned the landscape.

No human lights were visible on the peninsula. I then strode off toward the water, making sure I stayed in the weeds and grass. As best that I could tell, I didn't leave a trail.

I reached the water's edge in less than another hour. "I'm about a mile and a half from the cellar and over a mile from the south end of the peninsula," I surmised. "Time to turn right and walk in the weeds to the north."

Half an hour later, I stopped and looked around. A large log lay at the edge of a farmer's drainage ditch, just ahead. Weeds and bushes surrounded the old log. The water's edge and the end of the ditch was about fifty feet to my left.

"A plausible campsite," I decided. I took off my backpack and set it aside. I cleared out an area near one end of the log, dug out a small firepit with a stick and gently dumped the ashes from one of my Mason jars in the pit.

I found a few scattered branches lying around and collected them into a pile near the pit. "Looks like unused firewood," I said to myself. I then took out one of my empty cans and placed it near the firepit.

I proceeded to create a campsite around the firepit. I even made a bed from collected leaves. I finished in about fifteen minutes or so. "Not bad, Caroline," I said to myself.

My final touch was to make highly visible footprints in the soft earth and sand along the waters' edge, leading south. At the far end of the trail, I angled my prints up into the weeds and then doubled back to my fake campsite. "Looks like I headed south after leaving the camp," I said to myself with satisfaction.

I shouldered my backpack, turned north and used an old branch to wipe out my trail behind. After about fifty feet, I tossed away the branch and continued north in the weeds parallel to the water's edge on my left.

I looked up at the sky as I walked. The moon was nearing zenith. "That took about two hours," I guessed. "I have time to make two more campsites, both with false trails leading southwest." I did some mental calculations. "I'll need about three hours to walk cross-country back to my cellar." I looked up at the sky again. "You can do it, Caroline, and you'll be home before breakfast."

I made it happen. The last campsite was within sight of the gangster's buildings; I could see a couple of lights in the distance. I then angled southeast cross-country, doing my best not to leave a trail. The sky was just beginning to get light in the east as I trudged up to my cellar door.

I tidied up my camouflage, opened the door and went inside. "Whew!" I sighed. I had relieved myself far out on the trail, so I was done for a few hours.

After a brief meal of bread and water, I build up the fire and took a quick sponge bath. Afterwards, I sat on my bench a while, watching the flames die down.

Dressed in my flannel shirt and socks, I finally went to bed, just as the dawn light gleamed through the hole in the door. I passed out like turning off a light switch.

I woke up to the sound of rain. My cellar was cool and the fire was dead. I snuggled under my coat and burrowed down in the leaves of my bed. I had to go to the bathroom. "Oh shucks," I thought. "I don't have a bathroom."

There was nothing I could do but get up. I put on my jeans, coat and moccasins and looked out the hole in the door at the sky. It was already getting dark. I opened the door, went outside and did my thing in bushes and the rain. "Shortest bathroom break in history," I grumbled as I got back inside. I was shivering.

I used a couple of cigarettes, dry grass and small sticks for tinder and built a fire. Within a few minutes, the cellar began to warm. I took off my wet coat, jeans and moccasins. I draped the coat and jeans across my bed and placed the moccasins near the fire.

I was ravenously hungry. "How about chicken soup, Caroline?" I asked myself. "Sounds good," I answered. Soon I had hot soup ready. I ate my last piece of bread along with the soup and a drank a Mason jar of water.

Satisfied, I checked my remaining supplies. "Four soups, one beef stew, two corn and one bean," I summarized out loud. "Four day's supply left."

"What day is it, anyway?" I asked myself. I did a quick review. "It's Friday night, February 22nd." I answered. "I've been on this little excursion for six days."

The wind howled outside. I checked my firewood; I had an ample supply. "OK, let's settle in for the night," I decided. "The bad guys won't be out in this weather either, and I left plenty of dead-end trails and false campsites for their amusement."

My muscles were sore, so I stretched out on my bed. My coat and jeans had dried, and I lay on the jeans and used the coat as a pillow. I dozed, watched the fire and listened to the wind.

"Let's see," I thought. "If I were Black Widow Anna, what would I be doing right now?"

"She would be frustrated, because she hasn't found me," I concluded. "She knows I'm on the peninsula, and she has sixteen square miles to search." I thought a moment. "I would bring in more troops."

My train of thought continued. "She would like to capture me and extract information. However, if she can't do that, she must kill me, since I know her identity and her role in the North Side Gang." I followed the logic and decided that her men will be given orders to shoot on sight if they have any doubt about capture.

"A search of the peninsula would begin in the north and sweep south," I decided. "If my false camps and trails are found, the gang would concentrate on the west side for a while, but I can't count on more than a couple more days before they sweep the east side."

My thoughts turned to Hannibal. "He will be getting intelligence reports from the police, Capone's people and hopefully, from our friends in the Valley," my logic continued. "Gang members will inevitably go into town, and they may talk too much. If so, my friends may hear; they may investigate, and they will report to Hannibal." On that comforting thought, I snuggled down in my bed and fell asleep.

I woke up when light shined through the hole in the door. I was warm and cozy in my bed, but the cellar had cooled. I looked, and the fire had died down. I also had to go. I put off getting out of bed for as long as I could.

"OK, Caroline, rise and shine, you have to get out of bed." I got up, put my clothes and moccasins on and went out the door. The sun wasn't up yet, but dawn had arrived. I listened and looked around.

I saw nothing except my two neighborhood squirrels. "They are up early, and they are not disturbed," I concluded. "It should be safe to move around." I quickly walked into the bushes and did my thing.

As I headed back to my cellar, I heard a distinctive sound in the distance. It was an outboard motor. "Oh, good heavens," I exclaimed aloud. "A boat in the flooded bottom lands."

I then walked to a little rise in the terrain on the other side of the cabin site. I could see the flood water to the east and the south in the dim pre-sunrise light. Indeed, I saw a boat, about a mile or so away, near the shore. Someone was searching by boat. Who?

I went inside and packed my supplies in my backpack. I had to be ready to escape at a moment's notice. My supplies included two sealed Mason jars with water and all of my food except my last can of beans. I opened this can, ate its contents and drank plenty of water.

I also readied my weapons. I put my knife and pike in my cord belt, one on the left and the other on the right. My club went into the top of my backpack. I hefted my spear and set it in the near corner next to my backpack.

I was ready. Keeping a low profile, I crept up to my hickory tree. The squirrels were gone. As I watched the terrain to the north and west, the sun rose in the southeast. Light filled the sky. About two hours had passed.

After a half hour or so, I heard voices to the north. "Close," I concluded. "If I can hear them, they are less than a quarter mile away." I listened for another few minutes. The voices got louder and more distinct.

It was time to retreat. I retrieved my backpack, shouldered it, picked up my spear and slipped stealthily south. I crept low, just below the eastern crest of the north-south ridge line.

I stopped after about a half mile. I could see the water to the south. The peninsula ended in a narrow strip only about a hundred yards wide. I saw more boats. Some moved west, others stayed at the south end of the peninsula.

I looked out at the water to my left. Three boats now moved slowly north, close to the eastern shoreline. I could see two people in each boat, one by the motor and the other up front.

I stopped and looked back toward the root cellar. I saw several men moving about. "They have found my hideout," I concluded. "Time to move."

I continued south. I occasionally looked back over my shoulder. Two men moved out of the root cellar area in my direction. Two others went left, and two more went toward the eastern shoreline. With men on foot to the north and the boats in the water to the east, south and west, I was surrounded.

"The two walkers in the middle will be ahead of the other four," I thought. "I'll set an ambush."

I made sure that I left tracks as I continued to move south. I passed a clump of thick bushes and small trees, continued south for another dozen yards and then jumped left into tall grass. I made my way back to the thick bushes, took off my backpack and readied my spear and club. I left my knife and pike in my belt as weapons of last resort.

I crouched low behind the bushes and waited, spear in my left hand and club in my right. Voices grew louder; two men were following my trail. The wait wasn't long.

Soon I could see the two men through the bushes. One was a few yards behind the other.

I let the first man pass about two yards from my hiding place. The second had just passed when I jumped up. In an instant, I was behind him.

I silently drove my spear in his back. It met resistance from his heavy coat, and it didn't penetrate very far. He yelled in pain and tried to turn around. I lost my grip on the spear.

I saw an automatic pistol in his right hand. I swung my club, hitting his wrist. I heard bone snap. The pistol fell to the ground. Before he could recover, I raised my club and hit him full in the face and forehead. He dropped like a stone.

The first man turned and saw me. He raised a revolver and fired. The bullet whizzed past my head. Before he could fire another round, I was on him, club in both hands.

I swung my club left, right and left, dealing hard blows with each swing. He fell back, trying to protect his face. His revolver dropped to the ground. I switched my grip on the club to my right hand and swung it up high and then down.

Again, my blow hit my opponent in the face and forehead, right between his upright hands. He went down without another sound.

I heard yelling behind me. The other men to the left and right had heard the shot and the yelling. I looked frantically around the battleground for the two guns. I couldn't see them.

I did see my spear. I picked it up. With club in one hand and spear in the other, I ran straight south, through bushes and past trees.

A couple of shots rang out. The bullets made click-click sounds as they hit tree limbs. I kept going as fast as I could.

I covered a full quarter of a mile, stopped and hid behind a tree. I was totally winded; my chest was heaving, and I had to recover. "First battle over," I told myself. "Plan for the next."

28

THE BATTLE OF SAND RIDGE

After a minute or so, I had recovered my breath. Looking south, I could see that four boats had reached the shore at the end of the peninsula, about a quarter mile away. Boats were also going north on both the east and west sides of the peninsula.

I turned around and looked north, back along my trail. Four men were moving in my direction. They stopped at the prostrate forms of their two leading companions. They then continued toward me, slowly and cautiously. "OK," I thought. "I have a few minutes."

I looked around. I was on a little knoll with trees. "My attackers will have to come uphill from the north, south and east," I concluded.

I scanned the western terrain. The ground sloped down from my knoll, then up to the main ridge line. I looked carefully. No one was visible to the west. "The men from the boats on the west have farther to go to reach me," I said out loud. "Good."

"Defense," my mind raced. I looked around at my trees. Several were quite large. "The bad guys have guns; I have a spear, a club, a pike and a knife."

I looked carefully at the spacings of the largest trees. "Hide until they get close, jab with the spear at the nearest man, then run to the next tree." I played out the scenario in my mind. "If I lose the spear, use the pike, then the knife. Hopefully, their shots will go wild in the confusion, and I can make it from tree to tree."

"Stay in these trees as long as possible, then move west toward the main ridge," my thoughts continued. I made swift calculations of time. "If I survive the attack from the north, the east and south, I may have time to retreat west, to the ridge. I know my face had a wry smile. "Your odds are not good, Caroline."

I looked around one last time. "I have five, maybe ten minutes," I estimated. "Hide and wait." I crouched down on the west side of a big oak tree. Time seemed to drag. Voices echoed to the north. My body tensed.

Pop, pop, pop! Shots rang out. Then I heard Boom! Boom! The shots continued. It was like the Fourth of July.

I recognized the sharp pops; they were pistol shots. It took a couple of seconds, but I finally recognized the heavy booms. "Shotguns!" I exclaimed out loud. It didn't make sense. As best as I could remember, the North Side Gangsters didn't have shotguns.

The shots finally stopped. It dawned on me that none of the bullets or blasts from the shotguns were made in my direction. "What in the world?"

I stood up and looked around. Many men were striding toward me from north, south and east. I looked west. More men topped the ridge. I turned around and around several times, then hefted my spear, ready for the final battle.

I saw one tall man leading the group coming from the east. He wore a leather jacket, high laced boots and a fedora hat with the brim turned down. I saw his face. "Hannibal! Oh, my heavens!"

I stepped out from behind my tree. Hannibal strode toward me. He had his forty-five in his right hand. He stopped about twenty feet away, tucked his pistol in a shoulder holster under his jacket and smiled. "Need any help?" He asked.

I was transfixed for a full ten seconds. I'm sure my mouth was wide open. Finally, I dropped my spear and club and ran straight into Hannibal's open arms.

Hannibal hugged me tight for a long time. For the first time in over a week, I felt relief and security. It was wonderful. I cried a little, I couldn't help it. I felt Hannibal's chest give a big sigh.

I heard voices. Words rang out, back and forth, all around: "Here she is!" and "Make sure we got 'em all!" and "She's safe!"

I released Hannibal and looked behind him. The first face I saw was Frank Gardner. He stood just a few feet away. I hadn't seen him for over two years. He was older and more mature, but I instantly recognized his big grin. He was carrying a shotgun. "Hello, Miss Case," he said. He touched his hat politely.

At least another dozen smiling faces appeared. More men strode up from all directions. I recognized most of them. Some shuffled their feet and smiled, others tipped their hats and said variations on "Hello, Miss Caroline, so nice to see you again." I was surrounded by my river rat friends.

Suddenly, a flurry of gunfire popped, cracked and boomed in the distance to the north. My body tensed, and I moved back into Hannibal's arms. After a few moments, the gunfire ceased.

"Don't worry," said Hannibal softly. "My northern force is cleaning up back at the buildings where, I think, you were held captive." He paused for a moment, then added: "Eddie is there, leading another two dozen men, including the Parke County Sheriff and several deputies."

I stepped back and looked at Hannibal's wonderful face. I started sniffling again. "Control yourself, Caroline," I thought to myself. I took a deep breath, stopped sniffling and asked: "How did you find me?"

"It's a long story," replied Hannibal. "I'll save it for later." His eyes twinkled. He looked me up and down. "I like your outfit," he said. Chuckles echoed all around me.

I looked around at all of my friends. I then looked down at my open coat, overlarge flannel shirt, rolled up jeans, rope belt and handmade moccasins. The hilt of my knife and the end of my wooden pike thrust forward from my belt. I'm sure my hair was an absolute mess. "Caroline," I thought to myself: "You are indeed a sight to behold."

I then looked around at my audience and smiled with a confident air. I placed my hands on my hips, tossed my head back and turned around slowly. When I stopped turning, I was facing Hannibal.

"You really think so?" I said in my best self-assured voice. "I try to always dress for the occasion." My audience, including Hannibal, roared with laughter. It was a long-remembered moment for me and I'm sure for everyone present.

After the laughter subsided, Hannibal turned to Frank and issued some quiet orders. Mainly, he addressed the fallen North Side Gang members on the battleground that stretched along my trail to our current position. He then sent runners to the north, south and west with verbal situation reports and instructions.

I was fascinated with Hannibal's calm manner, concise instructions and military bearing. "Hannibal is a man who others will always follow," I concluded. I felt pride in 'my man,' and I'm sure my eyes were shining.

Hannibal finished in a couple of minutes. Frank and the others went about their appointed tasks. Hannibal then turned, looked at me closely and said: "Let's get you back to town, cleaned up and fed." He then pointed south toward the boats at the end of the peninsula.

"That would be nice," I replied. I suddenly realized that I was very tired, thirsty and ravenously hungry.

Hannibal stepped forward, put his arm around my waist and we walked together toward the boats.

As we walked the few hundred yards downhill, I asked: "Really, how did you find me?"

Hannibal was quiet for a moment. He then said: "Susie called me from Marshall Fields the moment she saw you being carried through the stairway door by the dressing rooms." He paused and then added: "She described two men and a woman in detail." He added: "She recognized the woman from our days in the Wabash Valley."

Hannibal continued: "I asked a few questions, and Susie remembered the flower truck. She looked out the window after you were gone, and she spotted it driving out from an alley below. She remembered that it was the same truck that was parked at our apartment building." Hannibal looked down at me, smiled and said: "You can be proud of Susie, you trained her well."

I thought a moment, then responded: "I see; you knew that the woman was Anna Nuardi and that the flower truck connected her to the North Side Gang." I looked up at Hannibal's face, and asked: "How did you know where to look?"

"That was a problem," replied Hannibal. "I cast a wide net in Chicago by calling Sergeant Watts and Joe from the Green Mill. They immediately spread the word. A massive hunt and intelligence gathering operation began."

He paused and then added: "I called Eddie and we both started calling friends in the Valley. Among others, we called Jim Hansen, the bookkeeper at Nuardi's car dealership, Blind Johnny, and Louisa, who now runs Valenti's restaurant in Clinton." He chuckled a little and said: "Word spread through the Valley like wildfire."

As we approached a row of boats on the peninsula shore, I asked: "How did you know they would hold me at the buildings where we rescued Kitty and Kathy a couple of years ago?"

"Those buildings were one of several possible locations," Hannibal admitted. "However, Blind Johnny solved the problem for us."

"How so?" I asked, as we reached the nearest boat. A smiling man handed me a blanket as Hannibal assisted me to a seat. "Thank you," I said, with a smile. I was grateful for the warmth.

I took my seat and pulled the blanket close. Hannibal sat beside me and said: "As you know, Johnny is still on our payroll. He visits speakeasies in the Valley and listens. He was in Scottie's old place in Lyford last Tuesday evening."

Hannibal paused, looked down at me and continued: "Several of the North Siders were in the bar. They let slip the location of their base of operations." He chuckled a little and added: "Apparently, you hit someone named Max in the nose, and they were joking about it."

"Oh!" I exclaimed. I couldn't help myself. I added: "Well, Max asked for it!"

Hannibal laughed and so did our boatman. Finally, Hannibal said: "Once I heard Johnny's description, I knew it had to be you."

I was silent for a while, as our boatman started his outboard motor and backed away from the shore. We turned around and headed across the flooded fields to the distant shore. Looking south, I saw the highway between the Clinton wagon bridge to the west and Lyford to the east. Several cars were parked along the highway.

I could also see the north-south earthen levee that paralleled the Wabash to the west. The levee had several gaps close to the point where the highway crossed over. Flood water passed from the Wabash through the gaps into the bottom land fields. Several more cars were parked on the crossing. I could see how Hannibal's 'navy' had crossed through the levee gaps from the Wabash into the flooded fields.

I looked back toward the peninsula. Boats were leaving the south point and were appearing from the north on both sides of the peninsula. I counted twenty boats, each with two to four men. "So many people came to my rescue," I said to Hannibal.

Hannibal nodded, smiled and replied: "You have many friends." He hugged me close.

I pondered a while. After a few minutes, I said: "I understand how you found out where I was held, but how did you find out that I had escaped and headed down the peninsula?"

Hannibal looked thoughtful for several long moments. Finally, he said: "I didn't know. I simply deployed enough men to cover all contingencies."

He paused again and then added: "I sent two dozen men under Eddie down the road from Highway 41 toward the buildings. I also sent boats up both sides of the peninsula and to the south end." He looked at me and smiled. "We had binoculars, and we scanned the peninsula from the boats and from the dirt road in the north."

"So, you saw me?" I asked.

"Not at first," replied Hannibal. But we did see men moving from north to south. He paused for nearly a minute and then said: "We heard the shot, and immediately converged to its location."

He squeezed me tight and with a slight choke in his voice, said: "When I heard the shot, I thought I had lost you." He looked into my eyes. I could see tears.

I reached up, kissed Hannibal on the cheek and lay my head on his shoulder. We stayed that way until the boat reached the south shore.

Saturday night and Sunday, February 24, were devoted to recovery. My ordeal had left me dehydrated, dirty, hungry and unable to sleep. However, thanks to Hannibal and my river rat friends, I was now safe. My body relaxed slowly, and the bad dreams subsided after a couple of nights. I would be OK.

Hannibal had set us up in the best suite in the Clinton Hotel. Immediately upon arrival on Saturday evening, I took a luxurious bath, washed my hair and manicured my nails. Later, I would go to a spa for a professional job. Hannibal, ever thoughtful, had brought along a couple changes of clothes for me from my closet back in Chicago. I felt human again.

After my clean-up, my first order of business on the 24th was to thank all who helped rescue me. I asked Hannibal, Louisa, Eddie and Frank to pass on my gratitude to everyone. Every time I think about the effort, concern and courage exhibited by all; I get a lump in my throat.

At first, I had to eat sparingly of wholesome food. My body required time to adjust; my recent diet was rather sketchy, to say the least. By Sunday evening, I felt much better.

Claude Robison, the Parke County Sheriff, visited Hannibal and me in our hotel room on Monday. He was a gracious man, very different than the corrupt Big Bill Johansson from my past. Sheriff Robison said that Big Bill's demise last year in a 'car accident' has yet to be resolved. No one in Vermillion County seems to care much; Big Bill had many enemies. Anyway, Sheriff Robison took my statement.

I also learned from the Sheriff that Anna Nuardi had survived the shootout at her hideout on Sand Ridge. She was now resting very uncomfortably in the Parke County jail. With my statement and others, her prospects were not good.

Only one other gangster survived the shootout at the hideout where I was held prisoner. Sam, the man who was reasonably gentle and thoughtful during my days in captivity, will spend weeks in the hospital, then jail awaits. Being a gangster is a high-risk business.

According to Hannibal and the Sheriff, the two gangsters whom I had smacked with a club on the trail also survived. Both had severe concussions and nasty gashes in their foreheads, but they were not dead. I must admit that I have mixed emotions concerning their survival.

Anyway, the Battle of Sand Ridge is over. After personal goodbyes and thanks to my many Wabash Valley friends, Hannibal and I will take a train from Clinton back to Chicago. It's time to plan the future.

24

OUR WAY HOME

On Monday, February 25, Hannibal bought tickets on the Chicago and Eastern Illinois Railroad. We would leave the Clinton Station on Wednesday for a six-hour trip to Chicago's Dearborn Station. Hannibal also called Susie, and she promised to have a car meet us at the station. We were going home!

Eddie planned to stay in Clinton for a few more days. He would make sure that the Parke County Sheriff had everything he needed. He also planned to spend some time with his aunt and uncle, Mom and Pop Valenti.

Mom and Pop were elderly now, but they were still active at the restaurant. Louisa and Antonio ran the operation, but Mom and Pop talked to customers and made a few specialty dishes. They dearly loved Louisa, one of my girls from the old days. Eddie, of course, was their favorite (and only) nephew.

Hannibal and I would have a pleasant train ride in a first-class coach and an excellent meal in the dining car. We had a lot to discuss. Since the Saint Valentine's Day Massacre, reform was in the air. The public wanted an end to the gang violence. What role should our forensic laboratory play in future Chicago police work?

Wednesday morning dawned clear and cold. Eddie, Frank, Johnny, Jim, Antonio and Louisa saw us off at the station.

I was dressed in a beige-colored cashmere coat with mink trim and a shaved mink liner. I also wore a matching mink hat, gloves and soft brown leather boots. Underneath, I had my burgundy-colored

Lanvin dress with a dark gray-colored silk scarf for flair. Hannibal had brought everything from Chicago, and he knew my tastes. "Good man, Hannibal," I thought to myself.

Of course, Hannibal was appropriately dressed in a charcoal gray cashmere top coat, matching fedora hat, leather gloves, black shoes and a classic gray business suit underneath. The gray at his temples provided a nice accent to his handsome, chiseled face. "What a man," my thoughts continued. "I'm a very lucky lady."

The porter took our day bags and escorted us toward our seats. "Very different than my surroundings on Sand Ridge," my thoughts continued. I shuddered a little, but not from the cold. Hannibal noticed, and briefly put his hands on my shoulders as we walked through the coach. I felt better after his touch.

Hannibal and I waved from our window as the train pulled away from the station. Eddie and the others waved back. "Such wonderful friends," I mused, as the train headed west through town.

After about half an hour, Hannibal and I walked to the beautifully appointed dining car. Soon we were seated in a small, U-shaped booth for breakfast. Several other well-dressed couples were already seated, and three or four black-tie waiters moved about, efficiently and quietly. The train clickity-clacked along the track through the wintery countryside.

As usual, our discussion began over a cup of coffee. After we ordered breakfast, Hannibal leaned back in his seat, sipped his coffee, and watched me for a moment. I expected him to bring up the future of our forensic laboratory. He didn't. What he did was totally unexpected.

Without taking his eyes off my face, Hannibal set his coffee cup down, reached into his jacket pocket and drew out a small white leather box with gold trim. It was about three inches square. He set it in the middle of the table. He then opened it. His eyes twinkled.

I looked at the open box. I'm sure my mouth dropped open. I put my hands up to my face. "Oh!" I exclaimed. The box contained a ring with the biggest cluster of diamonds I had ever seen.

Hannibal reached over, took my left hand gently in both of his and asked: "Caroline Case, will you marry me?"

My emotions ranged from total surprise to visions of our years together and finally, to tears of joy. I had never been so happy in my life. "I, I don't know what to say," I finally stuttered.

"Yes, would be nice," replied Hannibal. He smiled and said: "I love you dearly, Caroline. I have loved you ever since we met by your houseboat in the summer of 1921."

I cried; I couldn't help it. Between tears and sniffles, I said: "Hannibal, you are the best thing that has ever happened to me." I sniffled again, reached down with my right hand for my white linen napkin, and dabbed my eyes and nose. Finally, I got control of myself. "Yes, Hannibal, I will." I paused a moment and then added: "I love you, too."

Hannibal caressed my hand and said: "May I?" I nodded yes. He then took the ring out of its box and slipped it on my finger. It fit perfectly. He then said: "This ring is a family heirloom. My father gave it to my mother upon their engagement. I want you to have it."

Suddenly applause and cheers rang out all around. Words like: "Wonderful!" "Best wishes!" and "Lovely couple," interspersed the applause. Porters, waiters and patrons in the dining car were all smiling and clapping their hands.

Hannibal and I both looked up and around. Hannibal grinned. I'm sure my face had a combination of tears and a smile of pure happiness. Neither of us had been aware of our audience.

Soon breakfast was served. Our kindly old waiter said: "It's on the house." He grinned and added: "Best wishes to you both." He poured us each another cup of coffee and discretely moved away.

I hardly know what I ate. I kept looking at my beautiful ring, then Hannibal, and back to the ring. Finally, I asked: "Why, after all this time?" My eyes searched Hannibal's face.

Hannibal sipped his coffee and then set it down. He looked into my eyes and held my gaze for a long moment. Finally, he took my left hand, held it gently and looked down at the ring.

After another moment, Hannibal's gaze returned to my face. Moisture gathered in the corners of his eyes. He replied: "When I found you on Sand Ridge a few days ago, I realized what I almost lost." He paused and added: "I should have asked you to marry me long ago."

"But the ring," I responded. "You brought it with you from Chicago?"

Hannibal's eyes twinkled again. "Yes," he replied. "I have carried it with me for years, waiting for the right moment."

My mouth fell open again. After a full minute, I closed it and said: "You rascal!" You made me wait all this time?"

Hannibal laughed and said: "You are a very special lady. I was afraid you wouldn't accept my proposal."

I thought a moment and replied: "Good answer." I nudged him in the ribs, scooted around our booth, and kissed him on the cheek. "You are forgiven," I said.

Our train pulled into Dearborn Station mid-afternoon. Vincenzo, Harris, Susie, Silvia, Ruth and Mandy met us on the siding as we stepped off. Again, my mouth fell open. "What in the world?" I exclaimed. I turned to Hannibal. He just grinned.

Susie stepped forward. "I want to see the ring," she said. She giggled mischievously as she saw my amazed expression. "Word gets around," she added.

I looked first at Susie, then at all the others. I sniffed, tossed my head back in my most self-assured manner and gazed at everyone in turn. I then held out my left hand. The diamonds sparkled in the light of the nearby siding lamps. "Oohs and aahs" echoed all around. Words of "Congratulations!" handshakes and hugs followed. It was a wonderful moment.

After a couple of minutes, Vincenzo said: "My taxi is outside, along with a couple of other cars. Wait until you see." He looked first at Hannibal and then me. "Follow me, please."

Soon we were outside of the station. I saw a line of six or seven cars. Sergeant Watts and Detective Mulvaney stood by the first, which was a Cadillac police car. I saw another Cadillac at the end of the line.

Watts walked over, touched his hat, and said: "My compliments, Miss Case, and congratulations." He grinned from ear to ear. "The Chicago Police Department will escort you home."

Vincenzo came up and said: "My taxi is in the middle." I looked and sure enough, Harris stood by Vincenzo's taxi, holding open the passenger door. "The rest will ride in the other cars, Miss Case," said Vincenzo. "Are you ready?" He touched his cap politely.

I smiled, tossed my head back and replied: "Yes, I suppose." To the laughter and giggles of everyone, I put my right hand on my hip and walked slowly to my waiting "golden coach." Hannibal followed, laughing and shaking his head.

After a few minutes, everyone was ready. Our little parade left the station and headed north and east on city streets toward Lakeshore Drive. We arrived at our apartment building about thirty minutes later. Before I could open my car door, Harris was there. He moved ahead and opened the building door. Silvia and Ruth led the way inside to the elevator.

Everyone came in the lobby, but no further. Words like "Have a good evening," and "Congratulations" echoed all around.

Hannibal and I were left alone as we entered the elevator and rode up to our penthouse. Hannibal opened the door, picked me up in his strong arms and carried me across the threshold. A wonderful evening brought an end to a perfect day.

Saturday evening, March 2nd, 1929

Hannibal and I spent Thursday and Friday enjoying each other's company. Silvia discretely left us alone, except for late morning breakfasts and clean-ups. I was so thankful to be back in our apartment. The memories of my ordeal on Sand Ridge faded. It was time to think about the future.

Of course, I thought about a wedding. What girl doesn't? I asked Hannibal, and he agreed that sooner was better than later. He also said, somewhat mysteriously, "Check with Ruth; she may help."

I called Ruth on Thursday evening. "Of course, I will help," she said. "Thank you for asking. How about a June wedding?"

"That would be wonderful," I replied. "I've never organized a wedding before. I don't know where to begin."

"I have some experience," Ruth replied with a pleasant laugh. "I will call you in a few days."

So, our phone call ended. "What does Ruth have in mind?" I wondered.

I told Hannibal about my phone call to Ruth at breakfast on Friday. He smiled and said: "Ruth will take care of the wedding." He paused a moment and then added: "We need to concentrate on our future."

I thought for a full minute. Finally, I said: "I suppose we should end our detective work in Chicago."

"I agree," responded Hannibal. He gazed at my face, as if he could read my thoughts. Finally, he added: "We have been very fortunate. The North Side Gang may be disorganized and on the run, but they may have revenge on their minds."

I shuddered a little as flashes of recent memories crossed my mind. "Yes," I replied. I then sipped my coffee, and its warmth felt good.

Hannibal then added: "Right after the Saint Valentine's Day massacre, I talked with our forensic lab department heads and also to several people in the community, including Doctor Herman Bundesen, the Chicago Health Commissioner, Burt Massee, a prominent businessman, John Wigmore, the Dean of the Law School at Northwestern University, and most importantly, to Doctor Calvin Goddard, a respected expert in forensic science."

"You were very busy," I responded. I thought a moment and then added: "I suppose these men have an interest in the future of forensic science in Chicago?"

"Yes," replied Hannibal. "They are also men who can make things happen in this town."

"Does our lab fit into their plans?" I asked.

Hannibal thought a while and then said: "Yes; in fact, they would like to employ our lab people, equipment and expertise." He paused again and then continued: "Our small organization would form the core for training and methodology for a new, much larger lab at Northwestern University."

"Would all of our people, including Eddie, be part of the new organization?" I asked.

"Yes," responded Hannibal. "Goddard was particularly pleased. With both public and private funding, the new Scientific Crime Detection Laboratory, as Goddard calls it, would be able to provide increases in salary and career progression for all of our people."

I thought a moment, then asked: "What do the department heads and Eddie think?"

"They had many questions," replied Hannibal. He then smiled and added: "Not surprisingly, they were concerned about you and me, not themselves."

I got a lump in my throat, and not for the first time over the past several days. "Oh, Hannibal, we must make sure everyone is treated properly."

"I agree," responded Hannibal. "I explained to everyone that you and I would be fine." He paused and smiled again. "Once they were convinced of that, they were enthusiastic about the future."

I thought a few minutes while sipping my coffee. "What about you and me?" I finally asked.

Hannibal looked at me for a long while. Finally, he said: "As you know, we are financially secure. I have moved all of our investments into holdings that can weather any economic storm."

He paused and then continued in a somber tone: "From everything that I see with markets, banking and the world economy in general, a storm is coming, and it may last a long time."

I thought a while as I remembered my years of poverty and financial insecurity. I couldn't help myself. I asked: "How much are we worth?"

Hannibal smiled; he knew what I was thinking. "Well over one-hundred fifty million dollars," he replied. "Even with our life style, our net worth grows every year."

"Oh, good heavens!" I exclaimed. "I had no idea." I thought a moment, then added: "Does this mean I can go shopping?" I grinned mischievously.

Hannibal laughed and laughed. Finally, he said: "How would you like to go shopping in Paris on our honeymoon?"

30

WEDDING BELLS, TRAINS, SHIPS, CARS AND CANDLES

Saturday evening, March 9, 1929

Ruth called this morning, just after breakfast. "I have some ideas about a nice June wedding, Caroline. Could you join some friends and me for tea this afternoon?" Ruth spoke in her usual, calm, aristocratic manner.

I could hardly wait; I was so excited! However, I thought about proper tea times and responded politely with: "Of course, I can be at your apartment at two o 'clock. Would that be OK?"

"See you at two," replied Ruth. "I have also invited Susie and a fashion friend. We have some planning to do."

I dressed and primped for an afternoon formal tea. The process took until noon. From noon until quarter 'til two, I fidgeted.

Hannibal watched me fidget, laughed, shook his head and retired to our workroom. He was making plans with regard to our next move. We had agreed that we should leave Chicago; the danger was obvious. Where should we go after our honeymoon? Hannibal said he would explore options.

I wanted to concentrate on our wedding, and Hannibal understood. Ruth's tea party was the first step; I had no idea how to set up a wedding. I just wanted ours to be special.

I tried to estimate the time required between leaving my apartment, riding the elevator and arriving at Ruth's door. I left our apartment at five minutes until two and showed up at Ruth's apartment door a couple of minutes later.

Mandy opened the door. Frenchie was there, of course. He wagged his tail, sat and waited for me to scratch behind his ears. I did, and he scampered off, satisfied.

"Good afternoon, Miss Case; please come in," Mandy said with a big smile. "Mrs. Meltzer and the other guests are in the parlor." She then paused and whispered: "May I see your ring?"

"Of course," I replied, as I held out my hand. I loved to show it off at every opportunity.

The diamonds sparkled. I stepped into Ruth's tastefully decorated entryway. Low light sconces and beautiful paintings made me feel warm and welcome.

"Your ring is lovely," said Mandy. "Mr. Jones is a very lucky man. You are a special lady."

Such kindness! Mandy always knew just what to say. The contrast between my experience on Sand Ridge and the welcome I received at Ruth's apartment was hard to comprehend. I loved the changes that Hannibal and others had brought into my life.

Mandy led the way into the parlor. Ruth, Susie and another beautiful, fashionably dressed, silver-haired, older lady sat on comfy chairs around a coffee table. Large folios and pictures lay on the table. Mandy busied herself at a side serving table with tea, scones and other goodies. Frenchie sat next to the side table, paying rapt attention to Mandy's activities.

Susie grinned from ear to ear and said: "Hi Caroline, I'm so excited!" The other lady smiled and said: "Hello Caroline, I've heard so much about you." Her smile was genuine, and I immediately felt at ease.

Ruth rose to greet me and said: "Caroline, this is Amanda Cousineau, a friend from Paris." Ruth paused and then added: "Amanda has much experience in planning weddings; she's in Chicago visiting clients this spring and summer."

"Please call me Amanda," said the lady as she rose from her seat. "If you don't mind, Ruth said you might want my help in planning your very special wedding." Amanda stepped around the coffee table and walked over to me.

"Hello, Amanda," I responded. I didn't know quite what to say, so I blurted out: "I need all the help I can get."

Amanda laughed merrily, and she extended her hand. "Wonderful!" She replied. "I am so looking forward to working with you."

I extended my right hand, and Amanda took it graciously. She then said in a low, soft voice: "May I see your ring?" We were friends immediately.

The afternoon was spent in pleasant conversation about dresses, guest lists, invitations, locations, ceremonies and receptions. Mandy served tea and refreshments and contributed ideas. I had a wonderful time, and the wedding plan came together. By five o 'clock, we had finished. I couldn't wait to tell Hannibal!

Sunday evening, March 10th, 1929

I returned home on Saturday evening, from the tea at Ruth's apartment. After dinner, Hannibal and I settled on our sofa in the parlor. I curled up close to Hannibal, and he put his arm gently around my shoulders. I prattled on and on about wedding plans. I finally got around to a date. "Is Sunday, June 2nd OK with you?" I asked.

"Perfect," responded Hannibal. "I will use the June 2nd date as an anchor for other plans."

I told Hannibal what Ruth had already arranged with regard to location. "Ruth knows about the Spencer Hotel, of course," I began. "She also knows Willard Smolle, the Assistant Manager."

I paused, looked up at Hannibal and then continued: "Ruth suggested that we use a small ballroom at the Spencer for the wedding and a separate small ballroom for a reception afterwards." If you agree, Ruth and Amanda will follow up."

"Very nice," replied Hannibal. He smiled warmly, and his eyes twinkled. He then said: "I also have news." He paused and then continued: "I checked sailing schedules from New York to Europe. Cunard, Holland America and Compagnie Générale Transatlantique all have sailings in June."

"Perfect!" I replied. We celebrated with a glass of Chardonnay and watched the city lights come on through our parlor window. It was a lovely evening.

Wednesday evening, March 13ᵗʰ, 1929

Hannibal had more wonderful news this afternoon. I was in our workroom, going over photos of wedding dress designs. I had to make a choice very soon; the seamstress hired by Amanda needed time to create a dress.

Hannibal walked in, came over and kissed me lightly on the cheek. He then said: "We are booked on the Isle de France from New York to Le Havre on Friday, June 15ᵗʰ. We will board on Thursday evening, and the ship will sail just after midnight."

"Oh, my heaven!" I replied. "I can't imagine what it will be like; I have never seen an ocean liner before, except in pictures." I gave him a big hug.

Hannibal laughed and kissed me back. "We have a first-class suite. I have also arranged to put a car in the ship's hold. We will use it to tour Europe."

"I thought a moment and then said: "Tour Europe? I thought we were going to Paris." I'm sure my mouth remained wide open in surprise.

"Well, yes," replied Hannibal with a grin. "Paris will be one of our stops." His eyes twinkled. "I thought we might stay on the continent for a year or so."

He chuckled a little as he saw my expression of amazement. "What do you think?" he asked.

I sat still for a full minute. Finally, I stammered: "We can do this? I don't believe it. Oh, Hannibal!"

"Well," said Hannibal, "You'll have to buy clothes in New York for the trip over, and I still have to buy a car and put it on the ship. Do you think Saks on Fifth Avenue in New York will have anything for you to wear on the Isle de France?"

My emotions bounced around from confusion to pure happiness, but I tried my best to recover my poise. I replied: "A tough chore, but I will do my best."

Hannibal just laughed and kissed me again. He then said: "It will be summer, but the transatlantic crossing will be cool. You'll need a wardrobe with many layers."

"Tell me about the Isle de France," I responded. "I don't know anything about ships."

"Well," began Hannibal, "The ship was launched in 1926, so it's new. It can accommodate over a thousand four hundred passengers, with over 500 in first class."

"Tell me about our accommodations," I replied. "Knowing you, I'm sure they are special."

Hannibal then slipped into his military briefing manner. I couldn't help but smile; it was clear that Hannibal had planned for my question and had memorized an answer.

He began confidently with: "The ship passenger areas have the latest in art deco design. Each first-class cabin is unique. The grand salon is done in lacquer and gold. Forty Grecian columns surround a dance floor in the salon. Marble statues rest between the columns. The first-class dining room is the largest and most sumptuous afloat."

He saw my smile, blushed a little and slipped out of his briefing mode. He then grinned and added: "A friend at the booking agency mailed some photos; when they arrive, we can go over them together."

"You said we are taking a car? I asked. "How do we do this?"

Hannibal laughed. "Well, I have to buy a new car first and have it delivered to port in New York." His eyes twinkled again. "You can help me pick it out. How does a Cadillac touring car sound? Or maybe a European sportscar?"

"Expensive," I replied with a grin. "But very nice." I had seen advertisements in the Chicago newspapers. I thought a moment, then asked: "The ship can take our new car?"

"Yes," replied Hannibal. "The hold can accommodate sixty automobiles. Our car will be unloaded on the dock in Le Havre, at the mouth of the Seine River. We would have about a two-hundred-kilometer drive from our port to Paris."

"Kilo-meters?" I asked. "I have so much to learn," I thought to myself.

"Distances in continental Europe are measured in kilometers," Hannibal replied. "Two hundred kilometers converts to about 124 miles."

He smiled and then added: "Given a leisurely drive and an overnight stay at some quaint village hotel along the way, we could easily be at our Paris hotel in two days."

I shook my head in wonder for a few seconds. "Hannibal thinks of everything," I thought to myself.

To Hannibal, I turned my nose up, sniffed and said: "I don't suppose you have made reservations at a hotel yet. Only the best will do, of course." I tried to keep a straight face, but couldn't. I burst out laughing.

Hannibal joined me in laughter. "Not yet, but how does The Ritz at the Place Vendôme sound?"

I had heard of The Ritz of course, but I had never imagined staying there. To Hannibal I replied: "Well, I suppose it will have to do."

Hannibal laughed again and responded: "Only the best for you, my dear. I'll see what I can do."

I thought a few moments and then said: "The wedding is on Sunday, June 2nd, and we depart New York on the Isle de France on Saturday, June 15th."

I did some quick calculations in my head and then said: "Given a day or so in Chicago before we leave and a few days shopping in New York, we have to travel from Chicago to New York between about June 4th and June 9th."

Hannibal nodded. "I'll check on train schedules." He was quiet for a moment, and then he smiled and added: "You work with Ruth, Susie and your new friend Amanda on the wedding, and I will work on trains, ships, cars and candles."

"Candles?" I asked. I'm sure my face had a blank look.

Think about a candlelight dinner in Paris," replied Hannibal with a smile. "We may stay in Paris for a while, but I will also plan for travel on the continent." He chuckled and added: "You know, the wine country in France, opera in Vienna, the Grand Canal in Venice, Trevi Fountain in Rome."

Hannibal then got a mischievous look. He turned toward me and said: "I have also been talking to Ruth behind your back."

"What?" I responded. I'm sure the blank look on my face continued.

"Yes," replied Hannibal. "Ruth offered to rent us her villa in Tuscany whenever we want it. It's not far from Florence. Only her winery staff and servants will be there."

He paused a moment, then added: "Charles and other family members won't be going this year or the next. We can use the villa as a base of operations."

I thought about the situation with the Meltzer family after the case with Sydney. I understood. Somber thoughts passed through my mind. I was quiet for several minutes.

I forced my mind to return to good times and plans for the future. I had no idea what Europe would be like. Visions of luxurious travel and exotic places had never crossed my mind. "I, I don't know what to say," I finally stuttered. I'm sure my smile was radiant. I had never been happier in my life.

Hannibal smiled warmly and gave me a hug. "I want you to have wonderful experiences."

I turned to Hannibal and kissed him. It was a long and tender moment.

31

NEW ERA DAWN

Sunday evening, March 24, 1929

Great news! Eddie proposed to Susie! They plan to get married in the fall. Eddie has moved with the lab to Northwestern University, at a substantial increase in salary. He will be in charge of training crime scene investigators.

At first, Eddie's trainees will be employed by the laboratory under Doctor Calvin Goddard. Later, he will train Chicago police detectives. Eddie and Susie are shopping for a house in the suburbs.

Susie asked me if Silvia would be going to Europe with me as my maid. I had been thinking about it ever since Hannibal and I decided to leave Chicago. I asked Silvia if she would come with me, but she seemed reluctant. "Oh, Caroline," she said. "I would love to, but my life is here in Chicago."

Susie and I had a long conversation about Silvia. I told Susie about Silvia's reluctance to go to Europe. Susie solved the problem. She said: "Eddie and I will need a maid and eventually a nanny; we plan to have children." She paused and then added: "Would Silvia like to come to our house?"

"Oh, Susie, that would be wonderful!" I replied. "Let's ask her." We did; Silvia accepted, and soon I will be without a maid.

Sunday evening, April 7th, 1929

Last week, Hannibal took me shopping for a car. I have stock in car dealerships in Terre Haute and Indianapolis, but I had never shopped for a car before.

We looked at a Duesenberg Model J, a two-passenger Cadillac Roadster, a Packard Custom Eight Roadster, and a Ford Model A Deluxe Roadster.

We settled on the Duesenberg. It's a beautiful car. Hannibal said it was introduced at the New York Car Show in December of last year, and only a few were available in the U.S. According to the salesman, the Duesenberg marketing slogan is "The only car that could pass a Duesenberg was another Duesenberg – and that would be with the first owner's consent."

Only two Duesenbergs were available in Chicago, with one at the dealership. However, the dealer said that more were available in New York. Hannibal simply had one taken from the New York dealership. It would be delivered to the Compagnie Générale Transatlantique dock for loading on the Isle de France.

After a new cream-colored paint job, special burgundy-colored leather seats, a kit of spare parts, an extra set of tires and several special tools, it cost a whopping eighteen thousand dollars! "But it will be fun to drive in Europe," I thought to myself. "Maybe Hannibal will teach me to drive."

Sunday evening April 14th, 1929

Hannibal and I decided sell our penthouse in Chicago. We had two main reasons. First, Chicago was simply too dangerous for us, and we had decided to go to Europe. After a year or so, we will decide where we will go next, but that decision is in the future. Second, the housing market is good in Chicago right now. Hannibal is concerned that the economy will soon change. Best to sell now. Hannibal contacted an agent.

Sunday evening, April 28th, 1929

That was quick! We had three offers on our penthouse, including the furniture, within two weeks. After a brief bidding war and negotiations, Hannibal and I sold out with a tidy twenty percent return on our investment, after all expenses and fees.

We agreed to be out by May 30th. That means I have to pack my wardrobe and move out in a month. I will select some outfits to carry with me, and the rest will be packed with other personal items, books, china and a few furniture pieces. These will be transported on the Ise de France to Le Havre for storage until we need them . What a chore!

Hannibal and I spent last evening sitting on our sofa, sipping chardonnay and watching the lights of the city wink on. "I will miss the raw excitement, ethnic neighborhoods, skyscrapers and people of Chicago," I mused. "Most of all, I will miss my friends."

Hannibal put his arm around my shoulders. "I know," he replied. "We might come back someday; times will change." I snuggled close.

Sunday evening May 12th, 1929

This evening, Hannibal and I again relaxed in our parlor and watched the city lights. It was a cozy spot for us, and we both wanted to enjoy the spot as much as possible before we left Chicago.

After a period of silence just watching the lights, Hannibal said: "I made reservations at the Spencer for two rooms from May 30th until June 2nd."

"Oh good," I replied. "I will set up one room to do my bridal thing, and you can't watch."

Hannibal laughed and added: "We also have a honeymoon suite for the night of June 2nd through the morning of June 5th."

I giggled and snuggled. After a little while, I said: "I will have time for some last-minute shopping before we leave for New York."

Hannibal tensed a little.

"I want you to go with me, of course," I said. I know Hannibal was thinking about my abduction. I kissed him and added: "I have a desperate need to go shopping and try on clothes."

Hannibal relaxed a little and laughed. "OK," he responded. "I'll bring a lunch and several newspapers."

"Humph!" I muttered and gave him a dig in the ribs. "Men just don't understand."

Hannibal then said: "I bought tickets on the Twentieth Century Limited from Chicago's La Salle Street Station to New York's Grand Central Terminal. We leave Chicago at three in the afternoon on Wednesday, June 5th and arrive in New York at eight in the morning on June 6th."

"Overnight?" I asked.

"Yes," responded Hannibal. "However, we have a private compartment."

I was on a train once before I met Hannibal, and I distinctly remember the hard and uncomfortable seats. Our train ride from Clinton to Chicago was first class, but we didn't have a compartment. "What's it like?" I asked.

"Well," replied Hannibal, "We will have two fold-down beds, a sitting area with a table and two nice chairs, a couple of reading lamps, a tiny bathroom, and a place for our carry-on luggage." He smiled and added: "It's about fifteen feet square."

"It's so much better than just two hard seats in a regular passenger coach," I responded. I remembered the old days.

I lay back against the soft sofa and closed my eyes for a moment. "You are in a different world now, Caroline," I thought to myself. I couldn't help reflecting on how far I had come. I opened my eyes, looked at Hannibal and smiled. "You think of everything."

Sunday evening, May 26th, 1929

The wedding is only a week away, and I'm so excited! Susie will be my bridesmaid, Eddie will be the best man, and Harris will give away the bride. Ruth, of course, will be the matron of honor. The minister will be from the local Presbyterian Church; both Hannibal and I were raised as Protestants. We made a trip to the courthouse for a marriage license. So many details.

Amanda has been wonderful. She created and sent out invitations, set up fittings for the bride and bridesmaid dresses and made sure that Hannibal and Eddie will be appropriately dressed.

She also arranged for two adjacent small ballrooms at the Spencer, flowers and decorations, music during the ceremony and the reception, a beautiful cake and appropriate beverages.

Since Watts and Mulvaney will be guests, the punch will not, I repeat, not be spiked.

Wednesday evening, May 29th, 1929

Wedding in four days! Susie and I did our final fittings for dresses today. Both were designed by Jeanne Lanvin of Paris.

My dress is a modified robe de Mariée art deco gown made of white silk with a satin finish. It has a short train made of open weave shear tulle with light flower designs and a Chantilly lace veil and headdress. The bodice is simple, yet low to accent my figure, modest with a shear lace coverup to my neckline and long sleeves of the same shear lace. I have matching mid-heeled white shoes. Ruth lent me a lovely diamond-studded Tiera to hold my veil and headdress. I will also wear a blue garter for Hannibal's eyes only, and of course, my beautiful engagement ring.

Susie has a Lanvin dress, but it is a lilac-color and made of silk with a satin finish. The design is simple, with a low, square cut neckline and a shear lilac lace coverup. The dress has long sleeves of the same shear lace. Susie has matching mid-heeled lilac-colored shoes. She will wear her engagement ring. Like me, she takes every opportunity to let others see it.

Ruth has her own special outfit. It is also Lanvin, made of lovely, dark-blue embellished chiffon, with a round neckline. She will also wear a matching three-quarter sleeve jacket with black lace trim and a button front closure. She has matching mid-heeled dark blue shoes. Her accessories include earrings with diamonds and sapphires and a matching bracelet. Ruth looks slim, aristocratic and beautiful.

Sunday morning, June 2ⁿᵈ, 1929

My wedding day! It's six in the morning, and I am alone. The ceremony will be at three in the afternoon. Susie, Ruth and Amanda will arrive at my room at noon. Bath, hair, nails, lotions and potions: all must be done before they arrive to get me dressed. I'm as nervous as a schoolgirl.

"OK, Caroline," I muttered, as I paced around my bedroom. "Get control of yourself!"

I thought about the old days and my way up. "Poverty, saloons, sleazy back rooms, then a houseboat, and now a penthouse," I muttered to myself. "You have more money than you ever imagined, you've solved murders and you are about to get married. What a journey!"

I then thought about Hannibal. "He is everything in a man I could have imagined," I thought. "Really, Caroline," I continued, "Did you ever think you would marry?" I knew that the answer was no. "You are a lucky girl," I concluded. "Very lucky."

I relaxed a little, and the time passed with happy thoughts.

Tuesday morning, June 4ᵗʰ, 1929

Last Sunday, our wedding ceremony was a dream come true. Vincenzo served as the usher. We had about forty guests, all friends. The room for the ceremony was relatively small, so the seating filled the room on both sides of the central aisle. The room was lighted in a silver glow by two crystal chandeliers and sconces along the walls.

Amanda had arranged for a harpist to sit in the back of the room and play soft music. Selections prior to the ceremony included Arioso by Bach and Canon in D major by Pachelbell.

Our vows would be exchanged on a little dais in front of an alter with candles and a golden cross. Beautiful floral arrangements had been set on both sides of the dais.

The ceremony began with the minister, Hannibal and Eddie. The trio walked down the aisle to the dais. Susie and Ruth, the maid and matron of honor, were escorted together by Vincenzo to the dais, where they joined Eddie. After this processional, Harris walked me down the aisle to the softly played tune of the Bridal Chorus by Wagner. Susie carried my ring for Hannibal, and Ruth held my bridal bouquet during the ceremony.

The vows proceeded without a hitch, except that tears of joy came to my eyes and touched my cheeks. Everyone understood. Guests rose as Hannibal and I walked back down the aisle. I felt radiant.

After the formalities and congratulations, everyone adjourned to our second ball room for a dinner and reception. The harpist again provided music. Her selections included Ode to Joy by Beethoven, Horn Pipe from Water Music by Handel and Claire de Lune by Debussy.

Willard Smolle and his staff went all out with the food and service for dinner. Eddie, Harris and even Detective Lieutenant Watts offered toasts. I was so glad he had been promoted, along with Detective Sergeant Mulvaney. For dessert, Hannibal and I cut and served a beautiful wedding cake supplied by Giuseppe Costanzo's Bakery.

After dinner, dessert and many more congratulations, Hannibal and I slipped away to our honeymoon suite. Eddie took charge with our guests. Susie took care of the gifts given by many of the guests and sent by others who did not attend. She promised to send out thank-you cards once I make them out, which I will do before Hannibal and I leave for New York.

Of the many gifts, a special, unusual gift stood out. The gift was a beautifully wrapped, five-piece engraved silver English tea and coffee set and a matching serving tray. Included in the box was an envelope with a card. It simply said: "From your friends at the Green Mill. Thank you for everything. Best Wishes, Al."

Wednesday morning, June 5th, 1929

It's time to travel! The thank you cards are done, and I gave them to Susie for mailing. We had three wonderful days here at the Spencer, and we both packed our stuff. Hannibal and I will board our train at the La Salle Station for New York in a few hours. Hannibal also arranged with Smolle for a limousine. We will soon be off to new adventures.

Sunday morning, June 16th, 1929

We are at sea. Our suite is lovely, the dining room is wonderful, and the view is fantastic. I was worried about being seasick, but I haven't had a problem. What a relief.

Hannibal escorted me around B deck, which has a dozen or so French fashion shops. He said that the B deck Grand Foyer concourse was designed as a replica of the Rue de la Paix in Paris. The opulence is overwhelming. The sales ladies in the shops speak both English and French. I must learn French.

Hannibal promised a candlelight dinner in one of the four private dining rooms just off the grand dining salon tonight. What should I wear? I'll figure it out, I bought several evening dresses at Saks Fifth Avenue before we boarded the ship.

Monday morning June 17th, 1929

Last night, Hannibal escorted me to our reserved private dining room. It was set up for just the two of us. We had a dedicated waiter and his assistant. "What a wonderful evening!" I thought to myself.

As we entered our room, I noticed eight diners entering the room next to ours. They were dressed to the nines, and they were led by an elderly couple. The man treated their dedicated waiter with a condescending air. The woman, all aglitter with gems and the most ostentatious clothes I had ever seen, seemed sad, somehow.

I pointed discretely to the older pair as they entered their dining room. Our waiter rolled his eyes and whispered: "An American heiress and her companion."

He paused to make sure the group had passed into their room. "The two younger couples are son, daughter and their spouses. The middle-aged man is an attorney." He paused again and then added: "The attorney's companion is a New York socialite; I have seen her pictures in the newspaper."

"Oh," I replied as we moved toward our candle-lit table. Our chatty waiter went on about his chores. Soon we were seated. Our waiter gave us menus and poured us each a glass of champagne. He set the opened bottle in an ice bucket next to the table and left discretely.

I looked around our room. "Oh, Hannibal," I said. "It's beautiful."

"And so are you, Mrs. Caroline Case Jones," replied Hannibal with a smile. "We will have many new and exciting adventures."

We raised our glasses in a toast and then sipped in comforting silence. Our waiter came in and took our order for dinner. Hannibal ordered, since I was a novice with the menu in French. We both had bisque de Homard and salade du jardin. For the main course, Hannibal ordered Poisson loop de mer sauté for himself and classic sole Muniére for me. Dessert would come later.

Suddenly the lights went out. We had candles on the table, so we could still see. "What on earth?" I said.

Hannibal and I both looked toward the door. We expected our waiter to enter with an explanation. The lights came back on.

Suddenly, "Aheeeh! Eeeh!" This scream was followed by several thumps and the sound of scraping furniture.

Hannibal and I both stood and looked for the source of the sounds. "Next door!" I exclaimed.

Hannibal quickly moved to and through our door. I was right behind him. Several waiters were rushing toward the room next to ours. Hannibal and I were the first through the door.

I saw a table in the center of the room. Directly across, the elderly lady that we had seen earlier was sitting in a chair, staring right at us. Her body was tilted to the left, but it was held upright by the chair arms and back. I sensed that she was quite dead.

I looked around the room. Seven members of the dinner party were standing, all with expressions of disbelief on their faces. Several chairs around the table were overturned. I glanced down at the white linen and place settings on the table. Nothing seemed out of place.

Two of the three remaining women screamed and then started moaning "Oh! Oh!" The two male companions turned and tried to calm them.

Hannibal immediately moved around the table to the side of the woman in the chair. I watched him bend over, feel for a pulse and stare at her face. After about ten or twenty seconds, he raised up, looked to me, and said in a clear, calm voice: "This woman is dead."

Hannibal then glanced at each of the seven remaining diners, in turn, and added: "Please stay where you are." Next, he got the attention of one of the waiters standing by the door and said: "Go find a ship's officer immediately." He looked at another waiter and added: "Send someone to the bridge, and notify the Captain."

Hannibal's voice and tone had the air of command. Both waiters responded with: "Oui, Monsieur!" They immediately went about their appointed tasks.

While this was going on, I moved slowly around the room, taking in every detail.

Hannibal continued to give directions. He had the remaining waiter close the dining room door and stand outside. He had calming words for the two moaning women. They stopped. I could hear the waiter's voice outside as he told gathering passengers to please move on, go back to their activities, and everything is under control.

Two or three minutes passed. The door opened. A young ship's officer stepped inside. Hannibal walked over and whispered to him for a full minute. The officer nodded. He looked around the room and said: "I'll take over now." He then turned back to Hannibal and said: "Thank you, Major Jones."

Hannibal motioned for me to come. I did, and we discretely stepped outside the door. Hannibal then whispered: "I gave the young officer a brief description of what we heard from our room next door and what we observed when we entered this room." He paused and then added: "We have permission to return to our suite."

"Did you suggest to the officer that he preserve the crime scene for the Captain?" I asked.

"Very good," replied Hannibal with a smile. "Yes, I did."

"Can we have our dinner brought to our suite?" I asked.

"Good idea," replied Hannibal. He then turned to our waiter, who was standing by the door to our little dining room. Again, Hannibal gave instructions. We walked slowly back to our suite.

Within half an hour, our waiter and his assistant appeared with our bottle of champagne and dinner on a rolling cart that folded up into a nice little table. Champagne was poured, and dinner was served. The assistant left a dessert menu.

The soup, salad and fish were delicious. We tried to enjoy our dinner, in spite of the murder. As we discussed the events in the private dining room, our waiter returned. We ordered pompe aux pomme du Perigord with glace à la vanille.

Our assistant waiter soon returned with dessert, poured more champagne and then left. As we were licking the last of the dessert from our spoons, we heard a knock at our door. Hannibal got up and opened the door. A middle-aged man in a resplendent uniform stood in the doorway.

"Major Jones and Mrs. Jones?" He asked as he peered past Hannibal to me as I sat at our table. "I am Henri Villar, the Chief Purser."

"Please come in," replied Hannibal.

Villar stepped inside, looked at me and said: "Captain Blancart sends his compliments and thanks for your help this evening."

"You are welcome," I responded. "We will write up what we observed for you in the morning, if that is OK."

"Of course, of course," said Villar. "However, Captain Blancart is aware of your exploits in the American heartland." He paused and looked back and forth between Hannibal and me. "We would very much appreciate your continued help in solving this most perplexing murder."

32

EPILOGUE

Monday morning, June 17, 1929

At the request of Captain Blancart, Hannibal and I have decided to help solve the murder of "the American heiress" in a private dining room on the SS Isle de France.

Who knows how our investigation will turn out? Our work will be intense and probably scary; after all, we will be looking for a murderer in the closed environment of a ship at sea.

We dock in Le Havre in less than a week. I'm sure Europe will be filled with new sights and adventures. *Déjà Vu sur le bon navire Isle de France!*

ABOUT THE AUTHOR

My wife Linda and I live in the lovely Shell Point Retirement Community near Fort Myers, Florida. We travel the world doing research for my books. For example, in Chicago, the fabulous Spencer Hotel (1927-1945) was my setting for a fictional murder and later, a wedding in *The Blind Pig Murders*. Linda and I toured the hotel, which is now the Chicago Hilton, researched architectural drawings and studied the hotel decor, parties and guests during the 1920s. We also visited the Green Mill Jazz Club and The Hideout; both were Chicago speakeasies during Prohibition. Linda and I have already toured Europe to research places and historical events for *The Cat in the Window Murders*, which will be published in 2021.

My stories are a combination of youthful personal experience, family history and intense, scholarly research. My early years began in Clinton, Vermillion County, Indiana. My father and I fished and trapped on the Wabash River for a major portion of our family income; I know the river and its colorful people. My teenage years were spent on a farm in Sullivan County. In the late 1940s and early 50s, my step-mother had an apartment house on Erie Street in Chicago. As an adult, my degrees include a BS in Electrical Engineering, an MS in Engineering Management, an MBA and a PhD in Economics. I served 23 years in the U.S. Air Force. I had another 22-year career as a scientist and engineer, building large scale systems for the Department of Defense. My publications include seven books and a number of papers in scientific journals. I traveled to and lived in many places around the world, but I am still a Hoosier at heart.

CAROLINE CASE WILL RETURN IN
THE CAT IN THE WINDOW MURDERS

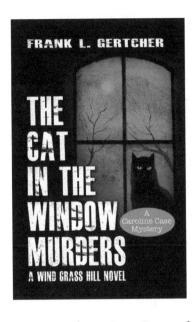

Independently wealthy Caroline Case Jones departs Chicago for Europe in 1929. She and Hannibal, her enigmatic new husband, enter a war-scarred continent embroiled in social turmoil and political upheaval. Solving murders is the name of the game. Intrepid Caroline acquires a new nickname, 'la Chatte dans la Fenêtre,' which translates to 'The Cat in the Window.' Caroline and Hannibal meet fascinating historical characters and experience newsworthy events and scenes in Le Havre, Giverny, Paris, Marseille and other ancient European towns. Caroline retains her cool, resourceful detective skills under intense pressure, and justice, legal and otherwise, prevails.